The Islanders

Also by Christopher Priest from Gollancz:

Fugue for a Darkening Island
Inverted World
The Affirmation
The Glamour
The Prestige
The Extremes
The Separation
The Dream Archipelago

The Islanders

■

CHRISTOPHER PRIEST

GOLLANCZ

LONDON

JB-

A short extract from *The Drone* was previously published under the title
'Fireflies' in *Celebration*, ed. by Ian Whates, NewCon Press, 2008
A different version of *The Trace* appeared in *Interzone* 214,
ed. by Andy Cox, 2008

The right of Christopher Priest to be identified as the author
of this work has been asserted by him in accordance with
the Copyright, Designs and Patents Act 1988.

First published in Great Britain in 2011
by Gollancz
An imprint of the Orion Publishing Group
Orion House, 5 Upper St Martin's Lane,
London WC2H 9EA
An Hachette UK Company

A CIP catalogue record for this book
is available from the British Library

ISBN 978 0 575 07004 2 (Cased)
ISBN 978 0 575 07819 2 (Export Trade Paperback)

1 3 5 7 9 10 8 6 4 2

Typeset by Deltatype Ltd, Birkenhead, Merseyside

Printed and bound by
CPI Group (UK) Ltd, Croydon, CR0 4YY

The Orion Publishing Group's policy is to use papers
that are natural, renewable and recyclable products and
made from wood grown in sustainable forests. The logging
and manufacturing processes are expected to conform to
the environmental regulations of the country of origin.

www.christopher-priest.co.uk
www.orionbooks.co.uk

To Esla

Introductory

by Chaster Kammeston

I find it ironic that I should be invited to write a few introductory words to this book, as I know as little about the subject as it is possible to know. However, having always maintained that what one feels is more important than what one knows, let me begin.

Here is a book about islands and islanders, full of information and facts, a great deal I knew nothing about, and even more on which I had opinions without substance. People too: some of them I knew personally, or had heard about, and now rather late in the day have learned something about them. There is so much out there, so many islands to discover, while I am familiar with but one of them. I was born on the island where I live now and where I am writing these words, I have never stepped off the island, and I expect never to do so before I die. If this were a book only about my home island I should be uniquely equipped to introduce it, but for quite other reasons I would then not agree to do so.

For me the visual aspect of this Archipelago in which I contentedly live is confined to the handful of adjacent islands I can see in the offing as I walk or travel about close to my house. I know the names of most of them – there are three or four that are too small or unimportant to be named – and I carry a vivid mental picture of them as they appear to me. In rain, sunshine or wind, these neighbouring islands are constant companions, the background scenery to my life. They are lovely and intriguing to behold, they induce moods in me that are always varied and unpredictable, and I never tire of staring at them. They infuse me with the spirit of island life, and thus infuse every word I have ever written.

I am however incurious about them. I assume that many of the people who visit my own island must come from some of them, and, no doubt, return to them afterwards. By reading the advance proofs of this book I have accidentally discovered a few unsuspected facts about one of these adjacent places, but on the whole I remain as ignorant about my part of the Dream Archipelago as always. That is how it is, and how it will remain.

Although I can describe nothing of what I myself know about the islands, I none the less have a commission to write about them here. Let me sum up what is more generally accepted and known. I have culled most of it from reference books.

The Dream Archipelago is the largest geographical feature on our world. The islands are found around the whole girth of the planet, spreading across tropical, subtropical and temperate latitudes, both north and south of the equator. They are placed in the only ocean we have: this is known as the Midway Sea and it too is circumambient of the world. The sea with its islands occupies more than seventy per cent of the total surface area, and contains more than eighty per cent of all the world's water.

The Midway Sea is mostly wide, but there are two comparatively narrow stretches which create troublesome local currents and disturbances as the tides rise and fall. The Sea is bounded and bordered to north and south by two continental masses.

Of these continents the larger, to the north, is unnamed. This is because it is the location of approximately sixty different states and nations, many of them landbound. Each of these nations has its own language and customs and lays fierce and argumentative claim to pre-eminence on the vast continent. The countries all have names by which they know the continent, but as these names are in a variety of languages, and emerge from many cultural, historical and folkloric roots, no one can agree on what they should all call it.

Some maps call this continent 'Nordmaieure', but this is more to do with the fact that cartographers do not like unnamed spaces on their maps. 'Nordmaieure' has no political or cultural meaning. Most of these quarrelsome nation states are found in the mid-regions, or along the southern plains, because north of the seventieth parallel all is permanently frozen and therefore more or less uninhabitable.

The smaller southern continent does have a name: it is called Sudmaieure (explaining the cartographical fiction of the north) and it too is as yet mostly unpopulated, and for the same general reasons of intense cold. Sudmaieure is a chill polar wasteland, lacking temperate or tropical latitudes. Much of it is under permafrost or deep icefields. The outer fringe, where the land meets the southern littoral of the Midway Sea, experiences some seasonal thawing, and here there are a few small settlements. Some of these are temporary camps set up by the various military factions who have an interest in Sudmaieure, others are related to scientific projects, or fishing or mining.

The political concerns of this world of ours are worrying. Many of the countries in the north are at war with each other – they have been at it for as long as I have been alive, they were at it for at least three centuries before I was born, and they show every eager sign of being at it for centuries more to come. The issues over which they violently disagree, and the alliances they have formed in an attempt to prevail, are often reported in our newspapers and on television, but few islanders seem to take much notice.

This is largely because in an act of unusual, not to say *unique*, far-sightedness, the elders of the Dream Archipelago long ago drew up and agreed a document called the Covenant of Neutrality. The Covenant is just about the only matter on which the various peoples of the islands have ever agreed. It extends to every island, small or large, populated or unpopulated, and it was intended to guarantee that the belligerent concerns of the north should not affect the people of the Archipelago.

Although there have been many attempts in the past to breach the Covenant, and it is by no means an untroubled document, it has by some miracle held firm. The neutrality established long ago still manages to hold today. Nor is it just a matter of treaties and conventions: neutrality is a way of life in the islands, a constant preference, an attitude, a habit.

Our neutrality is tested every day, because for perhaps understandable reasons the warring nations have drawn up their own

3

agreement of sorts. It reflects their particular and vested interests, not those of the islanders. This makes the islanders' Covenant continue to be necessary.

By their agreement, these northern countries draw back from invading each other, or from bombing each other's cities, or damaging their industries and valuable reserves of minerals and fuels, and instead confine their war-making to the battlefields of Sudmaieure. They send their armies down to the stony wastes and the terrible icefields, and there they kill and wound each other's young soldiery, they fire bullets and missiles and shells at each other, they bash and batter and shout a lot, wave their colours and blow their cornets, march around making a lot of noise and no doubt leaving a mess behind them. All this activity is more or less without harm to anyone else, and appears to satisfy those who take part.

To reach Sudmaieure, though, the armies and everything connected with them must pass through the Archipelago, so we are constantly traversed by troopships and naval vessels and auxiliaries. Our islands are over-flown by military aircraft. It happens that my house overlooks one of the channels regularly used by troopships, and from my study window I can see the grey ships cruising slowly by. I try not to imagine the conditions aboard. The sight of these ships, with their cargo of young lives heading to war, has haunted me all my life and indirectly has helped give the essence to every book I have written.

I have also been asked to say something about the physical facts of the Archipelago.

For the purposes of this Introductory I have been trying to discover how many islands there are in all, since a statistic of that sort seems to be what matters to the kind of people who compile books like this one. They refer to it from time to time by the technically accurate description of gazetteer, because what we have here is a long list of names of islands.

It is however an incomplete island gazetteer, something which the compilers would be the first to admit. Logically, one can easily understand that if every island in the Dream Archipelago were to be listed by name in a book, the result would be of such immense size, and so full of trivial information, that it would have little practical use.

The same argument against usefulness may be made for an *incomplete* list, of course, compounded by the unarguable fact that an incomplete listing of anything reveals that a selection has been made, and any act of selection is of course political. So here we have partiality added to triviality, and they have made a book of it all while maintaining the conceit that a gazetteer is apolitical.

This is a conundrum I do not propose to solve for the no doubt industrious gazetteers who have produced this book, but it did lead me to try to find out, if only for my own amusement, what is the total number of islands in this world of ours.

There are many different reference books about the Dream Archipelago and I have several of them on my shelf. All the books make guesses about numbers, and all of those guesses differ from each other. Some authorities say there are hundreds of islands, but they count only the large or important ones. Others say there are thousands, but they are vague about how they define an island, and confuse island groups with individual islands. A few of these experts, by including half-submerged rocks and parts of reefs, say there are hundreds of thousands, and hint at even more.

After much browsing I reached the conclusion that the only thing the experts do agree on is that there are a great many islands.

Approximately twenty thousand of the islands appear to have names, but even this is uncertain. Some islands are organized in large administrative groups and known by collective names, or they are distinguished only by ordinal numbers. Others are in groups which are not named, while the islands in those unnamed groups, or some of them, are individually named. Other islands stand alone, and of these many are named but many more appear not to be.

Then there is the problem of the profusion of island patois.

Nearly all the islands have local names as well as the 'official' names that appear on the map. (Or they would do, if there were any maps. I shall return to this shortly.) Sometimes, there are two or more alternative patois names, some of which are based on

5

physical features of the island, but most of which are not. Where attempts have been made to standardize the nomenclature, further confusion has been created. Confusion is standard and normal, I'm afraid.

For instance, there is a group of islands called the Torquils, or the Torquil Group, or (occasionally) the Torquil Islands. They are situated at approximately 45°E, in the broad subtropical zone south of the Equator. The Torquils are apparently well known, much visited, famous for their beaches and lagoons. All the main Torquil islands have ferry ports, and the largest has a civil airport. The overall population at the most recent census was in excess of half a million people. There is no doubt that these islands exist and are well known by many people, other than the residents. The main text of this book, with its concern to provide as much information and detail as possible, makes several references to them. The Torquils therefore appear to be real, or at least really there.

However, it seems possible that there is another name for this group of islands, which is the Torquis, or the Torqui Group. As I'm accustomed to dealing with clumsy editorial work, I assumed at first that one name might be a mis-spelling of the other. However, the Tor*quils* are said to have the patois name which means EVENING WIND, while the Tor*quis* are said to have a patois meaning of SERENE DEPTHS. So many variables occur! How much is lost in translation from one patois to another, or in the oral traditions on which so much island lore is based?

To someone like me, who has not visited the Torquils or the Torquis and never will, there does not seem to be much that distinguishes one group from the other. They even appear to be in the same general area, or at least have similar coordinates. I suppose many people will assume they are one and the same.

I was willing to make a similar assumption until to my astonishment I discovered there was yet another group of islands, these called the Tor*quins*, which might of course be a further mis-spelling.

My reference books are more or less in agreement that there are one hundred and fifteen named islands in the Torquins, seventy-two named and twenty-three unnamed islands in the Torquils, and fifty-eight identified islands in the Torquis. However, in those allegedly separate island groups there are at least five islands in each with the same name, some of those have minor variations in spelling and a few appear to have been recently renamed in an attempt to capitalize on the presumed fortunes of somewhere else.

Some of the ones with the same or similar names have longitude and latitude references which are identical, or almost so, which would appear to be objective evidence that they are one and the same, until we discover that the Torquins and the Torquis, at least, are on opposite sides of the world, and that the Torquis and the Torquins are emphatically located in the northern hemisphere while the Torquils are just as firmly positioned in the south.

If the reader is at this point feeling muddled or mystified, let me reassure him or her that I am in the same state. I also suspect that many of these so-called experts who have written reference books have been just as bewildered by it all, and over the years have passed down their imbroglio for someone else to sort out.

The gazetteer does make an honourable effort to clarify this sort of problem, although as far as I am concerned it is a mystery on which I wish to spend no more time.

So I gladly join the general consensus of scholars and admit or declare that the Dream Archipelago contains a great many islands, and leave it at that.

But where exactly are they and how do they lie in relation to each other?

There are no maps or charts of the Dream Archipelago. At least there are no reliable ones, or comprehensive ones, or even whole ones.

There are thousands of charts which have been drawn up locally, mainly to enable navigation for fishing vessels and the inter-island ferries, but most of these are crudely drawn and graphically incomplete. They concentrate on depths of channels, hidden rocks and guyots, tidal passages, reefs, safe havens, coves, lighthouses, sandbanks, and so on. They show locally known prevailing winds. All this is plainly vernacular in origin, based on the seagoing experiences of local men and women, which is as it should be but is of absolutely no use to a global consideration of the whole Archipelago.

The problems of mapping the Dream Archipelago are well understood. High-altitude aerial cartography is more or less impossible because of the distortion caused by the temporal gradients. These gradients, impossible for me to explain here (there is an attempt later in the book), exist in every part of the world except at the magnetic poles. Even within a few degrees of those poles, which of course are in frozen land areas, the variations in what can be observed or photographed make reliable charting inconsistent and therefore unfeasible.

The only solution would be for mapping to be conducted on a scientific or consistent basis, concentrating on small or local areas, drawn at ground level or from an extremely low altitude, then combined by some central authority so as to produce a comprehensive worldwide map. Until comparatively recently no attempt on this mammoth task has been made. You will read about the modern efforts in this gazetteer. Maybe they will enlighten you, as they have enlightened me, although not by much.

The present-day cartographers use low-level aerial photography of the highest visual quality, but again because of the gravitational anomalies it has proved impossible to send out these pilotless aeroplanes in any planned or consistent way. The results are haphazard and random and it will be many years before anything approaching a definitive atlas of our world is produced. Until then the picture remains unclear and everyone continues to meander around in a way that is typical of islanders.

The dream-state of the Archipelago, which is what we islanders most respond to, and least wish to see changed, seems likely to continue without interference for a long time to come.

We are not at war because we have no disputes. We do not spy on each other because we are trusting and incurious. We travel short distances because we can see other islands around where we live and our ambitions are satisfied by going there. We rarely travel long distances for the same general reason. We invent gadgets and leisure activities and pastimes without purpose, because that is what we like to do. We paint and draw and sculpt, we write adventurous and fantastic literature, we speak in metaphors and we designate symbols, we act out the plays of our forefathers. We brag about our past glories and we hope for a better life ahead. We love conversation and sitting around, good food and passionate affairs, standing on beaches, swimming in the warm seas, drinking ourselves into contentment, sitting under the stars. We start making things then forget to finish them. We are articulate and talkative, but we only quarrel for the excitement of it. We are guilty of self-indulgence, irrational behaviour, illogical arguments, sometimes indolence, a musing state of mind.

Our palette of emotional colours is the islands themselves and the mysterious sea channels that churn between them. We relish our sea breezes, our regular monsoons, the banks of piling clouds that dramatize the seascapes, the sudden squalls, the colour of the light reflecting from the dazzling sea, the lazy heat, the currents and the tides and the unexplained gales, and on the whole prefer not to know whence they have come, nor whither they are destined.

As for this book, I declare that it will do no harm.

It is in fact to be commended. It is a typical island enterprise: it is incomplete, a bit muddled and it wants to be liked. The unidentified writer or writers of these brief sketches have an agenda which is not mine, but I do not object to it.

I did not write this book, although there have already been rumours that I did. This is the moment to aver that there is no truth in the rumours. I am in fact sceptical of the whole enterprise while liking it a great deal.

The book is arranged in alphabetical order and it is intended that it should be read in that order. However, as most people are supposedly expected to use it as a work of reference, or as a travel guide, then the order in which the articles have been placed is completely irrelevant. I do maintain, though, that few will be able to 'use' this book in the way it is presumably intended, so the alphabet is as good a basis as any from which to start.

One of the reasons for its lack of usefulness is something the reader should be warned about. Not every entry here is strictly factual. I found it surprising that in some cases the islands are described not by their physical characteristics, but by narratives concerning events that took place on them or people who did something while there. There is always a lot to be said for indirect truth, for metaphors, but if you are looking up a hotel in which you might wish to reserve a room, you probably do not want to read instead a biography of the proprietor. There is altogether too much of this kind of thing, but it is for some reason the chosen method of these gazetteers. I find it rather charming, but as a non-traveller I am always much more interested in the lives of hotel proprietors than I am in the rooms they have for rent.

Finally, it seems to me innocuous and even attractive to be urging travel to so many places at once, but it is in fact pointless when so few readers will act on the recommendation.

Any direction or travel plan within the Dream Archipelago more ambitious than being ferried across to the next island is usually a matter of guesswork or hazard. Because of the mapping problem, if you seek to land on any of the islands recommended by this gazetteer you will almost invariably turn up somewhere else. Furthermore, should you attempt to return whence you came, your difficulties will multiply.

Our history has largely been created by adventurers and entrepreneurs who arrived somewhere other than on the island they sought. The ones who landed where they intended frequently found that matters were not as they expected. Our history is full of people going, becoming confused, and then coming back or wandering off somewhere else.

Even so, finding any of these attractive places by chance, as that is the only way to appreciate them fully, will be a reward in itself, so it is my view that the foreknowledge these gazetteers are so keen to impart will always be irrelevant.

Prepare yourself by all means for the no doubt maddening and illogical local currency, be warned of the sometimes inexplicable local laws, know in advance the best spot from which to observe a cathedral, a mountain, or a group of mendicant artists, discover the patois name for the forest through which you plan to dawdle, brush up your knowledge of ancient arguments and abandoned diggings and installations of art, because you must be ready for anything that might occur.

None of it is real, though, because reality lies in a different, more evanescent realm. These are only the names of some of the places in the archipelago of dreams. The true reality is the one you perceive around you, or that which you are fortunate enough to imagine for yourself.

Chaster Kammeston

A Gazetteer of Islands

Aay

ISLAND OF WINDS

AAY is the largest of an arc of volcanic islands formed by the undersea Great Southern Ridge, close to the point where it crosses the Equator. It is known throughout the Dream Archipelago by the patois version of its name, ISLAND OF WINDS.

It lies a few degrees north of the Equator, at the furthest extremity of the arc. Aay's interior is dominated by three volcanic peaks, all presently dormant, as well as a series of lower foothills. The soil is extremely fertile. The island is heavily forested and there are still areas of the interior on the southern and western sides which are as yet unexplored. Two main rivers flow from the uplands towards the east, the Aayre and the Pleuve, which irrigate the coastal plain on that side of the island. A wide variety of crops and livestock are farmed. The principal town on the island is called Aay Port, and is in a sheltered position on the eastern side. Because of the island's great beauty and attractive physical features, tourists visit Aay all year round – to the west and south Aay has a vast shallow lagoon enclosed by reefs, and on the northern side, open to the sea, several of the beaches receive high surf. The tropical climate is pleasantly moderated by trade winds.

For all its tourist attractions, Aay is properly renowned as the location of the ACADEMY OF THE FOUR WINDS, which was set up two and a half centuries ago by the artist-philosopher ESPHOVEN MUY.

As a young woman, Muy was an enthusiastic traveller. She moved extensively around the Archipelago, sailing in small boats between many of the islands which lie between the horse latitudes and the doldrums, sketching and photographing what she saw and keeping a detailed journal. Her motives at first were wholly recreational or artistic, but as she travelled more she began making connections that were part inspirational, part delineative and interpretative, part social or anthropological, part mythological. For a while she made recordings of folk narratives and songs, and she kept detailed notes about the various different island patois in use.

She later wrote a two-volume work called *Islands in the Dream: Undercurrents of life in the Archipelagian Neutral Zone*, based on her notes and sketches. Although this was intended for an academic audience, a shortened version which followed a few years later became a mainstream title which sold strongly year after year. It permanently established her reputation and provided her with a solid income for the remainder of her life.

By the time the book was selling well, Muy had moved to the island of Aay. She spent the first twelve months observing, measuring and recording the geophysical nature of the island, as she had in other places. Her discovery about Aay was that its unique position and subsea geography place it directly adjacent to the two main oceanic currents. It is these that create its characteristic microclimate.

Muy noted that to the north and west of the island flows the warm current known as the NORTH FAIAND DRIFT, while to the south and east is the cold current called the SOUTHERN OSCILLATING STREAM.

These two oceanic currents are both parts of the global 'conveyor belt'. The Drift gains its warmth from a long circuitous passage through the tropical and subtropical regions of the Midway Sea. After passing the Aayian arc it separates into two channels, the smaller one continuing through the equatorial regions of the Midway Sea, but the larger and slower branch turning northwards and bringing a temperate climate to the southern areas of many countries on the northern continent.

The two channels are eventually reunited in a deepwater area of the Southern Midway Sea, the remainder of the warmth being released in a zone of intense storms. The current then becomes known as the Southern Oscillating Stream and passes through the icy oceans that surround Sudmaieure, where the salinity is much lower than average due to the amount of fresh water entering the sea from glacier calving.

Regaining salinity, the Stream moves slowly on towards the far side of the globe. It gradually sinks towards the deep ocean floor, passes far beneath the smaller of the two warm branches, then at last turns through a gyre and heads north towards the shallower stretches of the Archipelagian Midway Sea. It is still significantly cooler than the surrounding waters as it passes close against the Aayian arc of islands. Beyond Aay it turns east to meander through the main concentration of islands, tempering and cooling the more extreme aspects of the tropical latitudes, while starting to regain some heat for itself.

In this way, the island of Aay is uniquely impacted by two oceanic drifts, to the north and south, one warm, the other cool.

The currents were of course known to local people before Muy carried out her research – crude depictions of them appear on fishing charts that pre-date her birth by several centuries – but it was she who made the connection between the currents and the variety of winds that vent across the island all year round.

As well as the mild trade winds, moving in steadily from the north-east and south-east, Aay receives irregular winds from every quarter. Two major winds prevail, each brought in by the energy of the underlying ocean current: a rain-bearing breeze from the warm north-east, watering the land, enriching the forests and filling the lakes and rivers, and a cooler, fresher wind from the south-west, raising high the surf on the northern beaches, ripening the crops, sweeping protective cumulus from the skies and parching the summer streets and resorts.

When these winds meet, most often at night, violent and spectacular electric storms play around the summits of the central heights. Tornadoes cross the coastal plain at such times. But as well as these expectable winds there are many others, intermittent, surprising. Some arise from the hot flat islands to the north of Aay, others from the lagoons of the shallows to the south-east. One, bearing the heady scents of pines and resin, idles down from the northern mainland.

There is a föhn wind that prevails in the cooler months, sweeping from the summit of the mountains, through the high valleys and across the towns and river estuaries, bringing a seasonal island-wide lethargy and inanition. The suicide rate increases, people depart Aay to find other homes, tourists suddenly leave without explanation.

Less disruptive of everyday life, an equinoctial stream from the east precedes the autumnal gales, but seems not to be a part of them because it brings gritty air and a residue of fine sand to be left on the streets and roofs.

No one before Esphoven Muy had attempted to trace the sources of these winds, nor even take enough interest to try to find out which other islands they traversed, but she studied them and tried to distinguish one from the other. After a time she was able to make reasonably accurate forecasts of when they would arrive and the effect they would have on temperatures, rainfall, and so on.

The people who lived and worked on Aay began to depend on her forecasts. Other meteorologists, learning about her work, came to the island to meet Muy, to study with her, to seek her advice, to share ideas. That was how the Academy of the Four Winds was eventually set up, although for the first few years it was an institution that existed more in name than in bricks and mortar. It was informally based around Muy's house in Aay Port, then later in temporary buildings on the edge of town. Today, the Academy is established in a magnificent campus close to the centre of the Port. Wind turbines, the first to be erected in the Archipelago, are scattered discreetly about Aay, generating enough electricity for everyone on the island.

Once the winds of Aay had been identified and named, the Academy moved on to collect data about other winds experienced all over the Archipelago. The Academy was soon funded by the meteorological forecasts it produced, and to this day holds major contracts with industrial corporations, farming cooperatives, drilling companies, vineyards, tourism and sports promoters, and hundreds of other institutions with a vested interest in the predicted arrival of winds, seasonal or otherwise. In addition, the Academy has a less transparent source of income, unadvertised but never denied, from the many military and naval bodies which use or traverse the Midway Sea.

However, weather forecasting was never Muy's first interest. She charged the Academy with a purpose: the study of wind formation, of wind identification, of the social and mythological relevance of wind. The currents of air made up her universe.

The Academy is divided into several different faculties.

Astronomical and Mythological – the names or actions of gods, of heroes and explorers, of gallant feats of bravery, of epic tasks performed, of blessings and beatitudes bestowed. Thus, for example: the bleak polar wind that sweeps through the steep and unexplored valleys of the Western Fastness of the Sudmaieure continent is known to the islanders in that offshore area as the CONLAATTEN, named after Conlaatt, an ancient deity of the south whose breath was reputed to freeze victims to death. (In common with almost every wind in the Archipelago, the Conlaatten is known by other names in other contexts, and there are several patois names for it too.)

Natural World – winds that are named after the effect, benign or otherwise, on plants, animals, birds, insects, etc. Thus: the LENFEN, a breeze related to the island of Fellenstel, which every springtime carries young gossamer spiders to many different parts of the Archipelago. The WOTON is a wind that is said to hasten or ease the migratory passage of birds from south to north. Its companion or opposite wind, blowing a few months later, is called in the vernacular the NOTOW.

Anthropomorphism – winds which are described as having human characteristics: gentleness, jealousy, mischief-making, anger, mirth, pain, love, revenge, etc. Many of these winds are identified from folklore, or the oral tradition, and exist under a maze of different patois names. Some are related to necromancy (below). One area of learning is called Subjective Anthropomorphism, which collects data on the influence of winds on the human psyche: the föhn wind that causes depression, the sea breeze that promotes optimism and feelings of wealth, the lovers' waft, and so on.

Necromancy – winds which by repute are the product of evil, of witches' brew, of disastrous attempts to weave spells, of malign or failed attempts to make a deal with the devil. Notorious amongst these is a cold north-easterly hard blow occurring every five years or so in the Hetta Group of islands. Although this is conventionally sourced in the Faiandland mountains when there has been an unusual amount of snowfall, Hettans persist in believing that it is an accursed wind they call the GOORNAK. A woman being tortured on suspicion of witchery on the Hettan island of Goorn is said to have expired with a prolonged curse on her lips. Her dying gasp was a croak of hatred. It rose from her as an icy wind, froze to death every one of her persecutors, then swept northwards to the mountains of the mainland, where it is believed it lurks forever more. Even in the present day it is said that no one on Goorn will venture outdoors when the curse wind is blowing. The Academy has so far discovered and recorded more than one hundred different curse winds in the Archipelago. Naturally, most winds of this type are identified by islanders in the less developed regions of the Archipelago, and serious study of them involves detailed researches into folkloric matters. Many of the strangest and most evocative names for winds arise from necromantic sources: the COMBINER, the POISONER, the MANTRAP, the GARGLER, the ABYSS, and so on. These winds all have scientific names: for example, the Goornak is more correctly known as the FAIANDLAND BISE.

Scientific Observation – the study of storms, blizzards, smoke, gravitational influence, movement of sand or dust and the study of dunes, effects on oceanic currents, all as revealed by the passage of winds. Sandstorms are infrequent in the Archipelago, although they do occur in the Swirl. Unusually, the Swirl island group is close to the only part of Sudmaieure with a dry climate: the Qataari Peninsula. Winter blizzards sometimes affect the islands adjacent to the continental masses. Cross-faculty research can involve winds of other kinds. All over the Archipelago islanders welcome the summer wind known as the BREATH OF HOPE, which carries swarms of butterflies and ladybirds. Less welcome to the people of Paneron is the STIFLER, a humid wind that brings the allergenic pollen of carp-weed bushes from nearby unpopulated islands.

Military History – winds commemorated by their seeming intervention in times of war: the gale that dispersed one attacking fleet, the sudden expiry of a prevailing westerly that becalmed another, the heavenly wind that drove marauding ships on to a reef, the

20

unpredicted storm that prevented an invasive beach landing. Many navigation charts depict prevailing wind direction by incorporating a stylized figure directing the wind. Most of these symbols are ancient naval or military images: a schooner breasting waves, an archer aiming his bow, a whaler with his harpoon, and so on. The work of tabulating this material and cross-referencing it to military records that are often still secret, or locked away in archives in the north, is as yet hardly begun.

Navigation – every inhabited island or group of islands has created its own navigation charts of the seas, navigable passages, tidal surges, bays and shallows in its area. Each such chart or marine almanac contains information, often incorrect or distorted or based on guesswork, about the dominant winds in that region. However, these charts, almanacs and shipping logs also contain a wealth of vernacular first-hand accounts of great winds, sudden calms, bitter storms, as well as much documentary recording of the trade winds, the antitrades, the doldrums, the squalls, the headwinds.

Geography and Topography – the effects of equatorial heat and the creation of localized storm winds, mountainous islands with cliffs and ravines, the horse latitudes, Coriolis, the cooling of the poles, the temperate weather systems of high and low pressures, differential sea temperatures, the effects of the gravitational impact of the sun and the moon.

Esphoven Muy did not live to see the expansion of the Academy, because although she lived to a great age she departed from Aay in unexplained circumstances and never returned.

She was in her thirty-seventh year when the artist Dryd Bathurst arrived on Aay and set up a studio in the artists' quarter of Aay Port. At this time the Academy was still based around her own house. Town records show that Bathurst was resident on the island for less than a year, but during that period he created three of his most celebrated paintings.

Two of them are huge canvases. The first is what many people consider to be the masterwork of his early period: *The Raising of the Hopeless Dead*. This is an apocalyptic vision of a mountainous landscape – once you know that Bathurst was on Aay when he painted the picture, it becomes obvious that the terrible peaks are based on Aay's central range. In the painting, the mountains are being torn apart by a violent electric storm, with cascades of water, rock and liquid mud flooding down the slopes to engulf a fleeing population.

The second painting is no less epic and is held by some critics to be the greater of the two. *Final Hour of the Relief Ship* depicts a storm at sea: a sailing vessel is foundering amid gigantic waves, her sails torn into ribbons and two of her masts broken. A huge sea-serpent is apparently about to consume the passengers and crew leaping from the decks into the sea. Both of these major works are in the permanent collection of the Covenant Maritime Gallery, on the island of Muriseay.

The third painting from Bathurst's Aay period was a portrait of Esphoven Muy herself, and its whereabouts is unknown to this day.

Although the original painting was never exhibited on Aay, colour reproductions based on Bathurst's own print of it are familiar. It is on a significantly smaller scale than the massive oil paintings which were Bathurst's usual stock in trade. The painting of Muy was executed in tempera, the subtle colours employed to render her as a stunningly attractive woman, her light clothes in suggestive disarray while a mocking wind teases at her hair. Her smile, and the expression in her eyes, leaves little doubt in the mind of the viewer about what her relationship with the painter must have been. The painting, called *E. M. The Singer of Airs*, is unique in Bathurst's body of work: no other picture of his is so intimate, so sensual, so revealing of his love and passion.

Esphoven Muy is believed to have left Aay at around the same time as Bathurst moved on. She was popularly assumed to have followed him, and that her absence would therefore be short-lived.

Even as early as this in Bathurst's career, he was renowned not just for his fickle attachments to islands, but also to women. Work at the Academy continued but for the first two or three years after Muy departed the Academy seemed to lose a sense of direction. It was later reorganized when senior members of the academic body created a new managing foundation, and the Academy in its modern form started to take shape.

Muy herself, though, was never seen again on Aay and she had no further contact with the Academy.

She died some fifty years later. Her body was discovered in the tiny cottage in which she had been living, in a remote part of the island of Piqay. The people who lived near her had known her by another name, but when the authorities cleared her house they found many papers and books, and these identified her. She had kept a journal for all the years she lived on Piqay, and although most of the material has never been published the journals themselves are now kept in a closed case within the Academy Library, on Aay.

From the sole published section of her journal, which describes a period of roughly a year in length, a decade after she had arrived on Piqay, and from other papers which were found in the house and are available for inspection in the Academy, as well as certain artefacts discovered in the grounds of her house, it has become possible to gain a glimpse of the life she led in her self-imposed seclusion.

The journal describes her decision to plant trees on the hillside behind her home. For much of the year she writes about she is concentrating on this. Not every kind of tree was suitable to be grown in the Piqay soil, and she chose the hillside site because it was exposed to the wind, and this further restricted her choice of trees. However, the planting went on throughout the period of the journal, and quite clearly for some time afterwards. There is now a whole arboretum, mostly mature, on the Piqay headland where she lived. It has become a protected zone administered by the Piqay Seigniory on behalf of the Academy of the Four Winds.

Muy believed that each different species of tree responded to the pressure of wind in a unique way: the density and grain of the bark, the number of branches and the spread of them, the shape of the leaves on deciduous trees, the resonant qualities of the timber itself, the time of year that buds would appear or leaves would fall, the fineness and length of needles on evergreens, even the kinds of wildlife that might be attracted to inhabit the trees with their nests. All these would have an influence on the way the wind was received and responded to by the tree, and Muy believed she could identify many trees solely from the soughing they made.

She described the sound of a cypress as similar to the mild harmonies of a harp, a tall pine in full finery of needle as an ecstatic clarinet solo, an apple tree in blossom as a frivolous dance of clashing cymbals, an oak as a baritone voice, a narrow poplar bending to a gale as a coloratura.

The yard at the rear of her cottage was also put to use in the strong winds that flew across her headland. She hung one side of the yard with wind-chimes: wooden, glass, crystal, plastic, metal. They were rarely silent. More scientifically, Muy erected a number of wind measurement instruments. Five masts of different heights stood at the upper end of the yard, each bearing different types of anemometers and wind-pressure gauges. She analysed the results on data logging equipment in a specially built cabin, together with the readings from rainfall, humidity and temperature gauges. A tall lightning protector stood above everything.

Although this laboratory has since been dismantled, visitors may experience something of its unique concentration on the winds, because a reconstruction of it is in the Academy Museum in Aay Port. Normal opening hours apply.

Towards the end of the published section of the journals, Muy recorded a declaration that she wished to become a native Piqayean. According to the tradition of the island she said that she intended never to leave it again. She abided by that intent until the end.

In the light of her scientific discoveries the role played by Dryd Bathurst in this long final sequence of Esphoven Muy's life is now trivial. However, it seems that Muy did fall victim to an enigma of the heart. Although Dryd Bathurst never worked or set up a studio on Piqay, it is known that he arrived there not long after leaving Aay, and left again soon after. No one was believed to be accompanying him at the time, but the dates roughly coincide with Muy's arrival on the island.

The standard biography of the artist, *The Epic Canvas of Dryd Bathurst* by Chaster Kammeston, lists an astonishing number of women with whom the artist is known or believed to have had affairs. Esphoven Muy's name is among them, but Kammeston does not go into details.

Although Muy lived and worked on Piqay for much of her life, it is with Aay that she will always be firmly associated.

A springtime breeze that Muy often noticed during the years she was living and working on Aay, now bears her name. The VENTO MUYO is a light, warm zephyr, scented with the fragrance of the wild flowers that grow on the shallow cliffs to the south of Aay Port.

Aay is regularly served by inter-island ferries, but there is no direct link with the mainland. Standards of cuisine and visitor accommodation throughout the island are reportedly excellent. Seafood is a speciality. Daily guided tours of the Academy are available. Visitors require a visa and all normal inoculations – check with your personal physician before travelling. There are liberal shelterate laws, but property is expensive. Visitors should avoid the weeks of late spring as the föhn wind is most likely to be active then.

Currency: Archipelagian simoleon; Muriseayan thaler.

Annadac

CALM PLACE

One of the remotest islands in the Swirl, ANNADAC is situated close to the tidal anomaly that millions of years ago helped form the Swirl.

For the most part, continental Sudmaieure is an icy, snowbound waste, with only a few coastal strips adjacent to sea that melts for part of the year. There is, however, one peninsula, long and narrow, steep with mountains of volcanic origin, that extends to the north. This is the Qataari Peninsula, in the coldest part of which there are several glaciers, and these calve to the eastern side into the stormy Southern Midway. The turbulent combination of warm salty seawater from the Southern Oscillating Stream and the cold fresh meltwater from the drifting icebergs creates a churning and treacherous stretch of ocean, with a multitude of different currents. These, together with several thousand years of volcanism, threw up the hundreds of small islands that are now known as the Swirl. Annadac is one of these Swirl islands, far to the south and close to the continental mass.

With the coming of spring, a huge tidal bulge of water forms in the sea to the south of Annadac, every day, twice a day. This moves rapidly around the island. Over the centuries the phenomenon has caused serious coastal erosion and unpredictable weather patterns. The Annadacians are legendary for their forbearing and stoical nature.

Perhaps the most celebrated Annadacian of her era was the conceptual and installation artist named JORDENN YO.

From an early age Yo became enthralled by the rock and beach

26

formations that had been created all around her island by tidal movements and gale-force winds. Yo came to believe that the island was in essence a permeable being, that it was alive in some mystical sense, and that it could be moulded to react to the elements. She became fascinated by this idea, latterly obsessed by it.

Some of her first installations were cairns or dolmens built on exposed hillsides, carefully situated to catch the light of sunset or sunrise, or to present thrilling silhouettes against the sky, when seen from the most commonly used roads.

Many of these cairns still stand today and are in the care of the Annadac Seigniory offices. Three in particular are of interest to visitors, because Yo set them up in a configuration that would modify the pressure and direction of the wind, and set up a series of dust-filled twisters to march and scatter across the flat land around.

The site is open all year round, but the best time to visit the cairns is in the early fall. Then the prevailing CHOUSTER wind from the south-west, famous for its gusts and sudden changes of direction, will produce the wind funnels for about seven days and nights. Twisters appear other times of the year, but they are randomly produced and therefore the casual visitor cannot be guaranteed to see them.

Then as now, many young people on Annadac enjoyed the sport of tunnelling, and Yo was one of them. It was prohibited on many islands, but Annadac was still tolerant of the activity. Yo soon realized that tunnelling was a pastime that could lend itself to serious artistic activity. Her cairns had brought her work to the attention of the Covenant Foundation on Muriseay, and she was able to raise a small grant to drill some experimental tunnels.

The first one she completed ran from the south side of the island to the north, with a shallow turn at the midway point and a gradual narrowing throughout the length of the tunnel. The southern entrance was built below the tide line. When the tunnel was completed, and the buffer dam opened, the tidal waters began to flow through, twice a day. As the tunnel was opened in midsummer, the tidal effects were at first unexceptional, giving Yo extra time to run flow tests and make suitable modifications and improvements. A few months later, with the tumultuous rising of the spring tide, Annadac experienced for the first time the fantastic rush of water now known as the Yo TORRENT.

The Torrent pours through the tunnel at a terrifying velocity, emitting a thunderous roar that can be heard in most parts of the island. On the northern side, the flowing water bursts out into the rock-filled open sea in a great foaming sluice of ice-cold water.

Within a couple of years Annadac had become the destination of choice for thrill-seekers, as it remains today. Every year, in the three months of the highest tides, these people board rafts or don inflatable jackets, allowing themselves to be thrust excitingly and dangerously through the Torrent. Although the Annadac Seigniory imposes a number of safety regulations, every year brings an inevitable death toll.

Yo herself is not known to have ridden the Torrent. She left Annadac soon after the first of the spring tides, and is thought to have returned to her home island only once more, to attend the funeral of her father.

Out of season Annadac is a quiet island, dependent on farming and fishing, and offers few facilities for the casual tourist. Because of the proximity of Annadac to Sudmaieure, many of the young soldiers who become deserters pass through the island on their way north. However, there are strict havenic laws and most of the soldiers do not stay long. Ordinary visitors to the island will be unaware of them.

For those who intend to visit Annadac for the sport, the peak period is also the most expensive, and is usually fully booked by regular users. However, good torrenting is possible in the first two weeks of summer, the weather is warmer and the prices are lower. The authorities have ruled that visitors must carry full insurance and a cash deposit is demanded in case funeral arrangements become necessary. No vaccinations are required, but random medical checks are performed on all who use the Torrent. Some operators offer inclusive tours.

Currency: Aubracian talent; Muriseayan thaler.

Aubrac Grande
or
Aubrac Chain

The AUBRAC CHAIN is unusual in the Dream Archipelago, in that it has no discernible patois name, but instead is named after the scientist who discovered the true nature of the islands. His name was JAEM AUBRAC, an entomologist at Tumo University, who had taken on the field trip to replace an indisposed colleague. Aubrac left unfinished a laboratory research project on which he had been working, believing that it would be only a matter of a few weeks before he returned.

When Aubrac and his team of four young assistants arrived at the chain of thirty-five islands they and the operational staff set up a working base camp on one of the islands (then unnamed). It was not until some time later that they began to realize the island they had chosen was completely uninhabited.

Aubrac's journal records the discovery in what seems now to be an unexcited way, considering the reason for it that he later established. At first the team made the assumption that there would be settlements somewhere, if not on that particular island then certainly on some of the other thirty-four islands. They also kept in mind past experiences of remote islands, where indigenous people had been frightened of the new arrivals and kept out of their way. However, the team gradually realized they must have stumbled across a genuinely uninhabited part of the Archipelago.

Later explorations were to establish that nowhere else in the huge group of islands was there any evidence of recent habitation.

For Aubrac, the new islands were an entomologist's dream come true. Soon after he arrived he communicated to the head of his university department that his life's work now lay ahead of him. This turned out to be literally true, as he was never again to leave the chain of islands.

The number of new species of insects catalogued by Aubrac is simply vast – more than one thousand were identified within a year of his starting work. Although he was to die at a relatively young age, Aubrac is recognized as the leading zoologist in his field. He was awarded a posthumous Inclair Laureateship for his work. There is a monument to him in Grande Aubrac Town, which in the modern age is the administrative capital of the group.

Aubrac's name will be forever identified with one particular insect, not for its discovery as such but for most of the detailed research work that was to follow. The incident that began his research was an unfortunate contact by one of his assistants, a herpetologist named Hadimá Thryme. She was accidentally infected by one of the insects. Aubrac describes in his journal what happened to this woman:

In the early evening Hadimá wanted to observe her tree-snakes again, but no one else was free to accompany her. The snakes have a deadly venom, but Hadimá knows what she is doing and she carries antidotes so I gave her permission to go alone. She said the snakes are always torpid in the evenings. She had been gone for less than half an hour when her emergency bleeper went off. I took the GP vehicle, and Dake [Dr D. L. Lei , the toxicologist on Aubrac's team] and I drove at high speed to the site. We assumed of course that one of the snakes had bitten her.

Hadimá was barely conscious when we found her, and obviously suffering intense pain. We examined her quickly but could not find any sign of a bite, even in the area of her right ankle – she was bent double, holding the ankle tightly. Dake Lei administered about 2ccs of anti-crotalic serum, effective against most haemotoxic or haemolytic reptile venoms. We then put her inside the vehicle and brought her back to the base as quickly as possible.

We began emergency medical procedures, with Antalya [Dr A. Benger, the team physician] taking charge, and Dake and I assisting.

30

Although by this time Hadimá was only semi-conscious, she managed to convey to us that the bite was definitely in her ankle. Still we could find no puncture mark. The skin was slightly reddened, which we assumed was partly caused by the tight grip she had had on it. To be on the safe side, Antalya made an incision in that area, and a vacuum pump was pressed against it to try to evacuate any venom that remained. We applied a tourniquet above the knee. Antalya injected more serum, this time including anti-bothropic serum. Hadimá kept resurfacing into consciousness, and screaming in agony. She complained that the left side of her body was giving pain. The electronic monitors revealed that her blood pressure and heart-rate were both dangerously high. She said the crown of her head was hurting as if a knife blade had been thrust into it from behind. Her right foreleg swelled up, and became darkly discoloured. This was an indication of haemolysis: the haemoglobin in her blood was breaking down. Antalya injected antivenin, in an attempt to halt it.

The swelling continued to spread. Blood was flowing rapidly from the incision on Hadimá's ankle and she complained that it was almost impossible to breathe, even with applied oxygen. In a moment of rationality, Hadimá said she was certain a snake had not bitten her. She remembered brushing against a large black sphere on the ground, which she had thought was a seed pod. It was covered in short and bristly hairs.

This was familiar. I hurried to my office and collected some photographs taken a few days ago. I showed them to Hadimá and although she was clearly slipping into semi-consciousness again, she instantly confirmed that it was one of those she had touched.

I knew then that she had been poisoned by an insect, rolled into a protective sphere. I have not yet had time to do anything more than simply note the presence of these large arthropods, and take the photographs. I have witnessed the defensive rolling several times. The insects are everywhere around us, and although in an entomological sense they are fascinating, we find them repulsive to look at and sense a bite or a sting from one of them would be at least unpleasant and possibly dangerous. We are all keeping a safe distance from them until I have a chance to investigate them properly. I am planning to capture a few in the near future and examine them properly. Fortunately, the insects seem to feel as wary of us as we are of them, and scuttle off if we surprise them. I am now certain Hadimá must have brushed against one of them.

Her pulse started to vary wildly, from below 50 bpm to above 130 bpm. She voided her bladder incontinently and the liquid was highly coloured with blood. She complained again about the pain and appeared to be about to lose full consciousness. She was deathly pale and her entire body was covered in sweat. Antalya injected more stimulants, coagulants and antivenins into her. She made small incisions on Hadimá's arms and legs, to attempt to relieve the acute swelling. Blood, lymph and pale liquid gushed from these incisions. Her right leg was darkly discoloured for its entire length. Briefly, her pulse could not be detected and we carried out emergency resuscitation procedures. Further stimulants and coagulants went into her and although they increased the physical pain they restored her to consciousness. More discoloration was developing: on her arms, her abdomen and her neck. Both eyes were bloodshot. She vomited repeatedly, bringing up blood. Antalya administered further antivenin serums. Hadimá's neck and throat had swollen to the point where she could not speak, and was barely able to breathe, with or without the oxygen mask.

Fifteen minutes into her ordeal, a deep calm suddenly came over Hadimá and we feared the worst. I could see the way Antalya was reacting – it had become a matter of life support. Hadimá's pulse first accelerated, then calmed down again. She began to tremble, at first just her hands and feet, but then her whole body was shaken by tremors. The oxygen mask came off and Dake had to hold it over her mouth and nose by main force. We all felt we were losing her. But then she opened her eyes, and when Dake offered her some water she took it orally and kept it down. Gradually, the tremors left her. Her limbs were still discoloured and swollen. She shouted with pain if we touched her anywhere.

At the point where the sting or bite had been made a series of large blebs had appeared. These were hard to the touch but gave the patient no extra pain, so Antalya experimentally lanced one of them. A pale fluid filled with tiny black particles issued. Dake quickly examined these particles under a microscope, then on his urgent advice Antalya lanced the remainder of the blisters. The fluid that issued was carefully collected and stored in glass flasks.

Within another half an hour Hadimá Thryme was able to breathe unaided. For three days, under constant monitoring and light sedation, she was allowed to sleep while being fed intravenously. The swelling gradually went down, although the acute pains continued.

Aubrac ordered an emergency vessel from Tumo, and Hadimá was evacuated back to the university hospital. A few weeks later the team, who had remained on station, were relieved to hear that she had recovered from the poisoning and that all traces of the toxins were gone from her. She underwent a long convalescence, and afterwards said she did not wish to return to the expedition. She was replaced by Fran Herkker, a herpetologist from the main zoo in Muriseay Town, who arrived at the base a few weeks after the attack on Hadimá.

After Hadimá's departure, Aubrac set aside his pleasurable pursuit of butterflies, beetles, wasps, and so on, and concentrated almost entirely on research into the insect that had stung her.

In the first place, knowing it was a new species, he named it after Hadimá and gave it the scientific name *Buthacus thrymeii*. The genus was as yet tentative, because in general shape and ferocity the thryme was close to a scorpion, having two large and muscular pincers carried beside its head, and a curved tail rising over the body, tipped with a poisonous sting. But scorpions were of the arachnida class, having eight legs, while the thryme had only six. It was also significantly larger than any scorpion: most adult thrymes he eventually managed to capture were fifteen to twenty centimetres in length, but others he saw in the wild, which eluded him, appeared to be thirty or forty centimetres in length. From Jaem Aubrac's journal:

We have at last managed to capture three thrymes, after several weeks of danger and frustration. It took trial and error, and a substantial degree of risk to myself and Dake. Naturally we were wearing protective gear, but the daytime temperatures on this island are suffocating. We have discovered that thrymes are most active when the rains come, which is every afternoon for about three hours. There is no lessening of temperature during the rains, so any physical movement across the muddy ground is exhausting.

The particular problems of trying to trap a thryme (setting aside the fact that the mature insect is one of the most venomous insects I have ever encountered) are firstly that they can run for short distances at an amazing speed, faster than a running man, even when the ground is muddy or waterlogged; secondly, they vanish into underground burrows with astonishing alacrity. Neither of us felt willing to start digging to try to find their nests.

In the end the only way we could get hold of them was to make a sudden or alarming noise or movement, which would make most of the insects in the vicinity roll themselves up. This at least made them stationary, although they would unroll very quickly indeed, their stings raised and their mandibles open for a strike. However, by moving swiftly we were able to scoop up and trap the ones we wanted.

We discovered just how dangerous the insect could be when rolled: the bristles are as fine as hairs, but they are stiff and hollow and act as hypodermic needles for the venom they contain. The bristles of one of the first thrymes I tried to pick up easily penetrated the outer level of the handling gauntlets I was wearing, although the inner layer managed to block them. One of the insects Dake picked up unrolled in his hand, and spat venom directly towards his eyes – needless to say he was wearing visor protection, which saved him.

Once the insects were safely contained in laboratory condition, Aubrac began to examine them at close quarters. Although none of the team had ever been attacked by one of the thrymes, they were clearly ferocious. Aubrac's first enquiry was into the creatures' aggressive nature, or whether its fearsome weapon system was merely for defence:

I have created three test environments, each made of an escape-proof glass container, with a layer of moist soil and leaf-mould at the base. Into this I have introduced a number of different kinds of potential foes or predators, to see how the thryme would get on. The grim results are as follows:

1. A hawk-like predatory bird, seen by us to hover and dive against small animals or perhaps insects on the ground. The bird we captured for this test was approximately three times the size of the largest thryme. It panicked as it was thrust into the test cell, and was dead within four seconds. We have not repeated this experiment.
2. A pit viper, at least three metres in length: survived for forty-eight seconds.
3. A rat: killed within nineteen seconds. It survived so long only by fast attempts to escape.
4. A giant venomous centipede, with a heavily armoured carapace and one of the most pernicious venoms Dake says he has ever analysed: it vigorously joined the thryme in battle, but survived for only thirty-three seconds.
5. A large spider, seen to attack birds' nests and to display 'huntsman' tendencies of aggressive behaviour, and equipped with two large sacs of highly effective venom: dead within four seconds.
6. A huge scorpion, one of the largest I have ever come across: it attacked the thryme with instant relish, but was dead within eight seconds.

More alarming still was the discovery Dr Lei made about the system of venom carried by the thryme. It carried two arrangements of venom sacs: one in the tail, the other in tiny bladders inside its mandible. From the jaw it could envenom both by a bite and in some cases by spitting. This was a fairly conventional arrangement, although the venom was a peculiarly powerful cocktail of proteins, amino acids and anti-coagulants. Lei's analysis of the compounds was to a large extent frustrated by the discovery that the venom appeared to change its nature from one individual thryme specimen to another, and even then to change its constituents at different times of the year.

The impact of a bite or sting on a human being, as they had seen when Hadimá Thryme had been merely scratched with one of the defensive fine hairs, was a full-scale attack on not only the nervous system but also the blood and cells. Although standard antitoxins alleviated many of the symptoms if applied quickly enough, the venom was so intense that it was almost impossible, at least for a small team working on site, to know if an effective antidote would ever be possible.

However, an extra threat existed, as Aubrac described:

We have established that the really dangerous thryme is the female of the species. There is not much to distinguish male from female by outer appearance alone: the female seems to be slightly larger than the male, although as we have to work with so few specimens it's difficult to be certain. She has extra joints in her arthropodic shell, and her thorax is wider than that of the male. However, if coming across one of these dark, fast-moving beings in the wild, you would not be able to tell the difference from the superficial appearance. The obvious rule remains: if you see a thryme, keep well away!

The female carries her young in a marsupial pouch inside her jaw – at this stage they are microscopic grubs, or in some cases fertilized eggs. A bite from her could be either a venomous bite, an impregnation of parasitic grubs, or a mixture of the two.

I am now urgently concerned to know whether or not it was a female who infected Hadimá, because Dake tells me he has found traces of fertilized ova inside some of our captives' bristles. The news from Tumo is that she has made a complete recovery, so let us hope so.

A few weeks after he wrote that journal entry Aubrac was informed by the university on Tumo that Hadimá had suddenly fallen ill, suffering horrific symptoms of poisoning once again. The medical staff at the hospital had been unable to help her, and she died within two hours of feeling the first twinges of pain. No traces of venom were ever found. A post-mortem examination was begun, but her internal organs proved to be massively infested by parasitic maggots. All her major organs had been destroyed in this way. Aubrac immediately ordered that no more examination should be made of her body and that it should be kept in isolation in an hermetically sealed casket. He then arranged for Antalya Benger to travel to Tumo to certify her death. After this, Hadimá's body was removed from the mortuary and cremated.

Now realizing that the incubation period of the infestation was at least several months, Aubrac instituted a major program of incineration at his research station: every thryme they had ever had inside the laboratory, all the remains of any of the animals tested against the laboratory specimens, any of the soil media used inside the captive thrymes' cases, any organic thing at all that had had the least, most glancing contact with a thryme … everything was incinerated. The glass cases were treated with acid, then broken up and buried.

Staff at the hospital where Hadimá had died were moved into isolation until they could be tested negative for infestation. Fortunately, it transpired that no parasitic invasion to key workers had taken place.

Soon after Aubrac learned of the death of Hadimá Thryme, an unexpected change took place in the weather. Aubrac's journal again:

We have been getting used to the daily cloudbursts but about three weeks ago they became a thing of the past. We are now afflicted with a steady wind from the east, which is hot, dehydrating and relentless. It has the usual negative effect of an unwavering wind: we are all feeling short-tempered and depressed, we find it difficult to sleep and we are desperate for a change. Every day is now the same.

I have been trying to extract some information from the university about the climate of these islands, but they say that there was practically no knowledge of them before our expedition. All they could tell me was that because of the position – a few degrees north of the equator, with a lot of open ocean around us, to west and north – we are exposed to a prevailing wind known as the Shamal. There are many barren or desertified islands upwind of us. Paneron is the best known.

The relief from the endless mud and humidity was of course welcome at first, but all five of us are alarmed by the effect the sudden drought is having on the thrymes. Whereas until quite recently we would spot them on a daily basis, they remained shy and furtive. The dry weather has critically changed their behaviour.

For one thing they appear to be hungry. They are violently attacking anything alive – two days ago a seagull landed incautiously on the ground close to our base, and in full view of us was almost immediately overwhelmed by a horde of thrymes. There are now hundreds, perhaps thousands of them around us. It is of course impossible to venture out unless full precautions are taken, but because of the clumsy weight of our protective gear, and the hot wind and unbroken sunshine, we keep outside trips to a minimum.

This morning Yute [Yuterdal Trellin, the team's intercession scientist] had to go across to the storage building to collect some medications and other materials. When he returned there were three thrymes attached to the back of his protective suit, their pincers deeply buried in the protective material. Dake and I managed to get the insects off him, killed them by beating with the paddles we have kept for just such an emergency, then incinerated the bodies, destroyed the suit Yute had had been wearing, and gave him a thorough medical examination to determine if any punctures had been made to his skin. All is well. No one is more relieved than Yute!

Matters deteriorated over the next few days. Swarms of the thryme were seen outside the station and Aubrac ordered that no one should go outside. He discontinued keeping his journal around this time, because, according to Dr Lei, the entire team realized field work had become impossible.

They knew they were going to have to evacuate the base, and that it would be only a matter of time before they did. Accordingly, they began dismantling their laboratories and transmitted all their written notes to Tumo University. These included Aubrac's journal, which is how his record has survived.

Evacuation presented a serious logistical problem, as any activity at all attracted the attention of the thrymes. The GP vehicle, kept sealed up close to the main building, was secure enough, but transferring to it and loading it up was fraught with dangers. While the team prepared, a boat was despatched from Tumo to pick them up.

Aubrac's last message to the university summed up what he clearly felt at the time was the only significant discovery they had made: 'This island group is uninhabitable,' he wrote. 'No one has ever lived here, no normal human being ever will.'

They went ahead with the evacuation but it was almost a total disaster. Fran Herkker was attacked by two thrymes while trying to enter the GP – in spite of the protection she was wearing she died almost instantly. The team felt they had no alternative but to abandon her body on the ground just outside the base buildings. In the stress and anxiety of making their escape, they had no facilities for burying or cremating her body. Less than an hour later, while the GP was still heading towards the coast, Aubrac himself was attacked by a thryme, which had somehow managed to get inside the vehicle. He died traumatically and with horrifying swiftness. Although the remaining three felt that in the interests of science they should at least attempt to take his body back for post-mortem examination, they quickly decided the danger was too great. Aubrac's body too was abandoned.

Dake Lei, Yuterdal Trellin and Antalya Benger survived the journey to the coast and were safely picked up by the ship sent to save them. A few months later, Yuterdal Trellin died suddenly, and his body was found to be infested with parasitic grubs.

Thus the background story of the Aubrac Chain. Fifty years after the premature end of the expedition, the entire group of thirty-five islands was named after Aubrac, as was the largest island: Aubrac Grande. Other individual islands were named Lei, Benger, Trellin and Herkker. The Archipelago authorities declared the group a nature and wildlife reserve, and entry to the islands was prohibited on an absolute basis.

That is how the Aubrac Chain might have remained until the present day, if it were not for two unforeseen events.

The first was the discovery of several colonies of thrymes on some of the more southerly islands in the Serques. Until this, it was believed that the insects were found only in the Aubracs and would be contained there by natural processes. How some of the insects had emigrated, or crossed the sea, no one knew, but it raised the horrific spectre of the insect starting to disseminate throughout the Archipelago, with an all too easily imaginable impact on the lives of millions of people.

The Serque colonies were eradicated, although thrymes are still encountered on some of the more remote islands. As for wider dissemination, since the Serque discovery colonies of thrymes have been found on other islands and the insect is now habituated throughout most of the tropical zone. By rigorous culls and other precautions, thryme colonies have been effectively contained and controlled. Some islands have succeeded in eradicating the insect altogether, but in most places it has survived at a minimal level.

In general the thryme is feared more than it is encountered. It is true to say that most people are phobic because of its appearance and speed, its darting gait, the movement of its long legs. Practical fear of the consequences of an attack is of course another matter entirely. The insect is easily identified and people stay well away from it when it is discovered.

Local Seigniory departments have set up eradication squads, and most public buildings are routinely sanitized. Property sold on the open market is obliged by law to possess anti-thryme certification. Effective antidotes to the poison now exist, if applied quickly enough.

The Aubrac Chain is the insect's natural habitat. While the islands remained unused by human settlers the thryme was presumably dominant, as it had been before and during Aubrac's few months of scientific work. But the population of the Dream Archipelago was increasing rapidly and the need for living and working space was mounting. The availability of a huge expanse of undeveloped island territory, lushly vegetated and quite likely rich in mineral deposits, was too great a temptation.

Corporations from the new technologies identified Aubrac as the ideal location for a gateway hub, made the necessary arrangements with Seigniory departments, and started construction and re-zoning work.

From the outset, the environment of the Aubrac chain was planned on a non-enviropollutant basis, which is to say that every existing aspect of the natural habitat would be systematized and supplanted. All danger from the thrymes would be removed along with everything else. Natural rainforest would be converted to woodland parks, deserts would be irrigated and made arable, rocky shores and open plains would be turned into leisure and sports complexes. Wildlife would be introduced to game parks, if no natural wildlife was already present. New cities would be built. New industries would leap into existence. Prosperity would be guaranteed.

In the modern age, the developed Aubrac has become the dynamic heart of the Archipelago's booming silicon economy. The various huge IT corporations which now administer the islands are the engine-house of this prosperity, dominated by the creators and inventors of operating and networking systems. From the forest of gleaming towers, campuses and development facilities, all wrapped in landscaped parkland, the hidden infrastructure of today's world is reliably routed through a system of hi-def optical cables and digital links.

From Aubrac arise all IT service and support facilities, unified communications setups, telepresence opportunities, content delivery facilitators, troubleshooting guerrilla squads, web exchange activists, borderless optical networking, application management, corporate partnership consultancies, vid-conferencing suites, prestige data centre availabilities, immersive operability and anti-operability, gaming interfaces, collaboration experiences and implementative facedowns.

Many of the thirty-five Aubracian islands have been ecologically systematized and industrially managed as planned by the IT companies, but a few of the smaller islands were parcelled up into smaller tracts to be developed by private enterprise as dwellings. The corporate standards of infrastructure remain on these residence islands, with total commute accessibility to the hubs, digital holism and full leisure gateways.

One of the largest Aubracian islands, Trellin, has been redesigned as a tourist and visitor attraction, based on its large sweeps of natural rainforest (fully managed, but reconfigured as a wilderness activity interface area), and the spectacular cliffs overlooking the Midway Sea. There are no zoning controls or plans on Trellin, because of the input of many entrepreneurs from the distant island of Prachous. These powerful Prachoit families are the principal interests behind the booming economy of the Aubrac Chain. Their luxurious homes are of course not accessible to visitors, but some of them may be glimpsed from afar.

For the intending visitor, certain preparations are necessary.

Firstly, a minimum amount of convertible currency must be imported to the Aubrac Chain and spent while there. The local currency is of course the Aubracian talent. There is no official exchange rate with the Archipelagian simoleon, so currency should be bought before leaving home.

Full travel and medical insurance is obligatory, and this must include provision for funeral and crematorium expenses, and repatriation costs for relatives and other travelling companions. Every traveller, no matter what age, must be insured in this way. There are strict shelterate laws, and unless a work permit has been obtained in advance, no one is admitted to the Aubrac Chain without a recognized round-trip or return voyage certificate. Anti-importunation regulations are the strictest in the Archipelago. Erotomanes must be licensed in advance, but not all local values are acceptable on Aubrac – visitors should check with their home Seigniory before setting out.

Finally, some rather more informal words of advice to all visitors who, in knowledge of the history of the Aubrac Chain, might have residual fears about the possible danger of a thryme sting.

Here we use information from the *Official Aubracian Handbook*, copies of which can be obtained throughout the Archipelago from licensed tour operators. The *Handbook* describes life in the Aubrac Chain in comprehensive detail, but is in our view rather too vague about some matters. What follows has to be our unofficial interpretation of that which has been left unsaid. We merely observe a few facts.

Workers around the Aubrac silicon lagoon are amongst the highest paid and best treated in the world. They do, though, suffer an abnormally high mortality rate, and in most cases the cause of premature death is not revealed.

It is against Aubracian law to be anywhere at any time without a supply of antidote serum.

All depictions or descriptions or even mentions of deadly insects are prohibited by law. The word 'thryme' may not be used (and is not used in the *Handbook*). The ban extends to books, magazines and newspapers, public notices, warning signs and official literature. No drawings of large insects, or photographs or digital image files of them, may be made, held or distributed. The word 'thryme' may not be used in conversations, and use of the word 'insect' must always be either in the strict scientific sense, or to refer to butterflies, bees, and so on.

There is no such thing as burial of the dead anywhere in the Aubrac Chain: all dead bodies, human or animal, are invariably cremated. Organic waste is incinerated. Sewage is subject to intensive reprocessing.

A full medical examination (including in some cases exploratory surgery) is mandatory for all visitors, not only on entry to Aubrac, but also on departure.

All physical ailments which appear while in Aubrac, however mild, chronic or medically describable, will invoke deportation orders from the authorities, and these are invariably carried out.

Although our readers will draw their own conclusions, we should add in fairness that the Aubrac Chain remains one of the most intriguing and interesting destinations anywhere in our Archipelago. The swimming is superb and the sea is clean, there is no better cuisine anywhere else in the islands, all hotels operate at the highest international standards, uninterrupted web access is guaranteed ... and the golf courses, our researchers have reported, are incomparable. After a successful putt, though, visitors are not allowed to remove their golf-balls by hand from the cup. Automatic ball-retrieval devices, or trained staff, are always on hand to be of service.

Cheoner

RAIN SHADOW

From File No: KS 49284116, Criminal Records Office, Cheoner Municipal People's Court.

My name is KERITH SINGTON and I was born on the island of CHEONER, in the town of the same name. I am male. I am twenty-seven years old. I fit the description of tall, well-built, dark-haired, blue-eyed, no extraneous facial hair. I walk with a slight limp but have no other disabilities.

This interview is taking place in the offices of the Policier Seignioral, in Cheoner Town. Serjeant A is my interviewing officer. Caporal B is attending as Independent Policier Witness. The interview is being recorded and will be transcribed by Serjeant A.

I have no complaints about the policier treatment of me since my arrest.

I am not legally represented, but I was offered the opportunity of being represented *pro bono* by a member of the Procurator's Department in Cheoner Town, which I declined. I am of sound mind and body and am making this statement freely and of my own accord and not under duress.

I understand that I have been charged with murder and that this statement may be produced in court as evidence.

I have been asked to describe my personal background before I was arrested.

I was born on RAIN SHADOW [Cheoner]. I had two brothers and one sister, but one of my brothers died when I was still little. I went to school in the big town on Rain Shadow [Cheoner Town]. I was very happy indeed at school, and I think I did well. I was always popular with the other boys. All my teachers spoke well of me, and they are willing to come to court to give evidence on my behalf.

I did have some trouble with older boys, who were always picking on me. I deny that I got into trouble. I deny that I was accused of stealing things from three other students and one of the teachers. I deny that I was involved in the incident in which another boy had to go to hospital. I deny that I had to leave the school early.

My mum and dad always loved me, although after dad went to live on RED JUNGLE [Muriseay] I didn't see much of him any more.

After I left school I spent a lot of time looking for a job, but no one would employ me. In the end I got a job as a deckhand on one of the ferries that travels between Rain Shadow and Red Jungle. I liked this job but it never paid me much money. I used to do odd jobs to earn extra money. I deny that I was involved in any crimes. I do admit that I would sometimes take messages for other people, or carry things for passengers on the ferry if they didn't want to have their luggage searched. I deny that I made any money doing this. I agree that I earned extra cash from time to time in ways I am not willing to describe.

[Detained Person (KS) is shown a print-out from Muriseay Policier Seignioral, but Serjeant A has to read it to him.]

I agree that I have a record of criminal offences, but I will say on oath that they are all minor offences which were either committed by other people, or I was involved with the people who committed the crimes when I wasn't there. They weren't violent offences, except one or two of them were. I deny that I have ever physically attacked any policier officers. I do not carry a knife or any other weapon. I agree I was once charged with carrying an automatic pistol, but there were reasons for that and I was let off. I deny that it was mine.

I do not think that the policier are trying to victimize me or intimidate me. I have been treated well, given food and drink three times a day, I am allowed to exercise in the yard and I have experienced no punishments from the officers on this station.

I agree that I have been to SLOW TIDE [Nelquay] and CHILL WIND [Goorn], but I did not stay long on either island. Anyway I was working on a ferry which meant I called at many islands and I cannot remember all their names. I deny that I made friends on Slow Tide. I agree that I was questioned by the policier on Chill Wind.

I do have friends who are travellers. I do have friends who are known to the policier as street drinkers. I have never been a traveller or a street drinker. My friends travel about the islands and I agree that I have sometimes been seen with them. I agree that these friends are known to use narcotic drugs, and that all of them have served time in prison. I cannot tell you the names of these friends because I either did not know them or because I have since forgotten them. One was called Mack. I have never been to prison myself.

[Detained Person (KS) is shown a detention record from Muriseay Category 4 Prison, which he denies is his. Serjeant A reads it to him, but Detained Person (KS) claims it must be someone else with a similar name.]

When I went to the island called Chill Wind [Goorn is part of the Hetta Group], which is a long way from Red Jungle but it is on the route which my main ferry job takes me, I did not intend to kill anyone. I was short of money and one of my friends gave me some. I spent the money on food and the clothes I was wearing when I was arrested. I deny that I stole those clothes. The money that was found on me is mine. That is not the money my friend gave me, but some other money.

I agree that I tried a few of the pills my friends had with them, but they were medicines for headaches. I have many problems with headaches and blackouts. My friends often help me by giving me something for the pain. We also had several alcoholic drinks, and I drank a few of them myself. We were having a good time and a lot of laughs and I was not angry with anyone. I did not have another blackout that day or at any time that the offence was committed. I can clearly remember what happened and I promise I am telling the truth.

Until I was arrested I had never heard of the man called Akal Drester Commissah. I have never met Akal Drester Commissah. He has never done anything to me. I have never had any dealings with him. I was not angry with him about anything. I did not owe

47

him any money. I had not seen him before that night. I now know more about him. I have been told that he was a performer of some kind. I think he was an actor, but no one would tell me. He used the name 'Commis' when he was on stage.

I agree I was in the theatre at the time of his death. I deny that I went in without paying. One of my friends must have paid for me because I think he worked in the theatre. I agree that I went backstage.

I don't know how I found the sheet of glass. One of my friends must have given it to me. Three of my friends helped me carry it. It was me who told them where to carry it to. It was my idea all along. I am completely responsible for what happened.

I was angry with Mr Commissah but I can no longer remember why. He might have picked on me, but I don't know why. No, I could not carry the sheet of glass on my own. It was large, too large for me on my own. Yes, I am strong, but not that strong. It's not true that I carried it on my own, but I did tell the others who were helping me where to take it. We made a lot of noise but no one heard us because people in the audience were laughing and there was music playing. It was an orchestra, not a record.

No, I cannot remember what tune they were playing. Yes, I can now remember the tune they were playing. It was called *The Sea Flows By*. I know the tune because it is a favourite of mine. I recognize it from the recording you played me, but I could not remember the title until you reminded me.

It was me who told the others to drop the glass on Mr Commissah. Yes, they heard me over the noise of the music. My actual words were, 'Let's kill the bastard now.' I am certain those were my exact words. Yes, I am certain. I might have called him something else, more offensive. I can't remember exactly what I said. I agree I might have used the word 'asshole' instead. Yes, I am certain of that. Yes, I use both words to describe people I don't like. I often use words I'm not supposed to.

We were in the place above the stage where there are a lot of ropes and other stuff. I can't remember how we got up there. I think we climbed. I went first and my friends followed me. I can't remember how we carried the sheet of glass up. I think it was up there already. I don't know why it was up there. Yes, it might have been in the yard at the back of the theatre and we carried it up there. I think we climbed up ropes. If you say there was a ladder, then I remember we climbed that. I followed my friends up the ladder.

All I know for certain is that when I reached the top they were already there with the sheet of glass. Yes, I was wearing gloves, which is why my fingerprints do not appear on the glass. Yes, I always wear gloves when I am out with my friends. I don't know why. No, I don't have those gloves with me any more.

I can't remember why I wanted to kill Mr Commissah. I don't think I intended to. We were having a laugh. It was a sort of joke. The people in the audience were laughing. We held the glass until Mr Commissah was beneath us. Then I said the words I just told you, and we let go of the sheet of glass.

I can't remember how I escaped from the theatre. No one saw me as far as I know. I remember running away down the road. No one chased me. I can't remember where I ran to. I probably ran back to my ship, where I worked. I didn't see my friends again, and I can't remember their names. I think they were from Chill Wind. I think some of them were from Red Jungle, but I'm not sure any more. Yes, they were also from Slow Tide. They were all the same age as me, or older. They looked like islanders, not visitors.

No, I don't speak the patois of Chill Wind. No, I have never been to Chill Wind. I have never been to the town of Omhuuv. Yes, the ferry I worked on did occasionally call at Omhuuv. Yes, I do recognize the words *Teater Sjøkaptein*, but I don't know what they mean. Yes, they mean 'The Seacaptain Theatre'. That is the theatre I went to, where I murdered Mr Commis. I am definitely telling you the truth.

I was excited by what I had done, but I did not speak to anyone else about it. I saw something about it on television, and by then everyone knew all about it. I carried on with my life and had forgotten all about it until I was arrested. I am very sorry for what I have done. I didn't mean it.

This statement was dictated by the Detained Person (KS) in the presence of two officers of the Cheoner Policier Seignioral, and transcribed by Serjeant A, the arresting officer. It was read to the Detained Person, Kerith Sington, and all necessary corrections and amendments were made to his instructions. He has initialled every page of this transcript, and has placed his mark below.

X

his mark, Kerith Sington ......

From *Cheoner Chronicle*, 34/13/77:

The execution of Kerith Sington, the murderer of the mime artiste Commis, was carried out by guillotine this morning at 6:00 am in Cheoner Category 1 Prison. His execution was witnessed by a jury of twelve volunteers, and the death was confirmed and certified at 6:02 am by the prison doctor. All procedures of mitigation and appeal had been scrupulously followed and applied. Sington made a full confession to the crime and during the trial witnesses came forward to corroborate what he admitted. A last-minute appeal to the Seignior for mercy was turned down.

Gooden Herre, the prison governor, said to reporters outside the prison gate: 'With the execution of this evil young man, the entire Dream Archipelago has been rid of fear. The execution was carried out properly, expertly and in humane circumstances, and is intended as a deterrent to others.'

Sington was born on Cheoner, and educated at Cheoner Technical School. His parents separated while he was still a child. He began his life of crime while still a teenager and committed many different offences, some of dishonesty but mostly of petty violence, usually in concert with others. He spent many periods in detention, but after he found a job with Muriseay Marine his offending appears to have declined.

Sington's murder of the distinguished mime artiste, Commis, was carried out while Mr Commis was performing on stage in the *Sjøkaptein Theatre*, on the island of Goorn, part of the Hetta Group. Kerith Sington committed the murder with three others, but the identity of these people has never been established. Sington is known to have been the ringleader. All four were drug addicts and on the evening in question they had been drinking alcohol to excess. Members of the audience gave evidence at the trial that they had seen Singon running away from the theatre in the aftermath of the crime.

The policier are still searching for Singon's accomplices, who are believed to come from Goorn, or from somewhere else in the Hetta Group, or from Muriseay. There is also a connection to Nelquay, but the policier say they are no longer making enquiries there.

Extract from the Report of Judicial Enquiry into the Murder of Akal Drester Commissah, by Seignior Putar Themper, Attorney Supreme, Muriseay.
The murder of Akal Drester Commissah, followed by the confession, conviction and eventual execution of the perpetrator Kerith Singon, continues to cause concern. This concern is felt not only in certain sections of the judiciary and the press, but in a significant proportion of the general public. Several books of investigative journalism have been published about the case, highlighting evidence that was not available to the original judge and jury. More is now understood about Singon's background and mental state of health than was known at the time. Serious questions about the safety of Singon's confession have also been raised.

As senior presiding judge I have been commissioned to review all the papers and evidence that remain on file, and wherever possible to track down surviving witnesses.

As these events took place more than forty years ago I was not able to trace any witnesses who are still alive or capable of giving reliable testimony, so I have depended on the trial papers and other bundles of prosecution evidence. All the defence papers are intact. Because of the notoriety of the case the papers have been preserved in good order and I am not aware of any omissions or replacements since the trial was concluded.

The murdered man, Mr Commissah, appears to have been an innocent victim, who was in no way connected with the convicted man. It is not likely he did anything that would provoke an attack. He was respected and admired and to the present day the few performances of his that are available as visual recordings are appreciated and enjoyed by people of all ages.

I turn now to the background and character of Sington, which is where much of the anxiety about this case has arisen.

Kerith Sington was born in a poor part of Cheoner Town. His father, Ladd Sington, was a petty criminal, an alcoholic and a drug addict, and was said by many people, including neighbours, to conduct a violently abusive relationship with his wife. The wife, Mai Sington, mother of Kerith, was also an alcoholic and worked as a part-time prostitute.

The house in which Kerith grew up was always in bad repair, filthy inside and soiled with food waste and animal faeces. Throughout his childhood Kerith was the subject of neglect, abuse and violence, although none of this appears to have come to the attention of local agencies at that time.

Sington grew up to be a young man of exceptional size, with long arms and a large head. He was always tall for his age. Because of his unusual appearance and subdued manner he was bullied at school. Medical examination of Sington while he was in custody established that he was profoundly deaf in one ear, had a mild speech defect and because of a boyhood accident always walked with a slight limp. His eyesight was poor but he did not wear spectacles. His manner was reported by several professional psychologists to be meek and submissive, easily influenced and coerced. When drunk, Kerith was known to become loud, boastful and aggressive, and given to sudden outbursts of rage. He had a record of self-harm and both of his forearms were scarred.

He was a petty criminal, and made frequent court appearances. After the courts had tried a variety of non-custodial sentences, Kerith Sington did serve two short sentences in prison, both for acts of violence against the person, and while in the company of others.

His behaviour improved noticeably after he obtained a full-time job as a seaman with Muriseay Marine, for whom he worked as a deckhand on certain of their inter-island ferries. He remained impressionable and of a dependent character, and staff officers of at least two of the ships Sington sailed with filed statements about their concerns. When he was given shore leave of longer than twenty-four hours, Sington tended to drift into the company of others. On several occasions he returned shipboard in a drunken or drug-induced state, and was not able to perform normal duties for several hours. However, at least two of the officers stated that this was a recurrent problem with members of the ferry crews and that they had ways of rostering deck teams after shore leave. Sington was not considered to be a special risk to the ship or the passengers. He was in fact commended several times for his dedication to deck duties. In view of what soon happened, this trust turned out to be misplaced.

A serious but unrelated incident involving Sington occurred not long before the death of Mr Commissah. The trial judge disagreed with the defence that this event was admissible, so the jury did not hear it. I believe it had a significant impact on Sington.

Two weeks before the murder of Mr Commissah, the steamship *Galaton*, the inter-island ferry on which Sington worked as a deck-hand, was involved in a collision with another ship outside the harbour wall of Muriseay Town. Both vessels were holed below the waterline and they foundered as a result. There was loss of life on both ships: fifteen people died on the *Galaton*, and two crewmen were killed on the other ship, the *Roopah*, a dredger stationed outside Muriseay harbour. Prompt action by the master of the *Galaton* prevented any worse death toll, but it was a serious disaster which raised many questions about the volume of traffic using Muriseay harbour at certain times of day.

Sington was on duty as a deck look-out at the time of the collision, and afterwards he was taken in for questioning about his failure to raise the alarm.

According to the inquest report, after the accident Sington was inconsolable, intermittently blaming himself or one of the other crewmen (who was drowned in the incident), but in general admitting that the accident had largely been caused by his inattention. At the time of his arrest as a suspect in the Commissah case, Sington was still being investigated for criminal neglect causing death, but no prosecution papers had been drawn up or served.

Several independent journalists and criminologists have attempted to unravel the Commis mystery over the years, declaring it to have been a miscarriage of justice. Perhaps the most notable was the book called *Sington: Death in Error?*, which was the first to raise such doubts. The author of this was the remarkable social visionary, Caurer. It was a matter of fundamental concern to Caurer and the other journalists who followed her, as it is to the present enquiry, that none of the circumstances surrounding this marine accident was placed before the jury at Sington's trial for the Commis murder.

It was Caurer who revealed that the investigating officer in the *Galaton* incident, who detained and questioned Sington about his role in the collision, was none other than the policier officer known only as 'Serjeant A'. This officer appears to have been convinced that Sington was involved in some other illegal matter at the time of the collision, but Sington would not admit it. When Sington became a suspect in the Commis case, the officer made assumptions he should not, and obtained the confession from Sington about his alleged role in that.

Why Sington should deny complicity in a marine accident (albeit a most serious one) and yet be willing to admit responsibility to another offence (just as serious, but with drastic consequences for himself) has made the suspicion of policier intimidation too un-reliable as evidence. This was almost certainly why the trial judge ruled the matter as inadmissible.

It was Caurer who argued, and I concur entirely with her, that when Sington's impressionable and sometimes boastful psychology is taken into account, it becomes increasingly likely that this un-happy young man might have seen one case as providing mitiga-tion for the other.

In addition, it concerns me that I have been unable to locate any policier or court records dealing with the fatal collision between the *Galaton* and the *Roopah*. The only official record is the inquest report, but that of course mainly concerns itself with the manner in which the victims died. Why have these important records been lost, removed or in some other way made inaccessible?

I turn now to the concerns over Sington's confession.

In common with most indigenous island people, Sington in effect spoke two languages. Officially, his language of everyday function was demotic Archipelagian, the common linguistic currency. From the trial transcripts we can divine that Sington was not at all articulate, that he clearly struggled not only to understand what was said to him in demotic, but that he had difficulty in expressing himself. We also know, from the same school records, that Sington was illiterate in demotic when he left school. There is absolutely no evidence or commonsense chance that Sington learned to read and write after leaving school.

The language he spoke was the patois of urban Cheoner. We have evidence of this from school records. Patois is of course street vernacular. Patois is purely oral, with no written tradition.

The confession Sington allegedly made to the policier officer could not have been written down in patois. If Sington spoke in patois, then it must have been the recording that was later interpreted or translated by one or other of the policier officers, and written down in demotic. Yet the confession which was admitted to the trial was presented as his own evidence, dictated from his own lips and faithfully transcribed. The confession contributed greatly to his conviction.

Several observations can therefore be made about his allegedly written confession, all of which give rise to juridical anxiety.

In the first place, the confession was obtained by interview with two policier officers, at least one of whom, unknown to Sington, had already been involved in the search for Commis's killers as well as investigating the ship collision. We know that a recording of the interview was made, and then transcribed in some fashion, presumably by 'Serjeant A'. Was it then read to Sington aloud? In the demotic which he barely understood?

Sentences in the confession which begin with 'Yes' or 'No' look like the answers to direct or leading questions. There is also evidence that Sington was led or guided through certain other parts of the confession. For example, he cannot remember the music allegedly being played in the theatre at the time of Commis's death, until the officers play a recording for him and provide him with the title.

In cognitive screening applied to Sington after he had made his confession, but before the trial began, he was tested for his comprehension of certain terms. Sington did not understand any of the following words, all of which appear in the confession with relevant use: 'extraneous', 'procurator', 'duress', 'accord', 'victimize' and 'narcotic'.

Even more disturbingly, he was found not to understand the differences between the words 'deny' and 'agree', and appears to have used them interchangeably.

Sington was measured as being below ten per cent of average intelligence, and his mental age was estimated to be that of a ten- or twelve-year-old boy.

The results of these tests were not admitted as evidence during the trial, and therefore were not known to the jury.

Finally, I consider the actual events which led to the death of Mr Commissah. These were closely examined during the trial, but it is still uncertain as to what really happened.

All that is known for sure is that Mr Commissah, a professional mime artiste who used the stage name 'Commis', was performing his act at the *Teater Sjøkaptein* in the town of Omhuuv, on Goorn in the Hetta Group. At the time of year when this happened, *Teater Sjøkaptein* was used as a palace of varieties for summer visitors. During his performance, Mr Commis died when a large piece of plate glass fell suddenly from the rigging loft above the stage. It landed directly on him and he was killed instantly.

Several working men had been seen around the theatre in the days before this, they had been seen in the theatre on the day of the incident, and some of them, supposedly including Kerith Sington, were seen to be running away immediately afterwards. Several members of the audience, and representatives of the theatre's staff and management, all gave evidence in court to corroborate this. It was never clear what motives there were. Nor was it clear how the plate glass (which was exceedingly heavy) could have been carried up to the loft. And it was never clear how the glass was dropped on or aimed at the victim below.

In the end, the existence of the confession, garbled and self-contradictory as it might have been, was seen to be the principal incriminating evidence, and the judge directed the jury accordingly on the weight they should give it.

One of the matters that came up briefly in evidence at the trial, but was not followed up due to the absence of the crucial witness, was an incident that occurred shortly before the death of Commis.

It seemed that the ship of the line for which Sington worked – Muriseay Marine – had hove to in the fjord outside Omhuuv, and was undergoing routine repairs. It was alleged by the prosecution that Sington had been transferred to this ship after the *Galaton* was lost. All the crew, including Sington if he were part of it, were given shore leave.

It is then alleged that as was his wont, Sington fell in with a group of others. These young men had apparently been given casual labouring work by the *Teater Sjøkaptein*, which involved clearing rubbish, moving pieces of unwanted scenery, transporting performers' equipment to and from the station, and so on. They had the use of an antiquated truck. The job gave them access to the theatre and almost certainly accounts for the number of times they were seen in the vicinity of the building.

On the day of the fatal incident the young men were tossing some wooden flats on to the carrying compartment of the truck, and were making a lot of noise. This was witnessed by several passers-by, two of who later gave evidence in court. One witness said he was convinced the men were all drunk, or high on drugs. What then happened was that a third passer-by, irritated by the amount of shouting and banging going on, called up to the men to work more quietly. The group of men shouted back at him, using obscenities and taunting him.

The other witnesses, who did not become involved in the brawl that followed, were clear in what happened.

The third passer-by – to identify him clearly – was of distinctive, not to say eccentric, appearance. He was short and squat (one witness said he was heavily muscled), had a lot of facial hair, and was wearing brightly coloured leisure clothes, unsuited to the early-spring weather. Both the witnesses who gave evidence felt that his remarkable style of clothes almost certainly aggravated the situation. Several of the taunts that were heard were about the way he was dressed. In any event a fight quickly started, with all four of the young men, including, it was alleged, Sington, punching and scrapping in the street around the truck. The third passer-by fought violently and effectively, knocking at least two of his assailants to the ground and briefly winding the other two. At one point the third passer-by was himself knocked to the ground, but he recovered with what the witnesses testified as 'frightening furiousness'. Many other blows were landed, but the scrap was halted by one of the witnesses shouting that the policier had been called. At this, the four young men climbed into the truck and drove quickly away.

The third passer-by calmly picked up the bag he had been carrying, brushed himself down with his hand, then carried on walking away down the road. Although the description of him was clear and unambiguous, and several townspeople confirmed that they had noticed this oddly dressed man on other occasions, no one was able to identify him and he was never traced. He was not known in the town. He did not come forward in answer to the appeal for witnesses. Finally, it was presumed that he must have been a visitor to the town or a tourist, that he had no connection with Omhuuv and after the street incident had continued on his travels.

The salient point was that this man never came to court to give evidence, so neither prosecution nor defence was able to make much of the fight in the street as a preliminary circumstance for the alleged perpetrator.

However, with hindsight and access to the chronology of events, we can see that this fight happened only a few minutes before the main incident. The young men drove away from the scene of the fight, but then turned around and returned to the theatre. They made their way inside. As a performance was about to start, members of staff instructed them to leave. The four of them said something insolent and walked down through the auditorium, where most of the audience was already seated, waiting for the show. They were highly noticeable and intrusive for a few moments. They then made their way backstage. Having worked in the theatre for a couple of days, they knew their way around.

They were not seen again until immediately after the glass crashed down on to the stage, when most people in the audience saw them running away.

It seems to me that the fight in the street had a direct impact on the behaviour of these four young men. The prosecution said that it inflamed Kerith Sington into a homicidal rage, but they were depending on the unsafe confession to assume that Sington was one of the four. There is absolutely no evidence that he was. Even if he was one of them, now that Sington's background, mental state and general level of intelligence are known, it is just as likely the scrap had instilled terror in him. Whatever the reliability of those conclusions, his presence in the theatre on the day has not been proved beyond reasonable doubt.

The fact that the four young men ran away afterwards was emphasized as a way of incriminating all of them in general, and Sington in particular, but it's just as possible that they were running away because of the frightful event that had just taken place. It's worth noting that many ordinary members of the audience also ran away from the theatre in the immediate aftermath

So, taking all of these matters into account, the inevitable conclusion I draw is that Kerith Sington might or might not have had a part in the attack on Mr Commissah, but there was no evidence to incriminate him, and much of the evidence that was produced against him was flawed and unsafe. A jury in possession of all the evidence, and properly directed, would certainly have acquitted him.

When first arrested Sington claimed as an alibi that on the day of Commis's murder he was on the island of Muriseay being interviewed by the Policier Seignioral about the sinking of the *Galaton*. He maintained he was nowhere near Goorn or Omhuuv at the time. He later abandoned this alibi for an unknown reason, but it now appears to be closer to the truth than anything else that was said about him.

I therefore find and pronounce that Mr Kerith Sington was the inadvertent victim of the most serious kind of miscarriage of justice, and I shall pass the file to the Seignior's Department on Cheoner with the recommendation he be given an immediate posthumous pardon.

Collago

SILENT RAIN

An island of medium size, in the temperate zone of the southern Midway Sea. Formerly known for its dairy produce, COLLAGO is a place of low rain-washed hills, warm summers, windy winters. It has a rocky coastline with several landing coves or bays, and is blessed with attractive scenery which consists mostly of broadleaf tree coverage and an abundance of summertime wild flowers. There are few beaches and those that are suitable for swimmers are covered in shingle. The sea is unusually cold in this part of the Archipelago, because Collago lies in the path of the Southern Oscillating Stream.

There is only one large town: Collago Harbour, which as its name implies is the main port of the island. There is no airport. Outside the town there are few roads and motor vehicles are seen only rarely. There is a bus service, which circuits the island and crosses its width three times a day. It is not a remote island, but it is surrounded by many islands similar in appearance. Navigation channels are hazardous, and pilots must be used.

Collago is therefore an island of quiet pleasures, not an obvious choice for visitors seeking a hot climate or the excitement of night-life. Few would think it might become a place where people's lives are changed forever.

Collago's fate was determined by a medical breakthrough in a research clinic in the distant city of Jethra, the capital of the country of Faiandland.

Developments in gene-swapping and stem-cell modification, in the search for new or more effective treatments for intractable terminal diseases, led fortuitously to a process that would make any man or woman of normal good health into a physical immortal (or 'athanasian').

One hundred and fifty-two individual mutations in the human genome were identified, each capable of being personalized and therefore given a genetic signature. Suitably manipulated, these personal genomics would halt the rate of body ageing at the point the patient received the treatment. Thereafter, normal cellular decay or change would be replaced by rejuvenating cell growth, a process that would in theory continue for ever.

Practice has followed theory. The first human trials took place more than a century ago, and since then not a single recipient has appeared to age, has suffered any debilitating or degenerative disease, has fallen foul of any viral disease, or has died of any expectable or natural causes. Regular medical check-ups on a large sample of past recipients confirm their state of health.

However, not all of them are still alive: some have died in accidents, and several more have been murdered by non-recipients, for reasons of jealous anger, or for some other base motive we can imagine only too well. There are many advantages to being an athanasian, but the condition also has its drawbacks.

Hailed at first as a miracle of modern medicine, it quickly became apparent that the ability to create a group of immortal humans was attended by a host of moral, ethical, social and practical problems.

In the first place the treatment involved a lengthy medical process, with large nursing and psychological teams in support, as well as the need for uniquely complex scanning and monitoring equipment. This meant that each operation was expensive, clearly beyond the means of all but the super-wealthy.

The moral and ethical arguments for and against the process are now well known and often rehearsed.

If the majority of people know that there is a favoured minority who will survive them, resentments are inevitable. Many controversies have come to light over the years, and most of these have involved rich or celebrated or influential people who have tried to gain an unfair advantage. There have been cases of bribery, blackmail, threats, physical assaults. Rumours about this sort of activity are always current, always routinely denied.

There have also been several cases which were marked by circumstantial evidence: apparently miraculous cures for fatal illnesses, people who disappeared then were found to be living under new names and identities, film stars or other celebrities who managed to retain their beauty far longer than anyone might expect. No abuse has ever been conclusively proved.

Not so obviously, the athanasia treatment has had a subtle impact on the attitudes of employers to employees, on the way healthcare is provided to the normally ill, even on the way non-athanasians are insured against accidents, travel incidents, public liability, and so on. In every case, the notion that normal life expectancy is less than that of an immortal person has led to discrimination against the non-immortals.

Less a matter of public concern, but even so a cause of ethical debate: the recipient's memory is unavoidably wiped by receiving the treatment. He or she awakes to the reality of re-education in their own lives. It is the ultimate theft of identity. Many critics of the procedure point to this as the tool of experimenters, politicians, fraudsters, blackmailers and so on. However, the trustees of the procedure maintain that the rehabilitation staff are fully trained in the necessary techniques, that they are well practised and endlessly re-trained and appraised, and also that there are external audits and checks by independent outside agencies. They also point out that the rehab process has never been known to fail.

For all these reasons, practical and ethical, strict controls have always been necessary. After many controversial incidents, an independent trust was created to run the process, and this was established on the hitherto little-known island of Collago. The Lotterie Trust (or Lotterie-Collago as it became known) would not only perform and oversee the medical and psychological procedures, but would manage the financing.

Funding was through a worldwide lottery, open to all, which every month would produce a handful of randomly selected winners. They would receive the treatment, no matter who or what they were. Thus, along with the ambitious sportsmen and women, the brilliant musicians, the philanthropists, the rich, the glamorous, the ordinary working people, the unemployed, the young, the old, the happy and the sad, the promising, the ordinary, the disappointing, the unlucky, the lottery would inevitably select a random sample of criminals, paedophiles, embezzlers, rapists, thugs, liars and cheats. All were given the prospect of life eternal.

Inevitably, controversy ensued. Into it stepped the radical social theorist Caurer. Her powerfully written and compelling book *Lottery of Fools* simply narrated the life stories of ten recent athanasia recipients, what they had done with their lives before they were made immortal, and what they were likely to do after. Of these stories, seven were relatively uncontroversial: they were ordinary people in ordinary lives who had been given the treatment, some of whom had returned to obscurity, but two of whom had declared they would now devote themselves to good works. However, of these seven, six were married or in permanent relationships, and five had children. What, Caurer clearly implied, was going to happen to those families with the passing of the years?

Of the remaining three recipients described by Caurer, one was an alcoholic and another was morbidly obese. Caurer asked mildly that perhaps the geneticists should have looked around for more relevant gene mutations to personalize? The final recipient, identified only by the name 'Xxxx', was a middle-aged man with learning difficulties and deep personality disorders. He had already been convicted twice of rape and attempted rape, and was serving a prison sentence for arson. He was likely to spend the rest of his life in a detention hospital, and now the rest of his life appeared to be infinite.

Caurer concluded the book with an essay pointing out that all over the world there were people whose (finite) lives were already dedicated to the common good. She named no names, but suggested there were hundreds, perhaps thousands of eminent research scientists, inventors, religious leaders, social workers, composers, authors, artists, teachers, doctors, aid workers ... all of whom were in their individual way attempting to make the world a better place. Were the ten people whose lives she had described any more likely to improve on what these others were already achieving?

The consequence of her book when it was published was that the Lotterie trustees appointed a panel of international judges to sit annually. Every year they were to nominate a small number of people whom they had judged should be given the chance of an undying future. The cost of these extra cases would be met from Lotterie funds.

However, many of these so-called laureates, when their names were announced, unexpectedly declined the treatment. In the fourth year, one of these refusers was the philosopher and author VISKER DELOINNE.

Soon after he had been selected he publicly refused the treatment. He was not alone – four other laureates that year also declined the award. But Deloinne then wrote and published an impassioned book called *Renunciation*.

In the book he argued that to accept athanasia was to deny death, and as life and death were inextricably linked it was a denial of life too. All his books, he said, had been written in the knowledge of his inevitable death, and none could or would have been written without it. Life could only be lived to the full by the instinctive or unconscious denial of death, otherwise nothing would ever be achieved. He expressed his life through literature, he said, but this was in essence no different from the way other people expressed their own lives. To aspire to live for ever would be to acquire living at the expense of life.

Caurer came forward and said that Deloinne's book had changed her mind. She apologized publicly for her error of judgement, retired to her island home and never again uttered or wrote a word on the subject of athanasia. Deloinne himself died of cancer two years after *Renunciation* was published.

Lotterie-Collago reverted to its random selection of winners and within a few years the athanasia treatment was being carried out without publicity or controversy, lottery tickets were sold all over the Archipelago and in the countries of the north, and every week and month a trickle of lottery winners travelled slowly across the island-congested seas to the quiet, rain-swept hills of Collago.

Visitors are discouraged on the island, although there are no formal bans. Strict shelterate laws are in place, but havenic rules are comparatively liberal. Tunnelling has never been attempted on Collago but one can imagine that tunnellers would not be welcome. Some seasonal jobs are available on dairy farms but visas must be obtained in advance.

Currency: Archipelagian simoleon.

Derill - Torquin

SHARP ROCKS

Little is known of this place and we have been unable to visit it in the cause of researching the gazetteer. DERILL was formerly known as OSLY (patois: STEEP BANK OF GRAVEL) and is situated somewhere in the southern hemisphere. We know of no other islands in the alleged Torquin Group. (There happens to be an island paradoxically called Torquin in the Lesser Serques – that Torquin has become a 'closed' island due to the presence of a Glaundian army base.)

Occasional references to 'Torquin' as the name of a group or arc of islands should normally be treated as a spelling or typographical error.

There are persistent allegations that Derill, Sharp Rocks, changed its name in order to cash in on the perceived fortunes of either Derril or Derril (see below), but we know nothing of this and hold no opinions. We have never been there, have seen no pictures of it, have never met anyone claiming to have been born there, know no one else who has ever been there or heard of it and frankly do not care.

Derril - Torqui

LARGE HOME / SERENE DEPTHS

The largest island in the Torqui Group, also the administrative centre for the group, DERRIL is frequently confused with another more recently named island called Derril, in the Torquils. (See below.)

In this case, island patois is useful to learn and remember. The name Derril, in Torqui patois, simply means LARGE HOME. The Torquil Derril's patois name means DARK HOME or HER HOME.

Since confusion between the two islands is a constant problem for travellers, and because both islands in their different ways are extremely attractive to visitors, we believe the clearest way of distinguishing between them is to describe the island groups to which they belong. We are here to try to clarify.

The Torqui Islands (alternatively, the Torqui Group, or more simply the Torquis) lie immediately to the south of the city of Jethra, which is on the southern coast of Faiandland. The closest Torqui island to the mainland is called Seevl, and although it is not itself an important island it is well known to the inhabitants of Jethra. It lies offshore of the city and is of course always in view. Indeed, it can be said to dominate the city, as it is a grim, bleak and mountainous island which casts deep shadows across the Jethran offing during most daylight hours. In the past there were family and trading links between Seevl and Jethra, but these were discouraged by the authorities when the war broke out.

The Torquis are therefore northern hemisphere islands, and the Torqui Group covers a significant area of that part of the Midway Sea. Seevl, the northernmost, suffers a chill climate, exposed to constant winds from the mountainous land to the north and enduring bitterly cold winters. However, many of the other Torquis are so much further to the south, and in the main stream of the benign Archipelagian winds, that they enjoy warm or even subtropical climates.

The principal distinction between the Torquis (location of Derril, Large Home) and the Torquils (location of Derril, Her Home, Dark Home) is that the latter islands are in the southern hemisphere. The two groups are a long way distant from one another and different in some respects, but by a cruel coincidence their topography and climate are alike, not to mention the fact that even their geographic coordinates are uncannily similar.

As is well known, all map references for the Dream Archipelago are approximate. Because in this case they tend to confuse matters rather than clarify them, we shall not dwell on the similarities, nor point out any more of the awkward coincidences, for there are several. Let us simply say that the Torquis (patois: SERENE DEPTHS) occupy an area of the ocean roughly in the region of 44°N - 49°N and 23°W - 27°W, while the Torquils (patois: EVENING WIND) in the southern part of the world, are at approximately 23°S - 27°S and 44°E - 49°E.

It is probably best not to report the coordinates of the group allegedly called the Torquins, because they will only make things worse.

Derril, Large Home, the island with which we are concerned here, lies a long way to the south-east of Seevl, at the furthest extremity of the Torquis. It is not only the largest island in the group it is advantageously placed as far as the main shipping lines are concerned, it has two deepwater ports and is rich in mineral deposits. Industry thrives on Derril. The landscape is hilly rather than mountainous and much of the interior is given over to farming. Derril is in short a prosperous place and has always been influential in Archipelago affairs.

No greater influence was exercised and enjoyed than in the years the COVENANT OF NEUTRALITY was being planned, drawn up, and ultimately ratified and accepted by virtually every island group in the world.

The history of the Covenant is well known in detail, perhaps exhaustively to any child educated in our islands, so it need not be repeated here. But for centuries the Covenant has been the constitution, the bill of rights, which governs and directs life in the Dream Archipelago.

Although modified innumerable times by courts and legislatures on individual islands, to take account of particular cases or circumstances, the imperative holds good. The Covenant recognizes the individual identity and uniqueness of each island, or self-declared group of islands, grants delegated rights of self-governance, and ensures that the Archipelago remains neutral in all non-island concerns.

It has not prevented disputes between islands, although in practice there have been relatively few, but it has ensured that the islands do not become embroiled in the intractable and violent war being fought by the countries in the north.

At the time the Covenant was being planned, Derril attracted jurists, diplomats, philosophers, politicians, journalists, pacifists, historians, academics and sociologists from all parts of the Archipelago. Negotiations were complex and took more than eight years to conclude. There followed an administrative period of another five years, during which the organizing clerks translated the Covenant into every main language of the islands. It was also rendered into innumerable patois forms, to be announced orally to indigenous groups.

Another delay followed, for formal consultation and reflection, but then all the legislators, judges and Seigniory officials, and everyone else who had taken part in the negotiations, reassembled on Derril, Large Home, for the formal signing of the Deed of Covenant.

The signing took another twelve months – every island and island group was to take possession of original documents signed by all parties – but in the end it was done, and celebrations began.

In the present day the visitor will be delighted by the impeccably maintained Covenant Palace, where the negotiations and signing took place. There are several museums in the city where many of the original documents are stored, as well as a wealth of other material, such as formal robes, photographs, journals, paintings.

Conducted tours are arranged every day, using several different languages, and Derril City offers many hotels, pensions and guest houses at a range of prices.

The island has largely become a mausoleum to its own past, so other visitor attractions are few. There is a commemorative Yo Tunnel in the hills overlooking the bay, but it fell into disuse many years ago and no one knows how to make it function again. It can, however, be explored on foot. You will be required to use special footwear and headgear, but they may be rented at the site.

Long stretches of the coast have been industrialized – steel founding, ship-building and vehicle manufacture – and the inland areas are now dominated by intensive farming techniques. Much of the landscape is covered with plasticized cultivation tunnels, for the growing of the soft fruits which the island exports across the Archipelago.

On the far eastern side there is an area of the island which has always been leased, even in the years before the Covenant was signed. The Glaund Republic is the leaseholder and has a claim of inalienable right to use and occupy this immense tract of land. It has resisted all attempts by the Derril Seigniory to make it relinquish that right.

It is an ironic implied comment on the existence of the Covenant that the rentals paid by Glaund in effect underwrote the immense cost of forging the Covenant. Even deeper irony lies in the fact that on the island where neutrality was claimed, such a huge area should be operated as a military base.

Artillery and rocket ranges mean that the hills in that area are closed to walkers, in spite of a publicly declared Glaundian policy of openness to the public and a welcome to tourists. Now visitors are warned not to go anywhere near, because of a real danger from unexploded warheads and fragments of depleted uranium. The range is in use throughout the year. There are many submarine pens in frequent use, as are detention, interrogation and redaction centres, military training facilities and two huge airstrips. The whole area is sovereign territory, part of the Glaund Republic, but the matter is constantly in dispute.

Fifteen years after the Covenant was signed, and five years after the ratification process had ended, the Glaund base was shelled from the sea by units of the Faiandland Navy. There was much collateral damage to houses and businesses on the main part of the island. A naval and air battle ensued and an invasion of Derril followed, an attempt by the Faiandlanders to oust the Glaundians from their base. Militarily this failed. The native Derril people could only huddle in fear as their newly won neutrality was so cynically breached.

Fortunately, there has been no repetition of this in recent years. Glaund warships are constantly on station in the deep channels around Derril, and troop carriers come and go. The Faiand forces stay away from the area.

They too have their bases around the Archipelago. Neutrality is general but not yet universal.

The artist Dryd Bathurst was in residence in Derril City for a period. His gigantic oil painting entitled *Derril Nymphs in Succour* has never been placed on public display. It may be viewed strictly by appointment by accredited academics and art professionals. Information is available online, as are reproductions of certain details from the painting – the whole work is still considered too sexually explicit and debauched to be seen in one piece by the public. There are social reasons too: the families of the young models who so willingly posed for the artist are still reluctant to grant release of the images.

The building where Bathurst maintained his studio was demolished immediately after he left Derril, but there is a small and tasteful commemorative plaque on view in the public square opposite.

There are no shelterate or havenic laws, but because of Bathurst's sojourn on the island the anti-importunation regulations are strict. No visas are required for visitors intending to inspect only the Covenant Memorials, but those people wishing a longer stay should enquire at their local Seigniory offices before setting out.

Currency: all accepted and converted at market rates. The Muriseayan thaler is the official currency.

Derril - Torquil

Dark Home / Her Home / Evening Wind

The largest island in the Torquil Group, also its administrative centre, Derril traditionally depended on a mixed economy of farming and mining. In recent years the tourist trade and devotional pilgrimages have become the principal movers of the economy. In the case of tourism, certain recently lifted restrictions on travel (notably the erotomane laws) have opened up the whole Torquil Group to visitors. At the same time, the influx of pilgrims to Derril increases by several thousand people every year, and shows no sign of decline. The south-western area of the island, formerly given to arable farming, is now one of the most visited areas in the entire Archipelago.

Of the island patois names, the former, Dark Home, appears to be authentic and is mentioned in the historical record. The latter name, Her Home, is of more recent coinage and was taken up after the Manifestation. It seems that the formal name Derril also began to be used at that time, but we have been unable to trace any record of that.

The earlier name, Dark Home, came into use at the time the island was one of the main exporters of coal. The spills from the pits and the general discharge of smoke into the atmosphere led to many areas of the island being covered by a thin film of coal dust and tar. These spillages made Derril unattractive to visitors and unhealthy to residents, but strict pollution controls have been introduced all over the Archipelago. Because of them, the main island and some of the smaller ones adjacent to it, have been thoroughly decontaminated. Today, Derril is a pleasant, clean and healthy place to visit.

Mining activity, which was anyway confined to the northern part of the island, has now largely been discontinued, but local museums and visitor attractions are open all year round.

The west coast, which has magnificent rocky cliffs and wide sandy beaches, is a popular destination for vacationers. Inland, large areas of virgin forest are found. There is a danger zone on the eastern side, where Faiandland military forces manage a base. Because of constant training exercises, and trials of weaponry, we recommend tourists to stay away. In any event, the perimeter is patrolled day and night by armed guards, and there are abundant warning signs on every approach road.

Normal visitors need have no concerns about this base, provided they remain in known holiday areas. There are many facilities available for visitors to use, all of whom are allowed to travel to Derril by ferry, in the usual way.

It is important to remind intending visitors that before departure they should always check with their booking agent that they are travelling to the right place. The similarly named Torqui Group also contains an island called Derril, which is said by the people of Derril, Dark Home, to be an uninteresting and unattractive place. This is absurd, as Derril, Large Home, is unquestionably the birth-place of the Covenant. (See entry above.)

Even this historical fact has been challenged in the past by more extreme factions on Dark Home, or Her Home as these people pre-fer to call it. They also claim that Derril, Large Home, changed its name in recent times in an attempt to cash in on the Manifestation. Some of the more ultra-orthodox Derrilians even claim that Derril, Large Home, set up a Manifestation of its own, in an attempt to lure pilgrims.

This claim is probably based on the fact that Caurer, as a young woman, delivered a lecture at Derril University, Large Home.

Our gazetteer is not the place to attempt to mediate in an inter-island squabble that has been rumbling on for many years.

Private research suggests, incidentally, that the parvenu island is Derill, Sharp Rocks, in the Torquin Islands. (See entry above.) Until comparatively recently that Derill was called Osly, Steep Bank of Gravel. Not much is known about Derill/Osly. It is listed in the

Muriseay Register as a Category C island, although no reason is given. Category C islands are in general either not open to visitors, are unpopulated, or are believed to be hazardous in some way.

Let us move on to the main feature of Derril, Her Home.

This island is unusual in that it is one of the comparatively few places in the Archipelago to have a civilian airport. It is situated on the south-western peninsula and was built because of the ever-increasing pressure on the port facilities in Derril Town. Access to the south-western peninsula overland from Derril Town is now barred to visitors, so that visitors to the CAURER SHRINE mostly arrive and depart by air. Specialist airline carriers have been set up around the Archipelago, and they provide a network of reliable routes for Caurer pilgrims.

The Caurer Shrine is open every day of the year and no appointments are necessary.

Arriving passengers at E. W. CAURER INTERNATIONAL AIRPORT will be greeted by representatives of their tour operators, if they are travelling on one of the many available packages. If they are travelling independently they will find a number of efficient and inexpensive services available to them. Cars may be hired, buses leave for the Shrine at half-hourly intervals throughout the day, and there is a dedicated tram service whose route takes advantage of the many splendid views of the sea and adjacent islands.

Guides who speak most of the Archipelagian dialects are always on hand, and their fees are modest. There is hotel accommodation both at the airport and in the immediate vicinity of the Shrine. Pilgrims are recommended to stay at least one night when visiting the Shrine, or using one of the many healing institutes.

The story of the Manifestation is well known, but a brief factual summary of our own is something we believe we cannot avoid including here. As usual we leave readers to make up their own minds. Most of the pilgrims to Derril, Her Home, appear to accept it as literal truth.

In brief, two teenage girls, daughters of local farmers, are said to have gone missing during a particularly hot spell of summer weather. In the generally accepted version of the story both girls are described as entirely normal, but there is evidence that they suffered from learning difficulties. The older of the two had been lame since birth; the younger had endured a disfiguring skin infection all her life.

The names of these two unfortunates are not known for sure – their identity was concealed as a result of what happened to them. Local villages mounted a search for the girls as soon as they were missed, and the following day hundreds of volunteers from the locality joined the search. At first the families assumed the girls had wandered away from their home area and become lost, but as the hours of searching went by without result worse fears were aroused.

On the morning of the third day the girls suddenly returned, apparently unharmed. They had an unexpected story to relate. They said that while they were walking in a local gulley, which then as now was much overgrown with trees, they had come across a strange woman. She spoke to them gently and showed them many wonderful sights. They had walked with her and rested with her, and listened to stories of distant lands and miraculous events. At the end, when the woman suddenly left them, both girls discovered they had been cured of their ailments.

Later, when shown photographs by a reporter from a newspaper, the girls immediately identified the woman as Caurer. Neither of them had previously known anything about Caurer's life or work, and recognized her only from their meeting with the apparition.

Because Caurer's whereabouts at the time of the Manifestation were known exactly, and beyond a shadow of a doubt – she was delivering a series of lectures at the University of West Olldus, on the other side of the world from the Torquil Group – it was declared to be a miracle.

Caurer herself denied all knowledge of it. As the speculation grew, she refused to comment any further, beyond once more repeating her denial in the most forceful of terms.

Towards the end of her life, Caurer did reveal that at times when she was most in demand, she had occasionally used a physical double to stand in for her. This woman, a former journalist on the *Islander Daily Times*, was sent only when Caurer was not expected to speak, and merely added her presence to some occasion.

Researchers and witnesses soon produced a catalogue of past occasions when Caurer had been glimpsed only from afar, had been driven past in a vehicle, or had been seen standing on a podium, and when she had never spoken to anyone and refused all interviews. At the time, these occasions had added to her reputation for remoteness, and in many ways increased the curiosity about her. There had never been any suspicion of bilocation, though.

Caurer made this revelation on the occasion of the woman's death: her name was Dant Willer and she had become a trusted assistant to Caurer for about five years. In answer to a question from a journalist, Caurer added that this woman was not with her in her home on Rawthersay at the time of the alleged Manifestation, but neither was she anywhere in the Torquil Group, and certainly not on Derril.

After Caurer's own death an entry was found in her private diary, ridiculing the whole myth of a miraculous appearance on Derril, Dark Home, Her Home. The entry can be read in holograph in a display case at the CAURER FOUNDATION's exhibition on Rawthersay, and of course the complete text of the diaries has been in print for several years. The entry about Derril appears in all editions.

The same entry gives the only known insight into Caurer's attitude to the so-called Manifestation.

She asserts that the mystery of the young girls' disappearance on Derril was easily explained and rational in every way. She points out that the older of the two gave birth to a child about nine months after the incident. Whoever this child was or whatever it grew up to become, he or she has never laid claim to divine parentage or supernatural powers and it seems overwhelmingly likely that the reasons behind its mother's disappearance were of earthly origin.

However, by this time the Manifestation had become accepted as a true event by millions of people, and the astonishing growth of the miracle industry was in full swing.

As Caurer's reputation has continued to grow after her death, two charitable bodies have emerged. Each of these, in their profoundly different ways, seeks to represent her posthumously. Unsurprisingly, they are embroiled in a deep, permanent and apparently insoluble feud over her.

On the one hand is the strictly secular Caurer Foundation. This is based in Rawthersay, Caurer's home island, with administrative offices in the northern mainland city of Glaund. The Foundation was set up during Caurer's lifetime, and is usually accepted as accurately reflecting the ideas and wishes of the great woman's life, work and beliefs. About the alleged Manifestation on Derril, the Foundation's official stance is as follows:

Caurer herself never visited Derril, Dark Home, Her Home. No one connected with her work ever visited Derril. The woman who sometimes stood in as her physical double never visited Derril. Caurer herself never claimed to have the power of miraculous healing, and although she kept an open mind on the subject she never discussed it or wrote about it. She certainly never claimed to have divine powers. She believed that the story of the Manifestation had been innocently or naïvely invented by the two girls as a way of explaining away some other activity, and that other people had seized on the event afterwards in an attempt to capitalize on her name.

The opposing position is held by the Caurer Shrine Trustees:

They maintain that the Manifestation has been confirmed by elders of all the most important churches. Caurer has already been beatified and later is likely to be canonized. Her powers of healing have been demonstrated many times, both by people who have passed on Caurer's original laying on of hands, and the beneficial effects of the waters that flow through the Caurer Gulley. Hundreds of thousands of pilgrims confirm their lives have been changed for ever by a visit to the Shrine.

The Shrine Trustees also accuse the Caurer Foundation of attempting to undermine the economy of Derril, and therefore of the Torquil Group as a whole. The Caurer pilgrims support more than twenty hotels all year round, have indirectly financed the installation of modern infrastructure throughout the islands, as well as creating jobs all over the Archipelago in the travel and airline industries.

This gazetteer recommends non-pilgrim visitors to make their trips to Derril in the early spring or late autumn. The weather is at its best, and the island is less crowded than at other times.

Currency: all Archipelagian currencies are accepted at the Shrine and at the related facilities in the neighbourhood. The currency used in Derril Town: Archipelagian simoleon, Muriseayan thaler, Aubracian talent.

Intending non-pilgrim visitors to Derril are reminded of the confusion described above, and to take all necessary precautions. The usual inoculations for islands in the sub-tropical zone are not required, though. The island called Derril in the Torqui Group has strict havenic and anti-importunation regulations. On the contrary, on Derril, Dark Home, Her Home, importunation is freely bestowed.

Emmeret

ALL FREE

EMMERET is a small island, still underpopulated, which suffered devastating bush fires a century ago. After the fires the main settlements and principal house were rebuilt, under Covenant regulations.

There are few roads on Emmeret, but walking is pleasant and maps on sale in Emmeret Town show several recommended paths. The most frequented walk is the one from the port to UGGER PARK. Beyond the main landing point in Emmeret Town's harbour a well signposted narrow track leads through open fields and young woodland to CHUD ROCK, the highest point on the island. Chud Rock is famous for its limestone caves, which are open to the public. Tour guides take visitors through a series of spectacular rock and stalactite formations. Expert cavers may also enter the system of potholes at Chud Rock.

Beyond the Rock is Ugger Park, the seat of the Emmeret family, from whom have sprung several generations of important legislators. The fifteenth Seignior Emmeret was one of the drafters of the Covenant of Neutrality. The present Seignior Emmeret, the thirty-third, is normally absent. The house is at present closed to the public.

The history of the Emmeret family reveals many examples of the sort of eccentricity often associated with long dynasties. The twelfth Seignior is said to have banned children from the house, the eighteenth to have insisted that all house-guests should be permanently naked, the nineteenth Seignior, son of the naturist lord, is notorious for the many weekends of debauchery he and a band of regular guests enjoyed at the house; the twentieth Seignior, the son of the debauchee, devoted his life to the cloth. The twenty-third Seignior was obsessed with gardens, and spent much of his life at the house, landscaping and re-landscaping the extensive grounds. The present Seignior is said to take his feudal responsibilities seriously, is a kind and generous man, but he is rarely seen on the island that bears his name. He attends once a year for the formal collection of tithes.

During the thrall of the twenty-sixth Seignior Emmeret, Ugger Park was made into a haven for artists. Writers, painters, composers, musicians, sculptors, actors, dancers all made their long journeys across the Archipelago to take advantage of the liberal attitudes and free lifestyle they could luxuriously enjoy for weeks on end.

Some of the most famous artists of the time were semi-permanent residents in the opulent surroundings. Notable amongst them was the Mesterlinian poet KAL KAPES, who is said to have composed *Elegy to Squandered Passion* while staying at Ugger. A troupe of musicians, jugglers and illusionists travelled from the Qataari Peninsula and took up residence for several months. The world-renowned danseuse, Forssa Laajoki, then in the long afternoon of her miraculous career, over-indulged on the wine that was so freely available and eventually killed herself in a small room on the upper floor of the East Wing of Ugger. And the painter DRYD BATHURST stayed for nearly two years, the longest he is ever thought to have remained in one place.

Bathurst's well-liked epic landscape, *The Wool-Combers' Return*, was painted on the rear terrace at Ugger Park, although all of the eucalyptus trees in the distance, depicted by Bathurst, were subsequently destroyed in the fires.

Ugger Park was also the repository of one of Bathurst's most famous but least seen masterpieces. Simply called *The Shroud*, the artist executed this oil in the weeks after he first arrived. By repute, it portrays the artist as an aquiline-featured youth, glowing with health and sexual allure. Those who were able to see it declared it to be a true likeness, and that although Bathurst idealized himself it was none the less a substantial work of art.

Bathurst donated *The Shroud* in perpetuity to the Emmeret family on condition that it be kept in a closed room and never put on show to the public. The only people who were authorized to view the painting were members of the Emmeret family. With Bathurst's agreement, the painting was hung in a small room high in the East Wing. This was in fact the room where Forssa Laajoki's blood-soaked body was later found, on the floor in front of the portrait, the shaving razor still in her hand.

Dryd Bathurst's removal from Ugger House was sudden and sensational. His heroic painting, *The Wool-Combers' Return*, had been hanging in the main banqueting hall of the house for several months, provoking much excitement and admiration from all who saw it. One of the qualities of the painting, Bathurst's personal stamp, is the visual range it contains, from the vast sweep of land-scape and sky, mighty storms and cataclysmic events, together with tiny details, almost photographically exact, worked with the exquisite accuracy of a miniaturist.

Few of these details had ever been considered, in the context of the greater image. One evening, however, a guest of the twenty-sixth Seignior Emmeret, an art critic and commentator from a major heritage magazine, took a magnifying glass to the canvas. He looked intently at the detail, concentrating on a minute group of nature celebrants, cavorting and fornicating in the lush undergrowth. With great delicacy, considering the circumstance, the art critic managed to wonder aloud at the likeness of two of these ravished nymphs to, respectively, Madama Seigniora Mezraa Emmeret, and her daughter, the pretty and nubile Cankiri Emmeret, then only fifteen.

The twenty-sixth Seignior Emmeret was a man of calm disposi-tion, and after a brief session of his own with the magnifying glass he left the party without saying anything. He was not seen again that night by his guests.

Dryd Bathurst, who had been present throughout, later retired to his own chamber. Pulling back the sheets he discovered a forty-centimetre thryme, apparently not long dead. Serum was still ooz-ing from its mandible. Bathurst also was not seen again that night, nor ever again, on Emmeret.

Winters on Emmeret are warm; summers are hot. The ground is often parched by the sun. For unsurprising reasons the warn-ings about starting fires, and practical precautions against them, are evident all over the island. The humidity can be high in the hottest part of summer, but is normally at a fairly acceptable level. The many delightful beaches are open to the public but are an under-used resource. Visitors wishing to swim in the nude should exercise special care: the beaches were endowed by successive feudal Emmeret Seigniors, and have their own rules. On some beaches naturism is actively encouraged, but on other parts of the island it is severely frowned upon and there are penalties to be paid.

The Bathurst painting *The Wool-Combers' Return* is now on permanent display in the Covenant Memorial Gallery, on Derril. The painting is mounted at eye-level, so close examination of the canvas is not only possible, it is actively encouraged. However, whether it is because of time's great blurring, or the attrition of so much close scrutiny, or merely the restorers' art, the details that once alerted the twenty-sixth Seignior Emmeret to his house-guest's waywardness are no longer unambiguous.

In spite of Bathurst's permanent gift of *The Shroud* to the Emmeret family, it did not remain long at Ugger House. The Seignior despatched it soon after Bathurst's own departure, but it took several months for the emissary to catch up with the great artist. The meeting took place on the quiet island of Lillen-Cay, where Bathurst was enjoying a brief sabbatical. The transaction was swift: the painting was handed over to a member of Bathurst's entourage, a receipt was obtained, and the emissary began his long journey back to Emmeret.

Currency: Archipelagian simoleon, Aubracian talent.

Fellenstel

SPOILED SAND

FELLENSTEL is a large island in the southern temperate zone, long and narrow, running west to east. A range of mountains, Dentres dos Ilôts, divides the island into three climatic zones.

The southern coast is cool in summer, cold in winter, and troubled by sudden storms and unexpectedly powerful tidal flows. A brisk prevailing wind from the south-west, the HERBEAN BLACK SQUALL, brings sleet and rain, but ensures the southern faces of the mountains are always green and fertile. The Dentres range provides high alpine pasture, with deep winter snows and some winter sports activity. The northern side of the island, a broad coastal plain with several long sandy bays, enjoys a warm and stable climate: winters with a cool but pleasant rainy season, and a dry and sunny summer. Flowers and trees grow in profusion, the lush vegetation attracting holiday-makers all year round. The eastern promontory is a bird-watchers' paradise.

Although the principal economic feature of Fellenstel is tourism, there are many light industrial units in the small inland town of Juggre, providing employment for the local people and prosperity for the region.

Intending visitors require a visa, which must be obtained locally before departure. Standard inoculations are mandatory. Visitors should also be advised that Fellenstel has strict erotomane laws in place. Random searches and gene testing at port of entry can cause delay and in some cases embarrassment if the paperwork is not correct. Our general advice to intending travellers is always either to heed local laws or choose another destination – Fellenstel is a perfect example of this. It is a veritable paradise in many ways, but it uses retributive justice and the penal system is harsh. Being a visitor to the island is not regarded as adequate mitigation.

Tunnelling is prohibited throughout Fellenstel.

The search for the killers of Commis began on Fellenstel. Two men and two women, known erotomanes, were believed to have disrupted the artiste's performance when he was visiting Paneron. They also wrote negative reviews. How they were thought to have travelled halfway around the world to the scene of Commis's death was never revealed, but within a few days they had been arrested and taken in for questioning. The discovery of negative reviews of other theatrical performances on their computer hardware only made their situation worse.

They said nothing in answer to questions – the safest course of action given the harsh Fellenstel system of crime prevention and detection – and finally the policier were forced to release them. They remained under suspicion, however, and were unable to work for several months. Only once they had managed to leave Fellenstel were they able to resume their lives.

Currency: Archipelagian simoleon, Aubracian talent.

Ferredy Atoll

HANGING HEAD

Dear Sir,

I am twenty-one years old and I live on an island in the Ferredy group called Mill. I am here with my parents. I have just returned from university on Semell where I gained a First Class Honours degree in Island Literature.

I wish to inform you that during my three years at the university we were given many modern novels to study, and amongst them was your book *Terminality*. I was impressed by this novel and wanted to know a lot more about the other books you might have written, who you were, and so on. I spent a great deal of time trying to track down some other of your books, but unfortunately not all were available on Semell. I managed in the end to borrow three more titles, all of them apparently from your early career.

Let me tell you that I think they were very good. This led me to decide to specialize in your work, and my dissertation was on the subject of 'literary stasis', a phrase borrowed, of course, from your novel *The Tour of Circles*. I called my dissertation 'The Enigma of Staying: Immobilization and the Static Values of Chaster Kammeston'.

I know you must be busy and the last thing I want to do is interrupt your writing, but I do have a simple question I should like you to answer. I want to become a writer, a novelist, and I wondered if you have any advice you would be willing to give me?

From a devoted admirer.

Yours sincerely,

M. Kaine

Dear Sir,

Thank you for your reply, which took ages to reach me. Living in the Ferredy Atoll has many disadvantages. I hope that the lateness of this letter does not make you think that I reacted badly to the advice you have given me.

Let me assure you first of all that I have honoured your request and have destroyed your letter by burning it. No one else was allowed to read it. I am sure you have good reasons for wanting that, but I wish I could describe my feelings about having to burn something you had written. Every word you write is precious to me. But I respect your wishes.

In answer to your question: yes, I did get hold of the books of yours I could not find at first. My tutor admires your novels and was able to lend me his copies of the ones I did not have. Regrettably I had to return them when I left university, but since I last wrote to you I have been searching the internet. The only copy I have so far managed to buy is a rather old and battered paperback of *Escape to Nowhere*. Clearly it has been read by many people before me, but I am extremely pleased to possess it. I have made a special protective cover for it. I have read it twice since it arrived here. I find it intriguing and beautiful. The end always makes me cry. I have a thousand questions I would love to ask you about it, but I don't want to intrude on your time.

Thank you for the advice you offered me about becoming a writer. I must say it was not quite what I was expecting, and to be honest with you I found it disappointing. I intend to carry on in spite of your warnings.

May I ask: are you working on a new book now?

Yours sincerely,

M. Kaine

Dear Mr Kammeston,

I am so excited with the news of your new book! I can hardly wait to read it. Later this year I am intending to visit some friends who live on Muriseay, and I hope I will be able to catch up with all the books I want to buy while I am there. The Ferredy Atoll has only one bookshop. It is on the far side of the lagoon from where

I live and it is not exactly what I call a bookshop: it mostly sells magazines and a few best-selling romances, which are always a year or two old. Without the internet I don't know what I would do, but even the online dealers seem not to have heard of your books.

You say it will be another novel. May I dare to ask: is it another book in your 'Inertia' series? Can you tell me anything about it at all? I love everything you have written, but the Inertia books are special to me.

You want to know why I live here on Mill, and what it is like. I live here because I was born here and so it is my home. My parents are both social anthropologists. They came to the Ferredy Atoll before I was born to study and work with the indigenous people here. The Atoll is more or less untouched by the modern world and many of the tribal customs are unique. My parents have made several films about the people and they have written textbooks about the aboriginal culture here. My mother retired several years ago and my father now works mostly as a consultant, but they both love this place and don't want to leave.

However, since I was at Semell Uni for three years, which gave me the opportunity to see many of the other islands while I was travelling around. I confess I am restless to see more. When I go to Muriseay I am hoping to take several detours to visit some of the other islands. I notice that your island of Piqay is not far from Muriseay, or at least it would take only a few days on the ferries to travel there. Ever since we have been in contact I have been wondering if I might call in at Piqay and perhaps visit you? I do not want to disturb your work or trouble you, so if it is inconvenient I will understand.

Returning to Mill, there is not much I can say about it as a place. It is murderously hot here most of the year. We have snakes, hostile bats and large poisonous insects, but you learn to live with them. The 'winter' is short. The only difference between that and the rest of the year is that it rains day and night for three weeks. It remains almost as hot and the humidity is awful.

All the Ferredy islands are small. They are considered uniquely scenic and unspoiled. We have a few hills, hundreds of beaches, long stretches of forest, few roads, no railways, no airport. Everyone gets around by boat. The lagoon is fringed with many tall trees. Because the place is so photogenic you often see photographers or film crews working around the lagoon. They idealize the place but they would feel differently if they had to live here. My parents' house is in a shallow valley where there is a stream and a view of the lagoon. There is a small town on the other side of our island, with a dentist, doctor, a few shops, a hotel, not much else. I want to leave!

My first name is Moylita, and thank you for asking. It's a family first name, back through at least the last two generations. My mother is also called Moylita. I do normally sign my name with an initial, but I have been wondering, should I get any of my work published, if I should stay with that or use my full name. Do you have any suggestions?

You see, I am determined to ignore your depressing advice about not trying to be a writer! I am going to make good.

Yours sincerely,

Moylita Kaine

Dear Mr Kammeston,

I am extremely sorry I suggested paying you a visit on Piqay. I realize how presumptuous it must have seemed to you, and I will not mention it again. I know how busy you must be.

Yours sincerely,

Moylita Kaine

Dear Mr Kammeston,

I cannot tell you how surprised and pleased I was to hear from you again.

I assumed I had mortally offended you, because your last letter, nearly three years ago, was so terse and final. It is wonderful to receive your latest letter, sounding so full of life and at ease with yourself. I know that many good things must have happened for you in the intervening period, and I am happy to respond to your friendly enquiries.

But let me say immediately that although your last letter did upset me for a while, I soon realized I was the one who had over-stepped the mark.

I want to bring you up to date with what I have been doing, partly because you have so kindly enquired, but also because so many things have changed in my life.

Yes, I did travel to Muriseay as I had been intending. I stayed on for much longer than originally planned. While I was there I was able to buy copies of all your books, including *Exile in Limbo*, the one you told me you were writing. It is of course a marvellous novel, everything I had hoped. For me, reading it was even more thrilling than usual, having known just a little about it while it was in progress.

In addition, I found a job on Muriseay, I found a place to live and, after a few months of uncertainty about what either of us really wanted, a husband. His name is Rarq, he is a teacher, and although we live on Muriseay we recently travelled back to Mill because my mother has been ill. Your letter was waiting for me here when I arrived. We shall be staying for a while longer but if you choose to write back to me please send to the poste restante address at the top of this letter. We will be returning to Muriseay soon because Rarq has to start a new semester.

I do understand the explanation you have given me, in your most recent letter, about why you felt you had to pour cold water on my literary aspirations. You are completely right: I *did* half-expect you to write back, give me a pat on the head and tell me everything was going to be fine. I should have known that you of all writers would never do such a thing.

I could not say this before. When you tried to put me off I was at first saddened because I thought you weren't taking me seriously. But then I realized what should have been obvious all along, that you could not have read a single word I have written. It must be what you say to all young people who ask you about becoming a writer. I imagine you receive many letters of the same sort as mine. Once I realized that what you said wasn't personal I knew what I had to do. I guess now that it was what you intended all along. You made me think hard, made me consider my priorities, made me test my level of ambition and judge my ability as honestly as possible. In short you stiffened my resolve.

I am not yet a real author, in the sense of having a book published, but for the last two or three years I have been submitting poems and short stories to various magazines, and several of them have been accepted and printed. I have even made a little money. I don't suppose you have seen them and I'm not hoping, by mentioning them to you now, that you will ask to see them.

However, I have also started a little book reviewing, and I am wondering if you already know about this? Was it this that led you to writing to me again, and in such a friendly way? Because (in case it did somehow elude you) one of the first novels I was given to review was *Exile in Limbo*! And the review was not for some small-circulation literary magazine, but for the *Islander Daily Times*. I could hardly believe my luck when they offered the book to me for review. I now have two copies!

I hope you have read my review. If not I will certainly send you a cutting from the newspaper. I want it to please you, although I am familiar with something you said recently in an interview, that you never read reviews of your novels. Perhaps sometimes you are willing to make an exception to this rule?

All the time I was reading *Exile* I wanted simply to lay it aside and talk to you about it. My review is of course quite restrained and objective, but perhaps if you were to read it you would realize just how important to me this book really was.

Finally, the news that is for me the biggest of all. I said that I am not yet a published novelist, and I am not. But I am just about at the point of completing my first novel. If I hadn't had to visit my sick mother I should probably have finished it by now. I feel as if I have been writing it for most of my life.

I know I began it not long after our first round of letters, so you can see how many years it has taken. It is extremely long and fantastically complex. Sometimes I wonder how I managed to keep all the details of the story in my head as I wrote. It is largely based on the ideas and social theories of one of the people I most admire, Caurer of Rawthersay – I know you must know of her, because she has often cited your novels and your ideas in her essays and presentations. I have called her 'Hilde' in the novel.

Writers of course give invented names to their characters, but sometimes readers try to see through that. I'm aware that will probably happen with my book, but I hope and suspect that few people will be able to connect Hilde with Caurer. I genuinely believe I have assimilated Caurer's work and created Hilde as an embodiment of her ideas, rather than giving her Caurer's appearance or personality.

I feel safe in confiding this to you. I have always sensed that you are the moral and intellectual equal of Caurer.

Well, although I know nothing is certain, I am confident I will find a publisher for the novel. I now have a literary agent and she tells me she has already received enquiries from two companies in Muriseay. Naturally, I shall let you know the moment it becomes certain.

Meanwhile, I should love to know if you have ever met Caurer?

In closing, let me repeat how pleased I am to be back in contact with you. I loved receiving your letter and I have read it a dozen times already. I am sorry this reply is so long, but it is thrilling to me that we are writing to each other again.

We are both a little older than we were before, but one matter has not changed in any way. I believe you are our greatest living writer and that your finest work is yet to come. I am impatient to read it.

Yours affectionately,
Moylita K

Dear Mr Kammeston,

Nine months have gone by since I last wrote to you, and still you do not reply. I have learned from your unexpected silences that you are easily upset by the simplest or most innocently intended remarks, so I have to assume that something I said in that letter has offended you.

I have searched my conscience and scoured my memory, but I cannot think for the life of me what it might have been.

All I can say is that I am truly sorry, from the bottom of my heart. If I gave offence it was unintentional, or maybe just clumsy. I would ask your forgiveness, even though I realize that something complex and deeply personal has been disagreeable to you from knowing me. I have no idea what it might be.

If you feel unable to continue with this correspondence then I must of course respect your wishes.

I want to say in closing that I shall always treasure having exchanged a few letters with you. No matter what, I shall forever love the work that you do, and encourage other people to read it as intently as I always have.

Yours sincerely,

Moylita Kaine

PS: My publishers have just sent me my presentation copies of my first novel, *The Affirmation*. As it is dedicated to you I hope you will accept the enclosed copy, which I send in all humility and the hope you will understand everything that lies behind it.

MK

Foort

BE WELCOME

Foort is of medium size, one of the Manlayl group of islands in the northern subtropical zone. Its name in patois is rendered as Be Welcome, of which there is more to say.

Foort has several features which make it unusual, not to say unique, in the Archipelago. One of these is that it has a self-sustaining economy. It is almost entirely independent of other islands. It exports nothing and imports only essentials. Few people from other islands ever visit it; few residents of Foort ever travel to other islands. There is a ferry service but the ships that call do so at irregular intervals and are invariably en route to somewhere else. Foort is a brief stopping place, a port of call. In many ways, Foort is an island that is in but not of the Archipelago.

As facilities for visitors are few, and it has little of historical or cultural interest, we shall not devote much space to it in this gazetteer. One of our researchers did visit the island in the preparation of this book, so we know our information is up to date. For the sake of completeness, and the likelihood that some of our readers will have relatives living on Foort, here are a few facts about the place.

Firstly, its patois name is a fake. There never was an indigenous population who would make you welcome. Throughout the island you will see odd references to the island's mythical past, restaurants and streets and parking lots named after presumed indigenous greats or events of the past – our researcher noted in Foort Town that there was a 'King Alph' housing development, a market square named 'Victory Plaza', a bistro called the 'Old Castle Restaurant', and so on. All this is false. Until the modern property developers moved in, Foort was a barren island of sandy soil and rocky fore-shore, with a single mountain at the western end and a range of sand dunes in the east.

A more accurate patois name would be ISLAND OF CONDOMINIUM. The gleaming white towers of Foort dominate the skyline as you approach from any direction across the sea.

The only low or humble buildings on Foort are those of the people who have flocked to the island in search of work. They are the builders, cleaners, security guards, domestic servants, drivers, gardeners, shop-keepers.

There are twenty-seven golf courses on Foort. There are more than one hundred digital television channels. There are five private airstrips. Restaurants and wine bars are found in every street. Alcohol is inexpensive. Nursing and residential homes are numerous. There are three cinemas, one theatre, several dance halls and five casinos. There is a large lending library, with a range of books but a much wider range of videos imported from the northern countries. Every condo is surrounded by a gated private park. The beaches are clean and patrolled by security guards.

There are no massage parlours, strip joints, table-dancing bars or escort services, and there is no red light district. Violent crime does not occur on Foort, but there are occasional cases of dishonesty and these are dealt with effectively by the authorities. Havenic regulations are non-existent, but shelterate laws are in existence. Anti-importunate rules are strict, and erotomanes are not tolerated.

On the extreme eastern edge of the island there is reputed to be a sand dune which lights up at night. Speculating that this might be one of the coastal installations built by the artist Tamarra Deer Oy, who is known to have spent time on Foort, our researcher went to the location. He was unable to find it, or at least to pick out which of the many hundreds of dunes it might be. He met several people who claimed to have seen it, but two of them told him that the power supply was intermittent and in need of repair. No one knew how to do that. Oy himself left Foort a long time before.

There are few freshwater springs on Foort, and no rivers. All water on the island is either recycled or produced by the huge desalination plant on the north coast. A light pall of pollution, created by the plant, as well as by the heavy traffic and the thousands of air-conditioning devices in the condos, hangs over the island.

There is a network of roads that serve all parts of the island. Traffic is continuous, night and day. Every urban street has a track alongside it, used by the mobility vehicles of the halt and the elderly.

The biggest service and retail industries on the island are based on property: the supply of furniture and flooring, painting and decorating, garden maintenance, and so on. The demand from buyers for property is normally matched by the availability caused by death or incapacity. Almost the entire population is expatriate, people who have chosen to abandon the rigours of life under the wartime economies of the northern countries. Apart from the expense of buying property on the open market there are no immigration restrictions, although a return to the mainland is made difficult to the point of impossibility.

People from both warring alliances are welcome on Foort, and all mainland languages are spoken. Although the seignioral authorities maintain there is no zoning in Foort Town, people from the Faiand Alliance do tend to live in one part of the town, the Glaundians in another. There are expat-themed events all year round, with nostalgic playing of familiar music, cooking of traditional dishes and the wearing of folk costumes. Our researcher attended one of these events, and was surprised not only by how late at night it ran, but how uncontrollably drunk most of the people became.

Currency: all.

Gannten Asemant

FRAGRANT SPRING

GANNTEN ASEMANT is one of the smaller islands in the Gannten Chain. Its existence would barely be known outside the Chain if it were not for one remarkable event, which was a personal appearance by the artist Dryd Bathurst.

The occasion was a retrospective exhibition of his works, in which many of his smaller pieces were planned to be included, while four or five of his epic oils would also be hung. The gallery set the date for the private view and sent invitations to a select number of guests. Although there were not many of them they did live in many different parts of the Archipelago. Because of the distances involved, the invitations went out a long way ahead of the event. The select few were all known admirers of Bathurst's work, regular patrons or representatives of major galleries, or his professional acquaintances and colleagues. Because of Bathurst's itinerant ways, and his habit of arriving unannounced and departing in haste, few of these people had previously met him in person.

The press and visual media were not invited to the show. Bathurst had a lifelong aversion to publicity, both for himself and for his work. He never allowed TV cameras anywhere near him or his paintings, so no one present was expecting to see any of the television channels there. However, the almost total absence of print or internet journalists was surprising to some. It implied that Bathurst was entering a new and perhaps contradictory period of his life. The exhibition itself suggested he was seeking acceptance. The absence of the media indicated he wanted to shun fame.

In fact, one reporter did turn up, having blagged a ticket from another invitee. The journalist was a young trainee called Dant Willer, who was working on the local newspaper, the *Ganntenian News*. As events turned out, this young reporter's presence transformed what was intended to be a private party into an incident with many consequences.

The gallery was a small and until then insignificant one, called the Blue Lagoon. Before Bathurst's arrival on the island it was known only for local paintings by enthusiasts and amateurs, sold to tourists. For the gallery owner, a man called Jel Toomer, it was a genuine scoop, because at this time Bathurst's reputation, personal as well as professional, was a constant talking point.

His distinction as a painter of symbolic or portentous landscapes was never higher, with wealthy collectors practically fighting with each other to buy his huge canvases. In addition, there was a veritable industry of theoretical, analytical and academic papers attempting to unravel the enigmas perceived in the paintings.

His wider influence was also felt in the work of scores of young or emerging artists who were eager to identify themselves as *socius* Bathurst Imagists.

He was also routinely denigrated as an exhibitionist, a dauber, a plagiarist, a populist, a coxcomb, an obscurantist and an opportunist. Much else was said – privately, but in a more energetically vindictive and heartfelt way – by a string of husbands, fathers, fiancés and brothers, on a large number of islands throughout the Archipelago.

Dryd Bathurst's celebrity was not then wholly for his work. Endless tittle-tattle and gossip surrounded the more public aspects of his private life, filling the popular tabloids and celebrity magazines, which otherwise had no discernible interest in art. Stories about Bathurst's exploits, and alleged exploits, were told, re-told and endlessly embellished.

Photographs of him were rare – in fact, there was only one known to exist, taken years before, when he was an art student. It was still used to identify him: he appeared as a tall young man of slender build, narrow-hipped, with a chiselled face and lustrous fair hair. He looked sullen and aggressive, but also vulnerable.

Bathurst and his aides took extraordinary measures to disguise or conceal his features when he was travelling around. Travelling around was something he did almost constantly, of course. Should some enterprising photographer manage to obtain a candid shot with a long lens, or when Bathurst was caught unawares, then the painter would use any means at his disposal to suppress it: invocation of privacy laws or physical threats were instantly uttered, but most often he would resort to his vast wealth to buy the picture. Naturally, all this heightened the intensity of the attention around him.

It followed too that people were curious about his physical appearance. His enemies said that he had grown old, put on weight, that his flowing locks had thinned or fallen out, or that some cuckolded husband or lover had managed to disfigure him.

None of this was true, as the chosen ones who were allowed into the private view on Gannten Asemant immediately discovered. Although he was no longer the fragile youth blessed with classical beauty, Bathurst's body had filled out while maintaining a look of fitness and agility. His face remained aquiline and attractively angular, his fair hair flowed about his shoulders. He moved with feline grace and carried himself with an aura of manly strength. Fine lines of maturity that were forming around his eyes only emphasized the sensuality of his features.

His force of personality was extraordinary. Everyone present felt acutely aware of him, as if he was exerting a magnetic attraction. People could not help staring at him or trying to edge closer to him, eager to listen in on the few conversations he engaged in.

The temptations of the bounty aside, Bathurst was one of the most photogenic men they had ever seen. In order to remove temptation, all photographic equipment and cellphones were temporarily confiscated and secured in a guarded room along the corridor. The guests had to content themselves with gawping, and the lesser satisfactions of being able to tell their friends they had at least been there.

Even allowing for Bathurst's celebrity the canvases were still the dominant presence. The five large paintings, all completed comparatively recently and therefore unseen even by most of his entourage until this event, were hung on the gallery walls. The two largest were placed one at each end, the other three being hung side by side on the wall facing the window.

No catalogue was prepared by the gallery, so none of the paintings was identified. Was this Bathurst's own wish, or just a mistake by the gallery? No one seemed to know. However, we do know what paintings there were, because the enterprising young reporter from the *News* managed to elicit the titles from Bathurst or one of his close aides, and diligently recorded them.

With hindsight, we therefore have the remarkable information that this was the only known occasion when all five canvases of Bathurst's HAVOC SEQUENCE were displayed together.

Final Hour of the Relief Ship was on one of the end walls. Opposite, at the further end of the gallery, stood *The Breakers of the Earth*. Arrayed along the wall between them were the three paintings which today are recognized as supreme even amongst Bathurst's supreme canvases: *Virtuous Magnificence and Decadent Hope, Willing Slaves of God* and *Terrain of a Dying Hero*.

The mere thought of these five masterpieces being in one place at the same time still has the capacity to take the breath away.

However, even the presence of the five Havoc paintings did not provide the surpassing moment. Bathurst had promised to display several of his smaller paintings. Four of them were hung there, quietly filling the available spaces on the walls. Dazzled by the Havocs, the guests might have been excused if they had not immediately noticed the others. But there they were, four canvases placed unobtrusively at eye-level on a slightly uneven and not especially clean gallery wall.

Two of them were sketches for details in the Havoc Sequence: one of these was the head of the sea serpent from *Final Hour of the Relief Ship*. The other was the body of the naked woman about to be consumed by a burning tide of fast-moving lava, from *Willing Slaves of God*. Either of these so-called sketches would stand alone as a crowning achievement for any other painter. In particular, the draft of the serpent's head (which was in fact a full-sized canvas painted in oils) gave an astonishing insight into the close attention Bathurst paid to detail. With these two canvases set beside the ultimate paintings, it was possible to discern the artistry and technique that had been demanded of the artist.

Then there were the other two.

The first was *The Shroud*, which was being displayed openly for the first and perhaps the only time. *The Shroud* was a framed canvas of about fifty by sixty centimetres. The artist was depicted in such detail that it was almost a shock to see it. It was immediately obvious that it was based on the famous photograph, the one everyone had seen: the posture, the clothes, the facial expression – all were identical. The only difference was that Bathurst had painted himself older: the youth had been supplanted by the man. There was no hidden message in the painting itself. The guests could turn from a regard of the painting to see the man himself, standing a short distance away, almost the twin of his own creation.

The last of the smaller canvases stood out from the others, from the havoc, the shroud, the ever-constant sense that the artist was directly or indirectly placing himself in every image. This one was different. It was a portrait of a woman and the title was *E. M. The Singer of Airs*. One by one the guests came to this painting, stared absorbedly at it, apparently paralysed by its intensity.

All, men and women alike, were disconcerted and seemingly aroused by its fierce erotic clarity. Many stood before it for several minutes, neglecting the charismatic artist whose presence dominated the rest of the room, reluctant to move away, or to yield their place in front of the painting to another person. Some seemed embarrassed, others shocked. One man turned away, blushing. No one could ignore it, no one could deny its power.

At the time of this gallery view it's doubtful if anyone there had any idea who the sitter had been, who 'E. M.' might be. Now we know that it is almost certainly a portrait of Esphoven Muy. This is thanks to the detective work of Dant Willer, the young reporter. It was Willer who through later research into the Kammeston Archive was to establish the link between Muy and Bathurst.

It is also through Willer that we have a permanent, reliable recording of this painting. A tiny digital camera, concealed behind the lapel of Willer's jacket, snatched five images of the painting of

Muy. Like most of the people there that day, Willer was sensually overcome by the impact of the portrait.

Without the Willer frames the painting of Muy would never have been seen by anyone who was not at the Blue Lagoon. Those tiny low-resolution images, digitally enhanced and combined, have been the basis of every reproduction that has appeared since.

The painting of Esphoven Muy had never been exhibited until that day, and it has not been seen since. The Havocs were quickly reserved for collectors and national galleries, the sketches for the Havocs went to a museum on Derril, Large Home. *The Shroud* was not for sale, and neither was *The Singer of Airs*.

That loving portrait of Muy, an insight into Bathurst's past and his deeper self, his talent never before seen to such minimal but brilliant effect, remained the property of the artist. For that short time at the gallery view, a woman was briefly seen through the artist's eyes, a beauteous woman with wind troubling her hair and her clothes, and unspent passion troubling her eyes.

Bathurst and his entourage departed quietly from Gannten Asemant a few days later. It was never revealed where he was going, but Kammeston's biography suggests that it was to Salay, or one of the other islands in that group. Bathurst's life was destined to be long and he had many more islands to visit. The proprietor of the Blue Lagoon, Jel Toomer, became a wealthy man on his commissions from the exhibition. He donated the gallery building and all its remaining contents to the Gannten Seigniory, left the island and has not been heard of since.

The Blue Lagoon is still in existence and is open daily to visitors. Most of the paintings Bathurst exhibited that day are displayed in the building, but obviously only in reproduction, and in some cases fairly poor reproduction.

Dant Willer continued to work for the *Ganntenian News* until the period of apprenticeship was complete, but then moved away to Muriseay.

Ferry services to the Gannten Chain have improved in recent years, but it remains a remote part of the Archipelago. Hotel accommodation is not available at international standards, but inexpensive pensions can be found near the gallery and are recommended on that basis.

There are no shelterate laws anywhere in the Gannten Chain, but havenic rules should be observed.

Currency: Ganntenian credit, Archipelagian simoleon.

Goorn

CHILL WIND

THE SEACAPTAIN

It was not much of a course, but I was not much of a student. Choices of college education on my cold home island were always limited, unless you were able to win a scholarship to somewhere on another island. I was not, so in the company of many Goorn people of my age I headed for the technical college in Evllen. This town, sheltered by a range of hills in the surrounding countryside, and touched by the tepid last flow of a warm sea current from the southern reaches of the Archipelago, enjoyed a comparatively moderate climate. In Goorn terms this meant that it rained almost every day.

I completed my first year and then prepared for the obligatory gap year. A gap year was a way of saving expenses for the administration, while maintaining their grant-in-aid by keeping the student count technically higher. It was not for students an option. Most of my fellow students drifted off home, while the ones whose families had money set off on several months of vacation, the most popular choice being an extended sequence of island-hopping in the warmer island groups to the south.

I did neither of these because unexpectedly I landed a gap-year job in the north of Goorn.

My subject was practical stagecraft, the course I had drifted into by default, but which after the first week or two began to interest me. By the end of my first year I was sufficiently motivated to write several application letters, and when a temporary job in the town of Omhuuv was offered to me I jumped at it.

Omhuuv. I had never heard of the place, but soon tracked it down to a part of Goorn I never imagined I would visit. It was in the region known as the Tallek, in the mountains along the northern coast, a small port whose main industries the year round were the packing, smoking and canning of fish. Until I started applying it had not occurred to me there would be a theatre up there, but it seemed this was so. *Teater Sjøkaptein*, located in the heart of the town, closed its doors during the winter months, but maintained a repertory of drama and mixed entertainment throughout the summer. Tourism appeared to be the third industry in Omhuuv. Internet checks revealed that climbing, trekking, water sports, orienteering and tunnelling were all popular activities around Omhuuv's fjord, or in the surrounding mountains.

Once my place was confirmed I was anyway told that because of the winter closure there was no point in my attending until spring was due. I went home to Goornak Town, where my parents lived, and drifted through the cold months. Then, after an email confirmation from the theatre, I set off for Omhuuv on one of the round-island buses. The trip took four days.

My first priority was to find somewhere to stay. I had been browsing a college website which listed possible addresses, and in the weeks leading up to my departure I made provisional bookings at three of them. The one I chose after I arrived was an upstairs room in a house close to the seafront. The window looked out towards one of the smaller wharfside smokehouses, with a view beyond it across the smooth waters of the fjord. On the far side a mountain rose sheer from the water, and for the first few days of my time there the steep sides were patched with traces of clinging snow. Later, when the thaw settled in, the same mountainside was etched with white watercourses, as a dozen wild falls tumbled down to the sea.

I went shopping – there appeared to be only one general food-store in the town, but compared with the prices in Goorn Town and Evllen it felt inexpensive, at least for the sort of food I usually bought – then the next morning I walked through the narrow streets to find the theatre.

The centre of town was set back from the main road, so even the trucks, with their huge engines and deep-treaded tyres rumbling through towards the interior of the island, hardly broke the silence. In one of the side streets I found a large, almost monumental building: a white fascia wall, and two mock towers, castellated and painted deep blue. Across the white front was a long electric banner, presently unlit, with the words *Teater Sjøkaptein* picked out in electric bulbs. Next to the name was a stylized picture of a fishing boat, casting its nets, with the snowy mountains of the fjord in the distance behind. The grizzled face of a mariner, with a waterproof cape and cap, was superimposed across the view.

The main doors to the theatre were closed and barred, with brown paper pasted on the insides to discourage people from looking in. There were several glass display panels next to the steps, but I saw no announcements of performances, and there were no show cards visible. However, the building did not look at all derelict and was in good repair. The paint had been recently applied.

I pressed my face to one of the door windows trying to see into the foyer beyond. I rattled the handle lightly, not trying to force the door but to make enough noise to alert anyone who might be inside.

After a few moments a man appeared from within. He stooped to peer at me past one of the brown paper covers, then seemed to realize who I might be and unlocked the door.

'I'm Hike Tommas,' I said. 'I'm starting a job here.'

'Hike? I was expecting you last week,' the man said, but not in an unfriendly way. He extended his hand, and we shook. 'My name's Jayr. I'm the acting manager here. For the moment there's no one else on the staff, so we've a lot of work ahead of us.'

'What's to be done?'

He ushered me in, closed the door against the cold wind and led me through the lobby, where dust-covers had been laid over the carpets and counters, and down two narrow passages and a short staircase up. The theatre building was unheated and lit only by dim bulbs set high in the ceilings.

Jayr gave me a hot drink from the coffee machine he had set up in the tiny office behind the pay-booth. We sat casually in the cramped space, leaning against the edges of furniture.

105

'Do you have any experience in a theatre?' Jayr said.

'We had to do practicals in my course.'

I described some of them, naturally embellishing the facts to make them sound more impressive. In fact I had already set out my c.v. when applying, and I assumed Jayr would have seen it. Most of my real experience had been in watching other people working behind the scenes, but my interest in stagecraft was genuine and I had spent a lot of time reading the books and talking with other students.

I gained the impression Jayr was glad to have someone to work with him, and his questions soon sounded desultory to me. I decided he was probably unimpressed with his new assistant, but it did not seem to matter much. It was not he who had hired me, it turned out. We were both temporary staff, although I was more temporary than Jayr. He lived in Omhuuv all year round.

I slowly pieced together some idea of what the story was. The previous owners had sold the theatre to a new company, or there was a transfer of a trust document, or another kind of legal dispute. No one was officially the owner for the time being, so they needed staff to stand in temporarily and prepare for the season ahead. Although Jayr lived in the town he had not been born on Goorn, but on one of the other Hetta islands, at the far western end, a small industrial island called Onna. He had worked here the previous summer, more or less in the same position I was now in. He said he had been given a big chance, a fabulous opportunity to prove what he could do as manager. He told me the technical facilities in the theatre were as good as you would find anywhere. The official tech crew had not yet arrived and were not expected for a few more days.

He took me out to show me around the backstage area, giving me a guide to the main technical facilities. I took all this in without a problem: my course had given me a thoroughgoing background in stage management and theatrical craft.

The theatre was about to re-open after the winter break. Bookings had already started coming in. The *Sjøkaptein* was a popular feature of the town. The problem, Jayr's problem, was that the programmes were so unimaginative. He told me the previous year the season had included several plays, but now he was here he had discovered that this summer the main bookings were for variety shows, comedians who were famous from television, pop tribute bands, magic acts. There were problems with the need to hire musicians, finding out what special or extra lighting effects were needed, obtaining releases from TV companies, dealing with agents, all in addition to the normal concerns of staffing, safety measures, office paperwork, and so on.

The programmes at the end of the season were more to his taste. During two weeks towards the end of the summer a couple of plays were scheduled, and he was looking forward to those. In the meantime he was making the best of the rest. There was a renowned clairvoyant coming for a short season – Jayr was looking forward to her too. Clairvoyants always filled the seats, he said. And a mime artiste. Jayr liked mime. But he found the rest uninspiring. He told me there was plenty of scope for me to become involved.

Later, when Jayr had to make some phone calls, I wandered away on my own and walked down to the semi-dark auditorium. The seats were protected by vast over-thrown translucent plastic sheets. I sat quietly in the luxuriantly cushioned rows of seats, somewhere in the middle of the stalls. I leaned back, staring up at the ornately decorated plaster ceiling, the cluster of small chandeliers, the velvet plush on the walls. The building had clearly been renovated recently, but it still felt like a traditional theatre.

A sense of contentment spread through me. The only other theatre I had been in was the civic playhouse in Evllen, but that was financed and managed by the local authority, part of the leisure complex, with squash courts, a gym, a swimming pool and a lending library. The *Sjøkaptein* had the grace of tradition and years on it, but it was magnificent and alive, and dedicated to the calm illusionism of drama, entertainment, amusement.

The next day it began snowing again in earnest. The snow fell day and night, high, thin flakes blowing up the fjord from the direction of the open sea, drifting in the streets and against the houses, the wind gusting relentlessly from the frigid north-easterly quarter. Snow was an accustomed part of life for the people of the Tallek region. Snow changed the mood of everyone – snow had to be dealt with as a practical matter. Every morning and evening, and sometimes during the nights also, the Seigniory snow-ploughs and blowers were out, keeping the streets and wharves open, allowing the shops to trade, the fish to be landed, the trucks to enter and leave. I kept the stove in my room alight all day and night, as did everyone else in the town, fusing the billows of snow with thin grey woodsmoke. For me, Omhuuv took on a more rustic, medieval quality, feeling closer to the elements, deeper in a wild history.

I settled into daily routines. Jayr set me to work testing and checking all the mechanical equipment in the theatre: the ropes, the trapdoor, the rigging, the lights, the sound system. The scenery bay was cluttered with flats from last season's plays, and because we had no use for most of them I set about breaking them up, keeping intact the pieces that I could, or which Jayr said were standard pieces of scenery. I discovered I knew less about this kind of thing than I had thought, but because I was working alone I soon picked up what I needed to know. I carefully kept all the pieces of reusable timber, storing them in the scenery bay.

Jayr was concerned about the slow intake of his bookings: the theatre was due to open in the first weeks of spring, when the snow was supposed to be no longer falling, if not completely melted from the mountains. This was the regular schedule, but according to the records the bookings this year were unusually low. Jayr fretted and complained about the lack of audience support for some of the artistes, especially about the acts he favoured. There was one in particular: a man who worked under the stage name 'Commis', a renowned mime artiste. Jayr swore Commis would probably be the most popular act in the year, as he had been in the past, but at the moment his performances were being no better supported by the public than any others.

With two weeks to go before the first opening the blizzards still swept in every day, the gutters were blocked with ice, the roads were crested with dark and dirty mounds of old snow, compacted by their own weight and the endless passage of vehicles.

*

I began to like Jayr. He did not say much but he was always alert to my needs. He worked me hard but we took regular breaks and he often paid for lunch out of the theatre budget. I never really found out what he thought of me: sometimes I seemed to amuse him, sometimes to annoy him, but during most of our working days we were in separate parts of the building.

One day, during a break for a cup of tea, he said to me, 'Have you seen the ghost yet?'

'Are you trying to wind me up?'

'Have you seen it?'

'Is there one?' I said.

'Never knew a theatre without a ghost.'

'Is there one here?' I said again.

'Haven't you noticed how *cold* it is in the scenery bay?'

'That's because the doors are often open.'

I don't know what he was intending. It turned out that he had been in the *Sjøkaptein* for about five weeks before I arrived, often after dark, always alone, going into many of the deeper recesses of the large building, below and behind the stage, along the corridors, up to the high circle.

Everyone who worked in theatre was superstitious, Jayr said: there were plays the actors would never name, parts they would never accept, scripts they would not read without someone there to cue them, ropes the stagehands would never pull when working alone, the weird or sudden deaths onstage and offstage when mechanisms unaccountably failed, or the accidents with scenery or props, and the supernatural consequences of them all.

Jayr told me about hauntings reputed to be a feature of every other theatre he had worked in, but here, the *Sjøkaptein*, seemed to be entirely free of spirits, wild or sad or bereaved.

'Never knew a theatre without at least one ghost,' he said again at the end.

'Except this one,' I said. He was making me feel nervous, maybe intentionally.

'Wait and see,' he said.

I expected a cold draught to wind its way under the door and chill me, or an eerie cackling laugh to break out in the distance, but then the telephone rang and Jayr answered, speaking with his mouth full of food.

Every day, I would trudge through the narrow streets to and from the theatre, skidding and balancing on the rutted frozen snow, to do what I could to assist Jayr in his endless preparations.

Although he was dealing efficiently if unenthusiastically with the daily cascade of paperwork, Jayr's main concern was the non-arrival of the tech crew, whom he knew were trapped somewhere on mainland Faiand, held up by visa regulations, the weather and the irregular ferry service. Even if they should negotiate themselves free of the bureaucrats, much of the sea around Goorn, and the Tallek region in particular, was still full of ice floes. Although most facilities could be prepared before they arrived, the actual operation of theatre performances was impossible without a full crew.

Jayr became especially anxious when a message unexpectedly arrived from one of the first acts due to perform in the theatre. It was a magician, an illusionist, who styled himself THE LORD OF MYSTERY.

The message contained some straightforward publicity material (including obviously posed photographs of the great man performing, whose appearance and archness we both found amusing) and what appeared to be a standard list of demands he felt he had to make before he arrived: lighting requirements, the need for technical rehearsals, the raising and lowering of the curtains, use of stage apparatus and so on. There was nothing unusual in that, which would anyway be arranged in the technical rehearsals all performers underwent as a matter of course, but with it came a document that was obviously an extra item.

It consisted of a detailed drawing to scale, with measurements and angles drawn meticulously, of a large sheet of plate glass. At the bottom, written in capital letters, was the following:

'PART OF MY ACT HAS TO BE PERFORMED WITH A LAYER OF
CLEAN GLASS BETWEEN THE APPARATUS AND THE AUDIENCE.
THIS SHOULD BE OBTAINED PRIOR TO MY ARRIVAL, AS PER
OUR CONTRACT, AND MUST EXACTLY MATCH THE ABOVE

SPECIFICATION. ON MY ARRIVAL THE PANE OF GLASS MUST BE
FITTED TO THE APPARATUS WITH WHICH I TRAVEL, AND WHICH
HAS PRECISE MEASUREMENTS. LORD.'

'Do you suppose his parents gave him the name "Lord"?' I said.

'That's how he signed the contract,' Jayr said, showing me a
copy.

He seemed amused by the whole matter. The act had been booked
at the end of the previous season by the outgoing management. It
was true that it contained a clause written in verbose language,
presumably dictated by the Lord himself, about the venue's responsibility to arrange the supply and fitting of the glass.

Other than the contract, Jayr knew nothing more about this
Lord. He appeared to be resigned about it, saw it as part of the day-
to-day life of a provincial theatre, a problem to take in his stride.

One morning, when the snow was blowing fiercely down the main
street where I lived, I was as usual struggling towards the theatre.
Staying upright on the slippery ground was always a problem but
on that morning the difficulties were increased by the blustering of
the wind. I had long developed the technique of watching the icy
ground wherever I walked, but I also knew how to keep a general
look-out where I was going. Moving about was hazardous in the
snows of Omhuuv.

I was therefore not too surprised when I collided with a man
walking in the other direction, although I had definitely not spotted him coming. He was somewhat shorter than myself, and as we
bumped into each other his shoulder hit against my chest, spin-
ning me around violently. I managed, just, to keep my footing, but
I did so only by an ungainly manoeuvre with both legs spread and
my hands reaching down desperately to avoid the fall. I skittered
across the ridges of frozen snow, my chest aching from the blow
and for a moment I found it difficult to breathe.

The man I had crashed into, though, was much more affected
by the collision. As I was struggling to stay upright, I saw him first
bounce away from me, and then in some fashion seemed to fly
backwards, his arms flailing. He landed on his neck and shoulders

in a heap of soft snow deposited during the night by the blowers, his legs aloft. He was struggling furiously to release himself as I skidded anxiously over to help him.

'You bloody fool!' he shouted at me, shaking his head and spitting out snow. 'Why don't you look where you're walking?'

'I'm sorry!' I said. 'Here – take my hand!'

He clasped my wrist and after much pulling and shouting I managed to tug him out of the heap of snow. He clambered laboriously to his feet, shaking his arms and head, trying to bang the loose snow away from his clothes.

'You nearly killed me, you careless bastard!' he yelled, as the wind continued to howl around us. 'Look where you're sodding well walking in future, do you hear?'

'I said I was sorry.'

'Sorry isn't enough. You might have killed me.'

'Were *you* looking where you were going?' I said. His reaction to the accident seemed extreme, to say the least. Now he squared up to me.

'Where are you from, you bloody fool?' he said in a fierce voice. He leant towards me, as if trying to memorize my face. 'I don't recognize you. You don't talk like a local.'

I was still struggling to get my breath back. The man was thrusting his face pugnaciously towards mine.

Although his aggressive behaviour was frightening, I was struck, in the extremity of the situation, with the calm thought that in fact I had never seen him before, either. My way to and from work every day was always the same, always along this road, skidding on the frozen ruts, and I usually passed or saw the same people every time. I knew none of them, but in harsh weather a silent brotherhood of wintry endurance seems to arise.

This was the first time I had seen this bellicose little man. Although he was wearing a hood over his head, and a scarf was wrapped around his forehead, his eyes were visible – they were a pale and watery blue. He was crusted with frost and snow, but I could see he had dark and bushy eyebrows, a moustache that grew outwards and down, and a brown-red beard. More than this I could not see because he was, like me, wrapped up thickly against the cold.

'Look, I'm sorry if you were hurt,' I said, although the more I thought about it the less responsible for the accident I felt.

'Goornak Town, that's where you're from! I'd know that annoying accent anywhere!'

I tried to step past him, get away from him.

'When you come to Omhuuv, young man, you bloody behave yourself. You get that?'

I pushed past him, and staggered on across the frozen surface. He was shouting something after me, but because of the wind I could no longer hear his words.

I was shaken up by this unpleasant encounter, and not just because of the physical impact. Of course I was an outsider in the small town, a newcomer, but until that moment the worst I had experienced from local people was a mild curiosity about where I had come from and what I was doing in Omhuuv. In almost every case, the reactions were friendly.

I arrived at the theatre, warmed up in the office while drinking a cup of hot coffee with Jayr, then started my round of the daily chores. I was upset and preoccupied for an hour or two, but by the time we broke off for lunch I was back to normal.

As I walked home that evening, though, I kept an eye open for the man, distinctly wary of seeing him again.

The next morning, not far from where I lived, the man suddenly appeared. He seemed to have been lying in wait for me, because he dashed out of an alley that ran between two houses. He skidded forward like a man making a sports tackle, his feet thrusting at me and catching me on my shins. I fell violently to the side, on to the hard and impacted snow beside the edge of the road. One of the haulage trucks went by at that moment, narrowly missing my head.

I struggled to my feet, but my assailant was up before me. By the time I was upright again he had stumped off down the road, head low against his shoulders, his hands thrust deep into his pockets.

I hurried after him, grabbed his arm and spun him around.

'What's the matter with you?' I shouted. 'You nearly killed me!'

'Then we're quits, you bastard. Leave me alone!'

He pulled his arm away from me with surprising strength, and slithered on.

'Look – what happened yesterday was an accident. That wasn't! You attacked me!'

'Call the policier if you have a complaint.' He turned to look at me, and once again I saw that unremarkable but hostile face, the frosted eyebrows furrowed against the cold, the droopy moustache, the pale skin.

I grabbed hold of him again, angry and frightened, but with great ease he released himself from me and carried on up the road once more. He seemed immensely strong, for all his small build.

I brushed myself down, knocking the snow off my arms and chest. I tried to be calm, tried to put him out of my mind, but it was difficult.

I stared up the road after him, watching the way he moved. Everything about his body language evinced anger and hostility, a tightly coiled rage, compressed violently into his hunched body. I knew nothing about him except that from that moment on I resolved I would watch every step of the way when walking through the town.

Aching again from this second rough encounter, I stayed put. I watched him until he was out of sight, disappearing around a bend in the road, somewhere near the bus terminus. From the way he was waving his hands, I guessed he was still yelling at me.

Jayr said he was too busy to be bothered with Lord, so he delegated the preparatory work to me, as I had expected from the outset that he would. The great man's arrival was not long away.

His image was already part of our daily background as Jayr had placed several of Lord's rather ostentatious publicity photographs in the display cases by the theatre doors. I knew I had to buckle down to the task of obtaining the sheet of glass he had demanded.

My first problem was to locate somewhere that would supply plate glass of the high quality specified by him. There was nowhere at all in Omhuuv, and the businesses in the town I asked about this all told me that glass had to be specially ordered from a firm

114

of glaziers in the neighbouring town of Ørsknes. Because I did not want to risk getting any detail wrong, I borrowed Jayr's car and drove over to Ørsknes myself and contacted the glaziers. They were bemused by the exactitude of my requirements, but they obviously assumed it was for a shop front or window. Payment and delivery were soon arranged.

The fall of snow ceased during the night after I returned from Ørsknes.

When I was up and dressed in the morning I discovered that the long-awaited thaw had followed almost at once. The cold north-easterly wind at last dropped away, and had changed overnight into a balmy breeze from the south. For a day it seemed nothing in Omhuuv was going to change: the air trapped in the fjord had been chilled into what seemed to be a permanent freeze, and the snow in the streets and on the mountainsides was so deep, hard and solid that it felt that even a summer heatwave would never shift it. I walked the precarious streets with many of the other inhabitants of Omhuuv, still wrapped in protective clothes, sliding and skidding on the familiar frozen ruts, while a weak sun shone. But the hated north-easterly wind from the mainland was uncannily absent.

On the second day the thaw unmistakably began, with melt-water running through the streets, while the great frozen layers of impacted snow began to slide dangerously from the roofs. Seigniory workmen hurried from one building to the next, trying to control or manage the crashing of ice on to the pavements. Now at night I fell asleep to the burbling sounds of water running. There was water everywhere in the town, but most of it ran off into planned conduits leading down to the fjord.

All around the town streams and falls were appearing, and every day there were public warnings of likely avalanches in the hills above us. However winter was of course part of the normal life here, and long established avalanche barriers kept much of the danger out of the town. I was content to watch the steep mountainside I could see from my window, as it was transformed into a lacy pattern of white waterfalls.

On the third day the warm wind gave a daily rain shower, but it fell only in the late afternoons and helped speed the thaw. Every day was now a mild or even warm one, and the breeze from the south carried with it a smell that brought back to me memories of my childhood: somewhere in the warmer islands to the south of us the spring was already well established, and the wind bore scents of distant cedarwood, campion and herbs.

Jayr was more cheerful, because as the weather changed it seemed a signal of encouragement had gone out on some subconscious level. More bookings arrived with each delivery of mail or visit to the messaging service. Every morning he spent more than an hour on the theatre computer, selling and confirming seats for the long summer season ahead.

The sheet of plate glass I had ordered from the firm in Ørsknes was delivered as promised. It took the driver and his two mates, plus myself, to carry the bulky pane through the crowded back-stage space and place it in the stage area. The driver gave me some padded mounts to rest it on, but it was obvious that it could not be left where it was.

After the delivery men had departed I turned on some of the stage lights and inspected the glass.

In the Lord's specification he had noted the minimum distortion that he would accept, and I checked this with a special gauge – the glass was well within that spec. It was also exactly the right size, and the four bevelled slots where the glass was going to be attached were again absolutely correct. I checked and re-checked all the measurements, pleased at having made sure this was right. However, the bright lights revealed that the haulage of the glass, and our manhandling of it, had left several hand and finger prints, so I thoroughly cleaned and polished the sheet on both sides.

Jayr helped me move it on to the fly lines, and we slowly raised it into the rigging loft. I knew it would be secure up there, but it was discomfiting to know that the sheet of plate-glass was being held directly above the stage. It looked like a huge transparent guillotine blade, sharp, heavy and deadly.

In the town the thaw was continuing and I realized that in these early weeks of the spring the fjord became a place of great beauty and tranquillity. The mountains, which looked so barren when covered by snow, now brought forth grasses, flowers and bushes. White-water falls continued to course down the steep mountainsides, splashing into the dark blue waters of the fjord. The houses and shops, which looked so grim in the cold, broke out their seasonal colours: the people removed the wooden and metal shutters from windows, let their curtains blow in the breezes, hung flower baskets on the walls in the street, left their doors ajar. They painted and cleaned their houses, and tidied their gardens.

Visitors arrived, some in cars, many in buses. Shops and restaurants opened. During the days the streets of Omhuuv were crowded with pedestrians wandering around the newly re-opened boutiques and galleries, while the wharves continued their noisy work and the pungent odour of curing smoke drifted across the quays. More boats appeared on the fjord, but now they were pleasure boats, some bringing in more visitors, others simply sailing around. Two herons nested on the roof of the house I was staying in.

Inside the theatre also the seasons were changing. Our work was increasing daily, partly because bookings were now pouring in every day, and many members of the public called at the theatre with enquiries, but also because the tech crew still had not arrived. The ice cleared from the sea almost as soon as the thaw arrived, but there was some kind of visa anomaly that prevented so many people exiting the mainland at once. Because I had always lived in the calm neutrality of the islands it was too easy to forget that Faiand, the mainland country in the north closest to our part of the Archipelago, was a nation embroiled in war.

One day, shortly before our season opened I had to go to the trap room, the substage area, where one of the traps had proved to jam when I tested it. Jayr said I should try to find out what had happened – he was thinking of Lord, who was due to appear in the second week. Illusionists often needed to use a stage trapdoor, Jayr said.

The trap room in a theatre is sometimes used to store unwanted items, so out of season it can become cluttered. One of my first tasks at the *Sjøkaptein* had been to tidy up down there. By this time it was fairly easy to move around. There was little or no lighting when the theatre was not working, so I had to check the mechanism in darkness, leaning over the drive housing with a torch. The place was unheated, and cold draughts wafted against me.

My arm was down inside the housing, checking the clasps of the drive cover were tight, when I suddenly became aware of a silent presence. Somewhere near to me. It was as if something or someone had moved, dislodging air but making no sound.

I froze in position, my arm inside the machine, my shoulder and head pressing against the outer housing. I was surrounded by darkness, because I had placed the torch on the floor, the beam pointing through an access hatch close to the floor. I listened, not daring to turn my head.

The silence was complete, but the sensation of a presence was overwhelming. It was close to me, very close indeed.

Slowly, I began to slide my hand out from inside the machine, so that I could straighten and turn, look around, shine the torch about, make certain no one was there. The silence endured, but as I turned my head I became aware, on the periphery of my vision, of something white and circular, seeming to hover.

I sucked in a breath in surprise, turned fully towards it. The shape was a mask, a face, but it was horribly stylized, almost a child's cartoon of a face. It was frozen, immobile, but in some way I cannot describe I knew it was alive.

As soon as I was looking towards it the face backed away smoothly, disappearing into the darkness almost at once. It made no sound, left no trace.

My heart was racing. I grabbed the torch, swung it around in the general direction of the apparition, but of course there was nothing to see. I stood up fully, clouting my head against the low ceiling, the under-surface of the stage. The shock of it further frightened me, so I backed quickly away, hurried to the steps, rushed up to the wings of the stage. I was trembling.

A little later, Jayr saw me.

'I heard you making a lot of noise,' he said. 'Did you see something down there?'

'Shut up, Jayr,' I said, embarrassed at my reaction to something

I had only half seen. 'Was that you messing about in the trap room?'

'So you did see something!' he said. 'Don't let it bother you. Happens in every theatre. Sooner or later.'

The tech crew had at last received clearance from the authorities and were on their way to join us. But now the problem they faced was the multitude of ferries they had to board, the circuitous routes, the many ports of call where cargoes and mailbags were loaded and unloaded. We did not expect them to arrive until a day, or at best two days, before our opening performance.

I continued to work as hard as before, but now I had a background concern. I was worried by the sheer weight of the pane of glass we had lifted into the flies, hanging there, swinging sometimes if there was a draught of air when the scenery bay doors were opened. I quietly checked it periodically to make sure it was still secure in its harness, but other than that there was little I could do about it. Lord of Mystery was due to arrive for the second week's show.

Two days after I saw the apparition in the trap room, I had a similar experience. Once again I was alone, and again I was in one of the more inaccessible areas of the theatre. I had climbed up to the higher of the two loges at stage left. Jayr told me there was an intermittent electrical fault. The lights in the box sometimes flickered when turned on. It was probably caused by a simple loose connection, but the loges at the *Sjøkaptein* were popular, and were booked in advance for most performances. It had to be repaired before any member of the public could be allowed in.

As usual I worked beneath a dim overhead light from high in the ceiling of the auditorium, which barely shed any illumination and none at all inside the loges. Of course to work on the wiring I had had to isolate the current, so once I was inside the loge it was completely dark.

I was on my hands and knees, working with the torch between my teeth, peeling back the carpet to expose the wiring beneath, when once again I suddenly sensed there was something close to me that had not been there before.

My first instinct was to close my mind to it, concentrate on what

I was doing, hope that the feeling would pass. But an instant later I changed my mind and moved rapidly. I raised my head, sprang to my feet.

The white face-like mask was there again! This time it had appeared between the curtains that closed off the loge at the rear. I caught only a fractional glimpse of it, because once again it backed off, vanishing almost immediately.

I knew that behind the curtain was the access door to the loge, and beyond that was the upper side-corridor used by the audience as they found their way to their seats. I dived across the loge, snatched the curtains back then pushed the door open. I half-fell out into the corridor. This was a windowless part of the theatre building and Jayr and I never normally switched on lights along the corridor. I swung the torch in both directions, trying to see whatever it was that had intruded on me like that.

Of course, I saw nothing.

Shaken, nervous, a little frightened, I went swiftly down to find Jayr, who was working on the computer terminal in the office.

I said nothing, but collapsed into one of the spare chairs along the wall. I could not suppress a shudder, and I exhaled sharply.

'Was it a silent ghost or a noisy one?' said Jayr, without looking across at me. 'Does it moan, dress in ancient gowns, carry its own head, make a breathing noise, clank long chains, or does it just hover?'

'You don't believe me, do you? There's something out there. I've seen it twice now! It's really bloody terrifying.'

I was regarding my forearms, bare because I always worked with my sleeves rolled up. All the hairs were standing on end.

'Remember ... this is a theatre. Everything that happens in a theatre is *real!*'

With the last word, Jayr turned in his chair, lowered his head like a hunting animal, and made a snarling noise, baring his teeth.

At the end of that day, walking back to my room along the usual streets, I caught sight of my bearded assailant. His tense, hunched way of walking was distinctive, and the moment I noticed him I was on my guard. I held back, watched him for a few moments until I was certain he could not see me.

He was ahead of me, striding along in the same direction and did not turn back to look. It was certainly him but because the weather had improved so much he was of course no longer wrapped up against the cold. On the contrary, he was wearing rather large and loose beach shorts, bright blue, and a yellow shirt that flapped behind him as he walked.

Just the sight of him made me nervous, so I stood quietly by the side of the road, half concealed by a shop canopy, until the man had turned off the main drag, entering a side street at the other end.

The tech crew finally turned up. As soon as they had settled in their lodgings, and familiarized themselves with the facilities in the theatre, my working life changed. All the routine chores around the theatre – cleaning, checking, aligning and repairing – were taken over by others. I was impressed by the professionalism of the crew: four men and three women, who in just two days had the theatre prepared and technically rehearsed in time for the opening night.

That first week's bill was one of mixed variety turns. As the acts started to arrive at the theatre, roughly at the same time as the tech people, I was eager and curious to see them. The *Teater Sjøkaptein* was quickly being transformed from a cold, ill-lit and above all empty building into a place where a large number of people worked, bringing all the noise, companionship, squabbles, minor emergencies and sense of purpose that surrounds any group of people existing closely together.

Backstage, the building echoed with the noise of last-minute scenery building, lights being focused and calibrated, of tabs being raised and lowered, instructions shouted down from the balcony, and so on. Three musicians appeared, to provide the accompaniment. Meanwhile the front-of-house manager was hiring a temporary assistant to help with cleaning and preparing the auditorium, selling tickets and refreshments, and organized emergency medical cover for each performance. I was entranced by the sense of busy purpose, but my own working role was almost eliminated by these new people.

On our opening night I watched much of the show from the

wings, but I soon wished I had not. The acts were of the most basic and unimaginative kind, the sort of live entertainment I had no idea was still being performed in theatres. The show was compered by a middle-aged comedian who specialized in off-colour jokes, which were offensive mainly for being so unoriginal and therefore unfunny. The acts he introduced included a juggler, an operetta duo, a ventriloquist, a trick cyclist, a soprano, and a troupe of dancing girls. By the end of the show I realized I was staying on only because of these dancers. I thought one of them was rather pretty and seemed to be encouraging me with several smiles flashed in my direction, although when I tried to speak to her she cut me dead.

After that first evening I wasted no more time watching these acts, and was puzzled but rather relieved by how much the audiences seemed to enjoy them.

We were expecting the Lord to arrive halfway through this first week. The morning of the day we were expecting him – we had had to make a space for him in our already crowded vehicle park behind the building – I was sitting with Jayr in the office. He was entering the week's takings and expenses into the computer, while I sat idly by, rather enjoying the quietness.

A matinée performance was due that afternoon, but for the time being our temporary solitude was almost like those last days of winter.

'Have you been seeing your ghost again, Hike?' Jayr suddenly said, without turning away from the computer monitor.

'Not since the last time.'

'Are you sure?'

I had long wished I had concealed my earlier reactions from Jayr, as he had been teasing me repeatedly about my sightings of the ghost.

I stayed silent.

'I thought you might have noticed what's behind you,' Jayr said. 'That's all.'

Of course I turned to see, and to my surprise and (for an instant) horror, that impassive mask-like face was right beside me, lurking behind my shoulder. I could not help it: I leapt to my feet, startled, turning to get a better look.

'Hike, this is Mr Commis, our star turn the week after next.'

Standing next to my chair was the slight figure of a man dressed in a mime costume. He was clad from head to foot in some kind of soft, black, non-reflective fabric, hugging his skin. Only his face was clearly visible, and that was because it had been painted a brilliant, almost dazzling white. Every facial feature had been covered into blended invisibility, with stylized cartoons drawn in their places: he wore quizzically inverted eyebrows, a down-turned mouth, two painted black spots for his nose. Even his eyelids had been painted, so that when he blinked two stylized bright-blue eyes seemed to replace his real ones.

'Commis, this is my deputy Hike Tommas.'

The mime leapt into action. With an exaggerated motion he swept a non-existent hat from his head, swirled it elaborately, then crossed it in front of his chest as he bowed. When he straightened he momentarily spun the invisible hat on an extended forefinger, then threw it up in the air, waggled his head from side to side as the hat curled through the air, and with a sudden diving motion managed to get it to land on the crown of his head. Smiling, he bowed again.

'Er, good morning,' I said inadequately. Commis the mime smiled briefly, then turned away and with an agile motion jumped backwards on to the surface of a spare desk, and crossed his legs.

A moment later he began to eat an imaginary banana, peeling it slowly with precise movements, then pulling away the pithy strings that attached to the side of the fruity flesh. He ate it with great attention, chewing thoughtfully. When he had finished he licked each of his fingers, then tossed the peel away so that it landed somewhere on the office floor.

He raised a buttock, mimed a long fart, then wafted away the smell with an apologetic look on his face.

A little later he sharpened an invisible pencil, puffed on the loose shavings from the pointed end to blow them away, then used it to evacuate wax from his ear.

When Jayr and I took some drinks from the coffee machine,

Commis rejected our offer of a real one but suddenly produced an imaginary large cup and saucer, clearly full to the brim with a scalding liquid. He fussed over this, holding it gingerly, blowing gently across the surface, stirring it with an invisible spoon, tipping some of the liquid into the saucer so he could sip from that. He continued this performance until Jayr and I had finished our cups of coffee, then he put away his own cup.

When I tried speaking to him he made no answer (but cupped a hand behind his ear, pretending, I think, to be deaf). Jayr shook his head at me, discouraging me from what I was doing.

Later, Commis developed an itchy rash that appeared to travel all over his body.

He sat there and sat there, perpetually performing his imaginary feats.

Finally, not at all entertained by this self-centred behaviour, I decided to leave. As I crossed the office floor. Commis mimed intense fear and warning, shrinking back across the desktop in horror, pointing at the floor and imploring me with his eyes.

I could not help myself. I stepped carefully over the banana skin as I went into the corridor outside.

After that, Commis's presence around the theatre was a constant. He was due to headline the third week of our season, so his early arrival meant that he was underfoot practically all of the time. I found his endless pantomimes aggravating but harmless, and did what I could to ignore him. However, he was always there, sometimes mimicking me, sometimes leaping out in front of me to show me a cat he was pretending to hold or a photograph of me he had just taken, or trying to involve me in his fantasy world by throwing balls to me, or trotting in front of me, pretending to open and close non-existent doors. He never once spoke, never emitted any kind of sound. I kept expecting that I might one day see him out of character, but as far as I could tell he appeared to be staying and sleeping somewhere in the theatre building itself. He was always there when I arrived and was still there after I left at the end of the day. I never did find out what Jayr knew of him, what their relationship was, if any. It was obviously more than Jayr said, perhaps even close or intimate, but I was not that interested and did not enquire.

I realized that my work at the *Sjøkaptein* was now only marginal, and by agreement with Jayr it was to finish soon – in fact I was due to leave at the end of the following week, before Commis started his run of performances, when I would be paid off.

My final task before I left was to lend whatever assistance the Lord would need when he arrived. I was nervous about this: my weeks at the *Teater Sjøkaptein* had shown me that a professional interest in stagecraft was one thing, but a sympathy with the people who trod the boards was another.

The Lord's self-generated advance publicity was not for me a sign that he and I were going to work together well. However, to my surprise it turned out that in life he was a quiet, almost invisible presence, apparently shy and self-effacing. For instance, when he arrived in Omhuuv he let no one in the theatre know, so none of us realized at first that he was there. He and his female assistant had been waiting patiently in the foyer for so long, unobtrusively sitting in the chairs at the side, that one of the ticket office staff eventually went to ask if they needed any help.

When we finally saw him costumed and made up for his show he became impressive and extrovert, with an entire repertoire of theatrical gestures and loud and sometimes amusing remarks, and exuding endless confidence in his own powers.

His main illusion, with which he concluded his performance, was a set-piece which to the audience looked transparently simple, but which required careful and exact technical preparation.

He called the illusion 'THE LADY VANISHES'.

The effect seen by the audience was of a bare stage, backed by curtains, and dominated by a large, metal structure made entirely of steel rods. This consisted of four slanting legs, and a heavy cross-member across the top, strong enough to bear weight. The audience could see that this was the full extent of the apparatus: there were no curtains, no trapdoors, no hidden panels, just a skeletal steel structure standing in the centre of the bare stage. While performing the trick the illusionist could pass around and through and behind the structure and be seen at every moment. He would then produce a large chair, and this would be connected to the cross-member by a rope and a pulley.

His female assistant – transformed from a mildly attractive woman in her late twenties into a dazzling vision of glamour by her scanty costume, flowing wig and make-up – would sit in the chair, and be blindfolded.

As the small band in the pit played suspenseful music, with an insistent drum-roll, the magician would laboriously turn the handle of a winch, and the chair and Lord's assistant would rise towards the apex of the immense structure, twisting slowly. Once she was at the top, the illusionist would secure the rope and utter trance-inducing words. The assistant would slump in the chair, as if hypnotized. He then produced a large gun and aimed it directly at her! As the drums reached a climax the magician fired the gun. With a loud bang and a flash of light the chair would come crashing noisily down on the stage, its rope trailing behind it. The lady assistant was no longer in the chair, and indeed had vanished entirely.

The method was both much simpler and more complex than anyone in the audience would imagine. The illusion was achieved by a combination of stage lights and a mirror. Or in this case a half-mirror. Or in reality, a pane of clear glass, the one I had obtained for the Lord from the next town.

The glass was attached to the front of the metal scaffold. Because of the way the lights were shone on it, and with the assistance of more lights concealed behind the front struts, the glass was entirely invisible to everyone in the audience. Everything that happened inside the apparatus, or behind it, was completely visible. When the young woman was winched to the top, everything that could be seen was actually happening: she was really there, in the chair, and suspended from the cross-member.

However, at the firing of the gun (which by intention made a loud bang, emitted a huge flaming discharge and a cloud of smoke) two things happened simultaneously. Firstly, the lighting of the stage was switched. In particular the concealed lights inside the struts were turned off, and front lighting was increased. This had the effect of turning the sheet of glass on the front of the structure into a mirror. Because of the direction of the lighting, and the angle at which the glass was placed, it ceased to be transparent and now reflected an image of curtains (otherwise invisible to the audience) behind the proscenium arch. These curtains were identical to the backdrop curtains upstage, and lit appropriately. From the point of view of the audience, nothing inside the steel skeleton could now be seen. Meanwhile, in the same instant, the rope lifting the chair was severed by a small built-in guillotine beside the winch. This released the chair, so that it crashed down spectacularly to the stage with the rope snaking behind it. The assistant grabbed the cross-member with her hands and swung there out of sight. She hung on gamely with her hands, until the curtains closed on her and, out of sight of the audience, she dropped athletically to the stage.

All this was straightforwardly achieved, but it was also a technical challenge for myself, a stagehand called Denik and the lighting engineer. We worked for a morning and an afternoon, learning how to erect the frame (which Lord had brought with him in his property van), and arranging for the plate glass to be lowered from the flies then secured to the front of the structure. We aligned it with the hidden curtains and finally ran several repeated technical rehearsals, not only with assembling the apparatus but with the lighting cues. Although this was of course computerized, all the lights had to be set at the correct angles to achieve the desired effect.

Lord fretted over these preparations. The plan was that during a live performance, he would move in front of the main drop to perform small-scale magic, engaging members of the audience who briefly left their seats to walk up on the stage. While this was going on Denik and I walked on to the stage, behind the curtain, to lower the massive structure. We would secure it firmly, connect up all the concealed lights, run a brief test to make sure everything was working, then get out of the way to allow Lord to perform his climactic illusion.

We rehearsed it again and again.

During one of our final rehearsals, and entirely without our realizing it, Commis managed to find his way to the rigging loft.

He somehow clambered across to where the dummy curtains had been hung behind the proscenium. When the technician threw the switch to change the lighting, suddenly Commis was in full view of the auditorium, apparently now mounted on the top cross-member, a manifestation instead of a disappearance, scampering to and fro like a caged monkey.

Jayr had walked into the auditorium to watch this, and he applauded.

It was the last straw. I marched off the stage, headed towards the office. I wanted to collect my stuff and walk out.

I don't know how he did it, but Commis climbed down quickly from where he had been and hurried along the corridor behind me. He was still pretending to be a monkey, so he ran with a wide-legged waddle, his knuckles running along the floor.

I did something I was instantly to regret. Halfway along the corridor, I mimed opening an invisible door, passed through it, looked back. As Commis reached the door I slammed it in his face.

To my amazement he reared up in apparent pain and surprise, his face contorted as it collided with the invisible door, he tipped backwards and dropped like a felled tree. He collapsed in a supine position, arms and legs outstretched, completely motionless. For a moment I thought I had really hurt him, until I realized that the blankly staring eyes were the ones that were painted on his lids.

I wished I had not done that! I felt that I had somehow descended to Commis's level of aggravating playfulness.

I went on to the office and stood there by myself, feeling confused but also angry, still not sure why the mime should provoke me so. After a while Jayr came to find me.

I did not after all walk out of the *Teater Sjøkaptein*. Jayr was unexpectedly sympathetic, but he explained Commis's behaviour as the erratic actions of a highly tuned and sensitive artiste and told me I should be more tolerant of theatrical talent. We argued about that. I vented much of the irritation and frustration that had been mounting ever since I became aware of the man.

Finally, Jayr pleaded with me to stay until the end of the coming week, as the backstage work I was doing with the Lord's apparatus was crucial, and he didn't know if the technical rehearsals could be completed with someone else in the time that was left.

In the end I agreed and Jayr promised to keep Commis out of my hair. A mental image briefly tormented me: of Commis picking over my scalp with his monkey fingers, in search of salty excretions. I stayed on.

The Lord's first performance went smoothly. So did the second, and all the rest. Denik and I worked together well. The illusion was achieved every night and at the two midweek matinées.

Lord duly finished his week at the *Teater Sjøkaptein* and I helped Denik break his set, and carry the pieces of the dismantled frame to his van. The pane of glass was ours to keep, according to contract, and after Lord had departed Jayr and I briefly discussed what to do with it. Our options were few: we could give it away, or try to sell it, break it up and dispose of it, or keep it in the theatre somewhere. Jayr pointed out that we had been playing to almost full houses for most of the week, and if Lord wanted to make a return visit to Omhuuv in the next year or so the theatre would no doubt book him. If so, it would make sense and save time and money to retain the plate glass.

Accordingly, Denik and I put the sheet back into its harness of hemp ropes, and winched it up to the loft above the stage. There it hung, gleaming and deadly, swinging quietly like an immense blade whenever the scenery bay doors were opened and let in the wind.

I was now free to leave, so I packed my belongings, purchased a ticket for the long return journey on the circum-island bus, and then walked back to the theatre to say my farewells.

The conflict with Commis had tended to overshadow my last two or three weeks, and it took a conscious effort of will to appreciate that in fact I had benefited enormously from the experience. Even my negative feelings might one day serve me well, if a career in other theatres became mine. I was painfully aware that I was learning, that I had more to learn, that were still another two years of my course to run at the college in Evllen. Perhaps it was simply that as the least experienced member of the crew I had been subjected to a kind of initiation by the others. Thoughts on parting, probably too late. I still seethed with irritation.

I found Jayr straight away and he thanked me for the help I had given him over the weeks. I responded in the same way, acknowledging my debt to him.

Then I said, 'Tell me about Commis. What was all that about?'

'He's always miming when he's in costume, or rehearsing. You should have just played along with him.'

'I did,' I said. 'Only a little. How well do you know him?'

'No more than any of the other acts that come here. He's been performing at this theatre for several years and has a huge following in the town. We're almost sold out for next week.'

'He lives here in the theatre?'

'He rents a place somewhere on the edge of town, but when he's performing he moves into the same dressing room – the smallest we have, at the top of the tower. He rarely goes outside the building. You're about to leave – why don't you go and see him? Say goodbye. He might even speak to you, if you're lucky. He's a different character when he's not in part.'

'All right.'

He seemed to make normal everything the weird little mime had done around me. I shook hands with Jayr, thanked him again, then before I could change my mind I ran up the spiral staircase that led to the highest level of the building. I had rarely been to this area in the past. I had done some cleaning of the dressing rooms when I first arrived, but otherwise there was not much need to go up there.

As I clambered up the stairs I could not escape the thought that he would probably realize I was on my way. Sometimes he seemed psychic in his anticipations of me. I half-expected a new trick: Commis would hide somewhere, then leap out on me, pretending to be a large spider, or would mime throwing a net over me, or some other foolishness.

Slightly out of breath from the climb I rapped my knuckles lightly on the door, staring at the shiny star attached to the panel, and the name written neatly on a card beneath it. No answer, so I knocked again. Reasoning that with a silent artiste like Commis it might be wrong to expect a spoken summons, I pushed the door open. Full of apprehension I went inside and switched on the light.

He was not there, so I backed out immediately. I had glimpsed the usual mirror and table, the familiar sticks and cakes of make-up, the folding screen, the costumes hanging on the rack. The only unusual feature of the room was a narrow folding bed, placed along the wall. His outdoor clothes were lying on it.

I switched off the light and closed the door. Then instantly I opened it again. I turned on the light.

His outdoor clothes included a yellow shirt, and bright blue beach shorts. Now I noticed, lying on a chair beside the bed, theatrical disguise: a bushy red beard, a droopy moustache, false eyebrows.

I returned to the backstage area and saw Commis was alone on the stage. I was in the shadows, way back in the wings. I believe he did not know I was there, because for once he seemed to be concentrating on his work. He was moving about the stage, blocking in his moves. He used a piece of chalk to make minute marks on the boards, then made a brief practice of his mime in those places. I saw him start to struggle with an umbrella in the wind, I saw him trying to remove a piece of sticky paper when it landed on his face, I saw him prepare to take a bath. He did this quietly and expertly, without apparent consciousness of an audience, or of a colleague he wished to torment with his endless tomfoolery.

His presence in my life always made me take actions I might later regret. I could not ignore the discovery I had just made in his dressing room, that I had without knowing it already met Commis several times, out of role. I felt I understood him for what he really was. I realized all that as I went to the access stairs, even through my seething anger, even as deep down I recognized that what I was intending was wrong.

I reached the rigging loft, I found the hemps that held the huge sheet of glass in its place, I loosened two of the ties. I left them just tight enough to hold the glass safely. Probably.

When I looked down at the surface of the stage, I saw, as I had expected, that Commis's blocking marks were directly beneath the suspended pane of glass.

131

I went from the theatre at once, exiting through the scenery bay. I purposely left the largest door ajar, letting in a persistent draught. I felt frightened and guilty, but I would not, could not, return.

Outside the theatre, in the narrow streets of the town, the sun was shining and a brisk but pleasant breeze was coming onshore from the long fjord. There was still some time before my bus was due to leave, so I walked slowly by an indirect route, down to the closest wharf and then from there along a narrow lane that followed the shore of the fjord. I had never walked that way before and immediately wished I had. It was at a lower level than most of the town, closer to the water, and I could barely hear the noise of the traffic that passed constantly through the town.

It was a moment of symbolic liberation for me: I had abandoned if only temporarily the world of theatrical make-believe, of artifice and illusion, of light and shadows, mirrors and smoke, of people who played roles, who acted, who made themselves look and behave differently from their real selves.

The mime artiste was the extreme example of the common activity: his make-believe could never exist, even within the fantasy he created. Released from all that, I walked along the peaceful path, feeling the warm sunlight and being sheltered from the breeze, looking at the greenery of the spring's new growth, the sudden flowers, the signs of a coming summer. I was thinking of home.

Then behind me, disruptive and insistent, came the sound of footsteps. Someone was hurrying along the path behind me, a quick pace, almost a run.

I glanced back and realized that my pursuer was almost upon me. I could see his small determined figure, the bright-blue beach shorts, the fluttering yellow shirt.

When he saw me looking back, he raised a fist and shouted, 'I want words with you, pal!'

I suddenly realized how precarious my situation had become. I knew already the violence Commis was prepared to use when he was out of his role – here on the waterside path there were no houses in sight, there was no passing traffic, no other pedestrians walked along the lonely track. Just the trees and flowers, the deep and silent waters of the fjord.

I shouted no reply. I was genuinely frightened of the man, what he might be capable of doing to me. The guilt that was already in me deepened: perhaps he had already worked out the trap I had laid for him in the rigging loft above the stage.

I turned and ran, but behind me Commis started to run too.

I saw the path ahead: it showed no sign of coming to an end, of leading back to the main road, the houses of the town. It extended along the shore, at least as far as the next headland, created by the sheer side of a mountain as it met the water.

I was carrying some of my baggage, weighed down by it. Commis was closing on me.

Suddenly, I realized what I had to do.

I flung my bags aside and turned back to face him. He was now only a short distance away from me, and I saw him raising one shoulder, starting to measure his pace, just as I had glimpsed him doing that day he came skidding across the frozen ruts at me, felling me violently with a sliding tackle. I braced myself for impact, but in the same moment I lifted both my arms, strained at some imaginary weight, and raised a huge sheet of heavy glass between us.

I held it at the vertical, clinging to its sides, ramming it down against the loose gravel of the path, making a place where I could let it stand unsupported.

I leapt back and in the same instant Commis ran headlong into the glass. His body struck it first, but an instant later his head banged against it and he was thrown painfully backwards.

The glass collapsed down towards me, so I leapt back from it to avoid being struck as it fell. Perhaps it shattered on the stony surface of the path, but now there was nothing between Commis and myself.

He was standing away from me, turned to the side, slumping forward, holding his head in his hands. He kept moving one of his hands down to where he could see it, looking at the palm as if blood was pooling on it. He shook blood off the hand, emitted a low cry of pain. He pulled out a kerchief, mopped his brow, buried

133

his nose inside it. His head was rocking up and down. I could see him breathing heavily, and just as once before I was momentarily convinced I had really injured him.

In a state of bizarre contrition and concern I stepped back towards him, to see if he needed help, but as soon as I was closer to him reality returned to me. I heard the words he was using, a string of vile invective and threats against me.

I went away. I grabbed my baggage and hurried on down the path. In a short distance I saw a place where I could with some difficulty scramble up the slope through the undergrowth. I could hear traffic not far away.

As I started to climb I looked back. Commis was still where I had left him, still in the same pained posture of defeat. I gained the road, soon saw where I was, and found my way back into the main part of the town towards the bus station.

I heard nothing more of Commis. All my way back home, and for a long time afterwards, I kept thinking about him – for all I knew he was still standing there beside the fjord where I had left him, or he was not. And I often thought remorsefully about the heavy pane of glass hanging above the stage, or it was not.

Junno

PEACE EARNED

JUNNO is a small independent nation, comprising three islands lying in the subtropical zone of the Midway Sea.

Although mid-summer can be hot and humid, for most of the year the climate is moderated by the Southern Oscillating Stream. All three islands are heavily forested, with vast areas set aside as hunting reserves. The largest of the three islands, Junn Maio, has a range of mountains defining the southern coast: there are rich mineral deposits here, including iron, potash and copper. On the second largest island, Junn Secs, there are apparently limitless reserves of oil shale. These products are exported from the only harbour in the country: Junn Exeus, an immense industrial sprawl that disfigures a long stretch of the eastern coastline of Junn Maio.

Junno is one of the most prosperous places in the Archipelago – it is also the principal source of the world's atmospheric pollution, directly and indirectly.

It can be a difficult and unattractive destination for travellers, by air or sea, as apart from the local ferries calling intermittently there are no scheduled services. Because of its position in relation to the Equator, connecting flights have to be chartered privately. Only sub-vortical flights are allowed at that latitude, which causes delay. The sole working airport on Junno is operated by the Faiand military authorities. In theory, the Faiand Federation is under notice to relinquish their hold on the airport, but in practice most of the population of Junno is in favour of them remaining. There is brisk two-way trade with the base.

Our general advisory to intending visitors: take note of the difficulties and look for other destinations.

The semi-isolation from the rest of the Archipelago has made Junno into a haven for people with a dislike of centralized authority. Although there is a nominal Seignior, his family were violently exiled two hundred and fifty years ago, since when no tithes or tributes have been made and the three-island state has operated as a relatively stable anarchy. The islands have been declared 'open', allowing unrestricted havenic immigration.

When independence was first declared there was a flood of immigrants from every part of the Archipelago and it was these guest workers who were put to work in the mines. Their descendants are still on Junno, performing most of the manual labour. It is impossible to learn much about the conditions these people live and work under. We know they are paid extremely well but are not allowed contact with the outside world.

The Junnians abolished shelterate legislation at the same time and a steady trickle of deserters from the war in Sudmaieure still arrives in Junno every few weeks. The fate of these young deserters after arrival tends to fall into one of three groups.

The black-cap escouades of military policier are based at the airport and they are always on the alert to seize deserters from either side. They re-educate them all, then they return Faiand deserters to the front, and Glaundian soldiers are offered the choice of induction into the Faiand forces or a further course of re-education. Some of the fugitives from war, though, successfully avoid the black-caps and embrace the fiercely independent way of life in the nation. After what is usually a difficult period of habilitation, most of these young deserters settle down to remain in Junno. A third group, soon sensing that where they have arrived is not that different from what they have fled, take advantage of the lax border controls, and move on.

Unlike the inhabitants of almost every other island in the Archipelago, the people of Junno are armed to the teeth. There are not only more guns than people on Junno, there are estimated to be more than twenty guns for everyone, counting new-born babies, the elderly and the guest workers (who are prohibited from having their own weapons). More guns are acquired every year.

Apart from hunting and fishing, the main leisure pursuit on Junno is the thrice-yearly range war on the smallest of the islands, Junn Ante. The range wars are freely entered into by Junnian and immigrant worker alike. There are huge cash rewards for the guest workers if successful – their choice of weapon is said to be restricted and the guns lack the high power and accurate sights of those used by the Junnians, but there is never any shortage of participants. For the Junnians there are opportunities to gain land and other property from each other. Live ammunition is used.

The journalist Dant Willer was despatched as correspondent to cover the hostilities in the war taking place across the frozen plains and glaciers of Sudmaieure. For six months Willer filed horrifying stories about the extreme conditions suffered by both sides in those endless grinding hostilities, but then was recalled to Muriseay. On the return journey, Willer fell in with a group of young deserters who were travelling to Junno, to take advantage of what they imagined were liberal shelterate laws. Willer's touching descriptions of what these six young men had endured in the war, followed by the gruelling account of what happened to them once they reached Junno, won the *Islander Daily Times* a Prix Honorré for Investigative Journalism, and a cash bonus and promotion for the young reporter.

Willer later wrote a non-fiction book, *The Junno Range Wars: Earned Peace?*, and this too was awarded a Prix Honorré, in the category of Literature of Neutrality.

Currency: all trade on Junno is conducted with the use of convertible bonds, but we have been unable to discover what money would be used by travellers. We assume that the Archipelagian simoleon would be acceptable, and perhaps it would be possible to convert money at the point of entry.

Keeilen

GREY SORENESS

Close to the southern continent, Sudmaieure, KEEILEN was originally developed as a neutral garrison island. The idea at the time was to encourage the forces of the opposing belligerent powers to use this bleak, remote and previously unpopulated island as a base, rather than have them force the use of the more densely populated civilian islands elsewhere. Two large bases were partially built, at opposite ends of the island, encouraging occupation, but although Keeilen came to be used as a port of call, for refuelling, picking up supplies and so on, the garrison buildings were never used.

Later, the Keeilen authorities converted one of the sites into a civilian high-security prison. A tidal-flood cell was readied and set aside for Kerith Sington, the vicious killer of the much-loved mime artiste, Commis, but he was sentenced to death, so the cell was never needed. As it had remained unused for more than a hundred years, it was allowed to revert to its wild state. The prison was later downgraded to Category 2, for long-term as opposed to high-security prisoners.

Keeilen is free of mountains, but the south-eastern zone is a high plain, exposed to southerly gales. The bitter wind of the winter, the CONLAATTEN, brings heavy snowfall for several months. Modern settlements are in the northern quarter of the island, where there is some shelter from the cold.

Keeilen Town, the administrative centre, is where most of the prison officers and other staff have their homes. There is some manufacturing industry and a small fishing fleet ventures out when the sea is not frozen. It is a cheerless, wind-blown place where rain or sleet often fall. The sun is rarely seen. The sky remains dark and cinereous for most of the year. In the interior of the island there is mining of a deep seam of coal.

Because of its location so close to the southern mainland, Keeilen is a common first stopping-off place for soldiers trying to desert from the war fronts. The Covenant of Neutrality defines shelter-ate provisions, under which deserters are guaranteed a safe haven should they manage to reach any of the free Archipelago islands of their own volition. Traditionally, Keeileners make these desperate and unhappy young people welcome, but strictly speaking Keeilen is not a free island, as defined in the Covenant.

Because of the recent upsurge in hostilities, and thus because of a greater number of deserters, islands such as Keeilen have been experiencing problems with housing and employment. Now there is an unofficial policy of encouraging deserters to move on to other islands. Many stay, though, and as a result escouades of black-caps are often seen scouring the island. This is a breach of the Covenant, but there seems little the people can do.

Visitors are welcome because Keeilen is not a wealthy place, but in truth there are few attractions. For fell walkers the southern cliffs do provide a harsh challenge, but it is dangerous to move away from the marked viewpoints. The cliffs should not be attempted during winter as there are no emergency or rescue services on the island. The former tidal-flood punishment cells are well worth a visit, but only at low tide. Again, great care should be taken. Tunnelling is allowed on Keeilen, and there is a practice area close to the coal mines. Local architecture is vernacular; what few public buildings there are were built in the masonic style.

Currencies: Archipelagian simoleon; Ganntenian credit.

Lanna

TWO HORSE

Set alone in the tropics north of the Equator, LANNA is swept daily by the hot trade winds from the horse latitudes. Bisected north to south by a range of high mountains, comprising several extinct volcanoes, the island enjoys two distinct climates.

The eastern side, which receives the prevailing winds, has a varied terrain, some of it desert, some thick forest – the slopes of the mountains on that side are steep and bare. Two or three of the peaks are favoured by climbers and fell walkers because of the challenges they present and the amazing views of the Midway Sea. Every year there is an informal mountaineering convention, in which people new to the sport of climbing are given tuition on the nursery slopes, and the experts tackle the spectacular sheer faces and overhangs.

The western side of the island, in the rain-shadow of the mountains for most of the year, has a hot, dry climate tempered by spells of heavy rain in every spring. Then that side of Lanna is carpeted with a profusion of wild flowers, bringing visitors from many of the adjacent islands to enjoy the brief awakening to summer.

Lanna Town, a port on the westernmost side, has a natural harbour in the bay against which it was built. Although there is a modern section of the town, where banks and insurance companies provide local jobs, it is in the Old Town of Lanna that poets, painters and composers have congregated. There in the narrow streets, many of them climbing steeply up the hills from the harbourside, is a warren of small houses and studios which may be rented inexpensively.

It was to one of these that the brilliant Muriseayan poet Kal Kapes and his new young wife, Sebenn, moved late one winter. After a short period in which they settled in to their new house Kapes sent a message to his close friend Dryd Bathurst, inviting him to Lanna to see the display of flowers for himself.

To the Kapes' surprise, not only did Bathurst turn up when expected, he was for once travelling alone. The three of them spent seven days together, not leaving the Kapes' house on a single occasion. Many of their neighbours well knew who the new residents were, and also realized the identity of their house guest. Although there is no evidence for this, it seems likely that the visit would have provoked much gossip and speculation across the narrow streets of Lanna Old Town and in the taverns.

Bathurst was the first to leave, walking down quickly one morning to the harbour to catch the early ferry. He spoke to no one. His features were shrouded by a hooded cloak, in spite of the fierce heat from the sun.

Kapes and his wife remained, but still they did not leave the house. Ten days went by, with no sign of the poet or his wife and no indication of movement from within. Eventually, the neighbours felt enough concern to force an entry to the house.

It was the end of spring and the last of the wild flowers were wilting in the fierce heat from the overhead sun. The bodies of both Kapes and Sebenn were found immediately, in different rooms of the house. To the people who found them here was no sign of how they died, but a later post-mortem examination discovered that Sebenn had been strangled, and Kapes himself had taken a poison derived from the serum of the thryme.

A short poem was found in Kapes' notebook. It lay unnoticed with the rest of his property until some time later a researcher from Semell University was able to go through his papers in detail. Kal Kapes had earlier chosen Semell as his preferred repository for his papers and most of his original drafts, notebooks, letters, and so on, were already held in a special collection.

The discovery of this new poem, *Undreon's Way*, brought one of Kapes' finest last poems into the world. It was an old story, an ancient myth: from a time of gods and adventures and great deeds.

Undreon and Urcheon were brothers: they fought heroically in war together, but at the end of the war Undreon took Urcheon's wife and with her sudden and eager consent ravished her repeatedly while forcing his brother to watch. Undreon was consigned to hell, Urcheon murdered his wife, then submitted to the poison of a viper.

Fourteen lines. The date scribbled on the sheet in Kapes' hand was the day Bathurst had been seen in the Old Town, his face shrouded, his hasty steps leading him down to the port.

Luice

REMEMBERED LOVE

Deep in the southern hemisphere, Luice is a small but strategically placed island offshore from the eastern outer curve of the Qataari peninsula. Although it is in the rain belt of the subtropical region, its position in the shadow of the mainland and its high and otherwise exposed profile has created a barren, windswept landscape, with large areas of desertified rock and gravel. A hot wind (the Kiruk Akhisar, laden with grit and pollen) blows for about two-thirds of every year. There are no mountains, but the western part of the island is an undulating plain.

All the habitation is on the western side, where a natural port has been formed by a deep lagoon and a rocky reef. Luice appears to have been uninhabited before the outbreak of war, a fact repeatedly claimed by the Faiand Alliance who seized the island before the Covenant was drawn up, although archaeological research suggests otherwise. Whatever the reality, Faiandland has held the island for hundreds of years, using it as a way-station for the troops transported to or from the theatres of war.

Civilians may only visit Luice under military supervision, or if granted special permits. In any case, there is little to attract the casual visitor.

The non-military inhabitants are almost without exception immigrants from other parts of the Archipelago, who run service and infrastructure support for the military.

Luice Town is small and compact and does not extend much further than the area around the port. The wharfside consists mainly of huge warehouses, where war materiel is stored. There is a military hospital, a large cemetery and a few cheap food outlets. Several bars and brothels exist on the waterfront, and in the maze of narrow streets behind.

A metalled road leads to a busy airstrip inland.

A civilian ferry calls at Luice Town once a week. The troops use this if going on leave, or if after discharge they want to return independently to their homes in the north. Because of Luice's position, the closest islands of the Archipelago are at least an overnight voyage away – the ferries are large and comfortable, but too expensive for many of the troops.

Luice was the site of a devastating air disaster. Two troop transporter planes, approaching the airstrip from vortical altitudes and therefore not able to take full advantage of separation by air-traffic control, collided in mid-air. One plane contained two hundred constables from the Faiandland Border Policier, due to join the front line of a new assault. The other was carrying more than a hundred infantrymen, destined for the same planned salient. All were killed, as was everyone else on board: the planes' aircrews, senior auxiliary officers and civilian support staff. The total number of victims came to three hundred and fifty-two men and women, nearly all of them in their early twenties.

Although the collision occurred above Luice Town, by good fortune most of the wreckage fell into the sea or on to uninhabited land, so there were no extra fatalities on the ground. All the bodies were recovered, but most of the wreckage remains uncleared – one of the aircraft was transporting armour-piercing warheads made of depleted uranium. Where this wreckage fell, the Faiand authorities created an exclusion zone. The bodies of most of the victims are buried in a separate area of the cemetery in Luice Town.

Several relatives came forward to claim the bodies of their loved ones, and for months there was a trickle of these desolated arrivals on the island, usually exhausted after the long journey across the Archipelago. Often that complicated journey turned out to be a mere preamble to the maze of military bureaucracy they then had to penetrate, to gain access to the remains of their sons and daughters.

One such arrival was the author, Moylita Kaine. She later said that she had feared she would face more official obduracy than other people, for two reasons. Firstly, she was not a relative, but had come of her own volition on behalf of the sister of a young constable who had been killed. She was also no friend of the Faiandland authorities. A recent book by her had exposed the fact that both sides in the war were using psychosis-inducing gases. These had been illegal for many years, but they had been brought covertly back into use and deployed against each other's front line.

Her book led to a new abolition, surrounded by a storm of recrimination and controversy. Although she was a neutral, her book had been based on experiences in Faiandland, and consequently she had become *persona non grata* on Faiand territory. She was no stranger to their harassment.

Presumably, though, orders had come from higher up that she was not to be delayed on Luice, because the casket containing the young man's body was passed into her care soon after she arrived.

She was also given a badly damaged paperback book, the only possession they had been able to identify as his. She found his name, neatly written at the top of the first page inside. Much of the rest of the book was scorched and torn.

She had to return by the way she had come, with no special assistance from the Faiand people. Although Kaine was a modest woman with no interest in personal publicity, her literary reputation had spread throughout the islands and her brief visit to Luice aroused interest and sympathy amongst the people who lived there. As she waited for the incoming ferry to dock, she was photographed on the bleak, sun-scorched quay, with an honour escouade standing to attention behind her. In one hand she was holding the scorched remains of the paperback book, the other she was resting lightly on the flag-draped coffin.

As the gangplank was swung down to the quay, a young reporter stepped forward and approached her respectfully, addressing her by name. They exchanged a few words.

Then he asked her if the soldier who had been killed was a close relative, perhaps a son?

'No,' said Ms Kaine. 'He was just a friend, another writer. And he

145

wasn't really a soldier at all. He had been drafted into the Border Policier.'

Later, as the coffin was carried aboard the ship by the honour escouade, slowly stepping, arms linked beneath the casket, she was seen to be standing beside the gangplank, looking away across the harbour waters, weeping quietly.

Manlayl

HALF COMPLETED / HALF STARTED

A small island in the temperate latitudes of the northern Midway Sea, close to the northern continent, MANLAYL was for centuries known only for its fishing. The fishing grounds on the continental shelf in the Manlayl region are exceptionally rich and diverse, and the catches were exported to all parts of the Archipelago.

With the coming of the war, however, all islands in that part of the sea were surveyed for possible strategic usefulness. The Covenant of Neutrality was not then in place and many small islands found themselves requisitioned for the siting of observation and listening posts, for airfields, deepwater ports, training grounds and the like. In Manlayl's case, the Glaund Republic sequestered the island by main force and set about building an underground missile-launching site. The people of the island could only stand by powerlessly and watch.

The island's salvation came in the form of the hastily drawn up First Protocols of what was to become in due course the full Covenant. Protective neutrality was declared, the Glaundians departed with bad grace, and peace returned to Manlayl and many other small islands like it.

The Glaundians left a legacy of several deep tunnels drilled into the rock. Their excavations had revealed that the rock of Manlayl was mostly an old and stable formation of limestone, a soft but durable rock, suitable for ambitious tunnelling projects.

Word of this reached Jordenn Yo, the earthmoving installation artist. Using false documents to show she had claimed and won mineral development rights from the Glaund occupiers, Yo brought

147

in her equipment, hired the necessary artisans and tunnelling began. It was not long before news of her installations spread, and hundreds of freelance or mercenary tunnellers began arriving on Manlayl. Soon they had set up their own projects in competition with Yo.

Having seen or learned about what had happened on other islands, the Manlayl Seigniory Department invested most of the accumulated wealth of the island in a desperate lawsuit intended to protect the island from reckless tunnelling. After protracted and frequently adjourned legal proceedings they eventually won their case.

Jordenn Yo had already left Manlayl, realizing that if she did not her equipment would risk being seized by the authorities. She had already served prison sentences elsewhere. But many of the mercenary tunnellers carried on boring and digging until the last possible moment. Some were removed only after bailiffs were called in to take them out by force.

Finally, the battle was over and the last tunnellers departed. Some went into prison. Manlayl was made safe from tunnellers, and many other islands, feeling themselves at similar risk, used the case as a precedent for bringing in their own anti-tunnelling legislation. The life of the island slowly reverted to what it had been many years before.

Much irreparable damage had been caused, though, and more than half the island was now riddled with long, corkscrewing passages through the bedrock. Many of these had ingresses at mid-tide level, causing daily floods. Several of the smaller hills began to collapse, and part of the northern shore was crumbling into the sea with every tide. Inundation and subsidence extended a long way inland. Even today there are many large areas of Manlayl where it is unsafe to venture.

However, most of the south and eastern areas of the island are as they have always been, and commercial fishing has resumed. The island is a pleasant and interesting place to visit, with many historical markers. The main port, Manlayl Town, has several small hotels and pensions suitable for couples or families, and the cuisine, largely based on exotic seafood, is exquisite. Summer and autumn are the best times to visit, because the winter gales do still make Manlayl an extremely noisy and disharmonious place. It is not wise to reveal any interest in tunnelling.

Currency: Archipelagian simoleon, Ganntenian credit, Aubracian talent.

Meequa / Tremm

BEARER OF MESSAGES / FAST WANDERER

THE DRONE

The drones came in at nightfall. If she had completed her day's tasks at the observatory, Lorna Mennerlin would shut down her terminal then scramble down the uneven cliff steps to the beach. From there she could watch the aircraft returning as they flew in low above the sea.

When the sea was calm, the brightly coloured LEDs in the belly of each of the drones mirrored back from the surface of the waves. On some evenings the machines flew over one by one, sometimes separated by several minutes, but most evenings they arrived in such numbers that they swarmed towards the island in a glittering formation. As they passed over the beach and responded to the radar sensing of the rocky cliffs rising beyond, they would adjust their height in unison. In their wake was a breathy susurration from their silenced vanes, a feeling of secretive distances already crossed, covert explorations, unstated winds.

As a precaution against the security staff coming across her and challenging her for being on the beach at that time, Lorna always took the tabulator down to the beach with her, but this evening, as on most evenings, she did not switch it on.

The tabulator hung on its strap against her side. She could feel it vibrating gently in stand-by mode as it responded to the locating pulse of each of the incoming machines, separately identified. In this mode the tabulator's detection of the drones was numerical: so many of them recognized and logged, so many accounted for. She would return to evaluating the more complex quantified results the next morning, after they had been downloaded at the base and sent along the landline to the MCI's computers.

In the chartroom the staff would view the coverage of the ocean, then become absorbed in the task of tracing each drone back to its launch point, using the satellite returns to analyse its route. Working with the other cartographers, Lorna then laboriously transferred the images to the master data store. But even with a full complement of staff they were endlessly running behind – they were still trying to untangle the reports from more than two years before. Tonight's mapping data would probably not be properly evaluated for another two years or more. Gradually, the backlog was increasing.

Lorna should have left the MCI and Meequa Island several months earlier, at the end of her contract, but she felt trapped by Tomak's sudden disappearance. How could she leave until she knew what had become of him? Patta, her roommate, obviously thought it was time for her to move on, but that was for Lorna irrational and impossible. Tomak had left her with so many things unsaid, so many personal decisions unmade.

She still ached with love for him. Why had he left her that way? It was impossible to re-adjust until she found out what had happened.

She stared across the sea, under the scattering of drone lights, at the dark offshore island where Tomak had been posted. This was the real reason she came down to the beach every evening whenever she could, but it was becoming a habit. No longer a hope. Silence was the cruellest burden.

The other island had a name: Tremm, named after the mythological companion of Meequa, who was the bearer of messages. Tremm was Meequa's outrider, the guard, the protector, the fast wanderer who passes. But the island which carried his name was dark and low against the twilit horizon, stolid and heavy-looking, as much unlike a fast-moving wanderer as it was possible to imagine. Tremm was directly opposite the cove, an hour or more by boat from Meequa, across the shallow strait, and whenever the drones swarmed in she would see the paths of their LEDs veering to one side or the other of the island.

Tremm had been charted years before, but ironically it was one whose details were the least known because of the secrecy that surrounded it. It was one of several closed islands in the vicinity of Meequa, taken over by the military many decades before. The drones were programed to avoid it. No one could go near it without permission. Anyone who did go there had to sign security pledges, and never spoke about the use the island was put to. Most rarely admitted they had even been on the place. Officially it had ceased to exist. Even to look at it was, in theory, to break military law, although the civilian cartographers at the MCI, and the ordinary people who lived in the town, could and did use this beach.

On the map of the Midway Sea Tremm did not exist. No island was drawn in its place. It was shown as an area of the sea, a dishonestly blank zone south of Meequa. Someone had fancifully added oceanic depths, and blue contour lines. The legend said in small blue letters: DANGER.

Gradually, the chart of the Dream Archipelago was taking shape, but because the drones were self-guided on reactive principles (programmed to avoid each other and solid objects, rather than seek out certain targets) most of their data was produced along randomized paths and therefore much of it overlapped. The returns inevitably revealed unidentifiable stretches of ocean.

Digital images of land, or better still of coastline, were comparatively rare, a fact which often surprised visitors to the mapping institute. To most people, the sea seemed crowded with so many islands that it was unbelievable that it would be difficult to chart the areas of land. However, less than five per cent of the Midway Sea was solid land, the rest being ocean, lagoons, rocky shallows, beaches, and so on. This percentage was a working assumption. The actual figure would not be known until the mapping was complete. Satellite images, invariably unreliable because of the temporal distortion zones, had provided the working estimate, but drawing detailed, reliable maps was a matter of urgency.

At least the MCI was well funded. People who ran wars needed maps.

The terrain of many of the islands, viewed from above, was

unbroken forest, or unexceptional farmland with few distinguishing features. Many islands were desert. Where there were rivers they were usually short or narrow, or both, or overhung with foliage. Lakes were few. Mountain ranges were also a problem for a technical reason: the drones had a maximum working altitude, and when they approached that ceiling they were programmed to veer off. Coastlines were always more satisfactory to work with: the ports, peninsulas, cliffs, fort installations and river estuaries could usually be identified and located to particular known islands or even existing maps made by the locals.

The drones were programmed to detect and map roads, towns, railway lines, airfields, factories, homes, sources of pollution, and many more man-made objects. Mostly they found traces of sea.

Progress was therefore infinitesimally slow. When she began working in the Meequa Cartographic Institute as a young graduate, Lorna had imagined they would be mapping the whole shape and extent of the Dream Archipelago. As she quickly discovered, this gigantic task was still barely started, buried under an ever-growing mound of data. The only reliable trace they had was the individual path taken by each drone on each trip, and although this could be tracked against satellite data and computer records the amount of overlap and sheer number of indistinguishable images was overwhelming them.

More recently, as her youthful idealism was replaced by experience, she had found herself following the example of her colleagues. She started to concentrate on a single group of islands, ignoring all other data or passing it to colleagues.

Her chosen speciality was the cluster of cays, skerries and small islands in the southern seas close to Paneron, known informally as the Swirl, which comprised more than seven hundred different named places. Her first task had been to tabulate the names, itself a mammoth task. Many names were duplicated, many islands were named in different ways, and throughout the Archipelago, the Swirl being no different, local patois would use a locally recognized name while the inhabitants of other islands, some of them adjacent, knew the island by a different name. At least half of the known islands in the Swirl had no discernible name at all, yet her database had already passed five thousand separate names for the islands.

No one at the MCI had been to Paneron or the Swirl, no one at the MCI even knew anyone else who had been there. There were no formerly existing aerial photographs or drawings of the Swirl, and of course no charts were available. The satellite images, randomly distorted as always, suggested a spiral of islands, those towards the centre made to look larger than they probably were, those on the outer fringes smaller, and the rest warped in proportions whose extent could not be calculated.

A hundred books described the Swirl, but some of the accounts were only vague or lyrical, while most of the rest were written in the seductive rhythms of Archipelagian literature. A collection of seafarers' yarns, told in archaic marine argot, happened to have become one of Lorna's most reliable guides. Sailors were used to navigating, measuring, keeping logs, for all their fanciful stories of monsters and mighty tempests. Names were the only certainties – the culture of the islands was oral and textual, not visual.

Occasionally, one of the drones passed over an area of tiny islands and crags, and every now and again Lorna could make a matching identification and fit one more piece into her slowly shaping jigsaw.

Out of the known seven hundred she had so far charted three Swirl islands.

Such was the task. She knew that even if she lived to be an old lady, and worked in the MCI until the end of her life, no more than a quarter of the islands of the Archipelago would by then have been mapped. Maybe all of the Swirl would have been completed, perhaps many of the large islands elsewhere. But not all. Even by then.

She and the other cartographers had only charted a little over two thousand accredited islands. Another five thousand maps were in preparation. Beyond these were at least ten or twenty thousand more islands of unknown size, importance or position. The entirety of the task was still dauntingly unimaginable.

*

As the last of the loose formations of drones passed quietly over-head, Lorna walked across the shingly beach to a spur of smooth rock. The pebbles crunched and ground beneath her feet. She balanced the case of the tabulator against the outcrop, then leaned back on the sloping surface that faced the sea. She let her hands swing at her side.

Tomak had been away, presumably still on Tremm, for nearly two years. Never once in those months had she received any communication from him.

He warned her before he left.

'They mute the islands they use,' he said. 'Tremm is shrouded.'

'But there must be a way to call.'

'It's enclosed in a communications shroud. No sounds or transmissions enter or leave. No one without authority is allowed on, no one is allowed to leave.'

'Then why should you go there?'

'You know I can't tell you.'

'Then please don't go.'

She had implored him throughout their last three weeks together, but one evening, after they had stood together on the beach to watch the drones flying in, he had been taken in a motor-lighter to a small ship waiting offshore. Before that final evening they spent a short holiday together, a tearful and frustrating experience for Lorna, but Tomak said only that he was unable to resist the force of military law. He promised that he would return as soon as he could, but so far he had not.

As a civilian she was abruptly excluded from his life. Not long after he departed, feeling betrayed by him, feeling abandoned, deep in loneliness, she took a kind of unintended revenge on him. Her physical affair with one of the graphics assistants had not lasted for long, and afterwards she felt a sense of crushing guilt and abhorrence at her own selfishness. Bradd Iskilip, the man in question, was still working in the institute, but whatever there had been between them was emphatically over. It already felt like a long time ago to her, although not nearly as long ago as Tomak's departure. More than anything she wanted Tomak to return so that she could quietly, silently, close the error for good.

As the darkness of the sky deepened, she took her binoculars from their case and held them to her eyes. She focused on the dark jagged bulk of Tremm, knowing that if one of the patrols happened to come along the beach and spot her she would be in serious trouble. Her status at the mapping centre would be small protection.

At first she could make out little of the island in the dark, its steep mountainous sides almost at one with the sky. Then, as her eyes adjusted to the gloom, she could discern the central mountains. Five of the highest peaks were visible from this shore.

Her practised cartographer's eye made an inward plan: the five peaks that could be seen, the three that were out of sight beyond those, the plain on the north side facing her, the rolling terrain on the far side, somewhere a town on the coast. The contours and features taunted her, because she would never be able to check them or plot them. DANGER, it said where Tremm stood.

The first of the fireflies glowed so quickly she almost missed it. She held the glasses steady, hoping for another. After a few minutes she saw a second one, then almost immediately a third. She reduced the focal length minutely, widening the field.

Bursts of light were appearing on the dark slopes of the distant island, a sudden silent flaring, like miniature explosions too distant to be heard. So far away from her, with no hint of the size. She began counting them, as she often did – she had spent so long quantifying data, so to her it was an automatic reflex.

Double figures in the first minute, then a pause. Twenty-five more followed swiftly, followed by another pause so long she thought the display had ended. Then a final outburst of flaring lights, always white and intense, now clustered together, almost a stream of lights, but there was no discernible pattern.

When she lowered the binoculars, she discovered someone was standing a short distance away from her. It was a man, his shape just visible against the white curve of the waters's edge. She had not heard him walking across the shingle.

Swiftly, she moved the hand holding the binoculars, trying to slip them down out of sight. Just in case he had not noticed them, although of course he had.

'May I look too?'

'You know it's illegal,' she said. She recognized his voice, of course. Relief, irritation, both coursed briefly through her.

'So do you.'

'I was monitoring the drones.' She touched the side of the tabulator.

'Oh yes, of course.' He stepped away from her, lowering his head, staring down at the surface of the beach. 'You would have to say that. I know why you're really here.'

'Leave me alone, Bradd,' she said.

'As you wish. Do you know what causes the flares?'

'No. Do you?'

'I see you most evenings, looking across.'

'Then you must be looking too.' He was stepping to and fro in an agitated way, but somehow he was managing not to make any sound on the shingle. 'They're something to do with the military. Or the drones.'

'Same thing.'

'The drones are ours.'

'We use the data from them. That's not the same as controlling them. If you or anyone else at the Institute had the freedom to decide about using them, would you make them steer at random? Why do they avoid the places we want to see rather than fly over them? You know who finances them.'

She wanted to get away from him, but he had contrived to stand between her and the shortest way back to the steps. She eased the tabulator strap over her shoulder, then walked down across the shingle, going around him. It was getting too dark now to make out details, only shapes, but she knew where he was and she also knew how he would be looking at her.

Her feet crunched on the shingle again, a curiously hollow sound, as if there were just a shallow layer of pebbles above a cavern. She heard Bradd behind her.

As she started to climb back towards the top of the cliff, she took one last look out to sea, towards Tremm. Without using the binoculars it was impossible to be certain, but she felt sure the flares were continuing. She paused, looked back down. Bradd must still be there but it was too dark to see.

She raised the binoculars to her eyes but now Tremm was once again a dark shape. That familiar blankness, unrevealing of anything except the one quality that could not be hidden: its real presence, there across the strait.

At the top of the steps lay the unkept garden that surrounded the Institute, and in the dark the breeze from the sea was more of a presence. It mingled with the scents of the night-fragranced flowers that grew wildly everywhere, slowly cooling as the short night began. Beyond the main bulk of the building, in the valley below that opened out into Meequa Port, the lights of the town were visible, a ribbon of electrical dazzle that followed the course of the river.

Lorna paused, taking a breather after the climb up the cliff, thinking that Bradd would soon catch her up.

The windows of the institute building were lit from within, but every pane of glass was curtained so that it was impossible to see inside. Lorna knew that at this time some of the cartographers would still be bent over their drawing tablets and terminals, but most would have stopped work for the night. Some of them would have stayed behind to use the bar, but a lot of the staff simply went home at the end of the day. Lorna and her friend Patta were unusual in renting one of the institute's small service flats inside the main building.

Beyond the Institute, the town, the inland heights of Meequa's range of hills. Sometimes, people who worked in the Institute went on hill-walks up there in the heights, but because of the friable nature of the rocks the hills were not safe for climbing or exploring. Lorna herself had never been far inland from the coast. She preferred to leave the dark peaks a private mystery in the background of her life, an unexplored enigma.

The hills held other more tangible riddles too: Meequa was an important part of the network of military installations and bases found all over this sector of the Archipelago. Large areas of the hill country were forbidden to the public, even to members of the MCI staff, who were nominal collaborators in the drone project.

Somewhere beyond the first range of peaks behind the town was the base to which the drones returned, where they landed, somewhere dark, unlit, controlled by computer robots, collecting and storing data, information that was more than just the mapped details that were passed on to the institute: military intelligence, mining data, probable oil reserves, weapons caches, sources of energy. None of that disagreeable practicality was any part of Lorna's own enigma. She sensed a deeper, more personal absence because of her loss of Tomak.

Tomak's disappearance was probably explained by the hidden interior of this island, rather than by the uncharted highlands of the other. But Meequa was for her an island like a thousand others in the Archipelago, harbouring a seashore mentality, a littoral culture, turning its back on the engine of military intention and strategy that powered the island economies from inland, looking instead outwards to the unmapped seas, carelessly idle in the warmth, languorous under the sun, dreaming in the days.

The drones went out again before dawn, whispering above the roofs of the town, heading out across the sea. By the time Lorna was awake they had all disappeared, but another swarm of drones sent out earlier would be returning in the evening. The drone journeys were long: the solar-powered batteries could keep the flimsy craft flying for days or weeks. Many never returned. Some were shot down by troops: the enemy, of course, but even friendly gunners were known to use the drones for target practice if they strayed too near a base or a fort. Others crashed when the software failed and they collided with each other or with something on the ground, while more ran out of energy when they strayed too far south or north, and became trapped in a night that was too long for their batteries to be revived by the coming of sunrise.

But there were others, and these were the ones that Lorna loved to dream about. People from all over the Archipelago told stories of drones that became trapped in their own software. They somehow wandered into an area of terrain, a range of hills, a stack of rocks, a pattern of islands that set up radar avoidance patterns in the directional controls, but also closed a loop from which the drone could never escape.

Lorna had heard of more than thirty islands which had acquired attendant drones, constantly touring or circling the mountain heights, or zooming along the seashore, or heading bravely out to sea only to be returned by the detected barrier of a neighbouring island. One pair of islands in the Aubrac Chain had fortuitously created a virtual figure-of-eight, around which the captured drone constantly flew, never escaping, day after day, night after night.

Sometimes Lorna imagined that if the mapping enterprise went on long enough, every island would eventually have its own drone, permanently circling with its flow of silent, silvered wings.

When she arrived in the office that morning she downloaded a fresh set of drone images for the general area of the Swirl – the date identifying them was nearly two and a half years earlier.

She began as usual with the preliminary scanning, which filtered out and discarded approximately ninety-five per cent of everything: these were the unworkable, unusable images of the surface of the open sea, or of unidentifiable patches of land, or were blurred by motion or simply out of focus.

The secondary level of search on the remainder involved the fragments that might be identifiable in some way, and therefore able to be matched with previously stored images: these were usually glimpses of shallower seas, lengths of reef, concentrations of fish, large isolated rocks, or on land surfaces they might be clear images of mountains, or part of a river, or dwellings, or even short stretches of coastline. There were scanning and matching programs which could handle these, so she transferred the images to the computer and left it to sort out what it could. Occasionally, once every few weeks, one of the computers would report a matching image, causing amused relief and ironic cheers from the staff.

The material that was left after all this filtering was for her to search manually. These were the coherent images, the ones that promised to be identifiable. This was the real work for her, where all her time went. Using complex imaging software on her terminal she tried to match and compare the main images.

This morning the most promising result had been produced by

a series of fifteen contiguous drone shots. These readily connected into an unbroken stretch of rocky shoreline, for which the computer reported more than a hundred and fifty possible matches with existing downloads. Lorna had to look at each of these herself, trying to match them against the new image. In this particular case, the problem was that many of the rocks appeared to be volcanic in source, which might mean that they had been ejected comparatively recently and therefore would not match with anything. The software made corrections for height, angle and colour variations, but even so the final decision was almost always hers, or one of the other cartographers'.

Then again, the shore might be part of one of the hundreds of Swirl islands she had not so far identified. Even beyond that, it was not unknown for the drone search pattern to be identified or labelled in error. Many hours of wasted search time were regularly lost on searches for the wrong island in the wrong part of the ocean.

The day passed with normal absorption into this routine work: she took a long break at midday and went for a walk with Patta, and towards the end of the afternoon put away the search work and caught up with some correspondence. Various universities were funding the Institute's cartographic project, and there was a constant traffic of information to and from research departments in every part of the world. All the cartographers in Lorna's section had to take on some of this daily work.

She was about to close down her desk for the day when her terminal quietly emitted an incoming-data warning and a large file began to arrive.

It was a detailed graphic, loading slowly. The time estimate was two minutes for completion. Lorna's first reaction was to leave it and examine it properly the next day. It was early evening and she was planning to walk down to the beach as she so often did, to watch the returning drones. As she looked at the screen, though, she suddenly realized what the graphic consisted of, or at least what the title at the top claimed it to be.

It was a highly detailed map of the island of Tremm. It was topographically exact with 3-D representations of the physical features, all towns and settlements shown, as well as roads and unidentified 'installations', which Lorna realized at once were probably the military bases. There was even meticulous nautical representation, showing all the offshore sea depths, position of reefs, navigable channels, and so on.

Although she had never seen any depiction of Tremm before, the general appearance of the map was familiar, using the same cartographic conventions they used on all their other work. One unusual marking though, which she noticed at once in her first look at the map, was the presence of many tiny dots, marked in black with a surrounding white emphasis. The map had a legend, which was of course so familiar to her she barely glanced at it. But the one for Tremm indexed the dots with the letter 'Y'. No other explanation was offered.

The illegal map glared out at her from her terminal, visible to anyone else who might be in the office. Trying to act as normally as possible, Lorna first saved the map to an encrypted section of her personal memory card, then printed a hard copy. As soon as this was complete, she folded it quickly and slipped both it and the memory card into her bag.

She gathered her tabulator and the case holding her binoculars, and headed out of the office, towards the path that led down to the beach.

The first drones were already approaching from the south. Halfway down the cliff steps, Lorna saw the cluster of gleaming LEDs swarming in across the darkening sea. She paused to look, as always fascinated by the weird beauty of the erratic formations, the dodging and weaving amongst each other, the kaleidoscope of lights, the reflections from the sea.

She was disconcerted and a little frightened by the unexpected appearance of the Tremm map on her terminal. She could have no legitimate excuse for receiving or keeping it: the existence of the forbidden zones was known to everyone on the staff, so she would be unable to pretend that she had not realized what it was. Even so, she wanted it: the map of Tremm was a direct link with Tomak, a possible way of finding out where he was, or perhaps even of tracing him somehow.

But it had subtly changed everything. Until the moment the map arrived, Tremm was an unsolvable enigma to her, a barrier. She could dream about the unknown Tremm, but with the physical details of the place in her possession that helpless fantasizing was now replaced by a sense that she should act.

She decided not to continue down to the beach, but returned up the steps to the top of the cliff. As she mounted the last short flight she saw Bradd Iskilip standing there, his large body silhouetted against the lights of the Institute. At that instant she realized who must have sent her the map.

'Is that what you were looking for?' he said.

'How did you get hold of it? I thought – '

'All the closed zones are accessible if you really want them. It was easy to locate. I also know how you can get across to Tremm. Do you want to?'

'I don't know. I haven't even thought about that yet.'

'Do you have leave coming up?'

Two of their colleagues were walking towards them across the untamed garden. Lorna glanced around in a guilty fashion.

'We can't talk about this here!'

'Is your roommate in the apartment at the moment?'

'Patta? No – she went out for dinner in the town.'

'All right. This won't take long.'

The first wave of incoming drones swept past low overhead, the breathy rush of air, the quiet whirring of the motors.

Bradd turned and walked ahead of her into the main building. Lorna realized he was leading her but of course that was just the way Bradd was. During those few regretted weeks with him last year he was always like that. He wanted to be assertive, decisive, controlling.

She allowed him to lead her to the door of her apartment, but then she went past him, pushed the key into the lock and turned to face him.

'I don't want you to come in, Bradd,' she said. 'I don't think that would be right any more.'

'So you think we should talk about a visit to Tremm out here in the passage?'

His voice was loud, unguarded. He intended that. They both looked from side to side along the corridor. It could hardly be more open to the risk of being overheard.

'If you come in, tell me what you know, then please leave.'

He nodded, but it could have meant anything.

Lorna opened the door and they both went inside. She left the light off in the passage, and instead led him straight to her own room. Once they were inside she realized with a second inner thrill of guilt how normal it felt for him to be there with her. At the time of their affair, he had been a regular visitor to this room. Patta, for instance, clearly became used to him turning up at the apartment. Lorna did not want all that to start up again. She was certain about that. But even so Bradd had been much more than a one-night stand, and for a while at least, in that dark time when she realized Tomak was completely out of contact with her, she had believed she might even grow to love him. All that came back as an unwelcome reminder, just from him standing there, being in the room again. But it was over now, had been over for months. It was Tomak she still wanted, only Tomak.

'You need to get across to Tremm,' Bradd said. He had kicked the door closed behind him. 'I know what's on your mind and I don't really care any more. You made all that clear last year.'

'I'm sorry, Bradd. I never meant to hurt your feelings. We said everything then. It was just a mistake – '

'Well, it's in the past, and I've moved on,' he said. 'I'm all for making a fresh start. I believe I can help you now. I've recently gained the use of a friend's boat, a yacht. I've been learning how to sail it and I've already made several long trips along the coast here. I think, I *know*, that I could navigate across the strait to Tremm without any risk.'

'You mean, without risk of a boating accident?' Bradd nodded to confirm this. 'But what about the security?'

'Where I found the map I sent you – that file also has a lot of information about the way the island is patrolled. In theory it's as tightly protected as the Seigniory Palace, but in reality security along the coast is lax. If we make the crossing at night, we wouldn't run into anything.'

'It's far too dangerous!'

'I don't think so. How closely did you look at the chart of the coastal waters?'

'Hardly at all. I only had the graphic on the screen for a few seconds. I couldn't leave it there.'

'The water is shallow, usually calm. The tidal surge is moderate. There are some rocks, but they're all at the western end of the bay. The bay itself has a wide beach where I could simply run the boat ashore. The only danger would be if the weather was bad, but we wouldn't even set out if that was the case.'

'Why are you doing this, Bradd?'

'All sorts of reasons.'

'Go on.'

'Well, for one thing, I feel guilty about what happened last year. We both feel bad about it, but you were on the rebound. I took advantage of you. I want to make amends. I hated what you said at the time but I realize now what Tomak means to you. In some ways I regret nothing because I was genuinely attracted to you. What happened shouldn't have happened.'

'Bradd, I told you I was sorry.'

A shadow of a memory was passing overhead, though, breathing a quiet menace. She had heard this from him once before, a different context, not in this room, another. Then it had come with unstated threats – his obsession that she could not cope without him, his repeated claims that she needed him. He built her up and knocked her down, undermining her confidence in herself, in her job, in her belief in Tomak, sometimes even in her own sanity. It had terrified her then, helped make up her mind about him. She had refused to go near him for several weeks. But that was then. A safer distance had grown in the months that passed since.

She said quietly, 'You said there were several reasons.'

'There was all that. What happened between us, and trying to make amends. That's the main reason. The only other one is more complex. It's because we're told we shouldn't go to Tremm, that no one is allowed there. That feels like a challenge to me. We're both cartographers, Lorna, we've been trained to believe that a map should be something of objective fact. If a place is there, if an island exists, then we should be free to chart it. The only reason Tremm is not on our maps is political. Some government somewhere has decided its national interest lies in putting Tremm under its domain, and suddenly the island ceases to exist. But it's not our government and it's not our war. It's one of the countries in the north that must have made some kind of deal with the Seigniory. These things go on. Anyway, the result is ludicrous. We can see the island with our own eyes, every day, every night. Everyone who lives on Meequa knows Tremm is there, so do thousands of other people. So why can't we put it on a map? To me that's the challenge. I just want to go there, walk around on it for a while.'

'And then you would come back here?' Lorna said. He shrugged his shoulders. 'What about me, if I went with you? Are you planning to leave me there?'

'What do you want to do if I can get you across?'

'I need to find out what's happened to Tomak. I know that sounds desperate, but I haven't heard from him since he left. Anything could have happened to him: illness, accident. Or maybe he was the victim of some kind of crime. I don't even know if he's still alive. I assume he is, but all I can do is assume that. I've no other way of knowing. But until you sent me the map a few minutes ago it never occurred to me I could go to the island. I haven't already worked out a plan, a list of things I must complete.'

'Then why don't we sail across one night, when the tide is right? We'll land there, walk around for a bit. That'll satisfy me, and it'll give you a feel for the place. We needn't stay long and if it's as easy as I think we can return some other time.'

'I don't know,' Lorna said. 'I need time to think about it.'

She was standing with the tabulator and her binoculars still slung over her shoulder. She wanted to put them down, but an instinct warned her that Bradd would see that as some kind of relaxation of her guard. He was rushing her, seeming to want a decision immediately. What would be the point of sailing across to Tremm? How would that help her find Tomak?

'I'm going to be in the bar for a while,' Bradd said. 'If you want to think things over, or know anything more, that's where you'll find me.'

He left then, and she followed him out. She waited until he had walked down the corridor and she could hear the swing doors close behind him, before she returned to her room. She closed the door firmly behind her, kicking it, just as Bradd had done. Only then did she ease the heavy tabulator and the binoculars from her shoulder.

She made herself a light meal in the kitchen, drank some tea. Patta would be home soon, so when she returned to her room Lorna made sure the door was closed and locked. Only then did she switch on her computer and put up the graphic map of Tremm. She regarded it at first with professional interest, noting the scale, the density of the contours, the level of mapping detail. But her eye kept being drawn by the undescribed installations. She knew that if Tomak was somewhere on the island, that must be where he was.

Poring over the details she noticed again the dots marked with a 'Y'. There seemed to be no logical pattern to them: just a cluster of them here, more elsewhere, several more scattered across the face of one of the central mountains. There were dozens of them in all, perhaps as many as a hundred.

When she heard Patta opening and closing the outer door, Lorna quietly shut down the computer, made sure the encrypted data stick was safely concealed in the computer case, then went to find her roommate. She discovered Patta had been involved in an argument with her boyfriend and was crying quietly in her room. Lorna stayed to talk to her for a while.

Afterwards she went to the bar in search of Bradd. It was late, and she was expecting him to have left, but to her surprise he was still there. He was sitting by himself at a corner table, working on his laptop. As she went across to him he swung the screen to shut down the computer and waved to her to sit with him. The bar was about to close – only a handful of people remained, and they were in a group on the far side of the room. The shutter had already been lowered over the counter by the bar staff.

'Have you decided?' Bradd said.

'Decided what?'

'Do you want to sail across to Tremm one night? I thought you realized what I was suggesting.'

There was a clatter of glasses from the bar area, and one of the staff started music through the speaker system. After a few moments it was switched off again, and someone behind the bar laughed loudly. No one was interested in what Bradd and Lorna were doing.

'I still don't see what would be gained by just visiting the island,' Lorna said. 'If it's night-time we wouldn't see anything, we wouldn't be able to travel inland and the chances are we'd be spotted and arrested.'

'So that's a no.'

'It's a maybe. But for now I'd like to find out if you know anything more than you've already told me. You said there were some files with the graphics.'

'I'll forward them to you.'

'Is there anything in them that will help me locate Tomak?'

'I don't think so.'

'There are those unmarked installations on the map. What do you know about them?'

'The same as you. You must have come to the same conclusion. They are the buildings used by the military. I ran a comparative scan. There's an old map in the archives, more than a hundred years old, and at that time there was just the port and a few houses along the coast. Those huts are more or less the only new development since. I don't see that they have any special interest, as buildings. People have to live and sleep somewhere. But living quarters aside, what the other buildings are being used for is a different matter. There's something on the island they want to keep secret, so I imagine what goes on in those buildings is part of it.'

Lights in the room suddenly dimmed – the familiar signal from the bar staff that they wanted to close for the night.

Lorna said, 'There's something else about the map I don't understand. Those dots marked with a "Y".'

'Well, I can tell you what they are because I looked them up. But I don't think they're going to help you find Tomak.'

'Go on.'

'Did you ever hear of the artist called Yo? The installation artist, who built underground cavities?'

'Jordenn Yo. Of course! We studied her work at school. And there was a module on her work at university.'

'She came from your part of the world, the area you're trying to map. An island called Annadac, in the Swirl. You probably knew that? All right. She had to leave Annadac under something of a cloud. I'm not sure what happened there, but it was not before she had obtained a massive Lotterie-Collago grant. She used the money to take out a long lease on Tremm. She was working on the island for about five years. She later called it her apprenticeship period. She used the island's mountains to practise tunnelling and caving techniques. She drilled many tunnels – different diameters, different shapes and depths. Some were simply drilled into the rock, but others penetrated the mountain from one side to the other. It was a huge operation. For a while she had more than a hundred people assisting her. Many of them went across to work for her from here, from Meequa.'

Lorna was feeling a sudden excitement. Art history had been a secondary or optional course for her, but she always considered Yo to be an inspirational figure as a woman who had built and continued her career in spite of endless antagonism and philistinism. There were many islands in different parts of the Archipelago where the intricate and sometimes terrifying tunnels drilled by Yo and her artisans were now recognized as major pieces of modern installation art.

She had achieved her work under a lifelong barrage of criticism and prejudice, sometimes also physical attack, with many of the more conservative islands passing laws that banned her from landing there. She had spent at least two years of her life in one prison or another. But anyone who saw her work today could not fail to be moved by the grandeur of her vision, the sheer scale of her achievement. Her memory was cherished for the great drilled mountains, the artificial valleys and passes, where tides and winds played the harmonics of the sea, the sky and the earth.

'I had no idea,' Lorna said. 'Jordenn Yo, working on Tremm! That's simply astonishing.'

'Yo said that she did not want anything she left behind on Tremm to be considered as an example of her real work. She described Tremm as her schoolroom, a test laboratory. She was experimenting with techniques, discovering how rock strata had to be worked with, learning how to turn or reverse tunnels deep inside the mountains, or to tune the passages so that they reacted to the wind. She left Tremm while the lease was still in her name. As far as I know the tunnels are still more or less as she left them.'

Lorna said, 'Where did you find this information? Have you known it all along?'

Bradd tapped the top of his computer. 'I looked it up this evening while I was waiting for you. Tremm itself is never mentioned. It's just like the maps. The censorship has been thorough. But Yo is documented in detail and although Tremm isn't named it's possible to work out her connection with the island. How many offshore islands does Meequa have, for instance? Only one, of course. That's the sort of detail that often slips past censors.'

'So did she ever return to Tremm after she was famous?'

'There's no record of it. But she kept the lease going until she died. After that the title to the island reverted to the Seigniory, and it was then taken over by the people who have it now.'

Suddenly, all the lights in the bar room went out, with just the bar area itself illuminated. The other group of customers had already dispersed. Lorna and Bradd made their way out.

In the corridor Bradd said, dawdling, 'Well, then.'

'Thanks for everything you've done, Bradd. See you tomorrow at work?'

'Lorna –?'

'What?' But she knew what he wanted. 'No, Bradd.'

'No harm would come of it. Just tonight.'

'No. It's not what I want. Nor do you, if you think about it.'

She turned away from him and walked towards the part of the building where the living quarters were situated. Without looking back she waved a hand as she turned on to the staircase. She half expected he would be following her, but there was no sign of him when she reached her door. She went inside quickly.

As she made herself ready for bed she could hear Patta in the other bedroom, moving around, playing music. Lorna went to see her. Patta was feeling better, but she was angry about her boyfriend now, not tearful over him. They brewed some tea and sat together companionably. After that Lorna went back and they closed the doors that lay between their rooms. It was silent in her bedroom, and soon Lorna was asleep.

She awoke suddenly, with a dread feeling that she was no longer alone. The air had moved, and something under the floorboards had creaked, a noise she recognized from whenever she moved in that part of the room.

There was a dim, residual light showing from beyond the curtained window, and Lorna saw the dark silhouette of a man standing there close to her bed. In terror she sucked in her breath, tried to make a noise, but she felt paralysed by fear. Her instinct was to sit up, but she always slept naked, so instead she threw an arm across her head, pulling up the covers from the bed, trying to hide everything of herself.

'Lorna?'

It was Bradd – she knew instantly it was Bradd.

She managed to speak. 'No, go away!'

'Lorna, it's me. Tomak. I still have a key. I didn't want to frighten you.'

'Tomak! No!' She disbelieved him. But the voice was not Bradd's. She knew it was Tomak, but the way he had come silently in the dark was still terrifying her. She could not throw that off. And for a few seconds everything was unreal. She was still half in the dream she had been in before she awoke, she was unable to move, and her breath was rasping.

She groped towards the bedside lamp, got it on. In the sudden glare of light she saw it was Tomak, or looked like him. He had thrown his arms up to cover his face.

'No! Don't put on the light!' His voice was urgent with fright.

He moved quickly, bending forward with one arm still clamped over his face, the other hand fumbling for the switch. For a few moments he was within touching distance of her, but something made her shrink away from him. His hand found the lamp and he switched it off almost as swiftly as she had turned it on.

Her eyes were dazzled by the after-images from the glare.

'Lorna – you mustn't see me.'

'Tomak, it really is you, isn't it?'

'Yes.'

'Then hold me! Come here! Let me see you. Put the light on again.' A sense of relief was sweeping over her, and she moved quickly so that she was sitting up. She felt one of her pillows slide away to the floor. 'I've missed you so much! Why haven't you –?'

'Lorna, you have to trust me. I can only stay for a few minutes and I don't want you to look at me. There was an accident last year. I was all right, not badly injured.'

'What sort of accident? Are you hurt now? Why didn't anyone tell me?'

'The whole place is – we aren't allowed to communicate off the island. I shouldn't even be here now. If they catch me I'm in deep trouble. I can't tell you what happened in the accident but I want you to know I'm over it. I'm all right now. I was close to an explosion, didn't get away in time, and there was a fire. It's healed up at last.'

'This is terrible! Are you burned? Tomak … come and sit here with me!'

'I can't. But I wanted to tell you this myself. I had to come to see you. I know a lot of what's been going on. On Tremm we have access to almost everything. I know what happened last year, when you were involved with that other guy, the one who works here. I understand all that. It doesn't matter. You must be free to do what you want.'

'Of course it matters! Where have you been and why haven't you at least written to me?'

'I can't tell you. We communicate as passive receptors – you know what that means. We aren't allowed to send. None of that is important, though.' His voice was coming out of the dark, so familiar, but sounding sonorous, stilted, alien to her. This was Tomak, whom she had loved so long? As her eyes adjusted to the darkness, she could again make out his shape. He was still standing

172

a short distance from the bed. There was never much light from outside at night, but there was enough to reveal the shape of him against the thinly curtained window. 'I know you think I've run out on you,' he added. 'There was nothing I could do, there *is* nothing I can do about that. But I also know you're planning to visit Tremm, and I've come to say you must not go there. Not under any circumstances. If you've made plans, don't carry them out. It's a dangerous place.'

'Please, Tomak. Just sit with me for a while. I want to hold you.'

'No.' They were both silent for a moment, Lorna shocked by the absolute refusal. Then he said, 'I shouldn't even be here now.'

'What's going on over there? On the island? What is it that has taken you away from me?'

'The danger. The importance of what's being built there.'

'Can't you even tell me what it is?'

'Officially, it's a communications network. That's all I can say.'

'Is it something to do with the tunnels?'

'What makes you think that?' Tomak's tone of voice had changed, confirming something.

'Or the drones. You used to talk about the drones, how useful they are, the potential they have. You always used to call them passive communications devices, passive receptors.'

'I can't say anything. I've got to go.'

'Please don't!' She started to get off the bed, to stand against him, but he seemed to sense what she was doing and moved quickly in the dark. She felt his hands on her shoulders, pushing her down. 'Couldn't you just put your arms around me?'

'Lorna, I needed to say this personally, because I want you to believe me. It's impossible to break it to you gently, but I won't be coming back. It's over. I'm really sorry, but that's all I have to say. Stay away from the island, stay away from me.'

He was already heading towards the door, because his silhouette moved away from the curtains. Lorna swivelled around, fumbled with the light switch and threw it on. For two seconds, three seconds, she saw Tomak in the electric light as he dived hurriedly for the door. He was wearing green-grey fatigues that made him

173

look bulky and overweight. His hair was long, rolling around his neck, but there was a bare patch on top. Something had happened to his head: it was larger than she remembered, a different shape.

As he reached the door, in the final half-second, he turned back to look directly at her and then she saw his face. Burn scars bulged and reddened and sucked at his features: he had become disfigured, scarred, broken for ever.

The door slammed behind him and moments later the outer door closed too. She heard a key pinging as it bounced across the wooden floor.

She sat there on her bed and almost at once she began to cry. The tears broke out of her, an unending outpouring of misery. She soaked half a dozen tissues, wept into her bed covers.

Then she stopped.

She remembered the time she had spent with Patta earlier that evening, consoling her friend. Quickly, her unhappiness turned to anger against Tomak, and she remained awake the rest of the night, loathing him for what he had just done and the way he had done it. Then, in distress, she would remember loving and missing him so much and for so long, and in hot confusion she would veer inwardly from rage to wretchedness.

When the sun came up she dressed and went to walk along the edge of the cliffs. Tremm lay golden-hued across the blue-white sea, glowing in the morning light.

Three weeks later, after several sweltering, steamy days of unbroken summer rainfall, Lorna and Bradd went down to the harbour in Meequa Town and loaded food and drink on to his sailing boat. It was much smaller than Lorna had imagined, but it was almost new and was fitted with modern navigation and steering devices. In particular Bradd pointed out the two main sails, which were of material that was non-reflective and almost transparent. Undetectable after dark by sight or by radar, he said, and made of the same material used on the wings of the drones.

The sun, heading down towards evening, was still radiant and waves of humid air rolled in across the harbour. Bradd pulled off all his clothes except a pair of shorts, and set to work preparing the boat to leave. Lorna also stripped down to her bathing costume, and sat half in shade, half in the blistering sunlight until Bradd said they were ready to cast off.

Once they were beyond the harbour wall there was enough wind to provide at least an illusion of temporary coolness. Tremm stood towards the horizon, green-brown in the distant shimmering marine heat.

Bradd steered the boat away from the town, hugging the coastline of Meequa, and within an hour they had reached a small secluded inlet where no other boats were moored. They anchored the yacht, then dived in and swam in the calm cove until the shadows from the setting sun were dark across the water.

Back on board, they snacked on some of the food they had brought. They both kept looking out to sea towards Tremm, where the mountains were catching much of the sunlight slanting horizontally from the west. As night fell the humidity seemed to increase. Lorna lay breathless on the prow of the boat, dangling an arm towards the water, watching the movement of phosphoresence in the shallow sea below.

Bradd went below decks and switched on his night-time navigation gear. Lorna continued to doze in the muggy air, feeling Bradd's movements in the cabin directly beneath her but thinking yet again about Tomak, what had happened, what he had said that night, the suddenness of everything. It continued to hurt, but it also made her feel resentful of him. It was torment if she dwelt on it but she believed she was recovering at last.

When Bradd emerged from the tiny cabin she sat up to look at him, admiring his supple back, his strong arms. She watched him working one of the hand-winches, liking the calm way he moved, the compact angles of his torso, remembering the times when they had been lovers, thinking the best of him.

By some unspoken accord this trip had been arranged almost as if it had been planned in detail and agreed in advance. Bradd announced two days earlier that he was ready to sail across to Tremm, and Lorna quickly said she would go with him. They had both taken days off work, not knowing how long they would be away.

Lorna told herself she needed a break, was owed some time off by the MCI.

There was only a single bunk in the confined space of the cabin. Lorna noticed this as soon as they were on board, but she said nothing. Too much had been said between them in the past. But then before they sailed Bradd casually showed her that in one of the lockers there was a hammock that could be slung on the deck in the open air. She was assuming nothing, and it seemed that neither was Bradd.

With the aid of the inboard motor they left the cove, then Bradd and she hoisted the nearly invisible sails and they began to move out to sea, silent but for the sound of the water against the hull.

Several minutes later one of the instruments gave a quiet warning signal and Bradd immediately used night-sight binoculars to scan the sea near Tremm. After staring through them he handed them to Lorna, indicating where to point them. It took a few moments for her eyes to adjust to the artificially enhanced image, but she was soon able to make out a long power launch, lying low in the water. Because of the foreshortening effect of the powerful lenses it appeared to be close against the foot of the Tremm cliffs. It did not seem to be moving.

Bradd took the glasses back and stared at the vessel for a long time. Meanwhile their yacht sailed slowly on, using the automatic steering device.

'What do we do?' Lorna said.

'Nothing. We're in international waters. We've every right to be here. In theory, we also have the right to land on that island. Every island in the Archipelago is neutral territory – that's what the Covenant is for. But in reality the moment we cross into Tremm's waters that launch will come out to find out what we're up to. It's a fast-response patrol boat, armed to the hilt. Those people have moved in, grabbed the island, and set up armed patrols to keep everyone else out. It makes me angry! They're abusing our neutrality by making it into their domain. They do what they want and we can't stop them, because if we tried to get rid of them they'd claim we were breaching our own neutrality by doing so.'

He glanced towards the sky: it was clear of clouds, but because of tropical atmospheric haze a pale orange wash from the sun, which was now below the horizon, was faintly visible against the stars. The air was warm, but both Lorna and Bradd had put on lightweight shirts. The breeze was steady.

Lorna continued to watch the patrol launch through the glasses. After a few minutes it began to sail away. The movement was also picked up by the navigation gear in the boat. The launch travelled fast along the coast of Tremm, and soon it was difficult to make out the shape of it against the dark rocky cliffs, even with the night-sight boost. Not long afterwards, Bradd's onboard navigation equipment made a different sound, signalling that the target the radar had picked up was now out of range.

Bradd continued to sail calmly, then as the darkness on the sea became more or less complete, he swung the wheel and the boat headed directly towards Tremm.

'Are you still intending to land?' Lorna said.

'Not this time. That launch is not the only line of patrol.'

Since Tomak, since his visit in the night, Lorna's inner determination to find out what was happening on Tremm had dwindled. Tomak had at least succeeded in that. It remained a deep impulse in her to find out where he was and what had happened to him, but it was an impulse she found easier to resist with every day that passed. The hurt he caused had stiffened into a defensive anger, now more or less under control, but that remained harder to put behind her than the sense of loss.

Soon after they left the shelter of the cove Lorna went aft to sit beside Bradd in the tiny cockpit, because of the boat's movements in the waves. The night was hot, making her feel breathless. She leaned back against the coaming, feeling the wind in her hair and the occasional splash of droplets – both cooled her deliciously, while the mild plunging and yawing of the yacht gave her an inner feeling of physical suspense. Her muscles were constantly tensed against the rocking. In spite of her earlier reservations she was succumbing to the sensual nature of this venture. Bradd was close beside her, often pressing up against her as he manoeuvred the boat. She was tingling with awareness of his body, and whereas only two or three weeks earlier she would never have admitted to herself any such response, she was relishing the feeling that somehow she was yielding to him, giving herself up. But it was free of persuasion and without conscious decision.

Here she was, here he was. She could smell the dried salt on his strong forearms.

The lights of Meequa Town had been in view for some time, but as a pale blur against the darkness of the inland hills. Tremm was much closer to them and the immense size of the central range made a dark block against the stars. There were hardly any lights visible on that shore.

'Something's moving!' she suddenly cried as she saw a light sliding low over the sea. It had appeared quickly from behind the bulk of the island. She realized she was tensed against discovery by the patrol boats. Bradd stared across, reaching down into the well of the boat to find the binoculars.

But before he switched them on he said, 'You know what that is! It's one of our drones.'

Lorna took the glasses from him but then laid them down. She stood up, balancing herself against the swaying of the boat. The steady, low movement of the aircraft was of course completely familiar, but never before had she been so close to one as it passed across the sea. It traversed their course ahead of the boat, vanishing into the night as the beam from its LED moved away from them.

Soon more drones appeared, heading towards Tremm from all distant directions. The first sight of them was as pinpoints of light, easiest seen when they were grouped together. At first Lorna tried to count them, as she had often done in the past, but was soon unable to keep up. Because of their proximity buffers, the drones always weaved around each other, like strands of wool in an unravelling skein. Before long the first group of them was passing close by their yacht, low and steady over the waves, the multi-coloured LEDs glittering. Lorna was thrilled to see them.

Bradd stood beside her, balancing on the deck over the cabin. The boat was rocking and Lorna held his arm.

He had brought the map of Tremm and now he turned on his torch and held the map so they could both see it.

178

'I just took a fix on our position,' he said. 'We're more or less here, still outside Tremm's waters.'

He indicated the shallow bay on the western side of the island. They were right at the edge of the map. Even though it was dark and much of the island was unlighted, Lorna could pick out the major features – in particular the steep crags of the mountains. The tallest of these, which was the one furthest to the south, was where Yo had carried out many of her test drills. Bradd pointed the torch at that part of the map, where there were the marks of dozens of Yo cavities clustered on the side of the mountain facing towards them.

The first wave of drones passed towards Meequa, some of them flying directly over their boat. Lorna gazed up at them. Their hyaline wings glimmered as they passed beneath the stars. The hush of their motors could barely be detected because of the sounds of the sea. She watched the drones as they wove away from her towards the main island.

'There are more coming,' Bradd said, pointing to the south.

Towards the horizon they saw another group of the pinpoints of light, turning in towards Tremm and Meequa. At this distance the lights of the LEDs all looked white, but as they gradually came nearer Lorna was able to see the many different colours. At first they were manoeuvring no differently from the first wave – they all steered around the landmass of Tremm, following the line of the coast, staying low above the waves – but without warning the leading group banked sharply away from the island and began to gain altitude, heading out to sea. Some of them appeared to be flying towards the yacht.

One by one the drones banked again, turning back towards the bulk of Tremm, then circled, continuing to gain altitude. Behind them, the other waves of the drones were beginning the same manoeuvre. For a minute or so the sky above the yacht was a mass of different lights, circling around, gaining height.

Lorna and Bradd stood together on the gently swaying deck, their heads craned back to watch the swarming planes.

At some unexplained signal, every LED on the drones was suddenly extinguished. A transparent darkness soared above them.

Bradd jumped down to the cockpit, retrieved the binoculars and tried to locate the now invisible drones. After a few attempts he passed the glasses across to Lorna, who also tried and failed to see any of the drones.

They could sense the machines were still circling around above them. The warm sea air seemed to hum with the light pressure of their passage.

As her eyes adjusted, Lorna realized she could just pick out a faint disturbance of the starlight, as wings of the drones passed high overhead. She pointed this out to Bradd and they stood together, faces turned skywards, seeing the stars shimmering through the drones' wings. When Bradd's hand slipped into hers, Lorna did not resist him.

The first explosion came while they were still trying to spot the drones above them. They heard a low, deep thud, then a rumble, but by the time they had turned towards the source of the sound all that could be seen was the residue of flames and fire-glowing smoke on the upper slope of the most southerly Tremm mountain. While they were still looking, there was a second explosion, and this time they saw the flash before the sound reached them.

'It must be the drones!'

Another explosion occurred before Lorna could reply. This was lower down the mountainside, almost at sea level.

'Are they crashing?' Lorna cried.

'There's nothing on board a drone to make it explode like that. It's just a motor, a guidance system and the scanning equipment.'

But now the explosions were occurring with such frequency that the side of the mountain was half-lit by the flames that had already erupted. Lorna grabbed the binoculars and focused on the mountainside where it was most brightly illuminated. The swaying of the boat, and the fact that she was having to balance, made it almost impossible to keep the glasses trained on any one spot, but she soon found that it was easier with the night-sighting switch turned off.

Bradd took the glasses from her for a minute or so, during which something like twenty more big explosions occurred, then he handed them back to her.

'Point them close to that high shoulder on the right,' he said. 'You can see the drones flying straight into the tunnels!'

Because of the high magnification, and her unsteady hold, Lorna was not able to spot any of the drones in the constantly jerking image. But in the light from the flames she could see that where the drones were crashing in was the area of many of Yo's tunnels. Lorna repeatedly glimpsed the dark apertures, oddly, precisely shaped: round, square, triangular, asymmetric, tall rectangles, wide rectangles, long ovals.

One bulged with devastating fire as she managed to keep the glasses steady. Something deep within the mountain was exploding or discharging when the drones went in.

The explosions did not continue for long. There was a sudden eruption along the lower flanks of the mountain, like the final flourish of a fireworks display, and then the mountain was quiet once again.

They became aware at the same moment that the navigation gear in the cockpit was emitting a steady warning signal. Bradd turned sharply, looked towards the south.

'The binoculars ... quickly!'

She handed them over, flicking on the night-sight as she did so.

'Climb down to the cockpit, Lorna! That patrol ship is coming for us.'

In the dark it was impossible to see unaided anything on the surface of the sea, but as soon as she scrambled down into the cockpit Lorna saw the radar display. A continuous signal revealed something large approaching them at sea-level, and at high speed. There was no doubt what it was.

Bradd crashed down into the cockpit from the deck, brushing hard against her. He grabbed the wheel, spun it about. The boat responded at once, turning away from Tremm, heading north towards Meequa.

'We'll never outrun them,' Bradd said. 'But this takes us further away into international waters.'

Lorna took the binoculars into the cabin and placed them somewhere out of sight. She returned to the cockpit.

When she looked back the patrol boat was so close it was possible to see the dark shape of it unaided. It was speeding towards them, throwing up a huge white bow-wave.

'They're going to ram us!' Lorna cried.

'I hope not!'

They were both shouting. Terrified, Lorna put her arm around Bradd's waist and held close to him. The patrol boat was on them in a few more seconds, veering away at the last moment, but passing so close that the bow-wave drenched them and flooded into the cockpit. There was no engine noise audible from the launch, just the rushing of the water.

The little yacht yawed and rolled violently in the immense wake of the larger boat, shipping more water. Lorna and Bradd fell away from the wheel, soaked by the deluge of seawater that flooded into the cockpit. Lorna landed face-down and Bradd fell violently on top of her, his uncontrolled weight forcing her face down into the water. After a struggle to regain equilibrium he managed to lever himself away. He helped her back to her feet, while she spluttered and tried to breathe again.

The patrol boat was already turning for a second run at them. All they could do was brace themselves with the cockpit rail and press against the coaming. When the launch passed this time it was even closer than before and it made a sudden turn, whacking their tiny boat with its grey hull just as the bow-wave lifted it. Bradd and Lorna screamed and shouted in terror as the yacht flew upwards, then side-slipped into the sea in a flurry of spray and a rush of incoming seawater. They were both thrown from the cockpit into the sea, floundering in the dark night and the turbulent water. They were thrust under the surface several times by the strength of the wake and the turbulence of the churning water. Lorna, still gasping for breath after being crushed in the cockpit, was terrified she would lose contact with Bradd, or whatever remained of the yacht, but as the rough waters subsided Bradd's head broke the surface. She swam to him and they held on, trying to reassure each other.

They found the wrecked yacht not far away. It was lying on its side, almost completely submerged but still afloat.

Bradd yelled, 'So long as I can get on board ... we'll be OK. The boat will right itself. Help me round to the keel.'

They swam to the side of the boat where the hull was showing above the surface. Bradd showed Lorna how to hold on to the gunwales, then he clambered over to the submerged cockpit. She waited in the dark, shivering with fright and the shock of being in the sea. After a while she could feel the boat moving as Bradd did something inside. There was a sudden grind of a motor and almost at once Lorna felt the hull sliding down towards the sea, as the vessel tried to right itself. She struggled to pull herself over the gunwales, but her strength was failing.

Bradd appeared, reached down to her, pulled her up. She slithered, half-fell, into the flooded cockpit. They huddled there together while water splashed around them. She felt chilled through, by fear, by the sudden immersion, by suffering the brutal and ruthless actions of whoever had been steering the launch.

When the boat was upright again, although riding low in the sea, Bradd set a bailing pump going and the water began to jet out of the side. As the flood level gradually fell they went around inside the cabin trying to establish what had been damaged, what might have been lost.

Most of the equipment on the boat was intact, although the navigation gear had been flooded and was inoperable. The auxiliary motors, used for self-righting and pumping, were undamaged. The binoculars were missing, as were most of the food and clothes they had brought aboard. The main inboard motor appeared to be intact, but would not start on the auto-ignition. Bradd kept trying, and after a couple of minutes the engine coughed loudly before running normally.

There was no longer any sign of the patrol boat.

They were intent only on reaching dry land and safety. They removed the sails, which had been damaged in the collision, and headed for Meequa Town under power. They stood together at the wheel, holding on to each other. Lorna could not stop shaking until she was safely ashore.

She remembered Bradd's house from before. When they went in the familiarity struck her – the piles of books, heaps of old newspapers, the photographs stuck on the walls, his three peculiar cats, the sense of affluent male chaos. The background smell: other people's places always have a background smell you can never identify but always remember. She was glad to be there, but she went and opened the windows to allow air to move around. It was hot in there – Bradd said his cooling fans were broken. She stood by the window, making herself calm. One of the cats walked over to her and nuzzled her leg. Noise of traffic rose up from the street below; music was playing in the restaurant opposite. Because of the lights of Meequa Town it was impossible to look out to sea: all appeared dark out there.

Bradd put down what he had been carrying and went to stand beside her. He laid a light hand on her shoulder.

'Your clothes are still damp,' he said, and ran his hand down her back.

'Yours are too.'

'Shall we take everything off?'

So they did and so it happened again. She was not in love with Bradd, but he was familiar and they had gone through something together and survived it. She liked him more now than she ever had. He was making an effort and so was she in her own way. Anyway, she was an adult and he was always good in bed.

In the morning when she woke up next to him, Lorna left the bed and went to stand at the open window, watching the businesses in the town start to open. Traffic was as yet light, and she smelt the scent of flowers on the warm breeze. The sea was silver and glistening in the early sunlight. She could see the dark shape of Tremm, out on the horizon, there but not there.

They made love again, then dressed and went down to the restaurant for breakfast on the terrace, overlooking the harbour. Behind the street where Bradd lived the land started to rise towards the inland heights – because of its view of the harbour, sea and distant islands it was a sought-after zone and many more houses and apartment blocks were going up. It was some time since Lorna

184

had been in this part of the town, and she enjoyed the morning ambience of the shops and businesses, the light in the sky, the clattering noises, the endless sound of voices.

Later they walked down to the harbour to have a close look at the boat, and to work out what needed to be repaired or replaced. In the damp mess of the cabin there was hardly room for them both, so Lorna sat on the boardwalk while Bradd moved around inside. She was wearing a broad-rimmed hat to shade her from the sun. She watched the leisurely activity in and around the harbour, feeling happy for the first time in many months. Every now and then Bradd would emerge and place something next to her on the wooden planks. Once, she leant forward and kissed him. He grinned, then ducked down again into the boat.

A drone went over, its transparent wings glittering with silver highlights in the sunshine.

Lorna stared up to watch it, as did many other people around her. The drones were of course a familiar feature of life on Meequa, but they were rarely seen during the day. This one was flying parallel to the coast, but when it was over the harbour wall it banked steeply and flew out to sea. Lorna shaded her eyes to watch it. After about half a minute it banked again, this time going into a steep turn that directed it back towards the land. Within a few seconds it had passed over the headland and was out of sight.

Bradd emerged into the cockpit.

'The nav gear is working again,' he said. 'I just picked up a drone signal. Did you see it go over?'

'Yes.'

They thought no more of it, but that afternoon, as they walked through the town, a drone appeared from out of the heat haze, flying parallel to the coast. Lorna was immediately certain it was the same one. She rushed down one of the alleys that led to the harbour and watched as the drone repeated the course it had taken that morning.

Bradd looked up at the mountains and out towards the cliffs that rose to the east of the town. Mountains to be steered around, a complicated, jagged coastline with many rocky tors, other hilly islands in the vicinity. Plenty to avoid.

Later that night the drone again flew across Meequa Town.

By the time Lorna had returned to work at the Institute and was struggling once more to make sense of the photographic traces, the captive drone was a regular sight on Meequa. It went around continually, taking about seven and a half hours to complete its circuit, so that it usually flew overhead three times each day, but every now and then it appeared four times. It flew in the sunlight or in the dark, its iridescent wings refracting the stars or the sun, its motor running silently and faultlessly, the green-glowing LED in its nose sending a brief glimpse of purpose as it swept overhead, the air responding to its passage, and when the place was quiet it imparted a sense of unexplained mission, an unending task, a quiet breath of secrecy.

On Tremm, the nightly explosions continued.

Mesterline

DRIFTING WATER

MESTERLINE was the birthplace of the poet and playwright KAL KAPES, who is widely regarded as one of the island's most cherished sons. Although he frequently made long tours through the Archipelago, speaking and giving readings of his work, Kapes returned to Mesterline whenever he could. He met his wife, SEBENN HELALDI, also a poet, during one of his visits. They maintained a permanent residence on the island, in the heart of Mester Town.

The nature of Mesterline is that of providing a refuge, an instinct that permeates most of the people who live on the island. The native Mesters are open-minded, tolerant and incurious. They instinctively feel protective towards others, especially those who come to believe themselves cast out by the unreasonable expectations of others, or by pressure from authorities, or by laws they feel unreasonably restrict their behaviour. Although Mester people are themselves law-abiding they are tolerant of those with individual, unfashionable or unpopular ideas.

Ever since hostilities have been fought across Sudmaieure, Mesterline, although relatively distant from the landmass, has become a natural recourse for deserters because of the liberal attitudes on the island. The young men and women, frequently frightened, disillusioned or in some way damaged, drift towards Mesterline all year round. In many cases they arrive only after long and complex journeys, and often with the help of the island underclass.

When shelterate regulations were introduced throughout the Archipelago, a handful of islands immediately opted out. Mesterline was one of the first, although not, of course, the only one. By the time Kapes was born, the tradition of sheltering young deserters was well established, but while he was still a young man there was a sudden surge of deserters arriving on the island, and for a while a few of the islanders wanted a change. Kapes became actively involved in the controversy, maintaining that Mesterline's great tradition of tolerant welcome should never be allowed to die.

Today, deserters may safely live on Mesterline, never at risk of being turned in by the islanders, nor subjected to pressures to move on to somewhere else. The price the Mesters pay for this lenient attitude has been the frequent searches of the island by the black-cap escouades. The Mesters remain forbearing even of this intrusion, mainly because there is nothing they can do. They have none the less devised innumerable secure hiding places for those deserters who need to use them. From time to time the black-caps inevitably discover one of these refuges, and although a few of the deserters might be grabbed and taken away, because of the existence of the Covenant the islanders themselves are immune from reprisals. Invariably, new bolt-holes are prepared every time an existing one is exposed.

Mesterline is an island with low hills, broad valleys, wide meandering rivers and long beaches of deep-yellow sand. The Mesters have a love of viewpoints, so along the stretches of coastline where there are tall cliffs, the people have built many houses against the sheer faces, with innumerable ingenious means for gaining access to them.

Mesterline is a rainy island with daily showers. It lies in the path of the warm westerly wind known throughout the sub-tropical latitudes as the SHUSL, and towards the end of most afternoons a brisk rain storm sweeps in, drenching the countryside and towns. The steep streets in the coastal villages have permanent runnels dug along each side, to drain away the water. The Mesters relish these intense showers. They will often interrupt business or family meetings to go outside to stand in the streets or public squares, turning up their faces and raising their arms, allowing the rain to course through their long hair and drench their lightweight clothes. Everyone is happier after the day's shower. It is as if the Shusl brings the signal for the day's routines to an end, because afterwards the bar-keepers and restaurateurs put out the tables and the musicians arrive, ready for the easygoing socializing through the long warm evenings.

The secret of Mesterline is an open one: there is something in the water, some unique combination of minerals, some consequence of the natural filtration beds.

Any new arrival on the island falls under the spell of the beneficent feeling within four or five days, and within a month sees no earthly reason to move to another island.

Kal Kapes, one of the few Mesters who regularly travels abroad, has often invoked the experience as a kind of metaphor for growth: what happens when you sail away, the grinding sense of loss, or fear of imminent death, that steadily increases until one day it vanishes and no longer hurts you, and what happens when you arrive, and succumb happily to the Mester experience, a change for the better, a shifting of earthly priorities, emergence into a higher state of being and understanding.

The two main Mesterline rivers arise from the drainage of precipitation, but both are fed by natural springs close to source. Water taken from either of the rivers has no great impact on the disposition of anyone drinking it, although after filtration and the usual treatment it has a faint but pleasant flavour and can act as a mild pick-me-up. The river water is mainly directed to industrial or irrigation uses, or as inexpensive mains supply to people's homes.

To feel the full Mesterline effect one needs to partake of the spring water, tapped from only three natural sources inland.

For centuries the water has been bottled at source, two senior families running the business on a not-for-profit basis, themselves as much a product of the Mester outlook as the people they were supplying. One of the springs, indeed, could be freely tapped by anyone prepared to clamber up through the foothills with a suitable container. Mester water can always be drunk in its natural state, a mild aeration giving it a delicious and refreshing sensation on the palate.

Such was the essence of Mester life, but there is always some outside influence ready to try to ruin everything. On most islands it is the weather that comes along, changing the season, bringing a sharp or cooler wind, or in places a tropical storm or hurricane. In other parts of the Archipelago it can be the unwelcome intrusion from one or other of the combatant powers. Mesterline's interruption was unique to itself. Some hundred years ago the Seignior of the day for some reason felt dissatisfied with the level of tithes he was receiving, and the open secret was turned into a business proposition.

An inter-island water supply company, apparently under contract to the Seigniories of several of the desertified islands to the south, opened negotiations to tap the Mester wells and purchase the water on an industrial scale. It involved the building of a large, mechanized bottling plant, new roads, several storage tanks, and the laying of a subsea pipeline away to the south.

The Mesters, dopily unaware of the consequences of what was happening, sat blithely in their cliffside houses, and sprawled on their beaches, sat serenely in their bars and along the sidewalks, watching the trucks trundling to and fro, and the construction workers spending money in the shops and bars, and the ships coming and going with building and construction materials. The local water became cheaper and more easy to obtain, and the Mesters cheerfully drank even more of it than usual.

Then one day the water was no more. The bottling plant moved into full production and the pumps were daily pouring unimaginable quantities of the precious liquid into a long pipeline that led no one knew where.

The trucks that once had taken construction workers to the mountains now came down from the heights, heavily loaded with crate after crate of attractively bottled water, bearing labels in foreign languages. The trucks went down to the port, where water-company ships bore the crates away. In the quayside bars and restaurants, in the local shops, in the homes and most of all in the bodies and minds of the Mesters, the water was no more.

Slowly the Mesters came to realize what they had lost. In parallel with that, and consequent upon it, the soothing, relaxing, cheering effect of the water wore off.

It coincided with one of the return visits of Kal and Sebenn Kapes. He, not feeling the familiar growth in him, the happy emergence

190

into the higher state, was quickly apprised of the change that had taken place. Poets are not legislators, nor are they warriors or agitators, but they can be good with words. Kapes made a speech one day in the centre of Mester Town, a passionate speech well equipped with excellent turns of phrase, and what followed was unprecedented, unexpected, inevitable and noisy.

The ruins of the bottling plant are open today as a visitor attraction and access is free all year round. The summer palace to which the Seignior of the day retired can also be visited, on the small adjacent island of Topecik, but a boat ride is of course necessary. Parents with small children are reminded that parts of Mesterline are now historical or heritage sites where large explosions occurred in the past, and care should therefore be exercised. Although the direct action took place nearly a century ago there are still in theory legal proceedings being taken against the estate of Kal Kapes and certain members of the Seigniory families.

The remains of the undersea pipeline are normally closed to the public, but access to the remains of the pumping station is possible, and there is also a heritage section of the pipeline. It is possible to explore this if permission is obtained in advance.

Samples of Mester water may be taken freely from the source, and more supplies may be ordered from any of the shops in town. Visitors are reminded, though, that there is a strict upper limit on the quantity of water that may be taken from the island, and that what is permissible should be only for personal use.

Currency: Archipelagian simoleon; Muriseayan thaler.

Muriseay

RED JUNGLE / THRESHOLD OF LOVE /
BIG ISLAND / YARD OF BONES

MURISEAY is many things, and there are many things it is not.

Although it is by far the largest island in the Dream Archipelago and is the most populous, it has the most powerful economy, the highest mountains, the densest forest, the hottest summer temperatures, has more lakes and rivers than any other island, has the greatest number of airfields, ports, railroads, businesses, criminals, TV channels, film studios, museums, and many other superlatives, Muriseay is not the 'capital' island of the Archipelago.

It does not have a seat of government for anything except its own administration, plus three regional assemblies in semi-devolved areas. Although Muriseayan banks are found all over the Archipelago, and its currency is accepted in most of the biggest islands, it does not control the economy of other islands, nor does it seek to do so. The same is true of language, cultural influence, policy towards the Covenant, and much more. Like most of the islands, Muriseay is run as a benign seignioral feudal state, inward-looking and socially conservative, but with a positive interest in market forces, and the freedom and human rights of the individual.

Although Muriseay has a civilian policier force and coastline guards it has no army, no air force and the only navy is a small fleet of fishery protection vessels. The civilian populace is banned from holding concealable weapons, and strict licensing arrangements cover sport and hunting uses. There are two military airfields, but each of those is used exclusively by one or other of the combatant allied powers. In this, Muriseay is in contrast with the smaller islands, some of which do maintain a standing militia or defence corps. Muriseay is constitutionally neutral even within the Covenant.

Muriseay's wealth attracts many more immigrants than does any other island – it has full shelterate and havenic laws – so that while being the wealthiest place in the Archipelago, Muriseay also has a higher incidence of poverty than anywhere else. The apartments and houses of the major cities, including Muriseay Town itself, are crowded and in many places in poor physical condition. Some of the streets are all but impassable with traffic, mopeds, roadside enterprises and pedestrians – in other parts, especially in the Colonial Quarter, there are many fine buildings and open squares, and a network of old streets where restaurants, cinemas, houses and small privately owned shops are found. Many of the streets are lined with jacarandas and eucalypts. Air pollution is serious, especially in Muriseay Town. Crime is rife, particularly amongst ethnically varied immigrants. Huge shanty towns surround the outer city. There are numerous deeply entrenched social problems related to overcrowding, drug and alcohol abuse, prostitution, racial prejudice, child neglect and cruelty, homelessness, violent crime, and much more.

However, the most disruptive influence on Muriseayan life is the island's ambivalent relationship with the combatant powers. Both of these have immense military bases on Muriseay, established illegally and by force and occupied in resistance to all political attempts to have them removed. The large, heavily fortified camps are used for training, planning, interrogation and R&R. Because the camps are situated at opposite ends of the island they rarely come into contact or conflict with each other. Both bases employ local people, so their presence has a positive influence on the economy of the island. As well as having the military camps in place, Muriseay is also an invariable port of call for the many troopships passing through the Midway Sea, heading to or from the battle zones of Sudmaieure. These frequent visits have a disruptive effect on lives in the ports, adding to the social problems already in existence, but also bringing a source of income to many inhabitants.

However, for all the industrial and social complexities Muriseay is one of the most physically beautiful islands of all. The central massif has snow-capped mountains for most of the year, and its deep gorges, rivers, rock-faces and alpine pastures are a source of pleasure for inhabitants and visitors alike. Because of the island's proximity to the equator, and its adjacency to the strongest tidal flow in the Midway Sea, Muriseay has many beaches that are an irresistible attraction for pleasure-seekers, from quiet beaches suitable for young families, to the famous Wookat Beach, where the extreme sport of rock-surfing is carried out all year round.

Muriseay Town itself is in the south-western corner of the island, situated in a broad bay which is the outlet for two of the island's largest rivers. It is surrounded by tropical forest, of such complexity and denseness that beyond the limits of urbanization much of it remains unexplored, even in the present day. It is known or thought that the Muriseayan rainforest was the cradle of life for many hundreds of different species now found dispersed throughout the islands. No thryme colonies have ever been found on Muriseay. Parts of the forest are open to visitors in a range of sensitively designed and managed visitor and camping complexes, while the wilder and more remote regions are accessible to hardy bush-walkers. The forest extends over most of the southern half of the island and remains undamaged for most of its extent. There are rumours of 'lost tribes' still eking out a primeval existence somewhere in the deepest parts of the forest, but all evidence for this is anecdotal and scientific surveys have so far discovered nothing. The Muriseayan Council has for many years resisted attempts to commercialize the forest or to exploit areas of it for timber.

The forest is ringed, but not traversed, by modern highways and railroads.

Perhaps the greatest influence Muriseay has on the rest of the Archipelago is its heritage of arts. Almost every great composer, artist, writer or actor in the world was either born on Muriseay or studied there at some time, or at least has reflected Muriseayan influence in his or her work. Much of the island's great wealth has been poured into support of the arts – every Muriseayan city has a major opera house or concert hall, while Muriseay Town has two of each, endlessly in competition with each other. Galleries, theatres, museums, workshops, studios, libraries abound. Large artistic communities continue to thrive in all parts of Muriseay – there is an unusual arrangement in that no recognized artist resident on Muriseay is expected to pay tax, but contributes to the economy on a tithe basis, enriching galleries and public buildings with an ever-expanding variety of books, paintings, sculptures and musical compositions.

Of course, artists being of essence temperamental, there are those who have rebelled against the Muriseayan artistic hegemony, or were never accepted into it.

Of the writers, perhaps the must notable and luminous exile was the great Piqayean novelist Chaster Kammeston. He not only never visited Muriseay but actively disdained its influence, would not allow Muriseayan artwork anywhere near his house and never received nor of course ever applied for any Muriseayan grant aid. When awarded the highest literary accolade in the world, the Inclair Laureateship for Literature, Kammeston accepted, but on discovering that the ceremony was traditionally held on Muriseay he belatedly attempted to decline the prize. Such was his standing that the Laureateship Committee decided exceptionally to make the award on the author's home island. The entire committee plus an attendant horde of publishing and media people travelled at their own great inconvenience to Piqay. Kammeston did then rise magnanimously to the occasion, accepted the Laureateship humbly and thankfully, and made a gracious acceptance speech in which he praised a number of his fellow authors.

The mime artist, Commis, refused for years to take his perform-ance to the island. He never gave any reason. It is thought that his short Muriseayan season of live performances was booked either in error or against his wishes by his agent. The agent died in mysterious circumstances shortly afterwards, and Commis himself was mur-dered before he could reach Muriseay to fulfil the contract. Because of the unusual nature of his murder, it was cynically rumoured at the time that he had staged or falsified his own death to break the contract, but this is an outrageous suggestion. It remains none the less that his work is unknown on the major island except, ironic-ally, by word of mouth.

Rascar Acizzone, the tactilist master, was a native of Muriseay, but he was sent into permanent exile after a period of imprisonment. Although his work is still officially disapproved, the museums and galleries in Muriseay Town do have examples of his extraordinary paintings in closed case, for examination solely by academics, historians and genuine students.

A similar exception to the rule was the landscape painter and portraitist Dryd Bathurst. He was permanently barred from entering Muriseay after some incident during a visit in his youth. It appears that there was a policier or probation element to this ban, not an artistic one, because his work hangs prominently in several galleries on the island. And Jordenn Yo, the earthmoving installation artist, tried several times to enter Muriseay but was refused entry every time.

However, these people are the exceptions and the Muriseayan artistic influence remains the most important in the world. Visitors intending to take advantage of this immense heritage should plan an extended stay on the island, or make repeated visits so they might fully appreciate the huge range of material the island has to show.

Currency: all accepted in Muriseay Town; elsewhere the Archipelagian simoleon, Muriseayan thaler and Aubracian talent may be used at commercial rates. Forces' paper money is also accepted in the port areas of the big coastal cities.

Nelquay

SLOW TIDE

A small, obscure and largely unvisited island, NELQUAY is situated in the cool northern latitudes, part of the Torqui chain of islands. The economy is agrarian peasant, although a speculative construction project is under way to build a marina, hotel and casino complex.

This controversial and ambitious development attracted scores of migrant workers from neighbouring islands – notably from the adjacent Hetta Group – many of whom remained on Nelquay when the construction work went into abeyance. The financial backers of the project were not known, and the marina became subject to scrutiny by Covenant administrators. It would have involved the building of a new harbour immediately adjacent to one of the military shipping lanes. As that put the island potentially in breach of the Covenant, the entire project has been put on hold until more is known about who is behind the project and what their intentions are.

After the murder of the mime artiste Commis, the search for the killers soon focused on Nelquay. This was because there is a direct ferry route between Nelquay and the town of Omhuuv, where Commis was killed. A group of itinerant workers who were known to have been on Nelquay for the marina construction were seen in the vicinity of the killing at the time. They left Omhuuv just after the murder and there were witness accounts of them boarding the ferry to Nelquay.

Officers of the Policier Seignioral from the Hetta Group visited Nelquay Town and raided the address where these men were known to have been lodging. None of the men was present – to date they remain fugitives – but a great deal of incriminating material was discovered in an outhouse at the back of the property. A lot of construction equipment and materials had been concealed there, and this included a sheet of plate glass, similar, according to policier forensic scientists, to the sheet that was used to murder Commis.

Later some men were arrested in Nelquay, but were released without charge.

A dry, blustering katabatic wind called the Sora, which rises in the cold plateau of the mainland not far to the north of Nelquay, sweeps across the island most nights. Livestock on Nelquay is hardy, the main crops are beets, potatoes, carrots, leeks, swedes.

Kal Kapes visited Nelquay once, seeking imaginative exposure to the colder, more undeveloped and therefore more challenging areas of the Archipelago. He had always responded to the myths of the barren north, the great quest sagas of the seas and the legends of the frozen heights. He stayed for three months but there was no university or library on Nelquay, no one he could talk to, nothing to inspire him but the cold sea, the grey landscape, the seabirds and an almost unvaried diet of boiled mutton. He persevered, but he was alone. One night, close to the harbour in Nelquay Town, he was beaten up and robbed at knife point. He departed the next day.

Currency: Archipelagian simoleon.

Orphpon

STEEP HILLSIDE

Although there are vineyards on many islands throughout the Archipelago, the island of ORPHPON is the producer of some of the finest wines. Traditionally sold in cask form and never bottled on site, the wines are shipped to specialist distributors where they are repackaged. The white wines called ORSLA, from the hilly districts of Orphpon, are sharp, bright and dry. The AETREV of some of the neighbouring islands are a little sweeter, and vary in colour from a rosy yellow to a greenish gold, and have a bouquet reminiscent of spice and berries. These are the wines most eagerly sought by connoisseurs.

The wines from the southern coast of Orphpon are a coarser red, generally deemed undrinkable at the table, and are shipped to blenderies on the northern mainland where they are mixed with other table wines, or used as the basis for fortified aperitifs.

Olives are grown in the same region. On several of Orphpon's neighbouring islands the income from olive cultivation exceeds that of the vineyards.

Many people move to the Orphpon group of islands because of the presumed congeniality of the ambience, the warm summers and what is thought to be the spirit of good neighbourliness amongst the islanders. Much of this would appear to be true. However, there are strict shelterate laws and unadvertised visa restrictions.

Only by travelling in person to Orphpon will you discover that your stay is to be restricted to fifteen days, even should you have a firm booking at a local hotel or other resort, and that you will not be allowed to return for another two years. Outsiders and casual visitors rarely understand the reasons for these strict rules and every year there are attempts to breach or ignore them. Such visitors will then discover how strictly enforced are the laws. The prison regime in Orphpon Town is downright unpleasant and rigidly enforced (we write with some experience), and the authorities routinely maintain several empty cells throughout the holiday season in readiness for would-be visa deniers.

However, most of the cells in the prison do command an attractive view across the harbour and adjacent islands.

Unusually for the Archipelago, Orphpon is not a feudal state with a bill of rights for the freedom of the individual, but is a family-run fiefdom.

The family has extensive business interests throughout the Archipelago. The current Monseignior owns a vast fleet of luxury yachts, and a controlling interest in two of the largest inter-island ferry services. The family owns a large arms manufacturing company in the state of Glaund, and much of the gambling organization that runs through the Archipelago is owned and run by the Monseignior's extended family.

The artist, Dryd Bathurst, visited Orphpon when still a young man. He began a series of sketches for later development as oil paintings, but was forced to leave when his visa expired. There is something of an unsolved mystery about this, as his visa would not have been on a different basis than anyone else's, yet he is known to have remained on Orphpon for nearly a year. When he finally completed his celebrated Orphpon Sequence, some three years later, the paintings were recognized as modern masterpieces and they now hang in the Museum d'Artistes in Derril City.

It has recently been discovered that Bathurst had been allowed to stay in the Monseignior's Winter Residence on Orphpon, because even at his comparatively young age at the time his fame was widespread and his artistic reputation secure. It was while he was in the Residence that he drafted his sketches for the paintings that later made up the Sequence.

It is also known that Bathurst at least visited the prison in the town. The Bathurst Archive maintains that he went as a celebrated visitor who had been invited to inspect the facilities, but during our own brief internment we discovered from other inmates that there is one particular cell that for many years has been known as the Bath-House.

The identity of the tantalizingly unclad young model depicted in the two most admired Orphpon Sequence paintings is officially unknown. The Archive maintains that she was an imaginary muse for the great artist. However, one of the Monseignior's young nieces is known to have been staying at the Residence at approximately the same time, and after Bathurst left the island she was never heard from again.

Currency: Ganntenian credit, Archipelagian simoleon, also barter on a scale fixed by the Orphpon Seigniory.

Piqay (1)

FOLLOWED PATH

Piqay is the island of traces. A small and pretty wine-growing island, famous for its elevated views of the surrounding sea and other islands close by, Piqay is renowned throughout the Archipelago as the place no one can or will leave. In practical terms this is untrue, because there are no prohibitions on travel, and like most islands Piqay has a busy port constantly trading. Ferries depart every day for the adjacent islands. None the less there is a tradition amongst Piqayeans for staying. They are rarely encountered anywhere out-side their own island.

In the minds of the superstitious, Piqay is a place of unrested spirits, of unquiet souls, caught languishing between the here and now and the great hereafter. They are the traces of life. In the minds of the rational, Piqay is a place of unresolved hopes, of unfinished work, of unbroken attention. They are the traces of the living. Both irrational and rational are trapped by their condition.

Wider understanding of this phenomenon came from the work of the Inclair Laureate for Literature, Chaster Kammeston. His early novels, all set on Piqay, were at first misunderstood and neglected, because of what was taken to be the psychologically implausible behaviour of his characters.

Kammeston's second novel, *Terminality*, is a perfect example. *Terminality* takes the form of a murder mystery. In fact, it is not a mystery at all, since the identities of both the murderer and the victim are made known to the reader from the start. And it is not entirely a murder, either. Ambiguity rests both in the victim, who seems to have a split personality, and in the murder itself, which is set up so that it might have been accidental. Equally, it might have been deliberate. The theatrical setting, where appearances deliberately deceive, adds to the feeling of uncertainty. After the death occurs, the killer appears to be incapable of leaving the scene of the crime. His escape is made possible and eventually achieved with the help of others, but although believing himself innocent of a deliberate killing he refuses to flee. He remains on the island until the Piqayean policier seignioral arrest him.

Although this was apparently normal behaviour to the character, most readers and reviewers found it perplexing and frustrating. Kammeston published eight such novels during this early period, then disappeared from view. Nothing more by him was published and his work was soon overlooked.

It was eventually realized that Kammeston had spent his many 'lost' years in a sustained period of literary output. He wrote five more long novels, but refused to let anyone read them. Even his publisher was not told of their existence until the last of the five was completed.

When they finally began to appear in print Kammeston was recognized as a world-class literary artiste. Through these five major novels, which took the outer form of a long saga involving several generations of two rival Piqayean families, Kammeston expanded, analysed and above all elucidated the Piqay concept of the trail of experiences, the trace of life, the echo of oral tradition.

This trail, this spoor, was individual and collective, emanating not only from each person but from the psychic heart of the island. Kammeston described Piqay as an island with an infinitude of criss-crossing paths laid by ancestors, sustained by stories about them and memories of them. To depart from the island was to become diffuse, wraithlike, a lost soul without trace. With the illuminating example of these five great symphonic works, Kammeston's earlier novels were correctly understood at last.

He continued to write, but what followed was of a different quality. They were not at all minor works, but books that revealed the author's diversity, the range of his concerns. He essayed two biographies. The first was the life of the controversial painter Dryd

Bathurst, from which most of the general awareness and appreciation of Bathurst originally arose. A shorter book, which Kammeston described as a chamber piece, told the story of the tragically short life of the poet Kal Kapes. He also published two volumes of poetry, wrote three plays, all of which were performed in his lifetime, and a huge amount of journalism and essays: reviews, sketches, satirical pieces, autobiographical fragments.

Kammeston depicted himself as a true son of Piqay and never left the island during his lifetime. Even the ceremony for the Inclair Laureateship was exceptionally performed in a hall on his home island.

He died less than three years after the Laureateship was bestowed, from respiratory problems following an attack of pneumonia. He was interred, not cremated, and his grave is in the local churchyard. Kammeston's house and grounds are now open to the public. The university library in Piqay Town is the repository of his papers, letters, books and personal effects, all housed in an extension specially built for the purpose.

It was during the transfer of the Kammeston effects that one of the library assistants came across the alleged testament of Chaster Kammeston's estranged elder brother, Wolter.

This is a controversial document, whose authenticity has been challenged several times, but it has undergone forensic tests which show that it appears to be genuine in many respects. For instance, we know that the document was almost certainly penned after Chaster Kammeston's death because of analysis results from the paper and ink.

The claims it makes about Kammeston are what cause the doubts about its veracity. It seems unlikely that a real member of his family would have written it.

It is certainly true that Kammeston had a brother called Wolter, but it was widely believed Wolter was Chaster's identical twin, and not an older sibling. They were rarely seen together, for reasons dealt with in the document, but the comparatively rare photographs of them revealed the doubling effect of an uncannily close physical likeness.

In any event the Kammeston family was notoriously secretive, even before Chaster Kammeston became so celebrated. Little is known about his brother.

Wolter did not stay in the family home after he reached adulthood, but moved to a small house in Piqay Town until after his brother died. It is also true that Wolter survived Chaster, because he was seen at the funeral. He was later Chaster's literary executor, but not for long. He died within a year of Chaster, which is the period in which he must have written the testament, if indeed he did write it.

If the document is a forgery, then we are left to wonder who might have made it and the reason for it. So it seems likely to be genuine. Even if that is so, we must always remember that passions can run high in families, and that grieving relatives sometimes grieve not only for the lost one but also as an expression of their guilt about what they see as their own misplaced actions or inaction.

Nothing now can detract from Chaster Kammeston's immense reputation and standing, his literary achievements, his popularity with so many readers around the Archipelago.

Piqay is situated in the temperate zone of the northern Midway Sea, blessed by a warm oceanic current and sheltered by other islands from a prevailing northerly wind. Summers on Piqay are long, warm and benign, and the island welcomes many visitors throughout that season. Winters can be cold, but with only moderate amounts of snowfall. The island is popular with walkers and climbers, as the central range is low but interestingly rocky. The views of the adjacent islands are outstanding, with many excellent viewpoints all around the long coastline. Havenic and shelterate laws are enforced. A small artists' colony, concentrating on the tourist trade, thrives in Piqay Town.

Currency: Archipelagian simoleon; Aubracian talent.

Piqay (2)

PATH FOLLOWED

[THE TESTAMENT OF WOLTER KAMMESTON. Reproduced by permission of the Collections Department, Piqay University Library.]

My name is Wolter Kammeston, and I was born and have lived all my life on the island of Piqay. My younger brother is Chaster Kammeston, the Inclair Laureate of Literature. I always loved my brother, in spite of the many events in our lives which have tested that love.

With his reputation secure and permanent, I have decided, with dread in my heart, that I owe it to posterity to describe what I know is the truth about him. This is not to try to deny his real achievements as a writer but to add a human context to the work.

The whole family – that is myself, my sister and both my parents – were aware there was something strange and difficult about Chaster all through his childhood. He and I were alike in many ways, but there was something deep inside Chas that would not come out. It was dark and unreachable and it always felt risky for us to try to approach it.

Our childhood was both difficult and easy. It was easy because Father was a successful businessman with a direct line of connection to the Monseignior of Piqay, so we were a wealthy family with many of the attributes of advantage and comfort and influence. We were educated privately, at first by a series of governesses, later at a private school on the other side of the island, and all three of us attended Piqay University.

But our lives were also difficult because of Chas's dysfunctional behaviour. He was taken several times to see doctors or analysts, and these people made various efforts to find remedies: allergy treatment, dietary control, psychological testing, and so on. He was almost always given a clean bill of health, with the general consensus that he was going through the growing pains of youth, which would resolve themselves in due course. Chaster himself, I feel sure, somehow manipulated things to achieve these non-interventionist verdicts.

When Chaster wanted to be charming he could bring down the birds from the trees, as our mother used to say. But when he was not in a mood to believe there was anyone in the universe apart from him, he was awful to know. He could be angry, sulky, threatening, selfish, deceitful, and much else ... all those child-ish tantrums everyone knows and which are fairly normal, but in Chas's case he could resort to them all at once, or switch between them, one after the other. I was often – usually – the target, and if it was not me then it was my sister, Suther, and if it was not her then it was both of us at once.

If these were growing pains we could hardly wait for the pro-cess of healing to begin, but with Chaster the progress was in the opposite direction. When we were small, his difficult nature only appeared briefly, almost undetectably: a likelihood of tears if he did not get his own way, a period of sulking, and so on. But these were always short-lived. Chaster's real difficulties began to emerge only as he headed through his teenage years, and every year it grew worse.

By the time he had reached his twenty-first year he was almost impossible. The least worst manifestation of his odd behaviour was his prickliness, the quickness with which he would take offence, his inability to warm to others, even briefly in a social setting. More disconcertingly, his behaviour was eccentric: he was always straightening or cleaning objects around the house, or counting things aloud, pointing to them pedantically, as if expecting those of us around him to check or confirm his result. Much worse than that were his rages, his threats of violence, his aggressive physical demeanour, his controlling behaviour, his attempts to undermine everyone around him, his constant lies.

He got through his university years somehow, perhaps by curbing this behaviour as by then we knew he could, at least to some extent, but he left university with only a poor degree. He blamed everyone except himself.

Then, several months after leaving the university, he suddenly announced that he had been offered a job and was intending to take it up. To be candid, my reaction, and that of the rest of the family, was relief. We all felt that a break with the family environment, fresh horizons, working with other people, might well induce a change in him.

There was no indication at all at this time that he might one day become a writer. He had never been particularly bookish, often declaring he could not be bothered to finish a book once he had started it. Nor did he have any apparent facility with the written word – indeed, for a time at school one of his teachers had thought a serious and lasting problem with literacy might be underlying his behaviour. However, this turned out to be a false alarm, possibly related to one of his darker behavioural periods. If Chaster had any ambitions at all, we assumed they would lie in the direction of Father's business. This of course has been my own route through adult life.

We were surprised to discover that Chaster's job was not on Piqay. It was in fact in a part of the Archipelago none of us had ever heard of, in the north, a small group of islands close against the northern continent, at least two weeks' sailing from home with many ports of call on the way. He would tell us little about the job, but he said he would be working as an assistant manager in a theatre. No sooner had he told us this than he announced the ferry was sailing that night. He hastily packed a couple of bags, our driver took him down to the port, and then he was gone.

He stayed away for a long time without any contact at all with his family. Naturally, we were concerned for him. It was all too easy for us to imagine this irascible, unpredictable, moody, short-tempered, sarcastic young man provoking something with strangers, and coming off much the worse for it. But it has always been our parents' method to allow us to make our own way in life, to learn by experience, while keeping a distant watch on us. In Chas's case, when he first went away, my father employed a private detective to locate and then to observe him.

The first report came back a few weeks later: Chaster was working every day in the town's theatre, he appeared to be happy and productive, he had found somewhere to live, he seemed to be looking after himself. My parents allowed another six months to pass before asking for a second report – it was much the same as the first. After that, they asked for no more observations. Perhaps they should have done.

The first sign that something had gone wrong was an urgent email from Chaster to me, not long after we had read the second report. He demanded I sail immediately to join him. A few minutes later a second message arrived, and in this he made me swear that on no account must I leave Piqay. He said he was returning home, but would not say when.

Then a third message. He warned me that people – he did not say which people, nor how I would recognize them – might come to the house asking questions. He pleaded with me that if they did I was to pretend to be him and to swear I had been on Piqay for the whole of the time he had been away. He told me nothing more.

Both parts of this request were in theory easy to fulfil. I could say with complete truth that I had been here at the family house on Piqay, and if necessary I could produce witnesses to confirm it: my parents, servants in the house, friends in the town. The second part was also not a problem, or not in practical terms. Chas and I look alike, and we had grown up with people constantly mistaking each of us for the other.

But to maintain both of these amounted to a lie, one made worse because I had no knowledge of what Chas had been up to, nor even a clear idea of where he had been.

I had hardly any time to think about this, because the morning after I received Chas's last email two officers from the policier seignioral came to the house, demanding to see him. With great trepidation, and with feelings of doubt and misplaced loyalty to a brother who for the past several years had been little short of a monster to me, I went down to meet them.

I lied as little as possible to them. They assumed I was Chaster, so I did not disabuse them: a lie by omission, but still a lie. I told them, truthfully, where I had been during the last few months. No lies there, except in what I again omitted. The officers remained respectful to me – which brought home to me the influence my father continued to have on the island – but it was clear they were suspicious of everything I was saying.

I was questioned for at least two more hours and everything I said was recorded, as well as being noted in writing by one of the two officers. They told me nothing about the reasons for their questions but gradually the mysterious unspecified spaces behind the interrogation began to take on a definite shape. I was able to piece together some idea of what might have happened, what must have happened, and my brother's assumed role in it.

It did not take me long to work out there had been a violent death at the theatre where Chaster said he was working. He was thought to have been in the theatre at the time, or at least in the same town, but they were not sure. He (I) was no longer there, but they did not know when he had left. The death was caused by some kind of failure or accident with stage machinery or props: scenery was involved, or perhaps a trapdoor. Someone had died on stage but the officers were trying to find out if it had been a real accident or a deliberately prepared attack on the victim, disguised to make it look like an accident. Again, my brother's role in this was uncertain.

The officers tried to lead me, implying that if I would only admit the whole thing had been an accident that would be the end of their enquiries. I said nothing. Terrified of saying too much I invented no details, did not depart from the broad outline of what Chaster had told me to say.

They went away at last, warning me that they might need to interview me again. They ordered me not to leave Piqay without informing them first. In fact, that interview turned out to be the end of the policier involvement, because I never heard from them again and neither, I believe, did Chaster.

He stayed away, sending only occasional messages that he was 'about to return home', and pleading with me once again to remain silent, or at least compliant to his wishes.

The problem for me was the fact that I had been forced to lie to protect my brother. Although the lies were minimal, evasive, partial, they were none the less lies, and clearly my brother had been mixed up in something serious. I brooded on this endlessly. With every day that passed I became more resentful of him and angry. Because he was not there I could not confront him, so the pressure inside me mounted.

I believed I could not live with him any more should he return to the island, so with my parents' help I bought a small house in Piqay Town, well away from home. I moved in, settled in, began a life I hoped would be my own, free of Chaster and his moods and his way of manipulating me. Had I never seen him again that might well have succeeded.

But one day he did return, slipping in to Piqay harbour on a night-time ferry, then walking all the way to the house carrying his belongings in a bag across his back. He was found in the morning by one of the servants, sleeping in his own bed.

Curiosity, mingled with undeniable relief that he was home again, made me forget my decision not to see him. I went to the house later that day.

Chaster was a man transformed. He looked leaner and healthier, and his manner was calm in a way I had never known before. Although he was weary from the long shipboard journey he was in an expansive, friendly mood. He embraced me in his arms – something that he had never done before. I could smell salt and marine engine oil on his clothes. He complimented me on how well I looked, said how happy he was to be home again. He asked why I had moved out of the family home and said how much he'd like to see my new house.

We went for a long walk together, across the grounds and through the girdling woods, to the clifftop path high above the sea. There we enjoyed the views of the neighbouring islands in the emerald sea, the gleaming waves, the shining sunlight, the swooping gulls, all familiar as background to our shared lives, full of reassurance and memories, a sense of joining up the present with the past.

We walked and walked, not saying much, but that was because it was windy. The steepness of the path, as it roamed up and down the cliff peaks, made talking difficult. We came eventually to a place we had often rested in before: a small valley in the top of the cliffs, where a stream ran through then plunged out and down to the rocky foreshore below.

Chaster said, 'Thanks for doing what you did, Woll. Getting the policier off my back.'

'You never told me what you had done.'

He said nothing, but stared away across the sea. We were looking south-west and it was mid-afternoon, late enough for the sun to be throwing shadows of the islands. Whatever else happened in life, there was always this: the view, the gusting wind, the great panorama of dark-green islands, the slow ships and the endless sea.

'I've made up my mind,' Chaster said after a while. 'I'm never going to leave again. This is where I'll stay for the rest of my life.'

'You'll change your mind one day.'

'No, I'm certain about it. Now and for ever.'

'What happened while you were away, Chas?'

But he never gave me an answer, then or ever. We sat there on the rough clifftop rocks, staring down at the islands, a great unsaid thing hovering around us. Eventually we walked back to the house.

Chaster's behaviour still made me nervous: I kept waiting for an outburst of his dark side. He had always frightened me when he was like that. In a sense it was more alarming when he assumed a pleasant persona, when he seemed to be approachable, because of the sudden way in which I knew he could change. That was how he was on his return to the family: he seemed reasonable, sensitive to the needs of others. It put me on edge. And because he would say nothing about the months he was away, I was still left with that unresolved sense of injustice, of having had to lie for him. Surely, at least he owed me an explanation?

I was not to receive that explanation for many years, and then only indirectly and not from Chaster himself.

His change in temperament on his return did appear to be

permanent, though, and in spite of my initial nervousness I gradually grew used to the idea. If the darkness of his behaviour was still inside him, that was where he kept it and he did so for the rest of his life. Whatever else had happened while he was away, somehow it had led to that. He was a reformed character.

Something else had changed, too, but it took longer to become apparent. Because by this time I was living permanently away from the family home, I rarely saw him and so was hardly aware of it.

Chaster became contemplative, thoughtful. He read constantly. He took many long and solitary walks through the grounds of the house, and further, around the cliffs, into the town. At some point he began writing. I knew nothing about this, and I understood from Suther that he almost never spoke about it at home. She said he was always there in his room at the top of the house, a quiet presence, integrated into the various family events, but always retreating afterwards to be alone, wandering away up the stairs to the study from which a long silence then emanated.

He finished his first novel and sent it away to find a publisher. Some time later, maybe a year or so, it was published. He presented me with a copy, dedicated and signed on the title page, but I confess I did not read it.

A second novel appeared, then a third, then more. This was his new life.

I too had a new life: I had married my wife Hísar, and soon we had a young family and all the preoccupations that go with that. Suther also married, and she moved away to the island of Lillen-Cay. She too had children. Eventually our parents died, the house and grounds became our joint property. Chaster was the only one of us who remained living there, alone in the large house with a reduced number of servants.

My first realization that Chaster was becoming a well known writer was when I came across something about him in my daily newspaper. It reported simply that he had a novel due to appear later in the year. I found this mildly startling, that the mere prospect of a novel from him was considered newsworthy. By then he had written four or five novels, and from time to time I had even seen them reviewed, but this was a notice of something as yet unpublished. I cut out the item and sent it up to the house for him, because I was not certain he would otherwise see it. He never acknowledged it, but by then we hardly communicated about anything.

Another sign of the change in his reputation came when Hísar started telling me of some of the gossip she was hearing around town. I heard none of this myself – I assume people kept their thoughts to themselves when I was there because they suspected it would get back to my brother. But Hísar was different: she led a sociable life in the town, had friends of all types, often went with the children to other people's houses, belonged to theatre groups, historical societies, a walking club, she worked one afternoon a week in a charity shop, and so on.

The story was that Chaster, who never married, was constantly being approached or visited by women who were fervent, devoted admirers of his writing.

Some of them came shyly, almost furtively. They would arrive quietly on the island, find somewhere to live or stay, then wander around the town and the island, apparently trying to contrive accidental meetings with him. According to Hísar these women were easy to identify, since they were just about the only people who would ever talk about him. They asked after him in shops, they would plague our local librarian with questions about his novels, or they would simply sit or stand somewhere in the centre of the town, reading one of his books with the cover held up to be seen. Sometimes this method succeeded – Hísar told me that Chaster had been spotted several times walking around the town or the harbour with one or other of these people.

Some of the women were bolder. They would go straight to the house and ask for him at the door – most times, I gathered, he would not agree to meet them, but sometimes he would. What would happen then was no one's business but Chaster's, but presumably he had normal sexual appetites and many of these women were allegedly young and presentable.

All this would be a matter of tittle-tattle, were it not for the significant visit by one such woman.

Hísar and I knew nothing about this event until afterwards, by which time she had long departed from Piqay. Her arrival in the

214

town had caused something of a stir, because she was easily recognized: it was the famous social reformer and writer called Caurer.

She arrived unannounced on the first scheduled ferry of the day, disembarking in the dawn light with the other foot passengers. No one from her staff appeared to be travelling with her. She was delayed on arrival and went through the dock formalities with everyone else, although by this time she had been noticed and recognized. The officials dealt with her transit papers quickly, while the other passengers kept a respectful distance.

On leaving the dock, Caurer walked straight across to the town's taxi rank and climbed into the first available car. She acknowledged nobody, did not respond to the ripple of applause that had followed her across the harbour apron. As the car drove away and up the hill towards the interior of the island, people stood by the roadside to wave to her.

She went to my brother's house and stayed there for a period of time, but I have never been able to establish exactly how long it was. It might have been for the rest of that day, she might have stayed for one or two nights, or even longer. The tongues that wagged disagreed on this, but the only thing that matters is that she was definitely there.

She left in the dark, boarding the usual overnight ferry towards Paneron.

Two weeks later Chaster came to my house. Hísar was conveniently out with the children, but they had only just left. It made me suspect Chaster had been waiting outside the house for them to leave. He and I greeted each other as if we had seen each other only recently, but almost at once he launched into what he had come to ask.

'Woll, I need your help,' he said. 'I'm in a terrible state. I can't sleep, I can't work, I can hardly eat, I can't settle down. I've got to do something.'

'Are you ill?'

'I think I'm in love.' He looked as embarrassed as only one brother can to another. 'Her name's Esla. I'm obsessed with her. I think about her all the time, I imagine her face, I think I can hear her voice. She's so beautiful! So intelligent and articulate! So

sensitive and understanding! But I can't contact her. She left me
and I don't know where she is or how I could ever find her again.
I think I'm going mad.'

'Do you mean Caurer?'

'Esla, yes. I call her Esla.'

Until then I had not realized Caurer must once have had a given
name.

Once he had started there was no stopping Chaster. He talked
endlessly, obsessively, with little chance of my interrupting. Any
question I managed to break in with only produced another outpouring of his love for this woman and the frustration she had left
behind her.

'You should go to her,' I said, when at last a pause arose. 'You
must know where she lives, which island she's from. She sometimes
calls herself Caurer of Rawthersay. Is that still her island?'

'I believe so.'

'Then it must be a simple enough matter to find a shipping route
to get there.'

He looked diffident. 'I can't do that. You know I can't leave
Piqay.'

'Why not?'

'Have you read any of the novels I've given you?' I responded
with what I intended should be seen as an ambiguous look, because although he had sent me a signed presentation copy of every
new book as it appeared, I had yet to read any of them. He went
on, 'I've created a kind of ... well, I call it a mythos. It's in all
my novels. I write about Piqay, describing it realistically, as it is.
Sometimes only as it *was*, because two of the books are set in the
past. But as well as being realistic, the Piqay I create in the novels
has a mythology. I call Piqay "the island of traces", a place that
holds its inhabitants in a spell. No one can leave, no one wants
to leave. Anyone born here is said to be forever trapped here. The
island is covered with psychological spoors, traces of ancestors and
ghosts and past lives.'

'It's not true.'

'Of course it's not true. It's a mythos. I invented it. I use it as a

216

metaphor, as symbolic language. I write novels, fiction! You don't understand, do you?'

'Not really.'

'Well, in practical terms it means I can't ever leave Piqay. Not now. All my books would become invalidated. And if the readers found out – well, it doesn't matter about most of them, but it matters like hell about Esla. She above all people must never know the truth. I can't go after her.'

He was indeed a man in love, deluded by his own passions. Now I knew him to be also a man trapped in his own fictional invention.

The afternoon went by. I let Chaster talk out his obsessive needs, partly because I genuinely wanted to help him, but also because I found it fascinating to see my own brother, about whom I had such mixed feelings, acting in a totally new and unprecedented way. He could barely keep still. He was always levering himself energetically from his chair, then prowling and pacing around my sitting room, waving his arms, grimacing, declaiming theatrically.

In the end I said, 'What is it you want, Chas? You said you need my help.'

'Would you go to find Esla Caurer for me? You are the only person I can trust. I'll give you every detail I know about her. The island, the people she works with, some lecture dates she said she had coming up. She travels a lot, but her appearances are usually publicized in advance. I'll pay for everything. All I want you to do is find her, tell her how much I love her, then plead with her, beg her, use any means you can think of to make her come back and see me again. If she won't do that, then get her at least to contact me. Tell her it's urgent, a matter of life and death, anything at all, anything you can think of. I'm desperate. I can't go on like this. I have to be with her!'

And I was meanwhile thinking: I have a wife and children, and a home to keep and maintain, I have a job with serious responsibilities. Does he truly imagine I am going to abandon everything and rush off on this fool's errand?

Once before I had gone out on a limb for my brother, lied on his behalf, tried to save him for reasons I barely understood, and all for what? Grudging thanks much later, and a long silence.

I thought about it, though, while he sat there in the sun as it poured in through the large windows, and I heard Hísar and the children coming noisily into the house at the side entrance, and the contentment of my normal life regaining its shape around me.

Finally, I said, 'All right, I'll do it.'

He looked at me in pleased amazement. 'You will?'

'There's a condition, though. I'll only search for this woman if you tell me why you made me lie to the policier for you. What were you mixed up in, back then?'

'What does that have to do with any of this?'

'For me, almost everything. Tell me what went on at the theatre. Did someone die? Were you responsible?'

'It's a long time ago. I was just a young man. It doesn't matter now.'

'It still matters to me.'

'Why do you want to know?'

'Because you made me lie to the policier. Do I have to tell lies to Caurer for you too?'

'No – everything I've told you about Esla is true.'

'Then tell me the truth about the other matter.'

'No. I can't.'

'Then I can't go off and look for this woman.'

I suppose I had expected the old dark Chaster to burst out again, to threaten me, wheedle at me, use some kind of blackmail or other manipulation on me, but on that day I realized he had finally and for good buried the old destructive demon.

He sat in the chair across from me and he seemed to slump. He cried briefly. He wiped his eyes, stood up, left the chair and leaned against the window, staring out into the street. He did not react when Hísar briefly entered the room – she left when she realized who was there with me and that something difficult was happening between the two of us.

'I'm sorry I troubled you, Woll,' he said suddenly, and moved towards the door. He would not look across at me. I stood up. 'I won't ask you again. I'll find her some other way.'

'Chas, this other thing at the theatre still stands between us.'

'Let it go,' he said.

'I can't.'

'And I can't understand why everyone is still so fascinated by all that.'

'Everyone?'

'Esla kept asking about it too.'

I should have realized then what that woman had been doing at my brother's house, but because I did not I said nothing.

Chaster left, and if anything I felt worse about him than I had done before.

The years that followed, broadly speaking, were a stable period for us all. Chaster presumably pined for his lost love, and he must have got over it eventually. Hísar told me that the trickle of his women literary adherents continued to arrive in the town, so I imagine he was able to find relief from his sorrows with some of them. I know not, and I care not.

Chaster went on writing, because books of his continued to appear. Our children slowly grew up and we suffered and relished the various crises and triumphs of a growing family. Hísar and I took several long holidays off-island. My job continued. All seemed well.

I decided it was time I caught up with Chaster's novels, so I read them all, slowly and carefully, in the order in which he had written them.

They were not, I must say, the kind of fiction I normally like to read. I prefer a strong storyline, a range of interesting and successful characters, a colourful or exciting background. I like adventures, intrigues, brave deeds. Chas's novels seemed to me to be about losers or failures: no one could succeed at anything in his stories, doubts were constantly expressed, the language was understated or ironic, everyone went in for perplexing actions that took them nowhere. As for the background, all the books seemed to be set on Piqay, and in the town in which I lived, but I found it hard to recognize the places I knew. One book even contained a mention of the street where my house was, but almost every detail was wrong.

One of the novels did briefly interest me, because it described a violent death that had taken place in a theatre. My attention focused sharply, but it soon became clear that this novel was much the same as all the others. If there were any clues in it about what had happened to Chaster in the past, I missed them all.

I was glad to finish reading his books but I felt my conscience was now clearer. At least I knew what he had written, even if within a day or two I could remember hardly any details about them.

I had almost forgotten about Caurer and her disruptive impact on Chaster, when unexpectedly she burst back in on his life.

The background to it was the execution of a mentally subnormal young man, for a murder he was alleged to have committed. This had happened several years before.

I had not taken any special interest in what happened, although I did remember the controversy that surrounded his execution. Capital punishment is not common in the Archipelago, but there are several islands where it is still carried out. It's a subject that always causes heated argument. I am personally against the idea of state-sponsored killing and always have been, so whenever I hear the news that another hanging or guillotining has taken place I get a sick feeling in my stomach, wish that it had not happened, but try to console myself with the thought that due process must have taken place and all appeals would have been exhaustively heard.

In this respect, the guillotining of Sington was little different from others. I knew from news reports that the evidence was over-whelmingly against him, that he had made a full confession, that he showed no remorse, and that on his island group the law and its remedy were clear. Beyond that, I knew few details.

Caurer, a famous liberal reformer and campaigning writer, had for some reason taken it upon herself to re-open the case and in-vestigate whether Sington had been the victim of a miscarriage of justice. Her conclusion, unsurprisingly, was that he had.

I saw her book on the subject discussed in the press and felt interested and pleased that this might persuade more people to my point of view. But because of Caurer's brief but disruptive impact on my brother's life, I could no longer treat anything by or about her with complete neutrality.

One day, not long after her book had been published, Chaster turned up at my house. It had been more than a year since we had seen each other, but by that time separations of several months at a time were not unusual. He did not stay long.

'Have you seen this?' he said loudly, holding aloft a hardback book with a pale cover. 'Why has she done this to me?'

He tossed the book towards me but as I tried to catch it, and failed, he was already heading back towards the street.

I picked up the book from the floor, and saw what it was.

'I don't understand,' I said.

'Read it, and you will. I can't believe I fell for that woman. I should have realized what she was up to, coming to my place that time. All those questions about the job I had in the theatre. Had I seen anything that happened? Did I know anything? I thought she was different from the others but I was a damned fool and besotted. I was taken in by her.'

'Let me read it,' I said, already sensing that the book contained information about my brother. 'Does it damage you in any way?'

'Just read the thing then throw it away. I never want to see it again.'

After he had stormed out I sat down immediately and read the book from beginning to end. It was not particularly long and was written in a terse, attractive style that I found readable and unusually compelling.

Caurer told the story of the killing that had led ultimately to the execution of Kerith Sington. She went into a great deal of background detail about the victim, a theatre performer called Commis, and also about the theatre where Commis's death had occurred.

Her skill in reconstructing the scene was remarkable. She followed the policier investigation carefully, referring back to original statements and interviews wherever they were available. Then she moved on to the story of Kerith Sington, how he had become involved, how a certain amount of circumstantial evidence incriminated him.

In the longest chapter in the book Caurer went into Sington's childhood and psychological background, and the kind of deprived and socially chaotic world in which he lived. She produced several

examples of other, less serious offences in which he had been involved, how he had been secretive about them at first, then bragged
to impress his friends. After she had analysed his alleged confession
in detail, the reader could have been left in no doubt that Sington
had been wrongly accused. She certainly convinced this reader that
an innocent man had died for a murder he had not committed.

Nothing, to this point, had any relevance to my brother, or so
it seemed. But in her final chapter Caurer tried to answer the question: if Sington was not the murderer of Commis, who was?

She examined the lives and backgrounds of other people who
had been near the scene of the crime at the time. There was the
manager of the theatre, the directors of the company which owned
the theatre, several performing artistes, the technical and backstage
crew, some itinerant manual workers, townspeople, visitors, members of the audience on the night when the killing took place.

And – 'a young man, employed on a part-time basis as a general
assistant backstage.' No name was mentioned. Later the young man
was brought into the story again. Shortly before the death, 'he had
been involved in a violent street scuffle with the murdered man,
but according to witnesses in the street it had appeared to be a misunderstanding and the two men parted amicably.' And again: 'the
young man had applied for the job under an assumed name, a fact
which greatly interested the investigating officers. Furthermore, he
left the island in mysterious circumstances, and at a time no one
was able to be sure about. These two facts made him the number
one suspect, at least for a time.'

Then this paragraph: 'The policier authorities later established
the true identity of this young man. Although he was then unknown, he later became a world-renowned writer of novels, a man
of unquestioned integrity and honesty who is entitled to remain
anonymous. Moreover, once his real identity became known, investigations were taken to his home island, where a conclusive alibi
was established.'

There was no other mention of this young man, either directly
or by implication. Of course I realized he was Chaster: the story
about a violent scuffle in the street certainly had a ring of truth
to it. At that age Chas had always been quick to ball his fists and

strike an aggressive pose, and as a teenager he had involved himself in arguments in Piqay Town several times, and been beaten up for his trouble.

Caurer ended her book with the statement that although it was impossible for her to identify the real killer of Commis, the central truth remained unchallenged: that Kerith Sington had been wrongly accused, convicted and executed.

At first, I was not sure how I should react to this book. Chaster was not named. Nothing in it implicated him in anything illegal, and the identification of him was so vague that the 'true identity' could have been one of several people – Chaster was by no means the only world-renowned novelist of his, or my, approximate age.

When he threw Caurer's book at me, though, he had clearly been upset, which made me wonder if there was more to know or tell than there appeared. Perhaps he was concerned that Caurer had revealed enough clues for other people to follow up. Surely there would be an interest in trying to identify who this mysterious young man had been?

I assumed that his anger against her was more or less the same as mine: that he realized now that she had gone directly to his house, not to seduce him or in any other way inveigle herself into his life, but simply to ask some questions, while she researched her book on Commis's death.

The fact that he had fallen for her so completely had probably helped her cause on the day, and was a matter of indifference to her afterwards.

As had become my habit for many years, I decided to say nothing to Chas, nor to ask him any questions about the book. I continued to feel angry with Caurer on his behalf.

A few weeks later, I was amazed to receive a card from Chaster, inviting Hísar and myself to the house for drinks one evening. It was totally unprecedented. I had not been near the old house for several years, so if nothing else I was curious to see it again.

When the day came, Chaster greeted us with great friendliness and apparent good cheer, introduced us to the other friends he had invited, and made us welcome not only with generous quantities of drink but a superb meal too.

I couldn't help noticing that a copy of Caurer's book was standing prominently on one of the bookshelves, its cover facing out. Later, I spotted another copy, less obviously on show, in a neat pile of books stacked on a reading table in one corner.

When I could I took Chaster aside and asked him outright what had happened to change his mind about her.

He said, simply, 'I love her, Woll.'

'Still? After all this?'

'More than ever. Nothing has changed since the day I met her. I think about Esla every day. I hope and plan to see her. I imagine that every letter that arrives, every email, every telephone call, will be from her. She is an inspiration to me, the woman I most admire and love. I shall never meet another like her. I live my life for her, I write every word for her.'

'But you were so angry with her about the book.'

'I was hasty. I thought she had betrayed me, but I realized later that in fact the opposite was true. She protected me, Woll.'

'So this means – do you have any plans to see her again?'

'All I know is that one day she will come back here to see me.'

Tragically, he was right.

Only three weeks after this evening meeting at the house, Chaster went down with an attack of pneumonia. He fought for life and the hospital did everything possible to save him, but he died in terrible discomfort a few days later.

Of course there was a funeral and following his instructions, whispered to me from his hospital bed, and later found in a sealed letter addressed to me in his study, Caurer was to be invited to be present.

She was then well into her sixties but she was one of the most beautiful women I have ever seen. She said hardly anything to the other people who were there, and always stood alone. I could not stop looking at her. I began at last to understand much that until then I had not.

We returned to the house after the funeral ceremony, and everyone had a few drinks. As the guests started to depart, Hísar and I stood formally by the main door to give our thanks and say our farewells.

When Caurer's turn came I felt overcome with a strange but powerful sense of wanting to hold her, embrace her, possess her in some way, however briefly. I did not want to lose sight of her, let her away from me. I was finally understanding the charismatic effect on which so many people had remarked, over the years and in so many different contexts.

She thanked us politely for our hospitality. I held out a hand to shake hers. She did not respond.

She said, 'He told me a lot about you, Wolter. I am pleased to meet you at last.'

Her voice had the unmistakable and always attractive burr of the Quietude islands, that picturesque but remote group far to the south.

I said, fumbling for adequate words, 'I'm sure Chaster would have been pleased to know that you were here today.'

'He certainly did know I would be here. This is the day when I should tell you that Chaster and I were in love for many years, although we only ever met once, years ago. He is the only person I ever allowed to use my given name.'

'He always called you Esla.'

'Indeed, but now no one ever will again.'

I noticed then that her right hand, which I had tried to take, had a reddish-brown smear across the fingers and palm and that she was holding it slightly away from her body. Hísar had noticed it too.

'Have you cut yourself, Madame Caurer?' she said. 'Let me have a look. We have a trained nurse here, so we could have it cleaned and dressed for you.'

'No, it's not a cut, but thank you.' She moved her hand back, further away from us. 'I hurt myself, that's all.'

Then she left, stepping across the gravel drive to the car that had brought her, which drove away slowly towards the town.

Wolter Kammeston died thirteen months after his brother. He was survived by his wife of fifty-two years, Hísar, and two adult sons. His funeral was a private ceremony at the local crematorium, the only guests being family and close friends.

225

Chaster Kammeston's grave may be visited in the church burial ground, close to the crematorium, where there is also a commemorative plaque for his brother.

Rawthersay (1)

DECLARE / SING

A small island in the southern Midway Sea, Rawthersay is sheltered from prevailing winds by the mountains on the curving arm
of the Qataari Peninsula that lies to the east. This area of the Dream
Archipelago is known as the Quietude Bay, because although deep
in the temperate zone of the southern hemisphere the shelter of
the landmass has created a vast and tranquil bay where storms are
rare and all extremes of weather are virtually unknown. Summers
are warm and delightful with nights that are short, and mild winters are endured in short days and chilly nights. Springtime and
autumn are periods of picturesque natural change.

Approximately five thousand islands of every size are found in
Quietude. All are fertile and inhabited, governments are stable,
industry is varied, trade between islands has been harmonious as
long as there has been recorded history. The creative and performing arts are practised at a high level of accomplishment. When
the Covenant of Neutrality was agreed, the people of Quietude
famously neglected to ratify it for more than a hundred years, not
affected by the urgent need for peace that was felt elsewhere in the
Archipelago.

Although not the largest island in Quietude, Rawthersay is one
of the most developed. Its patois name renders as Declare. It is
situated in the coolest part of the Bay, far to the south. The two
principal activities on the island are sheep farming and mining.
The tall but fertile hills of Rawthersay provide ideal grazing for
the hardy breed of sheep that thrives on the island. The wool the
animals produce is warm, soft and hard-wearing, and is a major

source of export funds. Coal is mined in the southern valleys of Rawthersay, where a separate patois is spoken (the miners call the island SING), and in the east there are large deposits of iron ore which have been mined for centuries.

Rawthersay is a university island, drawing its students from islands all over the southern reaches of Quietude Bay. Ostensibly specializing in the practical vocations of mining and animal husbandry, Rawthersay University has developed many challenging courses devoted to folk literature and music, with an emphasis on performance skills. Touring troupes of performers from Rawthersay regularly travel around all parts of the Archipelago, where they are much appreciated.

The social reformer CAURER is probably the most celebrated alumna of the university. Born Esla Wann Caurer, she was brought up in a small farmhouse in the central valley of Rawthersay, and educated at the local village school. She won a scholarship to the university when she was seventeen.

The farmhouse is open to visitors but an advance appointment is necessary as it is still partly occupied. Many of Caurer's toys and letters from her childhood are displayed in the public rooms. There is a small but excellent bookstore next to the main building.

Caurer founded the university's literary magazine, *Free!*, and edited the first eleven issues while still an undergraduate. *Free!* editorialized about the unfairness of the feudal laws that still existed in most islands and the need for universal suffrage and human rights. It also published a great deal of student poetry, reviews, stories and art. The most notable item, the one that ensures the magazine's immortality, is a long article written by Caurer herself and published in the ninth edition of *Free!*.

This was a review of *Stationed*, Chaster Kammeston's third novel. How the copy reached Rawthersay and Caurer's hands is still not fully understood, because Kammeston's early books were all but unavailable outside his native island, but nevertheless Caurer got hold of it somehow and the article was written.

Using the name 'Esla W. Caurer' – she did not drop the use of her first names until after she left university – she wrote a review that is now known to be the first extended piece of criticism of

Kammeston's work. From the text it is possible to discern that Caurer had read earlier novels by the same writer, but this was her first opportunity to discuss them in print. The review of *Stationed* runs for eight tightly printed pages, full of abundant praise for the novel, but also, notoriously, it contains many speculations and pointed insinuations about Kammeston's presumed motives, proclivities and psychology. More than a year later these immature, unwarranted but witty and highly quotable judgements provoked a hurt but intrigued letter from the author. By this time Caurer had graduated and was no longer at the university.

The letter, addressed to 'Dear Editor', was never printed in *Free!*, but the original is today displayed in a case in the foyer of the Caurer Memorial Theatre. The review itself has been widely anthologized, but a facsimile of its original appearance in *Free!* is displayed next to Kammeston's letter.

The remarkable fact of this review is that Caurer accurately identified, described and praised the unique quality of Kammeston's work, which did not receive wider critical recognition for several more years. At the time, Caurer's essay had a negligible impact: it was after all an obscure book by a more or less unknown author, reviewed by a student at a minor university.

After graduation, Caurer left Rawthersay. Her first work was as an assistant community consultant in the neighbouring Olldus Group. She took up the cause of the poor and immigrant classes on that heavily industrialized chain of islands and wrote the first of her three plays, *Woman Gone*.

Woman Gone is an undisguised attack on feudalism unmodified by human rights, and for several years put her life at risk of reprisals. There were many barons and lords with vested interests. Her powerful, flowing and poetic use of language was unprecedented, and although the play opened in a small theatre in an economically declining part of Olldus Town, within a year it had transferred to Le Théâtre Merveilleux in Jethra, Faiandland. After a long run in Jethra the play was produced in many other theatres around the Archipelago, and is still today regularly revived.

When islanders in all parts of the Archipelago began to demand reforms to the way they were governed, *Woman Gone* was usually cited as the liberating inspiration. Lines from it were adopted as campaign slogans, posters were created using the images of the central characters.

Caurer was soon recognized as a powerful and moving public speaker. She kept Rawthersay as her base and returned there whenever she could, but she travelled constantly to public meetings throughout the Archipelago, where she gained increasingly appreciative audiences. During this period her second play appeared: *The Autumn of Recognition*.

Against expectations, *Autumn* was a light-hearted comedy with musical interludes, although many critics were quick to point out a certain paradox. Beneath the flow of witty dialogue, the scenes of casual adultery and sexual mix-ups, there must be some inconsolable tragedy that the author was not directly addressing. Whatever it was she meant seemed impossible to grasp, but there were clues in the text throughout the play and several of the speeches had a seriousness that was out of key with the rest. The play was delightful entertainment and it played to packed houses, but this enigma at its heart sometimes left audiences puzzled.

Caurer herself rarely discussed her work but during one public speech, in answer to a question from the audience, she mentioned as an aside that if the four acts of *Autumn* were performed in reverse order, certain scenes were removed, the music was omitted, and all the characters were played by actors of the opposite sex, then the play's real meaning would be revealed.

Soon after this the play was re-mounted in that form, and it was seen to be transformed. These days it is rarely performed in its 'original' version, although the Caurer Memorial Theatre does revive it in workshop productions every few years.

Her third play appeared at approximately the same time as *Autumn* was being reinterpreted. Called *The Reconstruction* it was another tragedy: an immense work of some three and a half hours' duration without an interval. It was presented in the form of a series of heartfelt monologues, describing life on particular islands. Each monologue was reconstructed by the next speaking part, making what had just been stated much more complex, but also more comprehensible. The language throughout was judged to be some of the most graceful and resonant ever spoken on the stage. Audiences were almost invariably reduced to tears by the experience of listening to her prose.

Caurer unexpectedly disappeared from view not long after the first performance of *The Reconstruction*. Thereafter she made no more public appearances, but remained in her secure house on Rawthersay. Rumours went around: she was dead, she was in hiding, she had been abducted – the usual kind of thing, but rumours lose their power if they are based only on speculation. The reality seems to be that she sought seclusion, because she entered a long period of sustained literary output.

She wrote a string of books, each one a memorable campaign in a liberal cause. There was a polemic about the horrors of capital punishment, and numerous examples of miscarried justice. This was followed by a book concentrating on a detailed examination of one such case: the execution of Kerith Sington for a murder he could not possibly have committed. Long after Caurer's book was published, Sington received a posthumous pardon. Two books on the rights of the individual followed – Caurer campaigned endlessly to make every island adopt a bill of human rights. There was a book of interviews with deserters from the southern war. She wrote several books on feudalism, and although the system remains in place in most parts of the Dream Archipelago, numerous reforms in many islands have followed. The publication of her book *One for You, Three for Me* was crucial in impelling economic reform, manumitting millions from poverty. One of her most famous campaigns was for the social rehabilitation of women victims of the war, many of whom had been forced into prostitution. No other individual has been responsible for such effective and wide-ranging social liberalization and reform.

As well as the books, Caurer produced many articles and essays, often written in response to an invitation from one organization or another – she became notorious for the way in which she sometimes came up with a view or a position contrary to the ideas of the people who had commissioned the piece. These essays were the closest she came during this period of her life to answering questions, because after she retreated to the seclusion of Rawthersay she granted no more interviews.

The first of the Caurer Special Schools opened on Rawthersay when Caurer was in her mid-forties. It remains a principal centre for higher social learning. Other Caurer Schools have followed and now they are to be found on many islands.

She occasionally agreed to be present at the founding ceremony of some of these schools, but she never made a speech and always took a minor role in the celebrations: cutting a ribbon, symbolically capping a foundation stone, for example, then returning quietly to the shadows. It was this sort of event that gave rise to the speculation that Caurer was using a woman who looked like her as a stand-in. Because Caurer herself, and later the Caurer Foundation, never denied it, and these brief appearances continued, the speculation was probably correct and it was never seen as harmfully deceptive.

Caurer herself was positively identified in public only once more in her lifetime, when she ventured out from Rawthersay alone to attend the funeral of the author, Chaster Kammeston. She was noticed boarding a ferry in Rawthersay harbour – at the next port of call several journalists went aboard. More of them boarded the ship at every stop. She had booked a private cabin, so they only saw her when she went to the dining saloon for a meal. Later, she had to change ships at the island of Ia and on the new ship there were no private cabins. She sat out the voyage on the deck, or in the public areas, staring away as the cameras took shot after shot of her. She ignored every question. Later, after a plea to the captain of the ship, she was able to remain out of sight in crew quarters for the rest of the journey.

The return voyage was an even greater ordeal for her. Stress and unhappiness marked her features and although she was allowed to use the captain's quarters she was able to find only a little privacy. Finally, she agreed to make a statement to the press, and allow photographs, if afterwards the media would leave her in peace.

As the ship sailed between Ia and Junno she stood in the saloon before more than fifty reporters, television cameras and photographers. She simply said that she was devastated by the sudden death of one of her most admired colleagues and wished to be left to mourn alone. She moved back, signalling that her comment was finished.

The media harassment continued afterwards, in breach of the bargain, until a manager from the shipping line intervened and arranged a private flight for her from an airstrip on Junno. Her arrival home on Rawthersay was unobserved. She retreated to her house, the security staff closed the gates and the shutters and no lights showed.

What followed has always been uncertain and the subject of much critical scrutiny. Caurer was said to have died within a few days of her return from Piqay. No one outside her immediate circle ever saw her body and the death was certified by a doctor who worked on her staff. Her body was allegedly cremated immediately afterwards. The cause of death was recorded as: 'Natural causes – infection / infestation.' None of this has ever been proved, and there is a strong body of belief that Caurer used the aftermath of Kammeston's death to slip away to a secret haven on some other island.

However, her death was accepted as a legal fact. Most of her books and papers were left to the Museum Nationale in Glaund City, capital of the Federation, and they are stored there to this day. Found amongst them, and catalogued separately, was a large collection of Kammeston memorabilia, including a complete set of his books as well as many letters, photographs, notebooks and photocopies of diary pages. Most of this written material is either to or about Caurer. There is even a lock of hair which has been positively identified as Kammeston's.

Caurer never bore children and there is no surviving family. There are several touching tributes and memorials from people who worked on her staff: notable amongst these is the long essay by Dant Willer, the journalist on the *Islander Daily Times*. That has been published in many different forms, but the handwritten original is in the Museum Nationale. Caurer's house on the edge of Rawthersay Town is open to the public and many fascinating items of her property are on view, as well as more of her papers. The house, and all matters relating to Caurer's estate, are now administered by the Caurer Foundation.

Visitors to Rawthersay are always made welcome, but there is little on the island for the conventional tourist to do. For the serious student of Caurer's life and work, a visit is of course essential. No visas are required and there are no anti-havenic laws.

Currency: Archipelagian simoleon, Quietude obolus.

Rawthersay (2)

SPOOR

The Trace

The study was lodged high beneath the eaves of the house and it was imbued with traces of him. It had not changed much in the twenty years since I was last there – it was more untidy, a mess of papers and books, standing on, lying beside, heaped below the two tables and a desk. I found it almost impossible to walk across the floor without stepping on his work. Otherwise, the room was much as I remembered it. The window was still uncurtained, the walls unseeable behind the crowded bookcases. His narrow divan bed stood in one corner, now bare of everything except the mattress. I will never forget the tangle of blankets we had left behind when I was here before.

Being there again was a shock. For so long his study, this exact room, had been a memory, a hidden joyful secret, but now it was bereft of him. I could detect the scent of his clothes, his books, his leather document case, the old frayed carpet. His presence was in every darkened corner, in the two squares of bright sunlight on the floor, in the dust on the bookshelves and on the volumes that stood there in untidy leaning lines, in the sticky ochre grime on the window panes, the yellowed papers, the dried careless spills of ink.

I gulped in the air he had breathed, choked by sudden grief. It was incomprehensibly more intense than the shock I felt on receiving the news of his illness, his imminent death. I knew I was rocking to and fro, my back muscles rigid beneath the stiff fabric of my black mourning dress. I was dazed by the loss of him.

Trying to break out of the grief I went to his oaken lectern, where he had always stood to write, his tall shape leaning in an idiosyncratic way as his right hand scraped the pen across the sheets of his writing pad. There was a famous portrait of him in that stance – it was painted before I met him, but it captured the essence of him so well that I later bought a small reproduction of it.

Where his left hand habitually rested on the side, the invariable black-papered cheroot smouldering between his curled knuckles, was a darker patch, a stain of old perspiration on the polish. I ran my fingertips across the wooden surface, recalling a particular half-hour of that precious day, when he had turned his back on me while he stood at this lectern, absorbed by a sudden thought.

That memory of him haunted me as I set out on this desperate quest to reach him before he died. The family had delayed too long in telling me of his illness, perhaps deliberately – a second message I received *en route*, while waiting in an island transit lounge, broke the news I dreaded, that I was too late to see him. I had travelled across a huge segment of the Dream Archipelago with the unchanging mental image of his long back, his inclined head, his intent eyes, the quiet sound of his pen and the tobacco smoke curling around his hair.

Downstairs the mourners were gathering, awaiting the summons to the church.

I had arrived after most of the other mourners. It had taken me four anxious days to reach Piqay. It was so long since I had made the journey across this part of the Archipelago, I had forgotten how many ports of call there were on the way, how many lengthy delays could be caused by other passengers, by the loading and unloading of cargo. At first the islands charmed me, as always, with their variety of colours, terrains and moods. Their names had memories for me from last journey to Piqay, all those years ago: Lillen-Cay, Ia, Junno, Olldus Precipitus, but they were reminders of that sense of breathless anticipation on the voyage to meet him, or of the quiet, contented thoughts on the journey home. My recollection of the journey home, or experiences ashore, telescoped into one brief episode.

This time the charm soon faded. After the first day on the ship

236

the islands simply seemed to be in my way. The boat sailed slowly across the calm straits between islands. Sometimes I stood for hours at the rail, watching the arrowing wake spreading out from the sides of the vessel, but it soon came to be an illusion of movement. Whenever I looked up from the white churning wake, whichever island we happened to be passing still seemed to be in the same relative position as before, across the narrows. Only the seabirds moved, soaring and diving around the superstructure, and at the stern, but even they went nowhere that the ship did not, and no faster. I wished I had wings.

At the port on Junno I left the ship because I wanted to find out if there was a quicker passage available. After an hour of frustrated enquiries in the harbour offices I returned to the ship on which I had arrived, where they were still unloading timber. The next day, on Muriseay, I managed to find a flight with a private aero club: it was only a short hop by air but it saved visits to the ports of three intervening islands. Afterwards, most of the time I saved slipped away, while I was forced to wait for the next ferry.

At last I arrived on Piqay, but according to the schedule of funeral arrangements that arrived with the news of his death, there was only an hour to spare. To my surprise, the family had arranged for a car to meet me at the quay. A man in a dark suit stood by the harbour entrance, swinging the passenger door open as soon as I appeared. As the driver steered the car swiftly away from Piqay Port and headed into the low hills surrounding the town and its estuary, I felt the commonplace anxieties of travel slipping away. It was even relaxation of a sort. I felt able at last to surrender to the complex of emotions that I had managed to keep at a distance while I fretted about ships and arrival times.

Now they returned in force. Fear of the family I had never met. Apprehension about what they might know about me, or what they might not. Worse, what they intended for me now, the lover whose existence might undermine his reputation, were our affair to become publicly known. The bottomless grief still sucking me down as it had done from the moment I heard the news about his illness, then later his death. My defiant pride in the past. The untouchable sense of loneliness, of being left only with memories of him. The hope, the endless irrational hope that something of him might yet live for me.

And I was still confused about why the family had sent the messages. Were they motivated by concern, by spite, or by just the dutiful acts of a bereaved family? Or perhaps, and this was one of the hopes I clung to tightly, he had remembered me and made the request himself?

But above all these, that endless grief, the loss, the feeling of final abandonment. I had suffered twenty years without him, holding on to an inexpressible hope of seeing him again one day. Now he was gone and I was forced to face the prospect of a life finally, absolutely without him.

The driver said nothing. He drove efficiently. After my four days aboard ships, with engines and generators constantly running, the bulkheads vibrating, the car's engine felt smooth and almost silent. I looked out of the dark-tinted window at my side, staring at the vineyards as the car speeded along the lanes, glancing at the pastures, at the rocky defiles in the distance, at the patches of bare sandy soil by the roadside. I must have seen these the last time, but I had no memory of them. That visit was a blur of impressions, but at the centre were the few hours I had spent alone with him, brilliant and clear, defined for ever.

I thought only of him, that time. That one time.

Then, the house. People crowded around the gates, pushing each other aside to make a way for my car. They stared at me curiously. Some women waved as the car slowed, leaning forward to try to see me, spot who I was or who they thought I might be. The gates opened to an electronic signal from the dashboard of the car. They closed behind, as the car moved at a more stately pace up the drive. Mature trees in the park, mountains behind, glimpses of the cerulean sea and dark islands, far away. It was painful to look around at a view I had once thought I would never forget.

On arrival I stood silently in a reception room with other mourners, knowing no one, feeling what I sensed was their silent disdain. My suitcase stood on the floor outside the room. I moved away from the cluster of people and went to an inner door, from which I could see across the main hall towards the wide staircase.

An elderly man detached himself from the group and followed me. He glanced up the stairs.

'We know who you are, of course,' he said, his voice unsteady.

His eyelids fluttered with apparent distaste and he never looked directly at me. What struck me most was the facial similarity. But this man was old! In my sudden confusion I felt embarrassed, unable to make a polite guess as to who he was. My first thought was he might be the father, but no, that was wrong. I knew his parents had died many decades ago, long before we met. There was an identical twin brother he had told me about, but he said they were alienated. Could this now be that twin, a living likeness? Twenty years had passed and you never imagine what changes there might be in someone you have not seen. Was this how he had looked before he died?

'My brother left clear instructions for us to pass on to you,' the man said, solving the mystery, but too late for me to respond courteously. 'You are free to go up to his room if you wish, but you must not remove anything.'

So I made my escape and went quietly and alone up the staircase to this room beneath the eaves. But now I was trembling.

A faint blue haze remained drifting in the room, a vestige of his life. The room must have been empty for several days, yet the light mist of the air he had breathed remained.

With a sudden flowing of renewed unhappiness, I remembered the only time I had lain with him, curled up naked on the bed beside him, glowing with excitement and contentment, while he sucked in the acrid smoke of the cheroots and exhaled it in a thin swirling cone of blueness. That was the same bed, the one in the corner, the narrow cot with the bare mattress. I dared not go near it now, could barely glance at it without the pain of loss.

Five of the cheroots, probably the last he ever bought, lay in an untidy scrambled pile on a corner of one of the tables. There was no sign of a packet. I picked one up, slid it beneath my nostrils, sensing the fragrance of the tobacco and thinking about the one I had shared with him, relishing the dampness of his saliva on my lips. A delirious exhilaration moved through me and for a moment my eyes lost focus on the details of the room.

He had never left the island during his lifetime, even after the prizes and honours began to be bestowed. While I lay naked in his arms, exulting inwardly over the touch of his fingers as they rested on my breast, he tried to explain his attachment to Piqay, why he could never leave to be with me. It was an island of traces, he said, shadows that followed you, a psychic spoor that you left behind if you departed the island. If you did you would become diffuse in some way that he could not explain. He said if he followed me when I left he would never be able to return to Piqay. He dared not try, because to do so would mean he would lose the trace that defined him to the island. For him, the compulsion to leave was less powerful than the urgency of staying. I, feeling a different and less mystical urge rising in me again, quietened him by caressing him, and soon we were making love again.

I would never forget the time we had spent alone together, but afterwards, in the many years of silence that followed, I had never been sure if he even remembered me.

Too late I had the answer, when the first message arrived. Twenty years, six weeks and four days. I had always kept count.

I heard large cars moving slowly on the gravel drive outside the house, and one by one their engines cut out.

The blue haze was thicker now. I turned away from the lectern, aroused by memories, but despairing because memories were all they could ever be. As I looked away from the dazzle of the window it seemed to me that the blue air was denser in the centre of the room. It had substance, texture.

The haze swirled around me. I moved my face towards it, puckering my lips. I darted my face to and fro, trying to detect some response from it. Streaks in the old residue of smoke, denser patches, coalesced before my eyes. I stepped back to see them better, then forward again to press my face against them. Smoke stung against my eyes and tears welled up.

The swirls took shape before me, creating a ghostly impression of his head and face. It was the face as I remembered it from two decades before, not the one the public knew or the grizzled countenance of the old man glimpsed on his identical brother. No time had passed for me, nor for the trace he left. The features were like a mask, but intimately detailed. Lips, hair, eyes, all had their shapes, contoured by the shifting wafts of smoke.

My breath stuttered, halted momentarily. Panic and adoration seized me.

His head was tilted slightly to one side, his eyes were half closed, his lips were apart. I leaned forward to take my kiss, felt the light pressure of the smoky lips, the brush of ghostly eyelashes. It lasted only an instant.

His face, his mask, contorted in the air, jolting back and away from me. The eye shapes clenched tightly. The mouth opened. The lines of smoke that formed his forehead became furrowed. He jerked his head back again, then lunged in a spasm of deep coughing, rocking backwards and forwards in agony, hacking for breath, painfully trying to clear whatever obstructed him below.

A spray of bright redness burst out from the shape that was his open mouth, droplets of scarlet smoke, a fine aerosol. I stepped back in horror, trying to avoid it, and the kiss was lost for ever.

The apparition was wheezing, making dry hacking coughs, small ones now, weak and unhoping, the end of the attack. He was staring straight at me, terrified, full of pain and unspeakable loss, but already the smoke was untangling, dispersing.

The red droplets had fallen to the floor and formed a pool on one of his discarded sheets of paper. I knelt down to look more closely and trailed my fingertips through the sticky mess. When I stood again, my fingers carried a smear of the blood, but the air in the study had cleared. The blue haze had gone at last. The final traces of him had vanished. The dust, the sunlight, the books, the dark corners remained.

I fled.

Downstairs I stood once again with the others, waiting in the great hall to be allocated to one of the cars. Until my name was spoken by one of the undertaker's staff, no one acted as if they knew who I was or acknowledged my presence in any way. Even the man who had spoken to me, the brother, stood with his back against me. His hand was linked affectionately around the upper arm of a short, grey-haired woman, speaking quietly to people as they stepped outside to join the cortège. Everyone seemed daunted by the seriousness of the occasion, by the thought of the crowds waiting in the road at the end of the long drive, by the passing of this great man.

I was given a seat in the last of the cars, bringing up the rear of the cortège. I was pressed against the window by the large bodies of two serious and unspeaking adolescents.

In the crowded church I sat by myself to one side, forcing calmness by staring at the flagstone floor, the ancient wooden pews. I stood for the hymns and prayers but only mouthed the words silently, remembering what he had said were his feelings about church services. The tributes to him were formal, grand, spoken sincerely by illustrious men and women. I knew some of the speakers already, but not one of them acknowledged me. I listened closely, recognizing nothing of him in their words. He had not sought this renown, this greatness.

In the churchyard on a hill overlooking the sea, standing near the grave, back from the main group of mourners, hearing the words of committal distorted by the breeze, I was again alone. I remembered the first book of his I had ever read, while I was still at college. An inspiration for me, a constant guide through life. Everyone knew his work now, but at that time he was unknown and it had been my own deeply personal discovery.

The persistent wind from the islands buffeted against me, pressing my clothes against my body on one side, sending strands of hair across my eyes. I smelt the salt from the sea, and the fragrance of flowers, the promise of distance, departure, escape from this place.

Members of the public and the cameras of the media were only just visible, kept in the distance beyond a cordon of flowers and a patrol of policier officers. In a lull of the wind I heard the familiar words of the committal being uttered by the priest, and watched the coffin lowered into the ground. The sun continued to shine but I could not stop shivering. I could think only of him, the caress of his fingertips, the light pressure of his lips, his gentle words, his tears when I had had to leave him at the end. The long years without him, holding on to everything I knew of him. I barely dared to breathe for fear of expelling him from my thoughts.

242

I held my hand out of sight beneath the small bag I was carrying. The blood had congealed on my fingers, cold, an encrustation, eternal, the final trace of him.

Reever

HISSING WATERS

REEVER is the largest island in a group known as the REEVER FAST SHOALS. Close to the Equator, the Shoals consist of some fourteen hundred islands, most of them unnamed and unpopulated. If they could be seen from the air without visual distortion the Shoals would appear in the shape of a large sickle, curving out in a south-westerly direction across the Equator, before turning and stretching away towards the east. Reever and two of the other main islands in the group are in the northern hemisphere, but most of the lesser islands are south of the line. The sea throughout the formation is warm and shallow, serene and idyllic in appearance but made treacherous by rip-tides, guyots, whirlpools and reefs. There are only a few navigable passages. Some of the smallest islets are little more than protruding rocks which are covered at high tide.

The four main islands, Reever itself and Reever Dos, Tros and Quadros, are large enough to support populations, and away from the coastlines there are areas of forestry and a little farmland recovered from cleared rainforest.

On the northern side of Reever the sea is much deeper, and it is here that the North Faiand Drift passes during its brief transit close to the Equator. The combination of deep cool water and sun-warmed shallow feeding grounds means that the finest rod-fishing is possible. Reeverites claim their islands are the recreational fishing capital of the world, but in reality it is a sport only for the wealthier visitors: vacationing financiers, investment bankers, tax exiles, remittance men and others with less conventional sources of wealth are the main beneficiaries of this bounty.

The restaurants, clubs, bars and marina buildings along the seafront of Reever Town display many photographs of huge fish, some of them two or three times the size of the overweight men said to have landed them.

Because of its position close to the Equator, Reever affords one of the best places to observe the twice-daily vortices as they pass above.

This is a common but almost invariably misunderstood phenomenon. If you look up at the sky at the right time of day you will see apparently stationary jets and transports stacked overhead, pointing in every direction and drifting slowly together in a westerly direction. The stack can be seen in many parts of the world close to the tropics, but it occurs directly over the Equator. The aircraft fly at many altitudes, their contrails stretching out behind them across the blue sky, spiralling to the golden mean. This astonishing sight is the sole visible evidence of a passing vortex.

It was on Reever that the temporal vortex was first noticed, investigated, identified and measured, by a local man called DEDELER AYLETT. A small museum and observatory on Reever Quadros now commemorate Aylett's work. There are several working models to illustrate how the vortices affect our perception of the physical world.

Aylett made his discovery while sailing around the coast of Reever Quadros. This is the smallest of the four main islands, and its rocky shore is popular with shallow-water fishermen. By chance, the island lies directly on the Equator and is bisected by the imaginary line into two areas of roughly equal size. For this reason, the visual distortions are uniquely observable at sea level.

Aylett noticed something that generations of fishermen had taken for granted: that every time you circumnavigate the island, the appearance of the cliffs, the rocky foreshore, even the lie of the land, seems to change. The headland you were navigating towards is lower or longer than the last time you saw it; a certain group of rocks that are dangerous at high tide are no longer visible, even at low tide; a thicket of trees on the clifftop, which could be seen from the harbour now appear to be behind a hill you know would block the view from the quayside.

Without more than the crudest maps, sailors and fishermen could never be sure if what they were seeing was true, or if they were somehow misremembering from the previous sighting. People were always getting lost and there were many shipwrecks.

Aylett, though, took the phenomenon seriously and made repeated circuits of the island. He kept careful records of what he saw, and took hundreds of photographs. He then correlated these observations with date and time, position of the sun, tides, wind-strength, seeking a pattern.

Aviation was not then a widespread activity, because it was thought to be highly dangerous. The actual construction of aircraft was sound enough, but pilots were constantly getting lost and being forced to crash-land on other islands or ditch in the treacherous seas. Without knowing it they were early victims of the visual or temporal distortions. All aircraft at this time flew only at rooftop height, and as slowly as possible, enabling the pilot or navigator to maintain direction, but this was another factor which caused accidents.

Aylett was determined to test his theory and invested his entire savings with a pilot willing to take him on a series of flights across Reever Quadros, initially at low level, but at slowly increasing altitudes as their confidence grew.

Aylett discovered what is now commonplace. If you fly in one direction, looking down at the ground – say from north to south – a certain island will look a certain way: mountains here, a river there, a town, a bay, forest, and so on. However, if you fly over it a second time – east to west – the same island will look oddly different: the river doesn't reach the sea in quite the same part of the coast, the forest looks darker or larger, the mountains now have fewer peaks, the coast seems less jagged, or more. Has it actually changed? Or was your observation inaccurate the first time? You go round for a third look – north to south again – and the island has seemed to change its layout yet again, and is different in a new way.

Worse, if you set off across the sea to an adjacent island, then try to return home, the island you left will now seem to be in another place or direction entirely. Sometimes it will have vanished altogether, or that is how it appears.

Aylett's measurements and calculations began to make sense of this, calibrating the degree of distortion to longitude and latitude, and the position of the sun.

In the present day, modern aircraft make use of the vortical distortions. By flying high in the direction of the Equator, the craft pass through the distortion, greatly shortening the distance needed to be flown, even from one side of the world to the other. It makes all flights reasonably short in duration, with a great saving in fuel. Although aviation charts of the Archipelago airspace are as unreliable as every other kind of map, the air operators have worked out a complicated but effective system of physical markers, so that as the aircraft descend from the distorted zone the pilots are able to see these markers and navigate to their destination by dead reckoning.

Twice a day, as the two main vortices go around the world, people on the islands in the equatorial zone are rewarded by the sight of the stack of aircraft passing overhead, all of them pointing in different directions, the spiralling condensation trails spreading out across the blue sky.

The Aylett Observatory on Reever Quadros is one of the best places to see this phenomenon. There are daily tours and lectures, and a special section provides many projects for young people to set up their own observation stations at home or at school.

There is a small artists' colony in Reever Town, no longer as influential as once before, but RASCAR ACIZZONE, founder of the Tactilist School, painted here before he was arrested. Although he was late to the technique of tactilism – ultrasound microcircuitry adapted to blend into and work with pigments – it was Acizzone who perfected the technique and gave it the name by which it is still known. After Acizzone was taken into custody and later exiled, the remaining artists in Reever Town referred to themselves as Pre-Tactilists, less as an identifier of their work so much as a way of avoiding some of the fallout from Acizzone's disaster. The artists' colony continues to exist in the present day and although most of the current work in Reever is conventional one or two of the younger artists are producing work that is challenging, experimental and of the highest quality. None of Acizzone's work is on public view.

Tunnelling is prohibited, but deep natural caves may be explored on Reever Tros. There are strict shelterate laws and local taxes are high. The casino is a major attraction, and is a significant earner for the Reever Seigniory.

Currency: Archipelagian simoleon, Faiandland dollar, Federation credit. Local transactions (only) in Aubracian talent.

Seevl

DEAD TOWER

THE GLASS

I had known Alvasund Raudeberg all through our school days. She came back into my life at a time when I had all but forgotten her. Time seems to accelerate after you leave school, and I had gone away, an exhibitioner at Kellno University on the subtropical island of Ia. The sheer hard grind and intellectual stimulation of my course speeded up the change even more. I was glad to leave my home island behind, and move into what I considered to be the modern world. Alvasund, and everyone I had known as a child, drifted into my past.

Then my parents unexpectedly died and I had to return to Goorn, the Hettan island where I was born. I did so reluctantly. It was one of the years when the Goornak wind was gusting down, a time of omens for most of the people in the Hetta group. The icy wind brought a regression to many of the primitive fears and superstitions which lent our part of the Archipelago a reputation for backwardness. The Goornak is a freezing, blustering stream of air from the north-east, the vile breath of a witch, or so some of the Hetta people say. When the Goornak blows the curse wind is thought to have returned and many aspects of the modern world retreat from Hetta for the duration.

I had then been away for four years, absorbed in a course in glass sciences. Ia was a long way to the south of the Hetta Islands, covered in lush vegetation and bathed by warm seas, modern in all things, a place where young minds are trained, ideas are formed and technology is developed. At Kellno Uni I learned to respect science and engineering, to be sceptical of superstition, to reject the conventional but to value the past, to think for myself. I read widely and eagerly, met other people of my own age, fell in love, fell out of love, debated, questioned, argued, got drunk, sobered up, learned, lazed around. I was a student, not typical of everyone else but not so different from them either. I grew up while I was on Ia, leaving behind, or so I assumed, the unattractive mental and psychological baggage I had carried with me when I first left Goorn. I had been born on Goorn, so what could I know of the rest of the world?

I made the best use of my time at the university, where I became involved in an outreach placement. It was a commercial laboratory, working on a research project into a new form of BPSG, borophosphosilicate glass, developed for use in superconductors. After I graduated, the time I had spent gaining experience in the lab in Ia Town benefited me in two ways. It meant I received a First with Honours, and following from that I was offered a full-time job at the same laboratory.

I barely thought of home, communications across certain sections of the Archipelago being slow, unreliable and expensive. Hetta is one such area. It's a wild and ruggedly attractive place, thirteen medium-sized islands in a large bight, tucked up against the coastal range along the southern shore of Faiandland. In winter three or four of the smaller islands are temporarily joined to the mainland when the sea freezes, but unreliably: the ice is too thick for small boats to break through, and too unreliable for traffic to cross over it. There are traditional trading contacts across the straits, but since the war began most dealings with the Faiand mainland have had to be undercover. Strict border controls exist.

On Goorn itself, the second largest of the Hetta group but not one of those close to the mainland, the northern coastline is mountainous, broken by deep fjords. This is the region of Goorn called the Tallek. Among the Tallek's headlands, steep cliffs and long bays of freezing cold water there are several small ports tucked away, sheltered from the prevailing winds. The mountains that loom over the sea are bare in summer, iced-over in winter. Deep-sea fishing is the main industry in the Tallek. I went to the Tallek only once, when I was still a child – my father had a business meeting there and he took the rest of the family along. Afterwards, ever afterwards, my memories of that high, chilly landscape informed my feelings about my home island, even those of the dull plains of grazing animals around Goorn Town, where I lived.

I had been working at the lab on Ia for less than three months when I learned that my mother had died. I had known she was ill, but had not been told how serious it was. Then soon afterwards my father suffered a fatal heart attack. Numbed by this double tragedy I made contact with my elder brother Brion, who now lived on the mainland, but he was unable to obtain an exit visa. Therefore, alone, I took the slow sequence of ferries north, one island to the next, frequently delayed, arriving in Goorn Town eight days later.

Once I was home I had much to do, sorting out my parents' financial affairs, clearing the house, and so on. While I was away from Ia my job was still in theory safe, but one day my boss made contact – a sponsorship deal had fallen through, and all the people in my team had been placed on half-salary. There was no pressure on me to return.

The atmosphere of Goorn was all too chillingly familiar. The days were short, the skies permanently fuliginous, the temperature icy. Sooty clouds scudded across from the north-east. I had already lived in the subtropics long enough to wish I could be there all the time. Goorn and its constant wind depressed me. I glimpsed other people about the streets, not many, but the few who ventured out huddled against the wind, huddled against their own thoughts and, I supposed, their pagan fears. Cars went by slowly, the sombre light reflecting ominously from their windows. I felt crowded in by the ignorant beliefs I discerned, but also lonely because of them.

In this state of suspense, trying to complete my parents' affairs was all but impossible. The bank staff, the lawyers, the Seigniory Estates Commission either did not respond to my enquiries or they made excuses or they sent the wrong paperwork. Almost nothing was being done.

After a few more days I realized I was wasting my time until the Goornak ceased. I decided to travel back to Ia, where at least I could see my friends and find out the facts about my job. I would have to make the long return journey to Goorn when summer came. I began packing.

Seeing Alvasund Raudeberg again changed everything. She came to the house on the morning of the day before I was due to catch the ferry. I was not only surprised to see her, I was pleased and intrigued that she had sought me out. I had always rather fancied her when we were at school together. She entered the house in a flurry of fine blown snow.

'I realized you must be back, Torm,' she said. 'I was sorry to hear the news about your parents.'

In the house I made her a hot chocolate and we sat side by side at the scrubbed-deal table in the kitchen, sipping at our drinks, our shoulders touching companionably for warmth. The eaves of the house groaned and sometimes shrieked as the hostile wind blustered through the town. The outer door was creaking and the house felt cold.

'Tell me what you've been doing since school,' I said to her. 'Did you go away to college?'

The morning passed. We each had our stories to tell, catching up, but in a sense they were similar. Like so many others we had left Goorn to escape – we had both been forced to return. Neither of us had clear ideas about what we should do next.

Alvasund told me she had been living on Muriseay until recently, but she had lost her job and could not find another. She had returned to Goorn because her sister had just given birth to twins, and most of the family were there to celebrate. She seemed restless and anxious to leave. I mentioned I was about to head back to Ia, suddenly realizing how much I would like Alvasund to travel with me. I could not stop thinking about her, how much we had both grown up, that I had always liked her, the possibilities that were gathering. But after I had mentioned Ia a few more times, trying to make it sound interesting and attractive, I realized that it was not an option for her.

'I'm heading up to the Tallek region in a day or two,' she said. 'Do you know it?'

'I was there with my parents, when I was a kid. Just a couple of days.'

'Do you remember much about it?'

'A lot of mountains,' I said, wishing I could elaborate more. 'A constant smell of fish and smoke. I was cold all the time. Just like this, but I was there in the summer so I guess the Tallek is cold all year. Why do you want to go there?'

'Various reasons.'

'Such as?'

'I've never seen the fjords.'

'It must be more than that. It's so hard to get there.'

'It's all a bit vague. There's the possibility of a job, but I need to know more about it. And the other day I found out there's a Yo tunnel in the Tallek somewhere.'

'I didn't know she came to Goorn,' I said.

'She wasn't here long. They threw her off the island when they caught up with her, but apparently she was in the Tallek long enough to drill most of the way through one of the slopes. She never finished, which is why it's interesting. Anyone can go in and explore.'

Alvasund suddenly changed the subject and talked about her course. She had studied stagecraft, gaining skills in computer-generated three dimensional sets, perspective building and subjective animatronic modelling. She said it was called active intelligence, because stages dressed in this way were capable of responding, not just to the actors' lines but to the reactions of the audience. It was still a new technology, and many theatre managers were conservative about stage techniques.

Once she had gained her degree she discovered jobs were hard to find. She worked for a while for a TV company. They had sent her to a regional studio on Muriseay, but that job expired when the studio closed. She was unable to find work in any of the theatres on Muriseay.

Now she was planning to visit the north, before she went back to Muriseay.

'Would you like company on the trip?' I said suddenly, trying to make it sound spontaneous.

'I thought you were returning to Ia.'

'No urgency. I just don't want to be in this house any longer.'

'Can you drive a car?' Alvasund said.

'Yes.'

'That would solve a problem for me. If we rented a car together, would you be willing to drive?'

'Where would we stay, what would we do?'

She looked gravely at me – a sudden reminder of her intriguing seriousness in class at school. 'We'll work something out, Torm.'

Then she laughed, so I did too. There was now a prospect of intimacy, alone with her for some days. She told me there was a house she could stay in, something to do with the job offer. She wasn't clear about that. 'No one else there now,' she added, and laughed again.

She left soon after that, but she came back the next day and we discussed practicalities. I cancelled my ferry ticket, obtained a refund. She had located a car rental firm that was not expensive. We looked at maps of the fjords, picked out the places we might pass through.

The town we were going to was called Ørsknes, close to where Yo had been drilling. The absence of markings on the map of the surrounding terrain gave a chill impression of bleakness, wind-swept peaks. We packed warm clothes, bought food and drinks, and agreed to set out the following morning. I offered to walk with her back to her sister's house, but she said no.

North of Goorn Town there is almost nothing of scenic interest, and the road is straight. The car was buffeted by gusts of wind. We drove all day, stopping for a rest and a brief lunch, neither of us sure how long the whole journey might take. We did not want to be driving through the mountains after dark. We could see them ahead of us, a dark range capped by many snowy peaks. Although the car was a recent model the heater did not work well and the further north we drove the colder we felt. Alvasund wrapped her legs under a travel blanket, and I halted the car long enough to pull on my wind-cheater.

It was late afternoon when we climbed towards the first pass, finding the road ice-covered and treacherous in places. A heavy snowstorm started, whiting out visibility. It did not last long, but it was concerning. Old snow was already piled on both sides, and the fresh fall was settling on the paved surface. When about half an hour later we saw a small hotel set back from the road, we immediately turned in to stay the night.

We drove down from the high pass into Ørsknes. It was close to midday. The sun was low in the sky but brilliant, the sea was deep blue but troubled with many flecks of white, the mountains hung above us, snow-covered, perilously steep, rocky. There were signs of rockfall near the bases of some of the mountains, close to where the road ran alongside the fjord. Using a small, hand-drawn map, Alvasund directed me to the house we would be staying in. We climbed out of the car, assailed by the freezing wind. Small white clouds raced overhead. The streets looked deserted. The curse wind was felt here too.

The house was built so that it backed on to the first elevation of a slope, which rose steeply from a tiny yard at the rear. Alvasund walked quickly to the main door of the house, produced a key and we were in. We carted our bags into the house, our breath blowing white around us, even in the interior.

It was an A-frame building, furnished minimally. The large street-level floor was dominated by a wood-burning stove, with neat stacks of logs placed alongside the stone wall. A long couch and a hide rug were in front of the stove. There was a kitchen and bathroom. Everything was clean, tidy, functional.

The upper floor was a mezzanine, attained by narrow wooden steps. Beneath the sharply-angled roof a large, thick mattress lay on the floor, with quilts and bolsters folded neatly on the top.

Two hours later we had the place habitable. The stove was alight, filling the house with the sweet scent of burning birch, and the water jacket around the firebox was piping heat around the house. Alvasund warmed up some canned soup and we drank it sitting together on the couch, staring into the glowing fire.

We had found some maps of the fjord which showed that Ørsknes was a distance inland from the sea, with another fishing settlement called Omhuuv lying further along the same shore, closer to the mouth of the fjord. A larger-scale street map revealed that it was probably not going to take long to explore the town. There were just the two main streets, with a compact maze of side streets like the one where the house was situated. The harbour and wharf buildings ran for most of the length of the waterfront. We could hear the winches and cranes, even through the stone and doubly insulated wooden walls of the house.

We walked around the town before sunset, wrapped up against the icy north-east wind. It seemed to gain strength as it passed along the narrowing fjord. Alvasund showed me the building where she believed Yo had kept her studio – it was now a net store – but many decades had passed since the artist had been there. Her studio could have been in any one.

As we walked back towards the house we spotted a restaurant close to the wharves. The place was open, so we ate dinner there. Some of the other customers looked at us curiously a few times, but there was no hostility in their interest. Alvasund and I were learning to relax with each other, and several times we stopped talking and sat and ate in silence, glancing warmly at each other across the table.

Afterwards, we returned through the now dark streets, looking for the house, hearing our own footsteps echoing in the deserted streets. We glimpsed dim lights behind the curtained or shuttered windows of many of the houses, but there was little other outward sign of occupation. It was starting to snow, a thin, cold downfall, blown along on the turbulent Goornak. We leaned against each other, holding on as we slithered along the increasingly slippery paths.

I was assuming nothing about what might happen when we went to bed, but the knowledge that there was only one bed in the house had quietly illuminated the evening for me. I could not forget Alvasund's unexpected laughter when we first discussed this trip, the smiling implication of us travelling together, and the easy affection we had shared in the restaurant.

But the night before, when we stopped at the hotel in the

mountains, had been a surprise if not a disappointment. The moment I switched off the car's ignition Alvasund had leapt out and run through the swirling snowstorm into the building. She returned with the news that we could stay, and started pulling her bags out of the car. Once inside the building I discovered we were to be in separate rooms, but I did not ask, and Alvasund did not tell me, if this was at her own request or if those were the only ones available. That is how I had spent the previous night, comfortably enough, warmly enough, but alone in a single narrow bed.

Now we were in Ørsknes, in a house where it was plain we would be sharing a bed. Once inside the house, with our warm outer clothes removed and the fire stirred up into a burst of new radiance, we made some tea. We sat together, as before, staring at the fireglow. Alvasund had picked up a tourist guide in the restaurant so we now knew where the Yo tunnel was located and how we could find it. We made plans to visit it the next day.

With the tea finished Alvasund stood up quickly, said she would like a shower and asked me if I wanted to take mine first or after her. I opted to go first.

Afterwards, I went up the narrow steps, crawled on to the mattress, and pulled the quilt around me. I was full of anticipation, my senses tingling, my appetite and readiness for her growing. As soon as I was in the bed she came up the steps to join me. She was still in her clothes and stood where I could see her. She undressed with her back towards me, stripping unsensationally to her underwear, then pulled on a wrap and went downstairs to the cubicle. I could hear the water flowing through the pipes, the shower running below, the sound of the splashing changing as she moved around. I stared at the small pile of clothes she had left on the floor beside our bed.

After a silence I heard her do something to the wood-burning stove, then she turned out the lights on the ground floor and came back up to the bed. She was wearing the wrap, with her hair hanging damply about her shoulders.

She kneeled forward on the edge of the mattress, pulled out the bolster from where it had been laid, and placed it along the bed, down the middle, dividing it in two.

'You understand, Torm, don't you?' She was patting down the long, heavy pillow, making sure it extended the full length of the bed.

'I think so,' I said, kicking the thing where it had rolled against me. 'I can see what you are doing. Is that what I have to understand?'

'Yes. Don't touch me. Imagine there is a sheet of glass between us.'

She towelled her hair briefly, then slipped off the wrap. For a moment she was naked, standing there, within my reach, but she was already crawling forward, sliding under the quilt beside me. The bolster lay between us.

She turned out the light, pulling on the cord that dangled from the rafter above.

I turned it on again and sat up. I leaned over towards her. She was already lying with the quilt pulled tight up to her face. Her eyes were open.

'Torm –'

I said, 'I wasn't assuming anything, but you're acting as if you think I was.'

'It's obvious. What you're expecting.'

'Everything we did today – was I wrong?'

'We're just friends, Torm. That's how I want it to be. If you assume that, that's OK.'

'What if I want that to change? Or you do?'

'Then we'll both know. Please, for now just treat me as if we have glass between us. Everything is visible, but nothing can be reached. This was something I learned at college, about an audience and a stage. There's an invisible wall between the actors and the audience. You look and you see, but there's no real interaction.'

I said, protesting, 'A stage effect isn't the same thing at all!'

'I know. But for now, just for now, for tonight.'

'You want me to be your audience.'

'I suppose so, yes.'

I thought about that. She suddenly seemed to me rather naïve, adapting a concept some drama teacher had explained, but applying it inappropriately. I reached up and turned off the light, aroused and annoyed. Moments later I switched it on again. She had not moved and her eyes were still open. She blinked.

'You say I can look at you.'

'Yes.'

'Let me look now.'

Amazingly she smiled at that and without another word pushed down the quilt to expose herself. I raised myself on my elbow again, stared at her lying there so close to me, her neat, compact body, quite bare, frankly naked to me. She kicked the quilt completely away with one of her feet, then moved slightly, revealing everything of herself.

Almost at once it felt intrusive and somehow pointless to be looking at her like that, so I turned away. Still she did not pull up the quilt to cover herself but I turned off the light. Moments later I felt her move under the quilt again. She fidgeted a few times and finally lay still. I tried to relax too, lying back with my head on the large soft pillow. I was breathing hard but I tried to still myself, to be calm. The bolster lay between us.

It was almost impossible for me to sleep but I think Alvasund did fall asleep more or less straight away. Her breathing was steady, almost inaudible. She barely moved.

Of course what she had done had thrown me into a whirl of thoughts, desires, inhibitions, frustration. What was she up to? She appeared to like me, but somehow not enough. She let me look at her, seemed to invite it and even enjoy it, but I was not allowed near her, kept back in a kind of imaginary auditorium. I was dazzled and aroused by the brief glimpse I had had of her, the way she lay there close to me, relaxing her arms so her breasts were revealed, and parting her legs a little. She wanted me to see her, or at least would allow it.

She was not the first naked woman I had seen, nor was she the first I had been in bed with. I assumed she must know that, or could guess it. During my four years away from home, growing up rapidly, enjoying new freedoms, I had had girlfriends and lovers, and there was Enjie, one of the students, a young woman reading Economics in another department of the college. Enjie and I had shared an enthusiastic physical relationship for several months.

259

Nor was Alvasund an object of long-held desire, because she had barely been in my thoughts since I left Goorn. Her return to my life had been completely unexpected. However, she was attractive to me, becoming more so, I was enjoying being with her, and –

There was a sheet of glass between us.

I knew about glass, but the glass I knew about was not for looking through, nor was it a barrier. On the contrary it was a medium of transient, non-fixed effect, used to control or enhance an electronic flow at some frequencies, while at others it functioned as an insulator or compressor. Her metaphor did not work for me.

I was awake for much of the night, sensing her physical closeness, knowing that were I to move just a short distance, or to throw an arm towards her across the bolster, or to allow one of my hands to slip beneath the damned thing, she would be there, close beside me, reachable, touchable.

But I did not. I listened to the constant wind, scouring across the roof just a short distance above me. I must eventually have slept because when I was next fully awake it was daylight. Alvasund was not in the bed beside me. She had already dressed and was downstairs doing something in the kitchen. I dressed quickly and went to join her. Neither of us said anything about what had happened, or not happened. I touched her hand to say hello, and she put an arm around my shoulder in a brief but affectionate hug.

I supposed that now, for the time being at least, it was my sort of glass between us, not just hers.

The wind was less bitter that morning, so we decided to walk up to the site of Yo's tunnel. According to the leaflet Alvasund had found it was only a short distance from the town centre. It involved a steep climb along a fairly wide track with a frozen, crumbly surface, iced up in several places, loose with stones in others. A layer of snow covered much of the way.

We soon found the site of the tunnel, which had been created so that the opening could not be seen from below. As we climbed we suddenly came upon it, a short section of tunnel leading back from the rocky wall and then falling sharply downwards, curling away from the light. The tunnel was huge. A truck or other vehicle could have passed through it. Guard rails had been erected at knee and thigh height.

We stood and stared down into it. Alvasund seemed moved by the sight of it, but to be candid it left me unimpressed. It was a large hole in a mountainside.

'You don't get it, do you?' Alvasund said eventually.

'Yes, I do, I think.'

'Jordenn Yo is really important to me,' Alvasund said. 'As an artist, as a kind of ideal, a personal role model. She stood for everything I want to be. She lived for her work, and in the end died for it. Almost every installation she completed was managed in the face of objections, bans, threats. She was thrown into prison several times. Of course, everyone prizes her work now, as if none of that happened. Any island where she worked shows it off as if it was their idea. But in reality she was always being harassed by the same sort of people then, the ones who run islands now. This is one of the tunnels she wasn't able to finish. She later disowned it, said it had been ruined by the Hetta authorities. Can't you see what she meant?'

'What would it have been if she had finished it?'

'Longer and deeper ... it was supposed to reach the far side of the hill. What's unique about this one is there's a vertical spiral down there somewhere.'

We stared at the entrance for a while longer, then turned and skittered carefully down the slippery track, returning towards the town.

'Is that it?' I said. 'Have we done what you came here to do?'

'I don't know. I'm waiting to hear about the job offer, if it still exists.'

'Are they here in town, or do you have to make contact with them somehow?'

'I said I don't know.'

'We could always come back and look at the hole again,' I said. 'Nothing else to do.'

The way back took us straight from the mountain track to a steep flight of stone steps, thence down to one of the town streets. We passed through the central area. I was hoping we might see a shop open or perhaps a café, somewhere we could buy a newspaper then sit and warm up for a while. As we approached the house a young man appeared. He was about to pass by without noticing us, but Alvasund reacted to him at once.

'Marse!' She let go my hand, raising her arm in a warm greeting. She walked quickly towards him.

He responded to the sound of his name, looking at her with a startled expression. He quickly averted his eyes and looked as if he were about to stride on past us, but when Alvasund said his name again he acted as if he had recognized her all along. He lifted a gloved hand in welcome. It was a brief gesture, almost a warding off.

He said, his voice muffled by a thick scarf he wore across his mouth, 'Alvie ... is that you?'

'Of course it's me, Marse. Why do you say that?' She was still smiling with recognition, disregarding his scowling manner.

'No one was supposed to be here until next week. Have you been to the house?'

'You sent me the key. Or someone from the Authority did.' She was not smiling now. 'I arrived yesterday, a few days earlier than I expected. I managed to get someone to give me a lift.'

'All right.' He was backing away from us, seemingly anxious to leave. He had an evasive look – what we could see of his face was raw from the wind, and his hair straggled out from beneath his hood.

'But what about the job?' Alvasund said. 'That's what I came here for.'

'I don't know anything about that. I've quit the operational side. I just check the office here, part-time.'

'So what do I do about the job?'

'There's an appointment form. Was it in the house?'

Alvasund glanced at me, querying. I shook my head.

'No.'

'Then someone will send it.'

'I need to know if I can still get the job,' Alvasund said.

'I'll hurry them along a bit, the people in Jethra. But – don't get involved.'

'Marse, it's what we were trained to do. You know that. You kept urging me to apply. We were going to do it together.'

'That was before.'

'Before what?'

He took another step back. He was looking at neither of us. 'I'll contact the Authority,' he said. He flashed a furtive look at me. 'Have you applied too?'

'No.'

The young man turned and walked quickly away, his hands thrust deep into the pockets of his padded cagoule, his shoulders hunched, his chin buried in his scarf.

His last words were more or less the first acknowledgement by him that I was there. I was at Alvasund's side, shivering in the bitter wind, a bystander, excluded. It made me realize how little I knew of Alvasund, or what her life had been like before we met again.

'Shall we go to the house?' she said.

'I'll collect my stuff,' I said. 'I think I'll drive back to Goorn Town straight away.'

As soon as we were inside the house I moved quickly, finding my clothes and the other things I had brought, stuffing them into my holdall. I was angry with myself, but also furious with Alvasund. She went to the kitchen, made some tea. She sat at the table, staring down, holding the cup in both hands.

'What's the problem, Torm?' she said, when I went into the kitchen to pick up the coffee I had brought with me.

'You don't need me here. I drove you, but you can find your own way back.'

'What's brought this on?'

'Who the hell was that? What was his name – Marse?'

'Just someone I used to know at university.'

'A boyfriend?'

'Just an old friend.'

'And who the hell am I?'

'An old friend.'

'No difference between us then. Except I was the someone you found to drive you here.'

Alvasund blinked and turned away. 'I'm sorry I said it like that. I knew straight away it was insensitive.'

'Too bad. Too late.'

'Torm, you're jealous!'

I stopped pacing around then and turned back to her. 'What do I have to be jealous about? What do I lose by you meeting up with an old boyfriend? Not a damned thing. You've given me nothing—'

'I thought we were only just at the beginning.'

She rose from the table and pushed past me, through to the main part of the house. I followed. The stove was still alight, a deep-red glow behind the fireproof glass. The house was warm, rich with the smell of woodsmoke. The windows were translucent with condensation. She sat down on the thick rug in front of the fire doors, leaning towards the heat. I sat in one of the cushioned chairs, half turned away from her.

Alvasund immediately rose to her knees, leaned towards me and kissed me full on the lips. Her hand rested affectionately on my chest. I was too angry for that, and pulled away from her. She persisted.

Finally she said, 'Torm, I'm sorry. *Really sorry!* Please … let's forget everything that just happened. Marse is an old friend from college – I hadn't seen him for over a year. But he was acting weird, and I forgot what I was doing.'

In a cupboard she found an unopened bottle of apple brandy, distilled and bottled locally. She broke the seal and poured two glasses.

'I think you should explain what's going on,' I said. I was still residually angry with her, thinking of what had happened in the night. Nothing had happened in the night. The sheet of virtual glass she put up as a barrier remained a barrier. 'You didn't bring me here to look at a hole in the ground. What's the truth about this job?'

'I've never been sure the job is real,' she said. 'If it is, it would be ideal for me. The money's terrific and I'm qualified for it. But I've been getting so many mixed messages from Marse – he took a similar job last year. First he'd tell me the job was open, and urge me to apply – then I wouldn't hear from him for weeks. For a while he was pretending he didn't know me. Then he changed again. Finally he told me to come here. But you saw what happened, in the street.'

'What was he when you were at college? A boyfriend?'

'Ages ago. It's been over for more than a year.'

'A one-night stand?'

'No – more than that.'

'A long affair, then?'

'It's in the past, Torm. It's not important ... but no, it wasn't a long affair.' She sat up, moved back from me. 'We were together for about a month. Then he dropped out of the course after only a year and a half. He had been offered this tremendous job in Jethra. He told me about it, then left. I didn't think I'd see him again because it was on the mainland. That's when he started sending emails – he wanted me to join him. But Marse is a difficult kind of guy, so I kept saying I wanted to complete my course first. Then the messages became mixed. He seemed to be discouraging me, ignoring me. He had moved to work on an island called Seevl. I discovered that the people who had employed him, an agency called the Intercession Authority, were still hiring. They couldn't find the right people, but my qualification made me ideal for it. Marse changed again, urging me to apply. For a time it was irrelevant – I hadn't finished at college. Then I went to work on Muriseay, but after that went wrong I began wondering if I should try it. Anyway, in the end I did apply. I have to run a preliminary test, and then I'll be told if I've got the job.'

'Which island did you say it was?'

'Seevl.'

'I don't know it. There are so many islands to remember.'

'It's one of the Torquis. Like Hetta, it's close to the Faiand coast, but it's at the other end of the country. Offshore from Jethra. It's only a small island. Marse told me once it's similar to the Tallek: cold climate, short summer, subsistence farming and fishing. Well, the story is that there are some old constructions on Seevl, built hundreds of years ago. No one knows who built them, or what they were for. Most of them are still there but they're falling into ruin. They want to make them safe.'

'I don't see the connection with you.'

'I've been trained in perspective imaging. 3-D visualization. But I couldn't get much sense out of Marse.'

'What does 3-D imaging have to do with making a ruin safe?'

'That's what the test is for. The reason I'm in Ørsknes is because there's a similar ruin in the mountains here. What I have to do is go there as a sort of trial run, use my imaging equipment, write some notes and then they'll have something of mine they can look at. The point is that most of the ruins are only on Seevl, but there's one other that's the same. It's here in the Tallek. It was built at the same time and in the same way. People who apply to work for the Authority usually have to go there first.'

'Where is it?'

'I've been given directions. On my laptop.'

'So why didn't you tell me this before?'

'It didn't seem important until just now.'

We sipped more of the brandy, stopped arguing and enquiring. Alvasund went to the kitchen, made some food for us and we ate it while we sprawled in front of the stove. It was one of those days shaped by the chilly weather, the memory of having been cold while we were outside. Gradually, I began to relax with her again – maybe the brandy helped with that.

Outside it had started to rain, a heavy, steady downpour. I went to one of the windows, wiped a hole in the condensation with my hand and looked out at the dismal view of the street. We could hear the rain in every part of the house, the drumming on the wooden roof, the sheeting noise on the concrete path, the swirling sound as the water coursed away. A sudden onset of rain was supposed to augur the coming end of the Goornak, said to be the spittle of the curse-witch. At least the wind had died.

After we had eaten we sat together on the rug, my arm loosely around Alvasund, resting on the lower part of her back. When the logs settled suddenly, with a bright uprush of sparks, she snuggled affectionately against me.

*

But in spite of all that, when it came to bedtime Alvasund again acted as if a sheet of glass stood between us.

This time I let her take the first shower, so she was lying in the bed by the time I clambered up to join her. I stood naked before her, but she was lying so that she faced away and her eyes were already closed. I slipped into the bed and felt the bolster lying alongside. I left the light on, listening to the rain, to the quiet sound of her breathing. Finally, I turned out the light.

Alvasund said in the dark, 'Would you hold me, Torm?'

'Is that what you'd like?'

'Please.'

She turned over suddenly, sat up, pulled on the bolster and tossed it to the side. Then she lay down again and moved so that she was pressing her naked back against me. I tucked my legs against hers, pressed my face into her hair. I reached over, laid my hand on her stomach. She felt warm, relaxed. After a few moments she took my hand and guided it to her breast.

The rain poured down endlessly on the roof just above us, but in the warmth and security of the house it was almost a reassuring sound. Although I was excited and aroused by holding her like that, I soon drifted off to sleep. Her nipple was a stiff little bud tucked into the space between two of my fingers.

In the night, in the dark, she woke me up, kissing me and caressing me. At last we made love, and I happily imagined invisible shards of glass flying away harmlessly in all directions.

Three days later we drove out of Ørsknes, heading northwards through the mountains on the eastern side of the fjord. The rain had ceased before dawn and the streets of the town were for the first time clear of any snow or ice. The sun was shining in the cold air. The wind had died. Leaving Ørsknes and climbing up to the mountainous hinterland meant we soon crossed the snowline. The higher peaks of the Tallek region often stayed snow-covered long into summer. However, the roads had been cleared of all ice and we were rewarded by one vista after another of the great Tallek skyline, the vast range of peaks under an azure sky. Attendant white clouds clung like ethereal banners to the leeward sides.

Alvasund glanced at the view from time to time, but much of her attention was on her laptop. She was running through the program that built 3-D visualizations, then extrapolated and modelled from a library of artefacts. She had already shown me some of the demo routines: for instance, one in which a single fossil bone could be extrapolated into a complete skeleton of some extinct reptile, and another in which pieces of timber, joined using certain vernacular building techniques, could suggest the outlines of long-vanished buildings. Working with a real artefact was something she had not yet had to do, so as we drove through the mountains she was studying the online manuals and further demos.

We were approaching the northern coast of Goorn and already I had several times glimpsed the calm cold blue of the distant sea. The mountains were less rugged here. We soon crossed down through the snowline into a high area of barren rock and clumps of coarse grasses. We stopped to consult the map that had been sent to Alvasund by the Authority: they had finally authorized her to go ahead and complete the test assignment.

In the event the site was not hard to find. The ruined tower stood on a smooth bluff of land, facing towards the sea above a steep decline. We could see it long before we reached it: a tall, narrow construction of dark stone, all alone, no sign of any other buildings or activity around it.

I parked within walking distance of it. Alvasund gathered her laptop and digitizing equipment from the rear seat and then we sat for a few moments in the car, staring across the moor at the old building. There was something about the tower that gave me a feeling of dread – it was imprecise and irrational, so I said nothing to Alvasund about it.

Wearing our thick coats we strode across the uneven ground, beset by a strong breeze from the sea. I felt the sense of inner unease gradually intensify, but again I said nothing to Alvasund. As we drew closer to the ruin we could see how jagged and cracked were the stone walls, with a large gap near the top on one side – there was a glimpse of some kind of wooden floor or joists within, broken and hanging at an angle. Orange lichen spread across much of the south-facing surface. The tower looked solid but decrepit, the stones dark in the bright sunlight.

Once beside the tower we could see the huge, amazing view of the sea and the rocky coast. Far away on the coastal plain there was a modern road, bearing fast-moving traffic.

'It must have been built as a watch-tower,' I said, looking towards the sea.

'I've been reading about the towers on Seevl,' Alvasund said. 'None of those was built with windows. Just the outer wall and a roof. This is the same design. Whatever they did here, it wasn't to stare at the view.'

'It's giving me the creeps,' I said.

In response Alvasund came towards me and hugged me, her cases and holdalls banging against my arms. 'I feel it too,' she said. 'Let's get on with it.'

She started setting up her equipment. This consisted of a digitizing panoramic viewer on a steadihold bracket, a compiler with an aural sensor on a short mast, and her laptop computer. I helped her into the web of counterbalanced steadihold straps, with the battery pack and the harness for the digitizer. I watched as she booted up the equipment, running the self-test, satisfying herself that she was ready to go.

'I want to try to finish everything in one circuit,' she said. 'Unless you intend to be analysed with everything else you should stay out of range behind me.'

She took a few experimental lines with the digitizer, but the battery pack was in the way of her arm. She took this off and handed it to me.

She began a first circuit of the base of the tower, sidestepping around at an even distance from the masonry of the wall. I stayed with her, carrying the batteries. The ground was broken, with many stone pieces half buried, and in front of the tower there was a steep downward gradient. After she had stumbled a couple of times I held on to the harness at the back, guiding her.

Finally, she said she was ready. I stood close behind her, grasping the battery pack. We were close against the base of the tower and the feeling of unexplained terror was sharper in me than ever before. Alvasund looked pale, her hair blowing around her face.

She started recording, then moved around with a steady sideways step, holding the digitizer trained on the main wall. I shadowed her, warning her whenever a stone or some other obstruction was underfoot.

We completed the take at the first attempt. As she closed the activator a powerful feeling of relief swept over me, that we could soon leave this place.

I walked to the rest of the equipment to collect it up.

Alvasund said, 'We can't go until I've interpreted the image.'

'How long will that take?'

'Not long.'

She downloaded the material from the digitizer to the equalizer, then to the laptop. Nothing seemed to happen for a long time. She and I were standing beside the equipment, face to face, staring at each other. I could see the stress on her face, the anxiety to leave. I had never known anything like this before, a dread without any kind of focus or reason, a blank fright, an unknown terror.

'Torm, there is something inside that place. I could detect it through the viewfinder.' There was a kind of nervy tightness in her voice, newly there, that suddenly scared me.

'What do you mean, something in there?'

'Something alive. Inside the tower. It's huge!' She closed her eyes, shaking her head. 'I want to get away from here. I'm terrified!'

She signalled helplessly towards the electronic equipment, where the online lights were still glittering faintly under the unremitting sunlight.

'What is it? An animal?'

'I can't tell. It's moving about all the time.' Her voice was shrill. 'But it can't be an animal. It's much too big for that.'

'Too big? How big?'

'It fills the whole place.' She reached out a hand towards me, but for some reason I couldn't identify I pulled back from her, not wanting her to touch me. She must have felt something of the same, because in the same instant she snatched her hand back.

270

'It's like an immense coil. Round and round. Against the walls, or inside them somehow.'

Not far from where we were standing was one of the gaps in the masonry at ground level. Through this it was possible to see some of the way inside. I could see a mass of broken stone, brickwork and rotting pieces of timber. Nothing alive was in there, or nothing visibly alive. No coil of anything.

Just then the interpreter completed its run, emitting a brief musical note, and we both turned with a feeling of relief. Alvasund grabbed the laptop.

'Torm, look at this.' She turned the screen around for me to see. 'You can see it now. It's there!'

The sunlight was too bright and I could see hardly anything at all on the monitor. Alvasund kept moving it around, first to put the thing where I could see it, then to move it back so she could. I stood beside her and raised part of my coat to throw a shadow on the display.

What was on the screen looked to me like an ultrasound scan: a monochrome image, slightly blurred, with no guide as to left or right, up or down.

'That's a trace of the wall,' Alvasund said, indicating a large grey patch. 'That jagged line is the broken bit there.' I glanced up and could see how the display matched it. It was a kind of three dimensional X-ray of the interior of the tower ruin.

I looked more closely. There was a ghostly image behind the wall, grey and indistinct, but it was clearly moving. It rippled, a peristaltic thrusting from one side to another, a sort of immense pliable tube, compressing and expanding. There were several such movements, some higher up and only just visible at the top of the screen. The largest area of this horrific movement was close to the ground.

'It's a snake, a serpent!' Alvasund cried. 'Coiled around. In there!'

'But there's nothing. We can see that. It's full of old rubble.'

'No ... it's definitely in there! An immense snake!'

'Something wrong with the software, then?'

'This is what the program does – it picks up traces of viability. It's detecting something viable in there. Look – the thing's *moving*!'

She took a step back, suddenly, knocking the laptop against me. The trace had moved, upwards and across. I imagined a vast reptilian head, eyes and tongue and long fangs, rearing up to strike. I stepped back too, but there was still nothing visible through the small gap in the wall. Nothing there we could confirm with our eyes. Nothing visible, nothing *real*. My terror of it remained.

I was trying to think of an explanation: perhaps there was a cavity wall with something trapped inside. I was scared that if there was something in there that it would break out and come at us.

I took the laptop from Alvasund, turned away to get the best look I could get. I glanced back at her, but discovered that she was no longer standing beside me. Somehow she had moved away. I looked around, but I was alone.

'Alvasund?'

'Torm!'

Her voice sounded faint, all but carried away on the wind. Then I saw her. She was inside the tower!

I could see her dimly through the gap at ground level. She was facing me, calling my name. But no time had passed. Had I blacked out for a few seconds?

I put the laptop roughly on the ground and scrambled across towards her, fighting back the intense feeling of fear. In a few seconds I was there by the gap. I went down on my haunches to squeeze through so I could reach the interior.

The way was blocked. Something hard, transparent, cold, like a pane of thick glass, had been placed over the aperture. Alvasund was there, an arm's length away from me, but she was trapped behind this invisible barrier, inside the tower. She kept shouting my name. I pushed and banged against the glass, uselessly.

She kept on shouting. She had raised her arms, was shaking her head from side to side, and her mouth was turned down in a horrid inverse rictus of fear and pain.

As I watched helplessly, a swift and horrible transformation came over her.

She grew old. She aged before my eyes.

She lost height, gained weight. Instead of her lithe figure contained in bulky winter clothes I saw Alvasund overweight, sagging, unhealthy, thinly clad in some kind of shapeless nightgown. Her hair became grey, lank, greasy, pulled into an untidy plait that rested over one shoulder. Her face became pallid and swollen, with a rash across one cheek. Her eyes were sunk into their sockets, dark-surrounded. Her lips were blue with cyanosis. Saliva smeared her chin, blood ran unabated from a nostril.

She was being held aloft by unseen hands. Her legs were dangling beneath her. She wore black stockings. They had slipped down to reveal blue bulging tangles of varicose veins on her scrawny, pallid calves.

Not understanding, I stumbled back from the gap in the stone-work, tripped over one of the half-buried rocks, rolled to recover, then dived across to where the laptop lay on the ground. Almost not caring what happened, what the consequences might be, I pulled every cable out of it, then fumbled underneath, found the battery, snatched it out of its housing. The instrument died. No image remained on its screen.

I turned to disconnect the interpreter, but as I moved towards it Alvasund was already there! She was outside the tower again, frantically disconnecting cables from the device. I saw her familiar face, the thick windcheater, her warm trousers.

She turned and she saw me.

It was impossible to think of driving but we reached the car some-how, hauling the equipment any way we could. We threw the stuff carelessly on the rear seat, then scrambled in at the front, slamming and locking the doors. We held each other, shaking and trembling. Alvasund's hair fell about her face, hiding her. I could still feel, almost taste, the terrible menace of whatever there was in that ruin.

Alvasund was crying, or so I thought, but when I looked closely at her I realized she was still shaking with fear, her breath coming in shallow gasps, her hands and arms and head trembling con-stantly. I put my arms around her, pulled her close to me and for a long time we were just there together, bulky and awkward in our outdoor clothes, trying to recover from whatever it was that had happened to us.

Through it all the constancy of the dark tower, the dead tower, looming over us.

At last I felt able to start the car's engine, backed away slowly down the track until we were at a safe distance. The tower was out of sight beyond a spur of land.

'What happened to you?' Alvasund said. 'You just vanished suddenly!' Her voice still had the shrill edge I had heard earlier. 'We were there together, and the next thing I knew was that you had somehow moved into the tower itself. I was left outside! I couldn't reach you, or make you hear me!'

'But it was *you* inside the tower,' I said.

'Don't say that! You were in there. I thought you had died.'

The mountain wind was blustering against the side of the car.

Eventually I was able to tell her what I had seen. Eventually she told me what she had seen.

We had had identical but opposite experiences. Each of us had seemed to appear before the other, transported somehow into the broken tower interior.

Alvasund said, 'You suddenly looked old and ill, and – I couldn't get to you.'

'How old, how ill?'

'I saw – I can't say!'

Remembering her, remembering the image of her inside the tower, I said, 'You thought I was about to die.'

'You were already dead. It looked like, I don't know, some horrible accident. I could see blood all over your head – I was trying to get in to help you, but there was a sheet of something in the way, a piece of thick glass or plastic blocking the gap. I couldn't get past it. I turned around to get a stone or something. I was going to try to bash my way through. Then suddenly you were outside again.'

'And suddenly you were outside.'

'What the hell happened, Torm?'

I could not answer that and neither could she. The one certainty was that that psychic image of Alvasund in the final moments of her life would haunt me for ever.

*

274

We returned to Ørsknes.

Everything about us had changed because of what happened at the tower, although we did not admit it to each other. Suddenly it felt as if we had known each other for years. The urgency of learning about and of trying to attract each other had receded. We were still in the first days of our relationship together, a time when new lovers feel endlessly curious about each other, but our curiosity had died. We knew more than we should. The knowledge was awful. It was a subject which remained unspoken, unexamined. We simply understood it, and always found it too awful to put into words.

So the words were never said and the knowledge we had of each other was never admitted, but it did make us closer, it bound us with its terrible secret. The fearful memory of the tower loomed over us both.

A short period of inertia followed. We were uncertain whether we should return to Goorn Town, or stay on in Ørsknes until Alvasund received a response of some kind. She had gone ahead and sent in her notes with the recorded results of the test, but there was no reply from either the Authority or Marse. Marse himself appeared not to be in Ørsknes any more. When he made no contact after Alvasund emailed him, we tried to find him in the town. He had said he worked in the Authority office, but we had never seen such a place. We traced it to one of the buildings near the wharves. There were no lights on and the door was closed and locked.

It was tempting to return home, but Alvasund said that if she was appointed she wanted to take up the job straight away. Goorn Town was at the wrong end of the island for ferries to Jethra.

Outside, the spring thaw commenced, the little town sprucing itself up for the summer. We saw more people walking through the streets, and winter shutters and shelters were put away. Alvasund and I concentrated on each other, saying nothing but doing what we could.

Then came news of Alvasund's appointment.

It was six days after our experience at the tower, in mid-evening. We were both sleepy and we were planning to go to bed early.

When I had taken my shower and I climbed up to the sleeping loft, Alvasund was sitting on the mattress before her laptop, her legs crossed, apparently reading something online. She said nothing, so I lay on the bed beside her.

'I've been offered the job,' she said at last, and turned the screen around so that I could see it.

She scrolled the display. It was a formal letter from the Intercession Authority, based in the city of Jethra on the Faiand mainland. The writer said they had examined carefully all current applications for the vacant position of perspective viability modeller. Alvasund's qualifications closely matched their requirements. As they urgently needed to fill the vacancy, they were prepared to offer her a probationary appointment at fifty per cent of the advertised salary, provided she accepted immediately. If her work was satisfactory, the position would be made permanent and her salary would be topped up and backdated to the full amount.

'Congratulations!' I said. 'I assume you still want the job?'

'Oh yes. But read the rest and tell me what you think.'

The writer insisted that she must read again the original prospectus, and also read the conditions of employment below. There was a reminder that the work could be hazardous, that they would provide all statutory liability insurance, accident and interment insurance, and a guarantee. All these details required her assent.

'You're going to go through with this?' I said.

'I need the money, and the work is what I'm good at.'

'But after what happened?'

'Have you any idea what that was?'

'No.'

'The whole rationale of this job is that it's the first properly funded scientific investigation into what's inside those towers.'

'Are you sure you want to know?'

She stared at me for a moment, with a familiar forthrightness.

'I'll never get another chance like this again.'

'Doesn't it worry you, what happened when we went to the tower?'

'Yes.' She looked disturbed by my questions, or irritated, and for a moment she shrugged her shoulder up and against me, half

turning away. 'Maybe it's different on Seevl,' she said, but uncon-
vincingly. She scrolled the image on the screen again. 'I had only
read the first two pages before you came upstairs.'

I moved so that I squatted beside her. Together we read through
all the material the Authority had sent.

Alvasund indicated a paragraph at the end. Here was a claim
about recent developments. It said that it had become possible for
researchers to approach the towers in much greater safety than
before, enabling them to be protected from the psychic activity
that appeared to emanate from within the tower. There was also an
effective physical defence.

'If it's as safe as all that,' I said, 'why do they make all the other
warnings about hazard?'

'They're just trying to cover themselves. They must know what
the risks are, and they have come up with a way of protecting
against them.'

'Yes, but they don't say how.'

I was thinking about the 'psychic activity', in the words of the
document, that had 'appeared to emanate' from within the tower
we had been to. Like a remembered feeling of pain, it was hard to
imagine later how bad it had been, but the relief that I was away
from it was like a gift of freedom. I could not imagine ever willingly
surrendering to it again.

We read on.

The final document was an illustrated history of the towers on
Seevl, and what investigations of them had been made in the past.
According to what we read, there were more than two hundred
towers still standing. All were approximately the same age and all
had been damaged in the past, presumably by islanders trying to
demolish them. None of the towers was undamaged, and there had
never been any attempt to restore them. There were a few sites
where a tower had once stood, but had been successfully brought
down.

All the remaining towers were dangerous to approach and the
ordinary people of Seevl never went near them. Many myths and
superstitions had grown up, the towers widely regarded as supernatural in origin. They were often used as symbols of dread or

repression in Seevl literature and art. There were countless folkloric accounts of giants, mysterious paw-prints, nighttime visitations, loud screams, lights in the sky and alleged sightings of large or slithering beasts.

Past scientific investigations had invariably failed to produce reliable information, but out of the almost invariably hectic accounts that followed contact a consensus had emerged. Each tower appeared to be occupied by, or at least was a habitat of, some kind of living being or intelligence. No one had ever seen what it was. No one had any idea how such a being might survive, feed or reproduce. The sense of morbid fear, endured by all researchers, suggested a form of defensive or even entrapping psychic emanation, emitted by whatever was inside.

'Are you certain you want this job?' I said.

'Yes. It terrifies me, but – why does it worry you?'

'I'll be there with you.'

She was in my arms, suddenly. I had sensed that the appointment, if she accepted it, would cause us to split up. They wanted an instant decision, which meant by tomorrow morning at the latest. If I did not commit to her, she would travel to Seevl, I would return to Goorn Town, and from there, eventually, to Ia. We should probably not see each other again. This felt like a parting forced on us by circumstance, not choice. We were still too new to each other to feel a sense of emotional momentum that would carry us through a separation. I did not want to lose her.

So we made love. The screen of the laptop glowed on the floor beside the bed, the words of the job offer radiated unregarded into the night. Afterwards, we sat up again, feeling tired but now wakeful. Alvasund typed at the keyboard for a while, then showed me the message she was about to send.

It was an acceptance of the job on the terms being offered. She added in her message that she would depart from Ørsknes the following day, and would arrive in Jethra as soon as possible. She informed them that I would be travelling and staying with her, and that we would require accommodation for us both.

'May I send it?' she said.

*

She sent it, and afterwards we were charged up and feeling loving and lazy and aroused, so we made love again. We slept. In the morning we carried our property to the car, cleaned and locked up the house, dropped the key off at the Authority office (still closed), then we drove away towards the coast.

We followed the road that ran alongside the fjord, the mountains meeting the calm waters of the deep inlet at an almost vertical angle – the road was carved out of the side of the mountains, with sections of it on piles built out from the rock or standing in the sea. In other places there were short tunnels drilled through spurs and promontories. Alvasund loved tunnels and talked again about Jordenn Yo.

We passed through Omhuuv, finally reaching the coast at the islet-strewn mouth of the fjord. We drove east along the coast road, heading for the ferry port we knew was somewhere on the north-eastern corner of the island. Soon we glimpsed the dead tower we had visited, standing back from the sea on its rise of high ground, black stone, a fractured outline, bare, blighted earth around it in every direction. It was too far away from the road to exert its influence, or so we believed, but even so the mere sight of the gaunt edifice gave us a thrill of familiar dread.

We were soon past it, out of sight of it, on a main highway with traffic flowing swiftly in both directions. This was the modern world, a place of industry and clerks and bankers and scientists, of trucks and policier patrol vehicles and motorcycles, a world where the ether was busy with radio exchanges, wireless communications, digital networks, not the psychic tendrils of ancient or supernatural evil.

We played music on the car radio, took a long lunch at an inn on a hill overlooking the sea, and carried on towards the port.

On arrival we discovered we had just missed a sailing to Jethra. The next ferry did not leave for two days. We stayed overnight in a small hotel, but then learnt that to travel to Jethra we needed exit and entry visas. Jethra is the capital of Faiand, one of the mainland combatant powers, officially and actually in a state of war. To travel from our neutral territory required permission from Goorn to leave the Archipelago, and permission from the Jethran administration to disembark.

Three days were lost while we trawled around between the Faiand High Commission and the Hettan Seigniory Office. I was the problem, the main cause of the official enquiries – Alvasund had a job to go to, I was merely her companion. She began to fret at the delay. Messages went to and fro between her and the Authority.

We took a ferry to Cheoner, having been told there was an airport, but when we were halfway there we learned there had been a marine collision between one of the ships and a dredger. Many lives had been lost. Ferry services in and out of Cheoner were suspended.

We disembarked at the small island of Cheoner Ante, waited and waited. Two days later, when I think Alvasund had almost given up hope, everything fell into place. The ferries were sailing again – exit visas were available at the Seigniory office on Cheoner. We should be able to get a flight from there the following day. Against all our despondent expectations, seats on the aircraft were available, it took off on time, did not crash, climbed surprisingly high above the islands to take advantage of the temporal distortions, and within an hour was landing in Jethra.

We walked out of the airport into a hilly, forested terrain bathed in sunshine, caught a modern streetcar to the city centre, and after a long journey through many of the residential suburbs and newly built business departments of Jethra, astonishing us both – neither of us had been in such a huge city before – we located the downtown building where the Intercession Authority was based, and went inside.

The island of Seevl dominated the view to the south of the city, its long grey-green bulk hogging the horizon and seeming to produce the effect of an inland sea. Its high range of undulating moorland created a feeling of enclosure across the wide bay. The city faced across to the north side of the island, which was permanently in shade.

Jethra itself was built on a river delta, with level ground in the immediate vicinity of the main channel of the river and its distributaries, but with gentle hill country further away at the edges of the former flood-plain. We found that the way most Jethra people spoke was urbane, sophisticated and full of allusions that we struggled to understand or respond to properly. From the occasional remark we heard or overheard I realized many of the Jethrans we met found our island way of speaking, or our island outlook, charming but quaint. All the preconceptions I had formed about Faiandland over the years were gently subverted away.

Much of our island outlook was created by the presence of wars, in fact by these Jethran people's wars, as well as our islander habit of turning away from those who transited the Archipelago on the way to battle. I had formed a general impression that everyone in the north lived in countries ruled and dominated by military or extremist régimes, that their freedoms of movement or speech were curtailed, that armed troops daily marched through the streets, that they lived in joyless barrack cities or wasted away in camps in bleak or remote countryside.

While Alvasund was getting to know her co-workers, and training on the elaborate new equipment they would be using, I had plenty of time to wander alone through the streets of this war-mongering place. I found a busy, productive city, with wide streets and thousands of trees, a modern high-rise business section, a huge number of ancient buildings and palaces, but around the docks I saw areas that had been recently devastated, presumably by bombing. Other parts of Jethra appeared to have been untouched by the war. There was an artists' quarter I returned to almost every day.

In Jethra I became conscious of a sense of unending terrain: island life imbues in you an awareness of the edge, the shore, the littoral, the adjacent lives on other islands, but in Jethra I felt instead the lure of distance, of places I could travel to and people I could meet without crossing a sea, and an endlessly unfolding world of certainty. Islands lacked that. Islands gave an underlying feeling of circularity, of coast, a limit to what you could achieve or where you might go. You knew where you were but there was invariably a sense that there were other islands, other places to be. I loved the Archipelago but living for a while on a continental mass, albeit the rim of a continent, gave me a new and enthralling feeling of possibility. However, there was little time to explore the sensation.

Alvasund's induction was being fast-tracked. The team to which she had been assigned was the last to set out from Jethra – they had been waiting for her while we lost time on Goorn and Cheoner Ante, waiting for boats and visas. The other three teams had already transferred to their bases on Seevl, reporting back as they made preliminary surveys of some of the towers, and conducted tests on the equipment, all at safe distances.

Then the day came when we too were to depart for Seevl. I was more nervous about the prospect of this than Alvasund. She said it was because she was involved in the work, had responsibilities and co-workers and a purpose. I supposed this meant that I had had time to think, and when I did I thought about where she was going and what she was likely to be doing. I was filled with a deep sense of dread for her. I could never forget that fugitive glimpse of Alvasund's final moments of life, projected to me by the presumed living entity that now she was about to investigate – or to intercede with, in the jargon they used.

I needed something to involve me. I did not enjoy hanging around doing nothing while Alvasund was so active. In short, I wished I could find a job, but I was feeling indecisive about that. There were plenty of jobs available in Jethra, and with time I could probably find something that not only suited me but which I would do well. That, however, would place me permanently in Jethra, whereas I wanted to be with Alvasund on Seevl. Everyone I spoke to said jobs were scarce on the island, a place that had been depopulating for many years, and whose economy was mostly at subsistence level.

I wondered if I should make contact with the glass resources laboratory in Ia Town. They were still technically my employers but they now seemed half a world away. I was still trying to decide when Alvasund told me we would be sailing to Seevl the following day.

I had already met the other members of her team: six young

people, four men and two women. They were all graduates. One had a master's degree in psychology, another in geomorphology, another in biochemistry, and so on. The team leader, a woman called Ref, was a doctor of medicine, specializing in vascular anomaly. Alvasund was the only one of the team from an arts background, but her skills in imaging, perspective building and active viability put her second in the team, behind Ref.

Marse too was working in the Authority headquarters building – we were surprised to see him the day after our arrival. Both Alvasund and I were shocked by the change in his appearance. It was only a couple of weeks since that brief meeting on the street in Ørsknes, yet he looked haggard, neurotic, shrunken. He recognized neither of us, even though Alvasund made an effort to sit down with him and speak to him. He barely said a word, would not meet her gaze and answered her questions in subdued monosyllables.

Later Alvasund told me she asked Ref what had happened to him. Ref said that in the previous year Marse was on one of the teams who went to Seevl to carry out preliminary surveys of the towers. At that time, intercession workers were not provided with protective gear. He had been taken off the work when he showed the first signs of psychosis. The Authority staff found him alternative work to do while his condition was assessed – his posting to Ørsknes had been one of these jobs, but his health was now deteriorating rapidly. They were waiting for a place to come free for him at a neuropathology hospital.

'Do they know what he's suffering from?' I asked Alvasund.

She simply stared straight at me, without saying anything. Then I held her to me.

'It won't happen again,' she said. 'Not now. We have protective gear, probably because of what happened to Marse.'

'It's dangerous,' I said. 'Must you go through with this?'

'Yes,' she said.

The next day, early morning, we were driven to the harbour passenger terminal in an Authority bus, all of us on edge, anticipating, excited, perhaps fearful. I was the only extra person on the team: everyone else had come without their partners.

We transferred to a launch for the trip across to Seevl, although first we had to go through exit formalities. Expecting this to be merely a technicality the group of us entered the border control building in lighthearted mood, but as we tried to pass through the exit channel we were delayed. The officials took a particular interest in Alvasund and myself because we were discovered to be Archipelagian nationals. The officials were suspicious of why we had visited the mainland for such a short time. How had we obtained permission to leave the Archipelago and why now were we departing, and did we intend to make more short trips to and fro across the international border?

They eventually accepted that Alvasund was a paid employee of the Authority, which they appeared never to have heard of, but which qualified her for an exit visa. They wondered aloud and lengthily about who I was, who was paying me, what my intentions were. My role was in their terms undefined. The interrogation, masked in a false bonhomie, seemed to go on for ever. Nothing I told them in answer to their questions seemed acceptable to them.

However, we were all in the end cleared for departure. We walked down through a maze of stairways and passages, finally emerging on the harbour apron. A steel-grey launch was tied up alongside, where our crates and cases were being loaded via a system of conveyor belts. There was a short delay while that was completed. When everything had been stowed below-decks the captain started the engines and the boat moved quickly away from the quay. I saw Ref leaving the wheelhouse. She went to the cabin below, where the others were.

Alvasund and I remained on the upper deck. We both anticipated the presence of islands. We sat together close to the prow, staring ahead at Seevl's dark bulk.

From Jethra, even from the hotel situated in the centre of the business section of the city, well back from the coast, Seevl had seemed to be so close that it loomed against the city, but once we had eased out past the harbour wall into the choppier waters of the open sea, the island was no longer an oppressive sight. It now looked to be just another island, one of the hundreds Alvasund and I had each passed or sailed close to at different moments in our lives. It was true that the cliffs seemed greyer and steeper than those we normally saw, and that there was a fringe of white breakers around every part of the rocky shore, but to our eyes there was something familiar about it.

The only port on the island was Seevl Town, positioned at the head of a narrow inlet on the south-western corner. While we were staying in the hotel in Jethra I had examined a chart which was in a display panel in the reception area and I knew that to reach the port from Jethra entailed rounding a series of rocky cliffs and landslips called Stromb Head. Once we approached the cliffs in the launch it was apparent there had been many rockfalls over the years. The debris had created a series of shallow shoals stretching a long way out into the sea. A wide diversion was necessary. Also, I knew from the chart that the seas were often rough around Stromb because of a conflict of tides. The shape of the island caused a flow to north and south of it and the two tidal surges met up again near Stromb.

The launch we were in was a modern, stabilized boat, which moved smoothly and quickly through the waves. Standing next to Alvasund on the foredeck, I started to enjoy the voyage, with a pleasant sensation that I was regaining my sea legs after so long on solid ground. The high sides of the deck protected us from much of the headwind. As the boat finally turned past Stromb, it heeled over more sharply than we expected, the high superstructure catching the wind like a pair of sails. The skipper increased the engine revs and started to push at an angle into the waves, cutting directly through the swell.

The launch turned into the inlet almost before we realized we had reached it. The gap in the cliffs was unexpectedly narrow, although once we were through the sea-opening the waters widened and there was room to manoeuvre. The swell here was moderate – the skipper throttled back the engine. Seevl Town was in sight almost at once, a small township, ranked in terraces around the steep and hilly sides of the inlet, predominantly grey like the rocks on which it stood. We chugged smoothly towards it.

'Torm!' A sharp intake of breath. Alvasund gripped my upper arm.

She pointed across to the northern shore of the inlet. There stood one of the towers, dark and dilapidated, built on the steep slope of the cliff so that it commanded most of the waters. It did not break the skyline.

We looked around in all directions. I soon spotted another of the towers, this one on the southern shore, again overlooking the town but not high enough to stand out against the sky.

Behind us, Ref and the rest of the team were coming up to the deck from below. They too moved to the rail of the boat and gazed up at the surrounding steep walls of the inlet. Between us we had soon counted eight of the towers, looming over the little town like a series of radio masts. The fact that they appeared to have been built low, so they did not rise above the level of the cliffs, gave them a clustered, covert quality that added to the sense of menace.

Ref, through her binoculars, described each of the towers, distinguishing them expertly. She used an alphanumeric identifier, which one of the men noted carefully on his digital pad. He read back each code for confirmation. Some of the towers were cylindrical, tapering towards the top, while others, believed to be from an older period, were square in plan. There was one tower which looked at first sight to be another circular one, but Ref said it was one of the more unusual octagonal buildings. One of the men, standing beside me, said there were known to be only nine of the octagonal towers on Seevl, but all of them were better preserved than the others.

I said nothing about it to Alvasund at that moment, knowing we would have time alone later, but the closer the launch moved us towards the town, and the deeper we penetrated into the inlet, the more I felt the creeping sense of disquiet. The impression that the towers had been put up deliberately to surround or confine the town was one thing, but I was also suffering an all too familiar mental or psychic feeling, a reminder of our frightening experience in the mountains around Ørsknes. It was as if an odourless gas had been released into the narrow inlet around Seevl Town, one that numbed the mind and induced fear.

Alvasund's hand tightened in mine. I glanced at her face – her jaw was set, the tendons in her neck stood out with strain.

The boat docked. Thankful to have something active to do, we busied ourselves with unloading our baggage and the equipment the team would be using. The modern dock facilities used in Jethra had no equivalent here, so everything had to be carried ashore by hand. No one said anything but there was a new quietness that had fallen on us as a group.

The town was still, almost free of traffic. No one seemed curious about us as we clustered on the quay with our baggage. People walked by slowly, their faces averted, not acknowledging us. The stiff wind had become a light breeze now we were ashore. I was oppressed by the sense of gloom and fearfulness, I felt no interest in our surroundings, and above all I no longer wished to look any further or higher than the ground around me. I was in terror of what lay above, but I did not know what it was.

Ref said that the cars that were planned to rendezvous with us at the dock had not for some reason been sent, and she went to the harbour office to find out what had happened. Eventually she returned, complaining that it was almost impossible to get a cellular signal on this island. We stood indecisively, but a few minutes later two large vehicles did arrive to collect us.

It turned out that because Alvasund and I were travelling together we had been allocated to another Authority-owned property, a small apartment some distance from the central harbour but close to the water. This turned out to be to our advantage. After a long delay the others had to move temporarily into rooms over a bar in the centre of the town. There was supposed to be a larger building available, operated by the Authority, specially built and equipped for a long stay, but neither Ref nor anyone else knew how to find it. The representative from the Authority, supposedly at the dock to greet us, had not appeared. Seevl already seemed to us a place permanently in disarray, running on half power.

The moment we entered our apartment and closed the door behind us, the sensation of dread abruptly lifted. It was so abrupt, so noticeable that we reacted simultaneously to it. It was like the sensation of air pressure being released as a plane descended: a relief, a clearing up, a removal of a background sensation.

We quickly explored the apartment, exclaiming at the sense of new freedom.

'The building must be shielded,' Alvasund said, when we had looked into both main rooms and dumped our luggage in the bedroom. 'After everything else, I wasn't counting on it. But I was told Authority buildings here were supposed to have been screened. It seems they did it.'

'What about the others?'

'They'll be all right for one night.'

When we had unpacked some of our things we ate the food we had brought. We sat together at the cramped fold-out table in the kitchenette. The window there looked over the water, not far below us. Outside it had started to rain, a mist drifting up the inlet from the direction of the sea. We kept remarking on the feeling of relief inside the apartment, the welcome sense of normality.

Alvasund showed me what she said was the material they were using as a shield against the psychic emissions from the towers. It had been placed hard against each of the windows, but it was also possible to see that it extended to each side, and above and below, an unseen layer concealed within the walls.

Alvasund said the material was some kind of plastic, but the moment I looked at it closely I suddenly realized what it was. It was neither plastic nor conventional glass, but a sort of non-metallic alloy created by fusing a number of polymers with glass crystals. In other words it was BPSG, polymerized borophosphosilicate glass, closely similar to the material I had been working with on Ia. It was made so that it remained transparent, and could be used instead of conventional glass. It was also a powerful transducer of energy. When you touched it there was a feeling of tough resilience, like hard rubber, almost impossible to break or shatter, although it could be moulded.

I looked more closely at the BPSG that had been used in the apartment. I touched it again and peered at it by leaning down so that the light from the sky was refracted through it. I saw a faint web of tell-tale halation, a misting of the transparency. This would be normally undetectable in use, caused by the many layers of molecular mini-circuitry within, and visible only at certain oblique angles. The variant we had been experimenting with on Ia was to enable high-energy waves to be collected, condensed, then amplified. Practical applications were yet to be designed, although we were funded by two major electronics companies. We had been experimenting with polarization of the glass at the time I left.

Ever since the incident at the tower on Goorn the thought had been nagging at me that maybe that kind of glass, suitably polarized and strengthened, could be used to divert, transduce or even block whatever those terrifying emanations might be. Now I realized that someone else, working for the Intercession teams, must have had the same idea.

After we had eaten, and because there was still time before we were supposed to meet up with the others, we lay down on the bed and rested. It was good to be there together, undisturbed, affectionate and relaxed.

Neither of us wanted to leave the apartment, return to the unshielded streets outside, but finally we went in search of the rest of the team. We walked through the narrow streets and alleys of Seevl Town, already gripped by the horrible feeling of psychic dread, but because we knew there would be an escape from it when we returned to the flat we could put up with it.

We saw how decrepit most of the town appeared – there was none of the sense of industry and purposeful activity that we had seen in Ørsknes, let alone the thriving metropolis of Jethra. Most of the buildings had been constructed from the dark grey local stone. They looked thick and solid, perhaps an attempt to shut out the pervading gloom. They were also shabby. The windows and doors were narrow, with makeshift shutters and blinds. Galvanized iron sheets were laid roughly against many of the entrances.

There seemed to be no wildlife – we heard no birds, not even the gulls which were otherwise found in every port in the Archipelago. When we went down to the quay we saw that the water of the inlet had an oily, lifeless look to it, as if the fish too were repelled by the emanations from the towers.

I began to think that I would find it difficult living in such a place for long, at least without the shielding, but I said nothing of this to Alvasund.

We found the building where the rest of the team was staying overnight, and as I had suspected there was no shielding. The building was just a normal town bar, clearly on the point of going out of business. The team members were stoical about the arrangement, as they had made contact with the Authority and would be moving the next day.

Gloomily we walked with the rest of the team through the town in search of somewhere we could find a meal; worriedly we ate it; and afterwards we dispersed with unenthusiastic farewells.

Once Alvasund and I were in our apartment again, though, our spirits lifted with the closing of the door. It was like shaking off the memory of fog, or removing a bulky garment. In fact, we threw off all our clothes and went straight to bed.

In the morning Alvasund dressed for work. She took out overalls and gauntlets, and so on, from one of the large cartons we had brought with us. The garments were made of heavy fabric, camo green. She put these on over her own clothes, becoming shapeless. Finally, she pulled on a large helmet, which I took at first glance to be made of metal. It covered her entire head as well as her throat and neck. It had a glass visor, which she snapped down over her face, then she tilted her head in a familiar gesture, suggesting she would like me to kiss her. I went across to her, smiling at what she was doing.

She flipped open the visor, and tapped it.

'I'm protected,' she said.

'You're completely beyond reach!' I said, groping unsuccessfully across her cumbersome garments, and trying to push my mouth through the narrow slot to kiss her.

'You know what I mean,' she said.

I looked closely at the visor, and saw that it was made of the polymerized BPSG. I held her as affectionately as her thick clothing would allow.

'Don't take risks, Alvasund,' I said.

'I think I know what I'm doing. The others certainly do.' She drew back from me. Then she added, 'I want you to do something for me.'

'What?'

'All my friends call me Alvie. From now, today, tonight, for ever, I want you to call me that too.'

'You may call me Torm,' I said.

'I already do.'

She snapped down the protective visor, smiled at me through the transductive glass, and walked with wide and awkward steps to the stairs that led down to the road.

I gave her another clumsy hug, and then she was gone. When she was outside I watched her through the window of the apartment as she stood by the side of the street. Soon enough the Authority vehicle appeared with the others aboard, and they drove away towards the edge of town.

I began to feel trapped in that apartment in Seevl Town. Although Alvie returned every day, sometimes early, halfway through the afternoon, and she was as loving and physical with me as ever, inevitably our lives were drifting slowly away from each other. I was alone almost every day. Although there were, or I obtained, the usual distractions, like books, internet access, films, music, it was still a fact that I could only leave when I felt able to brave the psychic aura that drifted around the town. I had no other protection than the discreetly glazed walls of the building. There was no work I could do beyond maintaining distant electronic contact with my former colleagues on Ia.

Alvie rarely talked about the work they were doing, but as they settled into what I assumed were routines she and the others always referred to it as 'decommissioning'. One day a small freighter arrived in the harbour. A heavy tractor, the kind of thing used in demolition jobs, was unloaded. It bore Authority markings. The driver took it clattering and smoking through the narrow streets and up into the hills away from town.

For me, the weird threat of the towers was gradually being re-placed by a more comprehensible longing. In short I was missing the outdoor life I had enjoyed in the subtropical warmth of Ia. My early background on Goorn had created in me an inward habit, one of staying at home, keeping warm, spending time alone, but I had found, a few years earlier when I arrived on Ia, that I much preferred those benign sea winds, the open spaces and cooling heights, the tangled forests, the hotly glittering seas.

Soon I took to walking every day on Seevl, at first simply for the needed change of environment, then later with increasing interest in the area around the town. Of course, unprotected, unshielded, I took the full force of the psychic emanations from the towers, but I discovered that it was possible to get used to them. I realized that they weren't targeted exclusively on me and after that I could almost ignore them. I also carried the knowledge that at the end of my excursion there was a shielded home sanctuary in which normality would return, not to speak of a happy physical affair with an attractive young woman.

I relished my daily walks, felt myself coming alive again, and a feeling of physical well-being was growing in me. My senses were developing – I felt as if I was seeing, hearing, tasting better than I had ever done before.

After two or three weeks of these long walks, I was hardly noticing the sense of dread. In fact, I so much enjoyed striding across the blustery high moors, with the racing skies, the blown coarse grasses, the stunted brambles and clammy mosses, that any mood induced by the dead towers was easily overlooked.

One day, clambering through hills a fair distance inland of the town, I noticed deep and parallel clayey furrows left by caterpillar tracks, and I realized that I must be close to one of the places where Alvie and her decommissioning team had been working.

I wandered up the slope, following the tracks, interested to see what might be there.

I came eventually to a shallow declivity, a way down from the local summit of a rising moor, exactly the sort of site where the towers were usually placed. I could see no sign of any tower ahead of me as I walked, but this was soon explained. I came to an area where the ground was torn and furrowed by the repeated movements of the heavy machine.

Dark bricks lay all around, some of them broken by the violent act of demolition, but many more of them intact. I walked around the site, looking at the ground, the view, the glimpse of the sea that could be distantly made out. I sensed no concentration or intensity of the psychic emanation. I assumed that Alvie and Ref and the others must have succeeded in removing whatever entity or force there might have been. It just looked and felt like a place where an old building once existed.

In the centre of the rubble I saw a series of deep channels, trenches, arranged in an octagonal shape.

When I was back in the peace of the apartment that night I said nothing to Alvie about this. She was in a quiet mood, and later, when Ref came to visit, I overheard the two women talking quietly about the need to take a short break from the work.

Alvie said at one point, in a hushed voice, 'I think it's getting to me at last.' Ref replied softly, obviously not realizing that even in the next room I could hear her whispered words, 'Two of the guys have requested a trip to the mainland.' And Alvie said, 'Then I would come too.' Ref: 'What about Torm?' Alvie said, 'I think he likes it here.'

That night she and I made exuberant love.

But the next day, as soon as Alvie had been picked up by the team transporter, I put on my walking clothes and set out for the site of the demolished tower.

The fallen bricks had not been on the ground long enough for them to become embedded in the thin soil and therefore difficult to move. They were heavy, of course, and hard on my hands, but if I moved one brick at a time and rested for a few moments afterwards, it was a practicable task.

When I took a break in the middle of the day I had succeeded in returning many of the bricks to the octagonal trench, the original base of the wall. As I had hefted each one in, it felt so right and natural that every brick seemed to slip willingly into its place. By the end of that day, one row of bricks, neatly octagonal, was just visible above the surface of the ground, giving the semblance of a deliberate construction.

I returned to the tower day after day, intent only on working with the bricks that were mostly undamaged. I had no means of mortaring them, so I had to find a way of resting each new brick so securely that it would hold firm – in practice, the bricks seemed eager to nestle once more with the others.

Soon the octagonal tower stood slightly higher than myself, and I had used nearly all the intact bricks I had found lying on the ground.

I stood back from the new building, looked at it critically, walked around it, admired the view of the valley and the distant sea it commanded.

Then I clambered over the wall, and for the first time I stood within.

I was surrounded by the tower's walls. I could see nothing outside. There was only the endless wind, the rushing sound of blown grasses. I sat down, stood up again, stretched out my arms to see if I could straddle the interior with both my hands.

Then I sat down again, until it began to be dark.

Of course I returned the next day, and every day after, climbing over the wall, taking up my position inside the octagonal compartment, listening to the unceasing moorland winds. I liked to sit, but I also liked to raise myself up to see over the wall, to regard the area of the island my tower was covering. It frustrated me that I could not both sit down and see outside, but after a while a solution became obvious to me.

Amongst the rubble of bricks left behind by the tractor were several heavy wooden beams, clearly once used as joists or supports. If I were to make an aperture in one of the walls, used a beam to support the bricks above, then a crude window would be possible. I could afterwards crouch silently within, looking out at the view.

For that I would require glass, not only to shield myself from the constant winds, but to give me a way of concentrating the sensations that poured through me whenever I went inside. I was thrilled by the idea, and also by the other thoughts I was having. My sensations were constantly expanding. Whenever I was inside the tower I felt I could see everything, hear everything, within me and without, past, present and future.

That night I went to the Authority's works depot in the town, and there I found several sheets of the special shielding glass. I chose a piece of suitable size, concealed it overnight close to our apartment.

It had been many days since Alvie had left for Jethra with Ref and the others. It would be many more days before she came back. Now I barely thought of her.

The next day I carried the glass up to the moors, dreaming about how I might fix it in place, planning how to use it, imagining the concentration of my thoughts and senses emanating from the tower, intensified, condensed, enhanced, transduced and transformed by the polymerized material, a psychic triumph, a focus of all fears and hopes.

There in my tower behind the glass I would wait patiently for Alvie's return. I had much to tell her about, much to show her, from the past, in the present and into the future.

Sentier

HIGH / BROTHER

SENTIER is a semi-arid island in the sub-tropical region of the southern Midway Sea. It is dominated by the cone of an immense extinct volcano, whose name in island patois renders not only as HIGH (the island's local name), but also as BROTHER. The island is short of natural resources, and there is a constant scarcity of drinking water. Large storage cisterns can be seen all over the landscape, especially in the drier uplands. In summer the island is beset by a hot wind from the equatorial north, the ROSOLINO. This was once the strumpet wind of the south-eastern spice trade, ruthlessly used by mariners but never trusted, but in the age of modern shipping the Rosolino brings aridity and dust to the islands it sweeps disdainfully across.

Because of its remoteness and the liberal attitudes of the inhabitants, Sentier is favoured by the backpack generation. There are many cheap hotels and food places along the strip and around the port in Sentier City. In this transient population, the young men and women who are deserters from the war find a congenial and safe environment. Sentier has permissive attitudes towards the use of alcohol and recreational drugs, and has allowed all havenic laws to fall into disuse.

Sentier City is a city only in name: the harbour is quiet and utilitarian, with a small area set aside as a marina for visitors. Fishing goes on, but in a desultory fashion. There is little trade with other islands, although because of its rich volcanic soil Sentier wines are popular and bring in much currency.

Most conventional visitors and tourists head inland, to the small town of Cuvler. Here there are unusual ruins: Sentier was purged during the first Federation invasion, and all the then-inhabitants were either taken as hostages or liquidated. This was of course before the making of the Covenant. The troops were soon removed under treaty and the island was eventually repopulated, but much of the old flavour of the town has long gone. There was once a thriving artists' colony in Cuvler, and the small area of the town, close to the desiccated banks of Sentier's sole river, where the houses and studios were once occupied, is now a protected zone. It is open to visitors. There is an excellent museum and gallery which displays the best surviving examples of the work from the early days, as well as more recent work, including a large but mediocre Bathurst: *The Coming of the Revenger*. Some of the ruined buildings in the Old Town also contain fragments of artwork.

Oddly, for such a remote and in many ways primitive island, Sentier has a worldwide reputation in the sciences and in medicine, and all this is to be found in Cuvler.

It was in Cuvler that the astronomer PENDIK MUDURNU was born, and it was he who set in motion the thirty-year project to build the world's largest optical telescope on the lip of the crater of the mountain. Mudurnu himself lived long enough to use the main Brother reflector, and subsequently the existence of the telescope has led to the building of many more observatories on the summit of the mountain, and the installation of instruments of every kind. The presence on this island of the Brother centre, and all the various comings and goings of scientists and visitors, has underwritten the prosperity of the region for many years.

Illustrious sons of Sentier include the mime artiste Commis, murdered by unknown assailants during one of his performances, and the author and philosopher Visker Deloinne.

The island flower is the quadrifoil, which manages to thrive in spite of the arid conditions on the island, and whose pretty yellow sepals have hallucinogenic attributes after drying and curing.

Currency: Archipelagian simoleon, Aubracian talent.

SIFF

WHISTLING ONE

Although its location is known and certain, and there are several tour operators who will transport you to the site, no living person has ever seen Siff. It is an island unique in the Dream Archipelago, because it is the only one completely destroyed by its inhabitants. The last traces of Siff sank beneath the waves more than a hundred and twenty-five years ago. All that remains is a huge area of rocky waste and rubble on the sea bed, which although in relatively shallow and clear water, and which it is possible for divers to explore, can never be seen above the surface.

Most visitors now view the remains of Siff through glass-bottomed boats. Single boats for up to six people may be individually hired on the neighbouring island of Gençek. Larger boats carrying up to fifty passengers set out daily from the same island.

There had always been a tradition of freelance tunnelling on Siff, because of the suitable nature of the rock and a lenient approach by the Seigniory officials (many of whom were themselves enthusiastic amateur tunnellers). Major excavations did not start, though, until the arrival on Siff of the installation artist Jordenn Yo. Yo had already made her name with various works of earth-moving art in many other parts of the Archipelago. Although there was at first a surprising amount of resistance from some of the inhabitants of Siff, Yo brought in a team of geologists who declared that many valuable minerals almost certainly lay beneath the surface, and in commercial quantities. Yo was granted a limited licence to drill exploratory deep tunnels. It did not take her long to produce samples of gold, platinum, oil shale and copper. As the assayers in

298

Siff Town hesitated, Yo soon produced some rare earth minerals, including apatite, yttrium and fluorite. Her licence was quickly amended to allow unrestricted drilling. Because Siffians were largely ignorant of such matters, no one thought to question either where she had found the samples, or why she never brought any more to light.

Within Yo's lifetime, Siff gained the patois name by which it was popularly known. Much of the island's rock strata were tunnelled, with the passages contrived in such a way that a wind from any direction above a speed of about five knots would set up a harmonic note. In normal times the sound would be a pleasant background humming, like the drone from a reed pipe, but during the seasonal gales (Siff was in the temperate north Midway, where winter low-pressure areas were always on the move) the island gave off a high-pitched wailing sound that could be heard on many of the neighbouring islands.

Yo called this the music of the sea and skies, and declared her ambition was to render every island in the Dream Archipelago into a gigantic wind-chime. Every day the tune would change, she said, but it would bring harmony to the entire world. She died not long after making the grandiose claim.

It was during this period that Dryd Bathurst visited Siff. His apocalyptic masterpiece *Night of Final Wrath* was painted on Whistling One.

It is often alleged that the gigantic painting was itself a form of cipher, the images of wrath being derived from a caricature of the important politician Bathurst had travelled to Siff to cuckold. The godly wrath, in this interpretation, was no more than the fury of a man betrayed by a wife many years younger than himself. This theory has latterly been borne out. Recent forensic analysis using X-rays and other exploratory techniques have shown that the cipher theory was not far-fetched. For instance, layer analysis of the oil painting has revealed that some of the more intimate curves of Dryd Bathurst's pretty young mistress were contrived almost undetectably into the scenes of apocalyptic collapse and destruction. DNA profiling has also established that the actual hairs plastered finely into the painted image of the godly pate were human in origin, and traceable to his mistress.

Naturally, this theory had not been formulated at the time. Dryd Bathurst left Siff in the way which was commonly associated with him: suddenly and in conditions of urgent secrecy. He was never to return. But the popular success of his enormous painting brought Siff to wider attention throughout the Archipelago. Then as now tunnelling was a popular pastime with many people, but there were critically few places where it was allowed to be carried out. Tunnellers descended eagerly on Siff from all over the Archipelago. Soon tunnels were being excavated in every part of the island.

The first major collapse occurred about a century after Bathurst's painting became known. Siff Town, by then thoroughly undermined, had to be evacuated and within another half-century the island was entirely abandoned to the teams of tunnellers.

Although many tunnellers were to die in the years ahead, the honeycombing of the island continued to its tragic and inevitable conclusion. In its final years, Siff fell silent: even the gales and storms could no longer find a tune to strike from the broken, gaunt and crumbling crags that the little island had become.

Siff's final collapse was witnessed by only a few. There is a poor-quality video of the last few moments, and this can be viewed in the museum on neighbouring Gençek. It makes depressing viewing. More than five hundred tunnellers died in the flooded galleries and passages during that terrible day. Today, their only memorial is under the clear, shallow seas where Siff once rose above the unforgiving waves.

Smuj

OLD RUIN / STICK FOR STIRRING / CAVE WITH ECHO

**By Dant Willer, *IDT* Political Editor, writing for Travel
& Vacation Supplement, *Islander Daily Times*. Although
never published in the newspaper, this short essay has been
available online from the *IDT* website for several years.**

It began as a routine assignment for this newspaper, the sort of
travel story I have been writing on and off for many years. As readers will know my by-line appears more often in the main part of
the newspaper reporting politics or the economy, but all the staff
here at *IDT* are given occasional travel assignments. Someone, we
console ourselves as we pack our sandals and sun block, has to do
these things.

The reader we have in mind is someone who might be thinking
of taking a trip or a holiday. For those who are not we try to convey
a reliable idea of what the destination is like. Travel journalism is
not important in itself and only rarely has a wider relevance – for
each reporter it can be a gentle reminder that there is more to life
than trying to break a major news story.

My assignment, only the third in as many years, was to visit
SMUJ. Why Smuj? everyone asked, including myself before I set out.
Joh, the chief editor of the *T&V Supp*, said, 'Your question provides
its own answer. It's a place no one seems ever to have heard of.
There is no better reason for going there.'

So, in the spirit of seeking the hidden, the lost, the forgotten,
the unknown, the undiscovered, I set out to explore Smuj. The first
challenge was to find it.

301

As regular readers know, the *IDT* no longer publishes maps. The official reason for this is because most maps of the Archipelago are notoriously inaccurate, but our former policy was that an approximate map was better than no map at all. However, the newspaper had to revise this policy when a few years ago the *T&V Supp* inadvertently sent a group of retired church workers to a Glaund Army rest and recreation base on the island of Temmil. Perhaps that is largely anecdotal, but the lesson was learned. Instead of printing an unreliable map now we give details instead of how we travelled to the destination, and leave it to our readers to follow in our steps. This is always the hardest part of the assignment, as here in the *IDT* office we are not even allowed to use the unreliable maps printed by our rivals.

So my search for Smuj began. All I knew at the outset was that it is somewhere in the seas between Paneron and Winho, and is often said to be obscured behind the magnificent Coast of Helvard's Passion. As I began my search on the internet – a first resort for everyone – a website assured me that Smuj was so well hidden within its own mysteries that even today the people who come from there, should they leave their enigmatic homeland to venture into the wider, mapless reaches of the Archipelago, will maintain the fiction of its inaccessibility and lament the impossibility of their ever being able to return.

It is all, I am a little sad to report, a romantic fiction. Smuj can be found. Neither immediately, quickly nor easily, but it is there to be found. All that is necessary is to forage through the small print of the ferry services in the approximate area and you will find that regular services are there. Not advertised, I should add, but certainly there.

Because I wish to encourage you to follow in my footsteps, I can save you the task of foraging. I chose to travel to Smuj on the scheduled services run by the Skerries Line, one of the smaller ferry operators in that part of the Archipelago.

The ship picked me up as the brochure said it would, and it departed and arrived on time at every port of call. There are many of these stopovers but they are greatly varied. The comfort on board for passengers was plain but of a completely acceptable standard, and the ship neither sank, went aground nor played loud music on its public address system. The cabins were air conditioned. While on board there was full, if occasionally intermittent, internet access. The shaded decks were adequate protection from the sun, and the steward service was good.

At one point in the voyage I was so lulled into a sense of contentment that I even thought, given the time and the funds, that I should like to spend the rest of my life cruising slowly through the Dream Archipelago. I loved the endless cerulean seas, the beneficent breezes, the tropical warmth, the attendant seabirds and surfacing dolphins, and of course the passing show of islands and rocky passages and glasslike calms. At night too the spectacle continued: we frequently saw the diamanté glitter of the lights in houses and towns, sometimes burning a path of bright colours across the dark sea towards our ship. I was therefore not all that pleased to disembark on Smuj, but because in reality I have neither the time nor the money to spend the rest of my life on boats, I was not sorry either.

On arrival I found, as half-expected, a small island, charming and unspoilt, with many of the conventional, expectable attractions for visitors. The swimming is safe and there are several uncrowded beaches and coves to choose from. The scenery is modest but appealing. There are quiet mooring places for private yachts all around the coast. Scuba diving on the reefs is recommended. There is no casino, but once a year there is a horse-racing event. As for eating, the standard of cuisine in the restaurants I went to was normally better than adequate and at best of world-class excellence. Private or rental cars are not allowed on Smuj, but two-stroke mopeds may be rented on a daily or weekly basis. The proprietors of several of the hotels I went to in Smuj Port claimed to have recently installed internet access, but I was unable to confirm this.

Smuj is one of the few islands I have visited where there is interethnic tension. For some reason Smuj has inherited three different vernacular patois systems, but none of them is dominant over the other two. It seems apparent to me that should the tourist trade increase then the influx of visitors will have the same unifying effect on the locals it has everywhere else, but that has not yet

303

happened. One of the curious sights and sounds at the end of the long hot days on Smuj is the evening promenadá, where parading individuals and families exchange remarks, clearly mildly offensive, in street language the recipient probably does not understand, while the meaning is not in doubt. The mood is aggressive, but also somehow good-natured, almost a ritual. Rude hand signals do not a civil war make! Balancing this is the obviously high level of interested interaction between opposite members of sex in the young people. Perhaps within the next generation this conflict will die out, if only for this reason.

Meanwhile, it means that Smuj offers the sympathetic visitor an unusual social experience.

The patois divide also means that the name Smuj has three patois interpretations: 'old ruin', 'stick for stirring' and 'cave with echo'. These are by consent more or less interchangeable.

I was due to stay on Smuj for a whole week, but by the third day time was hanging heavy on me. There is little culture on the island. In Smuj Town there is a small lending library, containing popular novels and copies of recent newspapers. There is a theatre, but locals told me it had been closed for several years. Touring companies rarely visited Smuj, they said, and in any event the theatre building needed to be renovated. I went to the museum, but had exhausted my interest in its few exhibits in under half an hour. I found a cinema, but it was closed. The only art gallery was exhibiting colourful paintings of the town. Swimming beaches and coves speak for themselves, and photographs are enough.

Then, one day at noon, while I was in a bar cooling off from the blistering sunlight, someone asked me if I had yet visited the ruined city in the hills. I had not. That evening I found out what I could – it was thought to be more than a thousand years old, destroyed in an ancient war, abandoned by what inhabitants had survived, and thereafter the little that remained had been sacked and looted.

The next morning I set off on a rented moped and headed for the range of inland hills. There were no indicating signs, but the man at the rental office told me that once I was through the pass I would see a large wooded basin surrounded by the hills, and the ruins were probably somewhere there. No one apart from me seemed at all interested.

I was soon to discover why. There had certainly once been some kind of settlement in the valley, but the traces that remained, all wildly overgrown with creeper, moss, intrusive shrubbery, were not much more than patches of broken rubble. I walked around for more than an hour, hoping to find something that might once have been a recognizable building or open space, but the clustering broadleaf trees had taken over. It was clearly a site that would reward scientific exploration, but I am not an archaeologist so would not know where to begin. I still do not know for sure which era it represents, who built it, who lived there.

I retraced my steps to where I had left my moped, wondering what else there could possibly be about Smuj that would be worth writing about. And at the exact instant, I found it.

When I dismounted I had hardly noticed the building next to where I had parked the moped. Now, walking back to it, I looked at the house for the first time. It was more than just a dwelling: a mansion of some extent, surrounded by mature trees, almost shielded from the road by the thicket. Beyond the widened patch of the road where I had left the two-stroke was a tall, metal gate, clearly locked and intended to be secure: it was not instantly obvious from the road because it was set in the drive itself, which curved away. I walked over and read the sign with great interest:

SCHOOL OF CAURER INSTRUCTION
AGES 6 – 18
UNDER PERSONAL SUPERVISION
AND PARTICIPATION OF E. W. C.

It took a few moments for the meaning of this to sink in.

Of anything that I had expected to find on Smuj, a Caurer Special School was not it. My state when I arrived to confront that gate was that I was hot, thirsty, sweaty, bitten by numerous insects and in general frustrated by my visit to this small and obscure island. All these were uppermost in my mind as I stared in surprise at the sign on the gate. It was not an old sign – it looked recently made.

Did the phrase *under personal supervision ... of E. W. C.* mean what I had assumed in the first instant? That Caurer herself was here, working in the school, on Smuj? Supervising and participating in person?

It seemed unlikely. Caurer had died several years before, which would seem to eliminate her from everything. But the circumstances of her death were attended by a certain mystery that I well remembered. The death certificate revealed that she had died of 'infection / infestation'. In the shorthand understood throughout the Archipelago, this strongly suggested she had suffered a fatal insect bite, probably that of a thryme. The consequences of such an attack were so appalling that even though several hundred people a year were killed by the insects, there was still a stigma attached. Death after a thryme bite usually led to a hastily arranged cremation, often within twenty-four hours, and was always the target of speculation and comment.

These were the circumstances of Caurer's death, but because of her public renown, and the love and respect in which she was widely held, she could not pass quietly from view. Her life was praised, celebrated and memorialized throughout the Archipelago in every form of the media.

I too was involved as a reporter in the search for information after her death. I was sent to Rawthersay to speak to people who had known or worked with her, and my impression of the great woman was deepened by what I saw and heard.

But there were difficult questions unanswered. The principal one concerned the cause of her death. No thryme colonies had ever been discovered in the temperate zone of Quietude Bay, let alone on Rawthersay itself, so the revelation that she had suffered a fatal bite caused great alarm throughout the islands. However, the usual searches and precautions confirmed that no colonies appeared to have been settled. The death certificate was in its way unambiguous, and the professionalism of the doctor who had signed it was never in doubt, but even so there remained a feeling that we were not being told everything.

Throughout her life Caurer had enjoyed robust good health, which naturally would not protect her from a stroke or a heart attack, or one of many other underlying causes of unexpected death. Any of those remained a possibility, a genuine death behind the one that felt a little unlikely. It was tragic and heartfelt, she was widely and sincerely mourned, but I at least, and many other journalists, continued to feel a nagging sense of mystery.

My own researches turned up the surprising information that shortly before her death Caurer had travelled unaccompanied to Piqay to be present at the funeral of the author Chaster Kammeston. This in itself was unusual: Caurer travelling alone was almost unheard of. Although she had been subjected to intrusive media coverage while using the ferries to reach Piqay, it turned out that in practice most of the media outlets who had cottoned on to her journey were all from the islands along the fairly narrow zone of the Archipelago through which she had travelled. For some reason it had spread no wider, certainly not to me or to the offices of the *IDT*. At the time, it was the fact of Kammeston's death that had been the major news and Caurer was by no means the only famous or celebrated mourner at the funeral. When I looked through all the reports from the time, the identities of individual mourners were usually not specified: 'the great and the good' was the journalism shorthand employed by reporters who had not been allowed into the ceremonies.

I could not help wondering if the death of Kammeston might not have had something to do with what followed almost immediately after.

I was probably not by then the only one asking that question. After much travelling around, however, and after many further interviews, I came to the conclusion that although we had certainly not been told the whole story, there was nothing in the public interest about it, and that Madame Caurer was entitled to privacy, in death as in life.

Such thoughts rushed through my mind while I stood there by the sign that announced Caurer's presence. Then I stepped forward and pressed the intercom bell. I heard nothing.

After waiting for more than a minute I pressed it again. This time a woman's voice came faintly and tinnily through a small metal speaker. 'May I take your name, please?'

'I'm Dant Willer,' I said, pressing my face to the green-painted grille. It was hot from the sun and a number of tiny dead insects crusted the gauze.

'Madame Willer. I don't recognize your name. Are you a parent?'

'No. I'm a journalist.' I sensed asperity in the silence that followed. 'Would it be possible to come in?'

I heard the woman clearing her throat – a thin rasping noise in the speaker. She started to say something, but the words would not form. A quick popping noise came through the speaker. I could not help it: in my mind's eye I imagined an elderly woman, leaning forward unsteadily to the intercom microphone. Another rasping noise, as she cleared her throat.

'We never grant interviews. If you are not the parent of a student here, you have to make an appointment. But we have nothing to say to the press, so please don't be troubled by the effort.'

There was finality in her tone and I sensed that she was about to break off the contact.

'I was hoping to see Madame Caurer,' I said quickly. 'Not as a journalist. Would that be possible, please?'

'Caurer is not here. She is busy on other work.'

'Then she is normally here in the school?'

'No. That is incorrect. Tell me your name again and what it is you want.'

'I am Madame Dant Willer. The truth is that I am a journalist for the *Islander Daily Times*, but I am here on holiday. I'm not seeking an interview for the paper. I have read the sign on your gate.' The thirst and the endless blazing heat were making my own voice weaker. I didn't want to clear my throat, send a rasping noise down the intercom. 'Please may I speak to Madame Caurer? Or may I make an appointment to meet her?'

'I've remembered your name now. I think you wrote a book about the range wars on Junno. Is that right? Is that who you are?'

'Madame Caurer –'

But the background hiss of the intercom suddenly ceased and I knew that the brief exchange had ended. My senses were alive. I stood there limply in the heat, the fulgent, unrelenting sunlight, with the sound of the hot breeze passing through the tree branches around me, the insensible dashing of small birds, the stridulation of insects, the white glare on the unmetalled road, the sweat running down my back and between my breasts, the burning of the drive's stony surface through the thin soles of my sandals.

I suddenly realized I might perish there in the tropical heat because I was unable to move. I held to the metal bars of the gate by a force of will over which I felt I had no control. I tried to raise myself to see better, but from this position the only part of the main building that was visible was a brick wall, next to some white-painted outhouses.

I was convinced I had been speaking to Caurer herself.

I was certain she was there, inside the building a short distance away. I was unsure what to do, and anyway I was incapable of acting on any decision. I pressed the intercom button several more times without response, then sagged again. I felt the back of my neck burning and blistering in the heat.

Then she said, 'I think you will need this.'

She had appeared on the drive beyond the gate and was approaching me slowly. In one hand she held a tall glass tumbler, in the other a flagon of water. Condensation clouded the side of the jug. The weight of it was making her arm tremble and I saw concentric ripples darting across the surface. Caurer was there, actually there, an arm's length away from me. She poured the water, her hand shaking because of the weight straining her wrist. She filled the tumbler to the top, passed it to me through the bars of the gate.

Our fingers briefly touched as I took the glass from her.

She stood straight before me as I gulped the water gratefully. She was taller than I had expected, smooth-skinned, not smiling but not unfriendly, steady in her gaze, wearing a pale blue dress, a broad-brimmed white hat.

She said, 'I admired your book more than I can say.'

I felt overcome with amazed pride and contrary humility. 'Thank you, Madame Caurer – I didn't think you would know the book. That's not why I'm here –'

'How long have you been out in this heat?'

I just shook my head.

The gate slowly opened making a whirring noise, a motor somewhere hidden. Nothing now separated me from her. She still had
not moved – the frosted flagon of cold glass unsteady in her hand.
She stood erect, regarding me seriously and with a sudden intensity. I felt so scruffy, unsuitable, dressed in clothes not even good
enough for scrambling around lost ruins, let alone meeting this
woman. I straightened myself, to try to meet her steady regard as
equally as I could. Caurer of Rawthersay, standing there, an arm's
length away.

I had never seen her before, not even a picture. But I stared back
at her, dizzy with a sense of recognition. She was me, we looked
alike! It was as if a mirror had been thrown up in front of me. I
raised one hand. She lifted her own, the one not gripping the jug.
I felt the same intensity in me that I was sensing in her. My head
began to swim. I could not hold the upright posture, because something had happened to weaken me. I slumped, looking down at the
ground. I focused on my legs, my bare feet loosely strapped inside
the sandals, and was ashamed of the dirt and dust that begrimed
me, the black lines between and around my toes.

She stepped forward quickly, caught me as I fell. The flagon
dropped to the ground, and broke in a splashing crash on the hard
surface of the drive. She had caught me with one strong arm, her
body sagging to brace herself against my weight. Without the jug
in her hand she gripped me with her other arm, her leg jolting us
both as she changed position. I slumped against her, the fabric of
her dress against my face. I felt the tumbler fall from my hand. I
thought stupidly of all the broken glass around us. Then I smelled
her scent, a light fragrance of mint, or flowers, or something that
flew. The warmth of her body, the reassuring grip of her arms. She
shifted her weight again, so that she was able to hold me better. I
closed my eyes, felt safe, hot, dizzy, grimy, ashamed, thankful, but
above all safe in her arms. I knew my knees had given out, that
if she let go of me I would crash to the floor. The cicadas rasped
around us, the sun was an endless blaze.

I was next aware of being half carried, half dragged. Two strong
young men, one on each side, one shaved bald, the other straggle-
haired. They were encouraging me, trying to make me feel secure.

310

They urged me on with soft words. My bare feet scraped lightly along the dusty floor, my arms thrown intimately around the men's necks. It was cool inside the house, the shutters down, a draught of blown air, shiny boards with pale rugs scattered, tall potted plants, terracotta ornaments, a decorated screen, a cushioned bench, long fronds over the windows.

Caurer stood beside me, her wide-brimmed hat now knocked to an angle, not yet adjusted, my dirty sandals dangling from her fingers. She was a slender woman, grey-haired, pale-eyed, in the senior years of her life, a presence of immense but silent power. I was stunned to be with her. Still she wore that same serious, uncritical regard. I hardly dared look at her, this woman who looked just like me.

In the distance, somewhere above, sounds of movement. I was in a school.

An hour later I had almost recovered. I had taken a shower and Caurer found me some clothes I could borrow. I had drunk a lot of water, and eaten a light lunch. At times I was alone, as Caurer had work to do in the school.

But at the end of the afternoon she and I were alone together in her first-floor study, and I realized during that intense conversation that without in any way planning or rehearsing it, I had spent most of my life searching for this woman, to know her.

Later I returned on my moped to Smuj Town through the dusty evening heat and the overhanging trees, the swarming midges and emerging moths, the gradually quieting cicadas. In the town the evening promenadá was beginning, the measured ambling around the squares and along the shore, the gay colours and flamboyant hairstyles, the calling and gesticulating and laughing, the young men on their motorbikes, the busy cafés and restaurants, the sound of guitars.

The next day I packed my luggage, went to the harbour office for a refund on my ship's return passage, and then was driven in a taxi to the school on the plain in the hills, behind the trees, beyond the gate, next to the ruined city.

*

Postscript

I wrote most of my essay during the first two or three days on Smuj. I completed it later when I was living in the school house. I despatched it to the newspaper together with my resignation, and I never discovered if it was published or not. I suspect not.

Madame Caurer and I worked together for several years. Officially, my role was to liaise with the media on behalf of the Caurer Foundation, ensuring that what was printed or reported about the work still going on was accurate and true to Caurer's intentions and wishes. In practice, much of my real work was to act as her confidante, her personal assistant and at times her adviser. Once or twice, when she felt the strain of travel or the pressure of crowds would be too great for her, I went in her place, never speaking, never pretending more than the quiet illusion my features created. When Caurer's health at last began to fail, I became in effect her nurse, although of course she had a full medical team on her staff. I was with her when she died, having become, in her own words, her most trusted and intimate companion. We were of an age, we were so alike in every way.

It was seven years after her earlier, false death. The harmless imposture was over. This time there was a quiet burial in the grounds of her home, and the only attenders were the members of her inner circle.

Everyone at the Foundation says I still look just like Caurer, but I make no use of that any more. She is gone.

Winho

CATHEDRAL

WINHO is the so-called island of whores. It is a place of thrilling natural beauty, with a towering range of mountains rising from the western coast and occupying much of the interior. Thick forest covers the remaining plain and the lower slopes of the mountains. The island is reefed, with a series of encircling shallow lagoons, rich and diverse in sea-life. Many small towns have been built on the fertile strip between forest and sea. Until the second Faiandland invasion the traditional activities in this area were farming and fishing. Set in a subtropical latitude, Winho rejoices in warm and dry weather for most of the year. The rainy season lasts for only two months. The prevailing wind on the island is known locally as the KADIA, 'blowing upwards to the mountains' – in reality it is part of the system of equatorial trade winds.

Winho was invaded twice by Faiand forces in the days before the Covenant of Neutrality had been ratified or could be enforced. The first invasion led to occupation and fortification by Faiandland and it lasted for almost a decade. After a violently resisted counter-invasion by Federation forces, Winho was eventually liberated and demilitarized. Loss of civilian life was on a disastrous scale, and there was extensive damage to property.

For about ten years Winho existed under a relatively benign Federation suzerainty, but as the Covenant took shape and gained global recognition the Glaundians had to leave.

Faiandland almost immediately re-occupied Winho, allegedly because of an administrative error but in reality because of its strategic position. There were also unfounded Faiand suspicions that the

313

Federation was continuing to use the island as a base. By this time, the Federation forces were engaged elsewhere and Winho was left unprotected. In the name of retribution horrifying atrocities were performed on many of the inhabitants, including pseudo-scientific experiments on human subjects, physical mutilation of most of the women of child-bearing age and the deportation of all males over the age of ten years. In deep poverty, many of the surviving women were forced either to flee the island, or as large R&R camps were set up for Faiand troops they went into prostitution.

Even after the Covenant rules once again removed the Faiandland occupying force, the impoverished island became renowned for its brothel culture, heavily dependent on the passage of troopships to sustain the economy. Major efforts by people from neighbouring islands to lend assistance came to nothing, because the central problem remained unresolved: the abducted menfolk of Winho could not be located, and even in the present day no mass grave has ever been found. It is clear that they were massacred. The grim search for the final resting place continues.

Winho has been for many years a focus of concern throughout the Archipelago. Caurer visited Winho and set up one of her special schools, which still exists and is regarded as a beacon of hope for the long-term regrowth of Winho culture. Caurer said she was desolated by what she found, and said afterwards that if ever her work had to be directed towards one island instead of to them all, it would be to Winho.

At another time, both Chaster Kammeston and Dryd Bathurst were on Winho, during the period when Kammeston was researching his biography of the artist. He was on the island for nearly two weeks. This is the only known series of meetings between the two. Bathurst had set up a studio on the waterfront of Winho Town, where he was tackling three of the main canvases in his Ruination sequence. We have only Kammeston's account of what happened when the two men met, which he describes in taut and restrained language in the pages of the biography. What Kammeston does not reveal there is what he wrote in his diary, and later in one of his letters to Caurer: he was so disgusted by Bathurst's private life that he abandoned work on the biography for nearly two years, only resuming it when Bathurst's reputation as a painter of apocalyptic landscapes was without precedent. Persuaded by the greatness of the man's artistic gift, and of course by pressure from his publisher, Kammeston completed his biography. He said later that it was the least of his books. To this day it is never included in official listings of his published works.

Another visitor to Winho, whose presence on the island was not known until long after she had left, was the novelist Moylita Kaine. She and her husband moved to Winho Town and rented a house in the hills overlooking the main bay while she conducted detailed research into what had happened during the two terrible periods of occupation. When she and her husband left Winho, two of the women she had met in the course of her researches travelled back with them to Muriseay, where they remained afterwards with their two families of seven children.

Three years later, Kaine published the novel that was to establish her reputation: *Hoel Vanil*. It is an unchallenged masterpiece. HOEL VANIL is the local name for the steep valley in the hills behind Winho Town in which the Faiand KZ was built. It was from here the menfolk were shipped away, and it was inside its low, concrete buildings that the brutal experiments on the women were conducted.

Hoel Vanil is now known prosaically as River Valley, and all external trace of the camp has long been removed. Two underground shelters remain. These were built by the slave labour of the Winho men, before the remainder who survived the underground workings were taken away. The shelters were used for a short period by the Faiandlanders as an ammunition store. The people of Winho Town never go anywhere near River Valley.

The island's economy is still sustained mainly by the arrival of troopships heading north or south. As these belong to the combatant powers they are beyond the laws of the Archipelago. Winho remains in crisis, a tragic, deep-rooted problem with no foreseeable solution.

Strict shelterate laws exist, rigidly enforced. Recently, visa laws have been revised, allowing visitors to remain for a maximum of forty-eight hours only. Deserters are not allowed entry and are forcibly returned to their units if discovered.

Currency: all acceptable, including paper money paid to the troops. This is exchangeable at par with the Archipelagian simoleon.

Yannet

DARK GREEN / SIR

THE DESCANT

Two people came to the small island of YANNET – a woman and a
man. They both had curious names, and the names were curiously
similar, but until they went to Yannet the woman called Yo and
the man called Oy had never met in person.

They were both aware of each other. Yo and Oy were artists,
conceptual creators of installations that were misunderstood by
the public and condemned by critics. Both artists were harassed
and had their work suppressed by the authorities. Neither of them
cared. They thought of themselves as art guerrillas, one step ahead
of their antagonists, always moving on from one installation to the
next. As people they were otherwise unalike.

Yannet stood at a sub-tropical latitude in the midst of a cluster
of islands known as the LESSER SERQUES. It was politically little different from most of the other islands in the Archipelago, in that
it had a feudal economy and was governed by a Seignior in name
and the partially elected Seigniory in practice. There was only one
main area of population: Yannet Town itself, the capital and port,
situated at the southern tip of the peninsula the islanders called
HOMMKE (rendered in patois as 'dark green'). The town was a place
of light industries, electronics studios and games developers. Many
highly paid jobs were to be found in Yannet Town.

The woman, whose full name was Jordenn Yo, was the first of
the two artists to arrive. On disembarkation at the port she told
the Seigniory officials that she was a geologist, taking up a freelance position. That was untrue. She was also travelling under an

317

assumed name, and produced forged papers to back up her story. She told the customs officers she would be importing certain items of unspecified machinery for a geological project. She requested an open manifest, to avoid having to go through the bureaucracy every time, but at first the officers were reluctant to grant it. However, Yo was well experienced in dealing with these situations and soon obtained what she wanted.

She found and rented an apartment in the centre of Yannet Town, one with a small building attached that she could use as a studio. Once established she began her work straight away.

Outside the Hommke area Yannet was sparsely populated. Along the coastal plains to the north there was some farming, but most of the island was covered in dense tropical forest, a deep natural resource, protected from loggers and other developers by island ordinances, and managed as a wildlife preserve. The coastline of Yannet was untamed. There was broken water at all levels of tide. There were few historical or cultural associations and because of this tourists on Yannet were scarce.

Then there was the mountain, known locally as VOULDEN (whose patois meaning is 'sir'. Apart from a few low foothills Mount Voulden stood alone, an asymmetrical cone rising out of the forest at the northern end of Hommke. Trees grew on its lower slopes, but higher up it was covered in coarse grasses or was bare rock. There were no obvious paths to follow, so although the climb was steep for only part of the way it could be a challenging ascent.

The whole extent of Yannet could be viewed from the summit of Voulden, as well as a glowing panorama of other islands in the vicinity. The sea was silver and sapphire blue in the brilliant sunlight, the islands hommke green, dark and intense, fringed with white crests of breaking waves. Shadows of light clouds scudded over the choppy sea.

To this summit one day came Jordenn Yo. She had climbed without looking around her any more than she had to, determinedly saving the view for when she reached the summit, trying not to preview or glimpse it, but holding on to the paths and boulders as she scrambled up.

At first, recovering her breath from the long climb, she sheltered behind some rocks to stay out of the wind. It surprised her how cold it was on the top of the mountain. But the view exhilarated her. She gazed around at the islands. They were impossible to count – the sea was choked with many small tracts of hilly land. The light was bright, unyielding. She gulped in the view, trying to fill herself with it or the sense of it. She watched the traces of the wind on the surface of the sea, the overlapping hatch of vee-shaped rippling wakes from the ferries, the way the clouds took shape and shifted over the islands, drifting out over the sea on one side, others forming to replace them to the windward.

She took many photographs, turning through three hundred and sixty degrees, high and low, records of Yannet's own landmass, of islands and sky and sea. Then she began to contemplate her real work with Voulden, the mountain.

She measured the wind pressure that day. During the course of a year three winds prevailed over this part of the Archipelago. There was a mild westerly wind known as the BENOON, warm with rain, intermittent, most often felt in the spring, one that she could make allowances for, but not depend on. The other two winds were from the east. One of these was called the NARIVA, a hot wind that circled the southern horse latitudes then crossed the Equator and swept across this part of the Archipelago. The third was known as the ENTANNER, a steady flow from the mountains of the northern continent, bringing cooler evenings at the end of the long island summers.

Yo tested the wind that day with the portable anemometer she had brought, noting not just the direction but also the pressure – today was an easterly wind, too cool to be the Nariva, but maybe a spur from the Entanner? She needed more familiarity with the winds before she could be sure she knew them. There was never a day anywhere in the islands that experienced a typical wind, so she would have to work with a median, perform endless calculations about force, frequency, direction, and always make those necessary allowances for the irreverent variables.

Finally, she lay down on the rocky surface of the summit, feeling herself pressing against the peak of the mountain. While the cold wind blew, lifting her inadequate clothes and chilling her, she shivered and planned, but in the end she cried a little. Already she loved Mt Voulden, loved its height, its eminence, its grey solidity. Voulden was a calm mountain of strong, stable strata, hard but safe to drill through – now she was learning the winds that made it breathe.

She returned to her studio before nightfall, exhausted by the strenuous climb and by feeling the extremes of temperature between the windblown mountain heights and the sultry plain below. Her plans for the mountain were taking shape. Within twenty days she had completed her surveys and sent out her orders, instructing that the earth-moving and rock-drilling plant should be made ready.

While waiting for the massive equipment to be shipped to Yannet she made other preparations.

Meanwhile, there was Oy.

At this time Oy was engaged in a small but exacting installation on the tumultuous shores of the island of Semell. Yo and Oy were still more than four years away from meeting on Yannet. Semell was in a distant part of the Archipelago called the Swirl, a system of more than seven hundred small islands and atolls in the southern hemisphere.

Oy's full name was Tamarra Deer Oy, but he had become known by his surname only. A conceptual and installation artist, he had spent the years since leaving college touring the Swirl, searching for suitable islands. He experimented with his techniques and materials on every island he visited, using local aggregates to mix with resinous cements, seeking the hardest and smoothest compounds, ones that would withstand not just time and the elements but the inevitable attempts by others to destroy or damage his works.

Like his near-namesake Yo, Oy was often unwelcome in the places he visited. He had been forcibly expelled from half a dozen islands, although so far he had managed to avoid prison. Also like Yo, as his reputation spread he too was often obliged to enter islands incognito and work fast, completing as much as possible before being discovered or exposed, having to leave his work unfinished.

His first complete work, uninterrupted, was on the island of Selli, a fiercely hot tourist island with immense bays and beaches, and a legendarily exuberant nightlife. Oy arrived out of season on Selli, and soon discovered two holiday-let cottages built close together on a shallow pine-cooled slope overlooking one of the beaches. The trees helped screen him as he worked. He began on both cottages, first sealing them up with thick layers of cement on the inside, leaving the exteriors unchanged but the interiors no longer accessible. He and his artisans then set about erecting a conjoining piece, simulated walls and a roof, making the two small houses into three, or one, or none. Using carefully matched washes he painted the exterior of his installation in several coats of island whiteness.

He paid off his artisans and departed Selli before the artwork was discovered. Before he left he gave the installation a good and approving kick with the flat of his foot.

Other forays into the inhabited Swirl islands were to prove more difficult, but he managed to seal the main street of a village on the island of Thet, and converted a small church on Lertode into an aesthetically satisfying, impermeable egg-shaped dome, painted matt black.

His first shoreline piece was a stretch of rockfall at the foot of chalk cliffs on the island of Tranne. Working in the ebb tide, Oy smoothed and levelled the rocks and their pools by infilling with cement. It was an isolated, unvisited expanse of coastline. Few people ever wandered by or saw what he was doing. At first he worked alone, but the sheer size of the installation made it necessary to hire artisans from the local villages.

Within three months most of the installation was complete. The area of broken rocks had been converted to a white plain, so smooth a ball could be rolled across it, and so uniformly flat that not even the most sensitively calibrated spirit level could detect a slope.

Satisfied, Oy discharged the workers and spent a few days working alone on the final details. Two days later, as he was preparing to leave Tranne for another island, a large fall of rock from the overhanging cliff covered or destroyed everything he had done. He went to see the damage for himself, but left Tranne immediately after.

*

It was Oy who made the first personal contact. He had long known of Yo's reputation, of course, but they had never met. Then one of the trustees at the Muriseay Covenant Foundation mentioned her and gave him a contact address. A few days later he messaged her:

hi yo, i'm oy, i know your stuff and i bet you know mine, we should get together and try something, how about it?

Yo did not reply at once. About six weeks later she messaged him:

I'm busy. Fuck off. Yo.

At this time Oy was working on a large, curving staircase he had chanced to find in an apparently disused part of the back of the Metropolitan Hall, in Canner Town. He was converting it to a flight of irregular steps that could only be mounted from below, using ropes, and in a horizontal attitude. He filled in the former stairs above to make a smooth descent. It was a challenge of great intricacy, and every day he worked there he expected to be discovered by the Metro officials.

Then a second message arrived from Yo, a few days after the first:

You are anathema to me. I loathe and despise what you do. You are a NON ARTIST. I hate everything you conceive or draw or build or fill in or cover up or make smooth or correct or stand near or pass by or breathe in the locality of or EVEN FOR A MOMENT THINK ABOUT. What you do is anti-art, anti-beauty, anti-life, anti-anti. Your so-called work is an abomination to every artist who has ever lived, or whoever will live. I have nothing to 'try' with you, except I would like to spit on you repeatedly. Yo.

But an hour later the same day her third message arrived:

Pls send two photos of you, one of them naked and from the front and close up, but not your face. Yo.

Moments later came the fourth and last message from her:

Come and see what I am doing, Oy. I am not mad. I am on Yannet. Yo.

He sent some photographs, more than two, later that day. Yo never acknowledged them.

It took Oy the rest of the year to complete the horizontal staircase, and he left at once before he might be discovered. He travelled across the Swirl to the island of Tumo, where after a boisterous holiday he began to contemplate his next work.

The horizontal staircase was opened up by Metro officials. It became apparent they had known all along what Oy was doing. Inferring who he was they had made an unannounced and enlightened decision to allow him to finish. They mounted the staircase as a permanent installation in an exhibition of modern art that was created to occupy the rear area of the Metropolitan Hall. Although it was excoriated by the first critics who reviewed it, the staircase quickly became popular with the public and within a year people were travelling from all parts of the Archipelago to see it and to try climbing it. Oy's financial support from the Muriseay Covenant Foundation was substantially increased.

Yo was being delayed by Seigniory officials who objected to the two huge pieces of tunnelling equipment, currently in the hold of a freighter impounded in the port. Her open manifest had no apparent influence on their objections.

While trying to resolve this she managed to get several of her smaller earth-movers and bulldozers secretly ashore on a remote part of the Hommke peninsula, by using beach-assault landing craft she hired from the Faiand base on Luice. This operation used up most of her remaining money, so there was a further delay while she applied to the Foundation on Muriseay. By the time the new grant came through, which was much less than she had hoped for, she had solved the problem of the tunnelling equipment.

To the Seigniory assay consultant, a retired gentleman who held the post as an honorary appointment, she produced several examples of valuable mineral ores, explained that Mt Voulden contained so much wealth that life on Yannet would be transformed for ever, and pointed out that for obvious reasons her work must remain secret. She contrived to leave a small nugget behind on his desk, when she left his office.

The tunnelling equipment came ashore shortly afterwards. Soon she was training two teams of artisans for the work that lay ahead. Her location for the installation had been identified for months, so the teams moved to opposite sides of the mountain without delay. Working under Yo's detailed and strenuous instructions they prepared to chew their way mechanically through the rock towards each other.

This was for Yo the most stressful and exacting period. Every day she had to make repeated visits to each side of the mountain, measuring the orientation of each machine, checking and confirming the quality, accuracy and angle of the workings. Numerous test and access shafts had to be drilled. At first progress was infinitesimally slow – three months after she had employed the teams they were still mostly idle. They crept forward with immense caution, each making preparatory drillings, but both machines remained visible outside the mountain.

However, she was eventually able to give her orders to start drilling in earnest. Both sides moved forward into the mountain itself, the great circular drill faces grinding slowly through the rock.

It was not long before a familiar but major problem emerged, which was how to dispose of the broken rock that was removed as the tunnel progressed. Yo's first remedy was a method she had used on other projects in the past: she paid an off-island contractor to take away the tailings. Several large loads were disposed of in that way. She discovered, though, that the movement of the heavily laden trucks through the town, and the effect they had on the loading of the ships, was attracting unwanted interest in what she was doing. She soon cancelled the deal and paid off the contractor.

She calculated the likely size of spoil heaps, chose places where they might be positioned and soon the tailings began to pile up in the foothills around Mt Voulden. Yo decided against trying to landscape them. She thought that slag was something Oy might deal with for her, should he ever turn up.

The work went on slowly, with more than three years of drilling necessary.

While Yo tunnelled, Oy was moving almost as slowly through other parts of the Archipelago. He went to several islands, but either could not find a subject that engaged his interest or stimulated his imagination, or he had to move on when local people recognized him.

He managed to complete some pieces successfully. He went to the island of Foort, a dry, rocky island, which initially he thought uninspiring, but he was able to go ashore, find somewhere to stay and then to move around freely. Either they did not recognize his face or name or reputation on Foort, or they did not care.

On one of his travels around Foort he went to the low eastern end of the island, where the coastline was defended by ranges of huge sand dunes. The sharp contrast between the deep blue sky, the ultramarine of the sea and the dark dampness of the creeping sands at low tide captivated him immediately. For a week he returned daily to the dunes and sweltered under the relentless sun, clambering across their shifting heights, blinded by the dazzle of the sun, scorched by the dry exposed sand and its coarse grasses.

He went to work. He had never liked a hot climate so he planned to work swiftly, make a minor installation that would require only a few assistants.

The first stage was to excavate and remove one of the existing dunes to make room for one of his own. The vast amount of sand and gravel that had to be shifted was distributed as unobtrusively as possible amongst other dunes. With a patch of rocky base finally exposed, Oy's artisans drilled solid foundations, then built and raised the wooden framework of the new dune. The timber Oy was using had to be specially imported from another island, and every exposed part of the wood was treated with fungicide and several coats of insecticide.

The outer integument was moulded from the toughest kind of plasticized sheeting, guaranteed by its manufacturer to be almost indestructible. Oy tested it with fire, rifle bullets and diamond-bit scalpels, and only the last managed to break through the tough fabric.

The false dune was then coated with sandlike carbonized fragments, pigmented to appear identical to the real dunes all around.

When the artisans had been paid off, Oy settled down alone to the intricate work of setting and adjusting the electronics. Firstly, the dune had to be sand repellent. The wind always blew, and the sand around the installation was constantly drifting. He did not want real sand on his dune, so he devised a mineral loose-body repellent which temporarily polarized and repelled any grains that came close to the integument.

On the windier days his dune was surrounded by a whirling cloud of polarized quartz crystals, shot up into a funnel of stinging sand.

Finally, there were two extra features inside the dune, powered by a bank of rechargeable batteries and solar panels concealed near the apex. One was a sonic generator, which was designed to emit a terrifying electronic howl at random moments. The other feature was an array of internal lights which would switch on automatically every evening at nightfall, making the dune's integument glowingly visible all over that part of the island.

He tweaked and adjusted the dune until he was satisfied, finally sealed it up, and left. As he waded through the deep, loose sand of the nearest genuine dune, his sonic generator kicked in with the first-ever random electronic howl. It was so loud and unexpected that Oy fell face-down with surprise into the sand, and his unprotected ears rang for days afterwards. He was pleased.

Next to Ia.

Here he set about duplicating the work that had been spoiled by the rockfall on Tranne. He found a stretch of wild coast where there were many outcrops of rock, with shallow pools and dangerous escarpments at the bottom of the cliff. He worked swiftly, and soon the section of shore was smoothed in many places to a hard, level surface, with softly rounded mounds where the taller rocks had been covered. However, he had always disliked repeating himself, grew bored with filling the coast and left with the work only half completed.

He travelled to Himnol, where to his surprise he found the local officials sympathetic. They encouraged him to work on the broken wall of an ancient castellated fortress on a high hill overlooking the town. Oy soon sensed that they saw in him a means by which the failing structure might be inexpensively shored up with his infilling. Instead, he began to construct a mirror and glass maze in one of the dungeons, using high-definition cameras and concealed lights to distort perspectives and angles. He found this an involving challenge, but his work was interrupted by an unseasonable storm and the dungeon was flooded overnight.

Disillusioned and feeling frustrated, Oy decided at last to go to Yannet and try to find Yo.

The main tunnelling of Mt Voulden was complete. Yo had sold all but one of her tractors, but the two immense tunnelling machines remained without buyers. Now that she was past the burrowing and earthmoving part of her work, Yo had lost all interest in that. The finishing absorbed her, and the complexity of her tunnel was a thrill that coursed through her whenever she entered its mouth.

The tunnel was straight. It was in theory possible to see daylight from one end of it to the other, and she had viewed and measured it so, but for the time being she placed heavy shrouds across both entrances. When she turned off the access lighting, the darkness of the tunnel was profound.

She had completed the final grouting and polishing of the tunnel walls. Much of her everyday work now consisted of almost obsessive checking of the smoothness of the reinforced walls, and detecting and repairing any leaks or cracks that might appear. It was several weeks since she had found any of these, but she continued to check anyway. Art should not have to be maintained, once installed.

Three areas of the tunnel floor were flooded with polymerized fluid. In these sections of the tunnel, towards the eastern end, an added layer of false roof could be dipped from full height to a narrow slot above the level of the liquid. Here the fluid level could be adjusted so as to tune the wind as it passed through the aperture between the steady surface and the low apex of the roof. A system of ancillary vents gave extra flexibility with tuning. The physical barriers acted like reeds and they would harmonize once the tunnel was finished.

One evening, hungry and thirsty and covered with grimy sweat, Yo drove her one remaining tractor to her apartment and went to her studio.

A man was waiting outside the building, lurking in the twilight shadow thrown by the high wall. She recognized him at once and walked over to stand directly before him. She was taller and more heavily built than he was, but she guessed he was a year or two older. He had the wiry, muscular appearance that she had stared at covetously in the photographs he sent her.

'I'm broke,' Yo said, looking him up and down unashamedly. 'Have you brought me any money?'

'No.'

'Do you have any money at all?'

'Not for you. Just mine. I'm Oy, by the way. Pleased to meet you at last.'

'Can you drive a tractor?'

'No.'

'It doesn't matter. You'll learn. What else can you do?'

'What do you need?' said Oy.

'Ah,' she said. 'We have common ground at last.'

She took him into her apartment and they went straight to bed. They made love on and off for five days, stopping only to sleep, or to find food and drink, or occasionally to take a shower. They were uninhibited lovers, but Yo had one rule: she would never let him penetrate her. She aroused him and satisfied him with her generous hands and mouth, and there were no other restrictions, but he was not allowed to mount her. She did like to spit on him.

Soon the bed was sticky and crusted with spilled juices.

Near the end of their marathon session, Oy said, 'I think I know how to drive a tractor now.'

'I need to show you my tunnel.'

'I thought that was why you wanted me here.'

'Yes, that too,' Yo said, and once again spat deliriously on the ridges of his well-tuned abdomen.

Eventually she drove him up to the western entrance to her tunnel, making him cling precariously to the back of the tractor. She unlocked the chains that held the shroud in place and they walked into the tunnel mouth. It was totally silent inside, with not even echoes of their footsteps or voices. The air was stilled and cool. She powered up the generator, breaking the silence, and after a few moments the access lights came on, stretching away into the far distance.

328

The tunnel was painted white, a smooth glossy coat. Wooden acoustic baffles were placed along both sides of the tunnel wall. There were dozens of these close to the tunnel mouth, but deeper into the mountain their number rapidly declined. For most of the length that Oy could see there was none at all. He stared down the perfect perspective for several minutes, unmoving, beginning to understand. Yo was behind him.

'What do you think?' she said.

'I think I'd like to fill it in. You've left all those tailings—'

'You bastard!'

'It's what I do. I find holes and fill them. If I can't find a hole I make one.'

'That's the same as what I do. I made this hole.'

'How long has it taken you?' Oy said. 'Three years, four? And still not finished? I've made a dozen pieces in that time.'

'This is almost ready. What's the damned hurry, anyway. And who the fuck are you to criticize *me*?' Her eyes were flared wide with anger. 'I despise your *attitude*, the stand you take against art, your—'

Oy seized her violently, and took her neck in the crook of his arm. He silenced her by clamping a hand over her mouth. He had learned a lot about her in the last four days. At first she struggled and bit him, but then she licked the palm of his hand, nuzzling her face. He held her like that for a while longer, pressing his body against hers, then he released her.

'I'm not mad,' she said, moving away from him and wiping her saliva from where it had smeared around her mouth. She took a deep breath. 'Many people think I'm mad –'

'Not me,' Oy said. 'I did think that, but not any more. You're just weird.'

His fingers and palm were bleeding. He wiped the blood on his shirt, then gripped his wrist to staunch the bleeding.

She showed him the little electric trolley she used for her inspection runs through the tunnel. He took the controls and drove slowly to each of the particular points she demanded. At each one she made a close and prolonged examination of the quality of the smooth surface, and tested the seals.

329

Towards the far end of the tunnel they came to the first of the three places where the roof angled down towards the channel of polymer below. Yo pointed out the system of software-controlled adjustable vents and ducts that were designed to ease the airflow and enable tuning of the reeds. Oy examined everything alongside her, feeling admiring of her and trying not to sound grudging.

In truth he was thrilled by what she was showing him. He sensed a new standard was being set here on Yannet, but Yo's arrogance and violent disregard for anyone's work but her own made it impossible to discuss it with her.

With the inspection completed, Yo took over the driving of the trolley and they returned to the western end. She shut down everything, closed and secured the huge shroud, then drove back to her studio. As soon as they arrived she took him to bed again, and a night and a day passed.

One morning, some time later, Yo drove to the mountain alone, refusing to allow Oy to accompany her. She was gone all day. When she returned late that evening she was exhausted and dirty but in an exhilarated mood. She answered none of his questions. She showered alone, then insisted that Oy should take her into the Old Town for a meal.

Afterwards, they walked from the restaurant through the narrow streets to the port.

There were two ferries moored at the quay, with the usual noise and confusion of winches and cranes, the loading and unloading of cargo, the boarding of passengers and cars, and a stream of loudspeaker announcements about sailing times and import restrictions. They walked away from this hubbub and the floodlit apron, down one of the long jetties and into darkness. They stared across the sea towards the dark bulk of the closest neighbouring island. They could see tiny lights across its heights. Yo had said little all evening, and still she said nothing. She stared down at the waves as they broke against the rocks at the bottom of the jetty wall. Several minutes passed.

'The wind's getting up,' Oy said.

'So now you do weather forecasts?' she replied.

'I've just about had enough of this. I've got better things to do than hang around all day, waiting for you. I'm going to move on soon.'

'No you're not. I need you.'

'I'm not just your sex plaything.'

'Oh, but you are. Best I've had so far.' She pressed herself against him, rubbing a breast against his arm.

He moved back from her. 'I've my own work to do.'

'All right. But not yet. I want you here for this.'

A big wave suddenly struck the rocks, throwing up a spray. The drops flew against them stingingly, borne on the warm wind. It was refreshing and stimulating in the hot night – it made Oy think of the way Yo liked to make love.

'I read about the wind yesterday,' Yo said. 'This is the Nariva at last. It's been expected for several days. Listen – can you hear anything?' She was turning her head from side to side, as if seeking a sound. There was just the constant racket of engines from the harbour, the echoing of the loudspeaker voice, some shouting from the ferry marshals directing the traffic, the whining of a winch, the surge of the sea waves. 'It's too noisy here!'

She marched back along the jetty towards the town, with Oy following. The tide was rising and they were drenched by several more flows of windswept spray before they turned on to the apron of the main floodlit wharf, between the cranes, the lines of waiting traffic, the traffic marshals in their yellow jackets and shiny helmets, guiding the drivers and waving their torches.

Once they had reached the street where she lived, on the edge of the Old Town, the presence of the wind could barely be felt. They were sheltered by other buildings, but there were trees on one of the hills above and these were swaying darkly in the night. Yo was muttering furiously, striding ahead of Oy. Whenever he caught up with her she would shrug a shoulder angrily against him and increase her pace.

In the apartment, which was stickily hot after the long day, she went around and opened all the windows wide, bending her head beside each one, listening outside. Finally, she threw off all her clothes.

331

'Come to bed!' she said.

'What were you listening for?' said Oy.

'Keep quiet!' She crossed to him, sank to her knees and quickly undid his pants.

An hour later, lying naked side by side on the bed, listening to the peaceful sounds of the night-time town through the open windows, they became aware of a deep vibration, transmitted through the building.

'That's it at last!' Yo said, sitting up and moving quickly to the window. 'Listen!'

He went to stand beside her. The Nariva wind was blowing more strongly now, gusting across the town and along the streets, skidding litter around, but the vibration was rising through the ground. At first he could not discern any sound that was part of it, but soon he heard a deep, low rumbling, a constant note, a distant siren. The town remained dark and shuttered against the windy night. The droning note wavered with the gusting of the wind as it came down from the direction of the mountain, sometimes fading away but mostly gaining in strength.

After a few minutes of gradual crescendo, the note held at a steady volume, a loud, deep booming, basso profundo.

'Ah,' said Yo.

'Congratulations,' said Oy. 'I'm impressed.'

'Now *that's* why you are here,' she said, holding herself against his arm.

'Just so you could show off to me?'

'Who better to show off to than you? Could you have done this?'

'I might have done it more quickly. But I fill things in. I would never have even started.'

He had rarely seen her smile before.

The immense bass note throbbed unendingly across the town. Somewhere in a street adjacent to theirs a car alarm, nudged into life by the vibration, began to screech. Another followed soon after. A policier car, or some other kind of emergency vehicle, rushed unseen by them through the town with its own siren suppressed but with its warning lights blazing and flashing. They saw the radiance reflecting quickly off the tops of walls and roofs, before the vehicle sped off in the direction of the port. After a few more minutes of electronic screeching the car alarms switched themselves off. Mt Voulden continued to moan its single, dark note.

The mountain fell silent an hour after sunrise, when the wind at last slackened. Yo had been euphoric throughout the hours of darkness, alternating between manic proclamations of her own genius, and bitter, lacerating attacks on Oy's own perceived failings as an artist. He no longer minded her abuse, because he knew by now it was her way of working herself up into a sexual frenzy.

If he learned anything from that long sleepless night of the mountain's deep roaring it was that the time had indeed come for him to move on. In some way he barely understood he knew he must have been useful to her, perhaps as a foil. Whatever it was, it seemed to be over.

Yo fell asleep soon after the mountain went quiet. Oy left her in the bed, showered and dressed and packed his few belongings. Yo woke up again before he could leave. She sat up, yawning and stretching, her face drawn with fatigue after the mostly sleepless night.

'Don't go yet,' she said. 'I still need you here.'

'We agreed you were showing off. That's what you wanted from me. What you've done with the mountain is good, it's brilliant, it's incredible, it's unique. I'm impressed. There's never been anything like it before. I couldn't have built it myself. Is that what you want me to say?'

'No.'

'I really mean it.'

'But it's incomplete. I've hardly started. What happened last night – it was like someone picking up a musical instrument for the first time. Have you ever tried to get a note out of a trumpet? That's all I achieved last night. I simply made my instrument sound a note. Now I have to learn how to play it properly.'

'You're going to teach the mountain to play tunes?'

'Not straight away. But I can program a tonic sol-fa, at least. There are vents up there in the tunnel that will create vortices

333

when I open them. One will release a torus of air. I've no idea yet what they will sound like.'

'All right, but I've stuff of my own to do. Maybe I'll come back and see you later, when you've taught it to play the national anthem. How long is that likely to be? See you in another five years?'

'Don't be a bastard now, Oy. I need your help. I really do.'

'Anti-help, anti-art?'

'Come to bed and put me back to sleep.'

In the end Oy agreed to stay on with her. Yo remained as she was, difficult and perverse, often yelling at him for doing something wrong, sometimes abandoning him so she could work on her own, but her reliance on him did appear to be genuine. Every day they worked together on the tuning vents inside the tunnel. Oy found this interesting, the endless range of settings and combinations, harmonizing as the wind shifted direction and pressure.

Soon the mountain was responding to the opening of the extra vents. A strong wind was no longer necessary to produce a note – Yo had installed a series of Venturi tubes that increased the local speed at which the wind stream passed through the tuners. One night they lay awake as the mountain groaned and curled its tremendous rumbling notes, fading away and recovering as the erratic Nariva swept across the face of the mountain. It was gaining a sort of ponderous, elephantine beauty.

But much as Oy admired her ingenuity he found the endless deep droning of the bass notes uninspiring. People in the town had started complaining too, but so far no one appeared to have worked out who was behind the all-pervading sound.

If Mt Voulden had been one of his own pieces, Oy would already have left the island. He disliked hearing comment on his work.

One morning at dawn, after another wakeful night, he said to Yo, 'It needs a descant.'

'A what?'

'Another tunnel, shorter, narrower, at a different angle to the wind, playing a higher harmony.'

Yo said nothing but stared at him in silence, before she shut her eyes. Several minutes passed. He could see her eyes moving rapidly behind the closed lids. Her jaw was clamped tight and Oy could see veins in her neck, pulsing with pressure. He braced himself.

Finally, she said, 'Fuck you, you bastard. Fuck you, *fuck you!*'

But this time her abuse did not lead to sex. She dressed in a hurry, went to the mountain alone and Oy did not see her again until the following day.

When she was ready she took him up the mountain, much higher than the main tunnel, to a place where she had found a long ridge on the southern face. The wind was keener and colder there and made its own harsh whistling as it scoured across the bare rocks and deep crevasses.

'If I could somehow drill a new tunnel through this ridge, would you stay around and help?'

Oy was balancing on an exposed boulder, buffeted by the freezing wind. Far below them the first tunnel was moaning, but they could barely hear it up here.

'If you could somehow drill it, I would somehow fill it in.'

'Then what's the point?'

'Ah – that old argument about point,' Oy said. 'Art has no point. It only is. We could do both. You drill a tunnel and I'll fill it in.'

'I thought I was the mad one.'

'Yes and no. That's the other old argument.'

Yo gestured impatiently. 'Then what the hell?'

'What the hell what?' Oy stared down at the astounding elevated view, the hommke islands, the seething sea, the white clouds and the shafts of brilliant sunlight. A squall of rain was distantly moving across from the south. Two white-painted ferries were passing in the narrow strait between two islands. 'Some places don't need art,' he said. 'Look at what's here! How could you or I improve on that?'

'Art isn't just about pretty views. There's no sound from the view, for one thing.'

'There's the wind. Why don't we build a virtual tunnel? You drill it, I will fill it in. All at once. It starts here where we are now, it comes out on the other side of the ridge. You know what you will do if you drilled it, I know what I could do if I repaired it. We achieve parity. That's what real art is. Parity! Now shall we go back down before I get frostbite?'

'What about the descant? I need that now.'

'There are other ways.' He leapt down from the boulder, narrowly avoiding turning his ankle on the hard and uneven ground. 'You'll think of something. I'll be back in a year or two, to see what you have come up with.'

But ten days later he was still restlessly there. Yo kept finding things she needed to do in the tunnel, and thinking up ways of making him work with her on them. In one sense it suited him, as he had a destination in mind, but the particular ferry he needed to catch to Salay had sailed a couple of days before. Another was not due for a while.

Mt Voulden now played its bass song every night, in low winds and high. Yo declared herself dissatisfied with it. She wanted to keep tuning and adjusting the baffles, but the reaction against the booming music from people in the town was growing more vehement every day. They both knew it was time to leave, time to start other projects.

Irrespective of what Yo herself might be planning, Oy was intending, no matter what, to catch the next ferry to Salay. It was due to dock in the harbour in the morning. He packed his stuff as unobtrusively as possible while Yo was showering.

When she emerged, hair wet and with a towel plastered around her body, Mt Voulden began to drone its tuneless music. Yo abruptly turned on Oy, shouting that she knew he was about to abandon her. She accused him of betraying his own art as well as hers, of selling out, of trying to destroy what she was doing –

It was the familiar overture. This time, knowing it was to be the last, Oy did not allow her to pull him down on the bed. He stood up to her, yelling back. It was anger in the cause of expression, not real anger, but it was verbal slaughter. He gave as good as he had ever got from her, and more. She hated that. She spat at him, so he spat back at her. She punched him, he punched her.

Finally he allowed it to happen and they sprawled together on the bed. Her towel had been knocked aside while they fought, but now she tore off his clothes. It was aggressively passionate, lust not love, but as before it was all the action of hands and mouth. Mt Voulden roared anew. A wind-borne scale began, a slow tonic progression.

Yo suddenly yelled, 'In me! Do it!'

She guided him so there was no misunderstanding what she meant, and at last he entered her. She gasped aloud, a rasping shriek beside his ear. Her fingers and nails dug into his back, her mouth pressed hotly against his neck, her legs clamped around his back and buttocks.

The tunnel through the mountain attained the top of the scale, and the great interminable note began to grow louder. Yo climaxed with it, screaming, shrieking, the highest music of sexual pleasure.

Oy slumped over and across her but she continued to release her noise of pent-up passion. Every breath she gave was another note, sweet and high. She was waiting for the sounds from the mountain now, listening for its cue, breathing with it, harmonizing, a tuneful descant, a melody of the air and sky, of the winds that curled through the tuning plates and fanned the vents and crossed the seas and islands. Her voice was surprisingly pure and innocent, untouched by her violent moods and mercurial nature. She was at one with the music she created, and now she sang the wind.

Out there in the ocean of islands the winds that sifted the sand on the beaches, guided the currents and stirred the forests had their source. They arose from the doldrums, from the cooling impact of snow and the calving of bergs in the glaciers of the south, from the unpredictable high pressure systems of the temperate zones, the calm lagoons of humid air across the tropics. They followed the tides, swooped around the heights of mountains, changed the moods and hopes of the people they touched, brought rain and cleansing air, created rivers and lakes and refreshed the springs, they ruffled the seas. Nariva, Entanner and Benoon. Beyond them a score of others, trade winds and gales, hurricanes and monsoons and tempests, cooling squalls and the lightest of breezes, the warm winds of dawn, circling the globe, raising dust, making rhythms in memory, turning wind vanes and filling sails, inspiring love and revenge and dreams of adventure in people's hearts, slamming windows and rattling doors. The winds of the Dream Archipelago blew wild and parching across barren outer cays and crags, enlivened the humid towns, watered the farms, swept deep snows into the mountains of the north. Yo's clear soprano voice tapped this source, gave it a shape and a sound, a story, a feeling of life.

As the note from the mountain lowered in pitch, became quieter, then ceased, Yo's singing ended. She was breathing quietly, regularly, and her eyes were closed. Oy extricated himself from her embrace, levered himself away from the bed, walked unsteadily to the open window.

A soft breeze was moving through the town. He rested his hands on the sill, leaned forward to take the warm air. His hair was matted to his head, his chest and legs were sticky with sweat. He breathed deeply. The breeze had come in from the sea and the islands, across the land, around and through the mountain, down into the clustered streets of the Old Town. It was the middle of the night, the early hours, long before dawn, still warm from the day, anticipating the next.

The street below the window was full of people. A crowd had appeared in the area outside Yo's studio, spilling out along the street in both directions. More were coming from the houses and apartments close by, their faces turned up towards the distant mountain, a deep shadow against the night sky. They were listening for more of its music. A group of women were laughing together, children had come outside with their bedclothes clutched around them, lanterns flickered in the breeze, several men were going around with casks, pouring drinks.

Behind Oy, on the bed, Yo had fallen asleep. Her face in repose was unguarded, undefended by pride and ambition, now just exuding modesty and in a way he had never seen before, kindness. She breathed steadily and calmly, her chest rising and falling in a gentle motion.

Oy sat beside her until dawn, watching her sleep, listening to the happy crowd outside as the people slowly dispersed. The mountain was silent. As the sun came up Oy dressed, then walked down to the harbour. He did not wait for the Salay boat to come in, but caught the first ferry of the day, heading nowhere that he knew, out into the endless sprawl of lovely islands, down into the Archipelagian winds.